LOVE AMONG VINES

MADISON SCORE

That's What She Said Publishing, Inc.

LOVE AMONG VINES

ISBN: 979-8-88643-894-9 (ebook)

ISBN: 979-8-88643-895-6 (paperback)

madisonscore.com

062725

To my amazing sons, Oliver and Owen. May you always follow your dreams.

CHAPTER ONE

JADE

"To Ashley!"

Five shot glasses clinked together. Tequila stung Jade Gardner's throat as it slid down, leaving behind the taste of sweaty gym socks. It had never been her liquor of choice, but it wasn't her bachelorette party.

She shot a look at the other four girls. They were sitting in a circle around the coffee table in the den of Ashley's parents' summer home. Even though it was early October, the air conditioning cranked away. The unseasonably warm weather clung to the hills surrounding Hammondsport, New York, like a second skin.

"So, what are we playing?" she asked when the burn had subsided. If nothing else, the sweaty gym sock juice might help her forget that her life was in shambles.

"Never Have I Ever?" Ashley Moore, bride-to-be and aspiring pediatric oncologist, flashed a mischievous smile. Her blonde hair was pulled back into a messy bun, and there was a small champagne stain on the collar of her shirt.

"Yes," Kenya Jones said with a point of her manicured finger. A fitness influencer and arguably the most beautiful person Jade had ever seen, Kenya had served as Ashley's "yes man" for the entirety of the trip.

Penny, Jade's golden retriever, put a paw on her lap as if to question the decision. In fact, she had expressed her disapproval more than once over the course of the trip.

Maybe she should have listened to the rescue pup.

The wedding wasn't for another three days, and already this had been the most uncomfortable bachelorette party she'd ever attended. But that was probably because Ashley was marrying Jade's ex-boyfriend.

"Sounds great." Jade put up five fingers, then bit the inside of her lip.

She had climbed out Ashley's bedroom window to play Never Have I Ever on their Midtown fire escape on slow summer evenings in high school.

But that was all before. Before grad school. Before Nate.

"What do you think, Blake?" Kenya said pointedly to another girl, who was staring at her phone and looking bored.

Blake Chan, Ashley's friend from undergrad at Stanford University and current stick-in-the-mud, had spent the entire trip complaining about the rented party bus and yelling at her assistant on the phone. She had looked Jade from top to bottom on their first meeting earlier that evening and hadn't spoken a word directly to her since. She was either shy, or she had decided that Jade's denim overalls and overly enthusiastic golden retriever had already irrevocably tarnished the vibe of her Instagram stories for the weekend. So far, neither an unmatched playlist of 90s summer bops nor two glasses of champagne had loosened her up, but there was always hope.

"Sure." Blake lifted her hand with as much enthusiasm as someone prepping for a colonoscopy.

"Great idea, Ash," said maid of honor Camila Bettencourt. A fresh manicure in Ashley's wedding colors gleamed under the overhead lights. Her brunette hair was smoothed back into a low knot, and a strand of pearls curled around her neck.

A prickle of curiosity welled in Jade. Camila had FedEx'd everyone a calligraphed copy of the official wedding timeline and bachelorette party events, doled out personalized T-shirts like she was an Etsy shop, and led them through an increasingly elaborate series of bachelorette-themed games. What kind of crazy stories did the extremely type A New York City real estate heiress have under her belt?

Thank god Camila had covered most of the expenses for the trip. Between the thousand-dollar bridesmaid dress and her two-year hiatus from the art world, Jade was hovering on the precipice of financial ruin. But there was time to worry about that later. Her oldest friend was getting married. To Jade's ex.

What the hell was she doing here?

"Never have I ever..." Ashley's words derailed those thoughts. "Had a one-night stand."

Kenya snorted. She, Jade, and Blake drank.

Blake leaned forward to look at Jade. "You don't strike me as a one-night stand girl." She almost sounded impressed.

Jade paused. "Well, I didn't used to be. Now it's kind of my comfort zone, you know? Can't get hurt if you keep everyone at a forced distance." She laughed, but it rang fake in the cathedral ceilinged room.

Oops. The tequila seemed to have unlocked some word vomit.

"Anyway," Jade said, catching Ashley's grimace behind her Solo cup. "Never have I ever been to Dubai."

The game continued, with each claim growing more outrageous.

"Never have I ever given a blowjob under a table in a public restaurant," Ashley said with a look at Camila.

"How dare you?" Camila's hand flew to her chest like she had been accused of an egregious crime. She drank.

"Never have I ever..." Camila paused. Her neatly coiffed hair had started to come undone. "Let a man use the back door."

Kenya and Ashley drank.

"Jade, I'm surprised you haven't," Camila slurred. "Back door is like *such* a thing for Nate."

Jade jerked back like Camila had slugged her with her Prada purse.

Camila slapped a hand to her mouth. "I'm sorry," she said, suddenly more refined. "I don't know why I said that."

"I told you that in confidence," Ashley said with a panicked look at Jade.

Jade jumped up. "I'm going to get everyone some water. We'll need to be hydrated for the hike tomorrow."

Her heart hammered in her chest as she rounded the corner and entered a gargantuan kitchen that looked like it had never been used. The last thing she needed was more details on Ashley and Nate's sex life. Her fists clenched as she held back the memories that threatened to flood out.

Penny tip-tapped into the kitchen and nosed her hand.

Jade offered her a quick pat and went back to opening cabinets. Where the hell were the stupid water glasses?

Abandoning the search, she wrenched the fridge door open. She paused, hand halfway to a row of bottled water. There on the second shelf was the chocolate milk she had grabbed at a gas station on the outskirts of town. Her heart rate inched up another notch.

This random-ass chocolate milk was touted as the best in the state. Could this be the solution to two years of crippling painter's block? Or would it be another useless attempt on the list of fifty-plus failed solutions? She had meant to try it before bed when she could focus. But if this chocolate milk brought her muse back, at least she'd have something to talk about with the unending stream of Nate's pitying relatives.

She twisted the cap off and took a swig. The creamy liquid flowed over her tongue. It was damn good. But would it be enough?

She yanked her sketchbook out of her purse and closed her eyes, clenching a pencil so tightly in her hand that her fingers hurt. She put the tip to the paper and waited.

Waves of inspiration used to come to her from everywhere and nowhere. After hearing a beautiful song, or tasting a loaf of freshly baked bread, or even after spotting a couple sharing an umbrella in the rain. An errant gym sock on a nature trail had once inspired a series of six paintings. Inspiration was everywhere. So why the hell had it abandoned her so completely?

Nothing had been the same since the incident. She was a hollow, dried-up husk of her former self. She had stared at a hundred sunsets, tasted a thousand new and exotic foods, and spent just about every cent she had left looking for an experience that would unlock this crippling block. And nothing had.

"Jade? You good?"

A soft voice startled her. Her eyes flew open to find Kenya looking at her, brows contracted as she leaned against the kitchen island.

"Hey! Yeah, I'm fine. Sorry. I was just trying something."

Her face was hot. She wasn't doing a good job at hiding her emotions.

Laughter rang out from the den. Were they laughing at her?

"You don't need to explain anything to me. I know an artist's work is very mysterious...and apparently sometimes involves dairy." Kenya bent down to pet Penny, who rolled onto her back and exposed her belly.

Jade smiled but couldn't summon the inspiration for a proper response. She wasn't really an artist anymore.

"I just wanted to check on you. Overall, I mean," Kenya added. "I know this is a weird situation."

She grimaced. "It's fine. I don't hold any ill will towards Ashley. She's one of my oldest friends."

"Sure. Doesn't change what she did, though." Kenya glanced over her shoulder, voice barely more than a whisper.

Jade's stomach twinged. The chocolate milk sloshed angrily. "I know from experience how easy it is to get caught up in Nate."

Kenya crossed her arms and stared out the dark window. "You're a better woman than me. If my best friend stole my boyfriend, I'd never talk to that bitch again."

Was Kenya digging for dirt? Or maybe this was some weird friendship test? Either way, Jade wasn't prepared to discuss her messy breakup.

"Yeah. Well. Nate and I just weren't meant to be. But anyway, let's not let that distract us from the party atmosphere. We're all here to celebrate Ashley," she said with a smile that hopefully looked genuine.

Crack. Their gazes dropped to Jade's hand. Two halves of a graphite pencil clattered to the island.

Kenya reached over and squeezed her shoulder. She smiled sadly.

Great, everyone pitied her. The wedding would be even worse—she had no date, and she had gone from talented artist and girlfriend of Nathan Astor to washed-up has-been who couldn't produce anything more artistic than a signature.

This weekend was her last hope. Maybe witnessing her ex getting married would deliver a catharsis that finally unblocked her. If it didn't, she would be homeless at the end of December.

Jade swept the pieces into a trashcan and grabbed the bottled water. All she had to do was survive the next three days. Then she could get back to figuring out what to do about her dwindling funds.

CHAPTER TWO

———

RETT

Buzz.

Everett Rhodes drew his phone out of his pocket and sighed. Wasn't it too early in California for his parents to be checking in?

"Hi, Mom." He fought to keep an exasperated note out of his voice.

The last thing he needed was more interruptions this morning. He had two displays to update, a batch of Chardonnay to quality test, an infernal social media post to make, and a check-in with the viticulturist.

"Good morning, darling. How are you?" Teresa Rhodes's voice rang through the phone like a middle C on a perfectly tuned flute.

"I'm fine. Just have a busy day ahead. Lots to do even without accounting for the party planning."

The cash register chimed as he closed the drawer. Correct down to the last cent, as it always was.

"Oh, yes. Your father and I are so excited. Are you sure there isn't anything we can do to help?" she asked.

"It's all handled," he said.

"I have no doubt. Your grandmother would be really proud, you know."

An ember of anxiety stirred deep in his core.

"Would she?" he asked curtly.

The hardwood floors creaked under his dress shoes as he approached the last rack in the gift shop. Another thing he couldn't fix unless business picked up.

He pulled a wine bottle out of the crate at his feet and slid it onto the shelf in front of him.

"Don't worry, sweetheart. Business has always ebbed and flowed. This is just a temporary slowdown. And you know your father and I—"

"I appreciate it, but that won't be necessary, Mom. I have a plan."

"If you're sure, sweetheart."

"I am. How is your day? Are you on set already?"

He glanced at his watch. It wasn't even six a.m. in Los Angeles.

"Calling from hair and makeup," she said brightly.

"Good luck today. Not that you need it," he added.

His mom was a brilliant, award-winning actress. From the silver screen to Broadway, she dominated every production. It had meant that she wasn't always around when he was growing up, but she had always been there when it counted.

"You're too sweet. One more thing about the party," she started.

Rett glowered. He already knew what was coming.

"Your father and I met the loveliest girl last week. You remember my director?"

"I do," he said.

"It's his daughter. She's funny and smart and in school for film. I think you'd really hit it off."

He bit back a deep sigh. Was this the sixth or seventh time that his parents had tried to fix him up after the breakup? There was no time for romance. If he took his hands off the wheel at the winery for even a minute, everything would come crashing down.

"She sounds great, but I think her presence would make the woman I'm seeing feel awkward."

The lie was out before he even had time to process it. *Shit.* Now he was going to have to make up a lie for why this imaginary person wasn't at the party. Unless he could hire someone?

"You're seeing someone?" The delight in Teresa's voice was so visceral it was like he had announced he was running for President of the United States. "I can't wait to meet her."

"I'm not a hundred percent sure she'll be there, though. She's pretty busy."

"I see." She didn't sound convinced.

He racked his brain. Who around town would have a friend or niece that his parents hadn't met? Surely there was someone he could ask to the party. Anything was better than making some poor woman fly five thousand miles only to be disappointed.

Gravel crunched in the driveway. He glanced out the window. Elaine and Todd, married wine enthusiasts who had been at Rhodes even longer than he had, turned into the lot.

"Oh, look at that," Rett said. "Speak of the devil. She showed up with coffee. I'd better go. I'll talk to you later, Mom."

"Enjoy your coffee date," she teased.

"Thanks. Love you."

He hung up the phone before he could dig his hole any

deeper. Stupid, stupid, stupid. He didn't have time to hunt down a fake girlfriend.

"Morning," he said when Elaine and Todd opened the door.

"Morning. Let me get that, boss," she said with a smile.

"I'm almost done." Rett shelved another bottle.

Todd shook his head. "Did you even leave last night? Or did you sleep in the back room?"

"Very funny." Rett smirked. "Not only did I leave, but I had time to grab dinner from the Tavern before they closed."

"They close at ten," Todd said flatly. His collared shirt was a little wrinkled, but Rett wasn't going to say anything.

"I'm telling you, if you don't slow down, you're going to have a heart attack by thirty-five," Elaine said. She took a bottle from Rett's hand and shooed him away.

"You say that like I have a choice," he said.

"You're the boss. No one is making you work twelve-hour days, seven days a week. Why don't you take a day off? A week, even?" She slid the case away from him before he could protest. "You know we could handle things."

He turned his attention to another row. One by one he rotated the labels. Now he was being heckled by his employees. Why was it that no one seemed to grasp the enormity of the situation?

Probably because he hadn't told them exactly how troublesome things had become. If sales didn't improve by the end of the year, he was going to have some difficult decisions to make.

But that wouldn't happen. It couldn't.

"I'm headed to the barn," he said without answering her question. "Give me a call if anything comes up."

"What's going to come up? We're not even open for another hour," Elaine called as the door closed behind him.

Rett tugged at his collar and cast a glance over the sprawling vineyard in front of him. Sunlight streamed down from a cloudless sky. Leaves that were just beginning to shift yellow rustled in the wind. This weather was going to wreak havoc with the harvest if it didn't cool down soon. He marched down a row, inspecting the Riesling grapes as he went.

No sign of blight or pests, but he couldn't be sure until the viticulturist arrived.

He unlocked the side door of the large outbuilding and stepped lightly down the stairs to the cellar. The smell of oak greeted him like an old friend. He strode past rows upon rows of barrels and vats. No leaks, no disasters, perfect temperature. It was just as he left it the night before.

Metal gyropalettes loomed large in front of him. Hundreds of black bottles were inside, tipped at an angle. He ignored the twisting of his stomach and marched past them to another rack of bottles clamped tight with halters.

Sure, the wine had looked okay after the riddling process. But he wouldn't really know until the first bottle was cracked open.

He brushed a speck of dust off one of the bottles. His mother's words came back to him.

Your grandmother would be proud.

Valentina Rhodes would never be in this situation. As business-savvy as she was gifted in winemaking, the winery had flourished under her hand for forty-eight years. But then she had passed, and it had been rather suddenly handed down to him.

It had been a year and half, and the quality of the product had never wavered—in fact, some critics said it was the best in the entire region. But competition had increased. They were losing out to flashy pop-ups with axe throwing lanes, live music, and mediocre wines.

Valentina would have fainted if she found out people were throwing axes in her winery. But he was quickly losing the ability to keep things at her preferred status quo.

The sparkling wine in front of him was a huge, expensive risk. It was her last dream, one she never got to carry out before her death. A rarity in the Finger Lakes, it had the potential to change the trajectory of the business. But only if it was good.

Would the wine honor the feisty woman who sang in the kitchen and let him lick the beaters when she made brownies? Or would it be the final domino in the winery's downfall?

CHAPTER THREE

JADE

THE PARTY BUS CRAWLED UP THE LONG, STONY DRIVEWAY TO winery stop number three: Rhodes Vineyard. The first two stops had been fine. Ashley, Blake, and Camila had raved over their fleet of sweet wine tastings while Jade had enjoyed a glass of whatever dry reserve each winery had. They had all been at least medium-palatable.

But over the course of two years of producing exactly nothing, she had sampled a lot of vino. And none of today's wines had knocked her romper off. Rhodes Vineyard had mixed reviews on Yelp, but at least their listings leaned to the dryer side.

"Selfie! Selfie!" Ashley beckoned with both hands for the girls to gather around her. It was approximately the fifteenth time the bride-to-be had gathered them for a group photo. But whatever the bride wanted, she got.

Jade crammed in next to Kenya and smiled. They all wore matching blush-colored shirts with wine-related puns on them, while Ashley had donned a crisp white T-shirt with the phrase Bride on Cloud Wine. Thanks to the tequila the night before and the resulting hangovers, Ashley had cancelled the morning hike. Jade had taken Penny on a run instead while the other girls slept in.

They broke apart and gathered their purses as the bus lurched to a stop. Bachelorette parties had to be a winery's bread and butter. But how annoyed did the owners get every time a group of lightly toasted twenty-somethings passed through?

Blake, a New York-based fashion model with deep family roots in the industry, had unceremoniously cut off the bottom of her Hakuna Moscato shirt and turned it into a crop top. Camila had paired hers with her signature set of pearls, and Kenya had tied it to expose her ultra-toned midriff.

Jade had left hers exactly the way it was and slapped on a pair of sunflower-embroidered jean shorts she had found in a thrift shop in the East Village. Blake had again looked at her like she was a swamp thing that had crawled up from the depths of the lake. Jade's patience was wearing thin.

They exited the bus and followed the walkway up to the charming stone-front winery. Blake tripped and would have careened into a bush if Jade hadn't grabbed her by the arm.

"Thank you, Blade." Blake patted Jade on the head.

"It's Jade, and you're welcome." What were the odds she could train Penny to poop in one of Blake's shoes before the weekend was over?

"That's what I said," Blake insisted.

Sure.

The winery looked like an old country home from the 1800s. Expansive, yet homey.

She turned on the doorstep and cast another glance over the vines. The sun sparkled on the lake below them. Rows of vines stretched from the road to a tree line. A roof stuck out of the trees toward the lake. Must be a gorgeous place to live.

A tingling feeling crawled up her spine. She froze on the spot.

The tingle used to happen time and again when something around her wanted to be painted. But she hadn't felt it once since the day Nate walked out.

She groped blindly in her purse. Could it be?

"Coming?" Blake held the door.

Jade's fingers froze on the spiral of her sketchbook. This was probably a false alarm. She had never been a landscape painter, anyway.

"Yes, sorry. It's so beautiful here."

"It's no Napa Valley," Blake slurred with a note of condescension. Despite her attempts at snobbery, she had been more than happy to finish off Kenya's fruit-forward flight at the last winery. It was a good thing they were going to lunch after this.

Her comment seemed to have drawn the attention of a stupidly attractive man in a three-piece charcoal suit. He was on one knee, restocking bottles in a display. Piercing green eyes set under a furrowed brow lifted to meet Jade's.

Her breath caught in her chest. Had she stepped into some weird winery MRI machine? Because she swore he had just looked right into her core.

With her face growing hot, she shuffled off to the tasting room. They crowded around a table, and Jade sat facing the gift shop area where the man was still restocking. Her gaze was drawn to the bulge of biceps beneath his suit. She hunkered down to hide behind Kenya's springy corkscrews as their server chatted with them.

She was in her fifties, with kind brown eyes and a

midnight blue blazer. Did all their employees dress so formally? "This is our Blaufränkisch, a dry red with notes of black cherry and blackberry. You might also notice a distinct peppery taste that's unique to this varietal."

Jade was barely paying attention as she lifted the glass to her lips.

The velvety liquid washed over her tongue. There was the sting of tannins, but so much more. Hints of plum and rich spice. An earthy full body that warmed her from the inside out.

A memory hit her out of nowhere—crowded around a table with her parents in their favorite Italian restaurant in Queens, lifting glasses and toasting to her twenty-first birthday. Her mom's laugh lines stood out in the flickering candlelight. The scent of marinara was sharp in the air as her dad reminisced about the trials of sleeping in a chair at the hospital.

Her heart ached.

"This is amazing," she whispered. Her eyes were watering, and she sniffed. Memories or no memories, she would *not* be crying on Ashley's day.

The others turned to look at her. Ashley's nose had wrinkled. Camila pushed her glass to Jade. Kenya shrugged and downed the rest of her sample.

"That's great," their server said. "If you take some home with you, it pairs really well with hard cheeses and smoked sausage."

Jade, who regularly had a charcuterie board for dinner, nodded enthusiastically. She accepted the rest of Camila's wine and savored the hint of cedar on her tongue. She made a mental note to tell her CrossFit friend Lindon about this place. He was a food and wine critic for the *New York Times* and they had shared many bottles over the course of the last two years. But none of them had ever elicited a memory like this.

"Next we have a dry Riesling. This batch was produced by some of the oldest vines on our vineyard. They were planted in 1975 by Valentina Rhodes, an Austrian immigrant who came here with her husband to start a new life. Her family was in the wine industry, and they're credited with bringing some unique varietals to the Finger Lakes."

The Riesling hit Jade's palate like Pop Rocks. Stone fruits mixed with fresh citrus. The tingling feeling was back, racing up and down her spine like she'd sat on a live wire. Holy shit. She reached for her purse and quietly drew out her sketchbook. Could it be? All she had to do to throw off her artist's block was come to the Finger Lakes and sample some wine?

Her fingers trembled as she wrapped them around a pencil. The tip was dull, but it would have to do.

With notes of grapefruit and lime zest on her tongue, she cast a glance around the crowded tasting room. What would she draw? The view of the lake through the floor-to-ceiling windows? Sunshine filtering through the exposed beams on the ceiling?

Her gaze moved back to the mysterious man who was now standing and chatting with another employee. A laugh broke the grumpy mask of his face. His eyes crinkled in the corners, full lips embracing a row of white teeth. His dark hair was molded back into place, but she could picture it hanging over one eye, disheveled in the unseasonal October heat.

The pencil moved across the paper almost without a thought from her.

It was happening. Finally, something. Nobody was going to want to buy a sloppy sketch of some random guy in a winery. But even if it was absolute garbage, it was something. And something was so much better than nothing.

The server refilled her glass. Jade raised it to her lips and sampled greedily. It had the crispness of chardonnay, but less oak. Apricots teased her palate while her pencil glided over the paper, filling in a crease here, a line there. Shading above the brow—not too much.

"This wine is trash," Blake whispered loudly.

Their server faltered as she was pouring the next wine.

Jade broke out of her trance and squared her shoulders. For the past twenty-four hours, she had given Blake the benefit of the doubt. She had put up with the constant side-eyeing of her wardrobe, the self-important shouting on the phone, and the never-ending negativity.

But this was not her fucking bachelorette party.

As if some unseen force had taken over her body, Jade ripped the wineglass out of Blake's hand and slammed it down.

"This is not your day," she said. "If you don't like the wine, sit there and shut up."

"No," Blake said defiantly. She picked the glass back up and nearly tipped her chair over. "If you tried serving this in a Napa winery, you'd be laughed out of the state. My palate has been irrevocably compromised. I expect a refund. Can I speak to the vintner?" she asked their server.

Oh hell.

"She doesn't mean that." Kenya stared daggers at Blake.

Ashley's smile was frozen on her face. Even Camila had the good grace to look shocked.

"It's no trouble. I'll see if he's available." She turned to the man in the three-piece suit. "Rett?" she called.

Those piercing green eyes lifted in their direction. He

said something to the employee next to him and started their way.

Shit. Jade had a partially drawn likeness of his face in hand and Blake was about to insult what seemed to be decades of winemaking legacy.

She tossed her sketchbook in her purse. Her feet hit the floor, and she half-jogged to intercept the man before Blake could open her mouth.

"Hi," she said. Why was she breathless? She ran three miles every morning. "Uh, I'm Jade."

"Rett." He stuck his hand out stiffly and eyed the group behind her. His hand enveloped her, and shockwaves coursed up and down her body. What the hell was in this wine? Ecstasy?

"Excuse me," said a snotty voice behind her.

"Nope." Jade reached around without looking and shoved what felt like Blake's face back in the direction of their table.

There was a harrumph behind her, but Blake didn't speak again.

He—Rett, apparently—was even more handsome up close. The charcoal suit hugged the contour of his torso. His close-trimmed beard framed his face. Even though Jade was five-ten in sneakers, he looked down at her.

She glanced down in a way she hoped was casual. No wedding ring. Not that she was looking for a distraction while she was here. She'd probably never see him again. But something told her she'd remember this interaction for the rest of her life.

"Thank you so much for being willing to speak to us. I'm sure you're incredibly busy." Maybe if she poured on the charm, he would forget what Blake's loose lips had said.

"I'm never too busy to speak to customers," he said, but his clipped tone failed to back up the statement.

"Your wine is incredible," she began. "The best we—I've had since we arrived. I would love to know more about your winemaking process. Do you offer tours?"

Rett looked past her at the group again. He crossed his arms over a broad chest. "You really like the wine?"

She nodded enthusiastically, then flexed her fingers. Her skin still tingled like an electric shock had passed between them.

"Then why is your friend dumping Splenda in our award-winning chardonnay?"

Shit. Jade pursed her lips and glanced behind her. Sure enough, Blake was rolling her eyes and fighting with a packet of sweetener.

"'Friend' isn't really the right word. We're here for a bachelorette party."

He glanced down at her shirt. The frown line deepened.

"Who you surround yourself with says something about you, don't you think?" One of his dark eyebrows lifted.

"I—uh..." She had an apology ready, but his words cut her off. Her cheeks grew hot and her toes curled. Out of all the wineries to pitch a fit in, why did Blake have to do it in the one that was owned by a Greek god in human form?

"If there's nothing else, I have more trash to restock. We keep selling out." Rett jerked his head at the cases on the floor.

"I'm so sorry again. I really think your wine is—"

But he was already gone.

"What the hell just happened?" Jade muttered to herself. She had never been dismissed that way in her entire life. Shame filled her.

Spinning, she zeroed in on Blake. She stormed over and pushed the chair until it turned around to face her.

"What do you want?" Blake looked her up and down again like she had just watched a dog throw up.

"Outside. Now." She pulled Blake out of her chair and tugged her toward the front door.

"Get off of me," Blake whined, but Jade only tightened her grip.

Her cheeks burned as she passed Rett. The front door slammed shut behind them.

"What's going on with you?" she asked. "No offense, but you've been a bitch since we left."

"It's none of your business," Blake snapped.

"Really? Is Nate your ex-boyfriend too?" Maybe he had secretly dated all the bridesmaids.

Another memory hit her—Nate on a gingham blanket in Central Park. A hot, slow kiss in the July heat. The brush of a wicker picnic basket against her bare arms as he leaned her back.

She sucked her cheeks in. Nate flashbacks were not invited to this cursed weekend.

"No," Blake snapped. "I don't—I don't have a boyfriend."

"Girlfriend? Fiancé? Prison pen pal?"

"I got dumped, okay? A week ago."

"Oh." The wind promptly fell out of her sails. No wonder Blake had been such an abominable twat. "I'm so sorry. That's awful."

The other woman sniffed. "He was supposed to come to the wedding. But out of nowhere he just decided that 'this isn't working.'" She threw her hands up in quotations. "We dated for three years. He didn't even dump me in person."

"What an asshole."

"It's just hard. I had such a clear picture of what our

future was going to look like. Our wedding, our kids, our five-year plan. And he just threw it all away like it was nothing."

Jade grabbed Blake's hand. "I'm so sorry he did that to you. If he can't see what a gorgeous, fierce, badass bitch you are, he never deserved you in the first place. I know how hard it is to be completely blindsided."

Blake averted her eyes. "I know you do. Kenya told me."

She shook her head. "It's been two years. I'm over it. It's fine."

It wasn't, though. If everything was fine, her muse wouldn't have completely abandoned her after the breakup. But that was not the female empowerment that Blake needed to hear.

"Trust me when I say you are going to be okay," Jade added. "And if I ever see your ex-boyfriend in person, I will personally slingshot him in the balls."

Blake laughed—her first laugh the entire trip.

"I'm a mess too, if it makes you feel any better." She threw her hands up. "I'm attending my ex-boyfriend's wedding with no date. Does it get more pathetic than that?"

It did. Attending your ex-boyfriend's wedding with no date and a plummeting career was definitely more pathetic.

"Well," Blake said, "don't tell Ashley I said this. But I've always thought Nate was kind of a dick."

"He definitely can be." Jade probably shouldn't have been speaking ill of the groom on his wedding week. But he had also completely upended her life.

Not that she was thinking about that. There were more important things to worry about. Making it through this godforsaken weekend and fixing her financial crisis. Those were the only items she'd be entertaining for the remainder of the week.

"So," Jade said, "knowing that I'm right there with you, do you think we can try to at least pretend to have a good time? For Ashley's sake?"

Blake nodded. She stuck her hand out. "Fake it till we make it?"

Jade threw her arms open and pulled Blake into a hug. She stiffened, then relaxed. It was like hugging a beanpole, but still nice. "Let's get some lunch."

CHAPTER FOUR

JADE

THE FRONT DOOR SNAPPED SHUT BEHIND JADE AS SHE AND Penny stepped onto the dew-covered grass. She tucked her water bottle in the side pocket of her backpack and surveyed the front lawn. Once again, a hungover Ashley had cancelled the morning festivities. Camila was probably fuming. With the other girls still in bed, Jade and Penny were on their own.

There was something magical about this place. Not the house—though it was decorated nicely enough, it didn't feel like home. Home, in her mind, meant outrageous blooms of color, soft blankets, fifty scattered dog toys, and paint supplies in every nook and cranny. Not that she was currently using them.

The lake and the surrounding hills, however, held a promise she couldn't quite put into words. Maybe it was just the change of scenery or the fleeting moment of inspiration from the day before, but something felt different here. And she was going to run straight to the heart of it.

She and Penny set off in the direction of the charming small town they had passed through on their way to the wineries yesterday. Hills rose and fell around them. The lake was partially visible behind a mask of leaves that had just begun to turn yellow.

A memory crept in. She and Nate had spent their last spring break of grad school in the Catskills. He—or more accurately, his family credit card—had booked a stay in an absurd resort in the Hudson Valley. They had hiked for hours before tumbling into bed, headboard crashing against the old-fashioned wallpaper.

And now it was nothing but a memory.

She had loved him so damn much even though he was the opposite of who she had imagined her soulmate to be. In line to manage his dad's hedge fund, he wore suits to class and dragged her to galas. His family unironically had lunch at the Ritz at least once a month.

A middle-class girl from Queens, Jade hadn't really fit into his world of designer labels and charity events. But he had drawn her in with his easy smile and quick wit, offering his elbow and shepherding her through every family and society event for a year and a half.

A car zoomed past on her left, and she flinched. Pining over Nate had accomplished exactly nothing. He was marrying her best friend this weekend, and she needed to accept it and move on.

Her pace quickened as The Killers blasted in her ears. Penny galloped along at her side. Maybe if Jade ran fast enough, she could outrun the memories.

A side stitch forced her to slow down as they wound down the hill and into the town square. The morning sun glimmered on the lake to her right. To her left, pathways cut through green grass to a charming gazebo. People bustled up and down the sidewalks, waving at each other. The smell of fresh coffee and sweet cinnamon drifted over from a turquoise café with a sunflower on the sign. The yellow door beckoned, but the single dollar in her wallet begged her to reconsider.

It was friggen adorable.

She passed a row of historic-looking buildings and came to an abrupt stop. Was that a vending machine full of artisanal cheese? She all but pressed herself to the glass. The machine had a credit card reader. Surely her budget could survive one purchase. Maybe two flavors. What if it was the secret to throwing off her painter's block for good? It would be irresponsible not to try it.

Five minutes later, she and Penny trudged up the opposite shore with a backpack full of smoked cheddar and honey goat cheese. The two-lane road felt familiar. It must have been the one they took yesterday while winery hopping.

She tugged Penny in close and moved back into a run. It was harder here with the hills, but the exertion kept her mind from wandering.

Her lungs burned as they crested a hill. Rows of grapevines sloped up a gentle incline on her left. And there at the top was Rhodes Vineyard.

Her heart fell into her butt, and she pulled to a halt. Penny looked at her.

The wine that had unlocked her first glimmer of inspiration was behind those doors. But Blake's attitude had made a horrible impression on Hottie McWinePants. It wasn't really Jade's responsibility to apologize, but he deserved one regardless. Would he even be there this early?

Penny seemed to agree, because she raced up the stony driveway. Jade's heart rate kicked up a notch as they approached the door. This winery was dog friendly—there had been a French bulldog named Mina at the table next to them yesterday. But Penny had a habit of greeting people by leaping on them. That must be why Jade was nervous.

She glanced down at the now sweat-soaked T-shirt and bike shorts she had thrown on without a thought. It wasn't what she would usually wear to make a good impression. But she would never see these people again. Why did she care?

She cracked open the entry door, and a wave of air conditioning hit her. Thank god. Maybe it would dry out some of the sweat. Penny pulled her farther inside.

Elaine, their server from the day before, stood at one of the tasting tables, bottle of cleaner in hand.

"Good morning!" she said cheerfully. "Welcome to Rhodes Vineyard." Her smile faltered when she saw Jade.

Damn it. So much for an incognito visit.

"Hi, Elaine," Jade said. "I just came back to pick up some bottles. I really enjoyed our tasting yesterday. I'm sorry for the others in my group. I think they were just hungry."

Elaine brightened. "I'm so glad to hear you say that! Our vintner works really hard to honor his grandmother's legacy."

"Well, he has a real gift."

Someone cleared their throat behind Jade, and she jumped. Penny yanked on the leash and beelined for whoever was behind her.

Jade whirled around. *Shit.* There he was. Rett was slightly less grumpy-looking today, but his expression was equally serious. His navy suit was paired with a matching bowtie. How long did it take him to get ready in the morning? Did he have a professional collar-starcher on staff?

He bent down to pet Penny. She sat on his overly shined dress shoe and panted happily as he scratched behind her ears.

"Is there something I can help you find?"

His voice hit her like lightning. It was deep, grumbly, but refined. Something stirred in her soul.

Did he recognize her? Maybe he was hopelessly nearsighted and couldn't place her due to the fact that she looked like she had climbed out of a swimming pool.

"Yes, actually. I just came in for a couple bottles. The dry Riesling and the Blaufränkisch."

"Let me get those for you."

"Thank you." She waited awkwardly while he pulled two bottles off the shelves and slid them into paper bags.

She slung her backpack off and opened the neck to find her wallet. Before she could stop it, three blocks of cheese tumbled onto the counter.

Amusement sparkled in his eyes. "You know you should refrigerate those."

Jade's cheeks grew hot. Did he think she was an idiot? "I was planning to. I just ran past that cheese vending machine in the village and was compelled by an outside force to stop."

Rett nodded. Was that the hint of a smile on his lips? "We've all been there."

He rang up the total, and her stomach twisted as she handed over her card. This trip was bleeding money out of her. How far would two bottles get her? Maybe the wine plus the closure of the wedding would be enough to finally lift this black cloud from her life.

"You won't want to put Splenda in these, by the way," he said as he tucked the receipt in the bag and pushed them toward her.

Damn it. Her cheeks grew hot again. He definitely remembered her.

"I am so sorry about yesterday." Oh no, word vomit was

coming. "I love your wine. Seriously. This is going to make me sound like a crazy person, but it awakened something in me."

His eyebrows rose, but she couldn't stop.

"I know the girls I was with yesterday were assholes. Blake—the primary offender—was really going through something. Most of us are. It's sort of a messed-up situation, actually."

Penny whined at her side as if Jade was embarrassing her, but the runaway train kept going.

"You see, Ashley—the bride—is marrying my ex-boyfriend. And I'm the idiot who introduced them. I was so excited when they hit it off. They're both huge Knicks fans. We went to a game during March Madness in our last year of grad school. I could almost see him falling out of love with me after that, you know?"

Rett was frozen in place.

"But we still made plans. I was killing it in the art world at the time, and he was lined up to work for his dad's hedge fund right after graduation. We were going to move in together, a beautiful two-bedroom in Midtown. I saw my whole future written out in front of me. I'd be Mrs. Jade Astor with my own studio space and galleries fighting for my art. And then on move-in day, I walked in and there they were."

Her voice faltered. Rett reached across the till like he was going to comfort her but paused halfway and tapped the counter instead. Maybe he wasn't a stoic stick-in-the-mud after all. Or maybe he had been reaching over to strangle her and put her out of her misery.

"He didn't cheat on me, if that's what you were thinking. Not physically, anyway. I walked in and they were standing in the kitchen, arguing. He hadn't even brought any boxes with him. He knew that he wasn't going to go through with it, and he still let me sign the lease. He let me go on believing that he still loved me, even though I knew the second I walked in that room that he was already gone."

Penny jumped up her leg, and Jade patted her on the head.

"So now I'm a bridesmaid who has to stand at the altar and watch my childhood best friend marry the man I thought I was going to marry. And I'm going to have to go make small talk with his family without even a plus one at my side. Or a career to discuss. I have never been so pathetic in my entire life."

Rett frowned, but she plowed on.

"What I'm trying to say is I'm an artist who hasn't created any art for two years. Not even a doodle. I used to get this feeling—like a tingling sensation—when inspiration hit. My mom would call it the 'muse tickle.' But I haven't felt anything since that morning, standing in an empty kitchen and watching my boyfriend choose someone else. Until yesterday."

She put a hand on the top of a bottle at the register. "Something about your wine cracked me open again. The profile, the bouquet, the incredible and barely detectable blend of fruit and earthiness. It was a small tingle, and it didn't amount to much, but it was there. I can't thank you enough for *your* art. I don't know if it's going to be the answer to my problems, but for the first time in two years, I have a tiny bit of hope."

Someone sniffed loudly behind her. Elaine leaned on a broom, tears in her eyes.

"That man did not deserve you."

Jade smiled.

"Uh—thank you," Rett said.

Heat crept into her cheeks again. She had just spouted a veritable fountain of crazy all over this poor man.

"I'm really sorry for word vomiting all over you, and I'm sorry for what happened at our tasting yesterday. I just wanted to say, from one artist to another, your creation is transcendental. Thank you for giving me hope."

Before he could say anything, she turned on her heel and left.

CHAPTER FIVE

RETT

RETT FROZE AT THE COUNTER AS THE DOOR SWUNG SHUT. What the hell had just happened? The leggy brunette from yesterday's trouble group had waltzed in with the most beautiful dog he had ever seen, shared a sob story that could have been a plot line in one of his mother's soap operas, and called his wine transcendental.

Elaine stared at him with her eyebrows raised.

"I'll be right back." Before he could consciously decide what he was doing, he had pushed open the door and stepped into the humid midmorning air.

The woman was fast. She was halfway to the parking lot already, bottles clinking together in her backpack.

He broke into a light jog. "Jade, was it?"

She jumped and whirled around. Her brown hair was smoothed back into a ponytail, and her blue eyes were the same hue as a sapphire. Her legs seemed to stretch for days.

"Uh, yeah," she said.

Had she noticed his eyes dipping? Shit, what was he doing out here?

"How long will you be in town?" he asked.

It would be insane for him to ask a complete stranger to be his date to the anniversary party. It would be even dumber for him to ask her to be his fake girlfriend. And yet, something told him he would never forgive himself if he didn't.

"Just until Sunday morning. You know, after the wedding that I was incapable of shutting up about."

His heart fell, and he shifted his gaze to the lake. He should have known. Bachelorette parties tended to blow into town as quickly as a typhoon and leave a flood of Solo cups and plastic tiaras in their wake.

"Did you run out here to convince me to join your wine club?" she asked after a beat.

A laugh burst forth from deep inside him. Cute and funny. What idiot had dumped her?

"No. Although it is a great deal—four bottles a month for the price of three, first dibs on tickets to our events."

She cleared her throat. "I probably should have mentioned that in addition to being a sad-sack ex and a failure in my career, I'm also incredibly broke."

He looked into her eyes. Her tone was light, but it didn't mask a sense of deep suffering.

She shuddered despite the heat. Something stirred in him.

"I'm guessing you live in Manhattan," he said.

She nodded. "That's where the art world is."

The dog dragged her forward, circling once and sitting in front of him. She looked up with a goofy smile until he bent down to pet her again.

"Who's this?" he asked.

"Penny," she said with obvious warmth.

"It's a pity you're leaving," he said with a glance. "I was

hoping to give you that tour you asked about. It's dog friendly. There's a lot to see here in the Finger Lakes."

Jade's gaze moved past him to the sweeping hills. "I kind of wish I didn't have to leave. I honestly love it here. I've never seen anything like it."

Rett would never know if he didn't ask. Maybe he could present it as a mutual benefit.

"I have a proposition for you."

Her eyes widened.

"I think we can help each other," he said before she could reply. "You need a date so you don't have to show up to this wedding alone. And I need a date for the vineyard's golden anniversary in two weeks."

She blinked. "Your girlfriend won't be accompanying you?"

An involuntary flashback of Alexa hit him like a punch to the gut—blonde hair flashing in the sunlight as she ran laughing through the green vines.

He shifted his gaze back to the lake, and something hardened in him. There was no way he was ready to share that particular story. "No girlfriend. Let's just say I am intimately familiar with your situation."

"Oh." Her voice softened. "Why do you need a date for the party? Won't you be busy running around as man of the hour?"

"If you met my family, you'd understand. They've been playing matchmaker and hounding me about settling down since I finished school. I just want to be left alone. Luckily my parents live in California, so they don't know that I'm not actually dating anyone."

Jade shook her head. "I feel for you. I do. But I won't be here in two weeks. I have to go back to the city and figure my life out so I don't go homeless."

So much for that idea. But he couldn't give up without a fight.

"You could come back," he suggested.

She bit her lip. "I can't...drive."

Rett stared at her. "You don't know how to drive?"

She crossed her arms and frowned. "I've lived in the city my whole life. Do you have any idea how expensive and unnecessary it would be to have a car in Manhattan?"

He hesitated. It was clear this wasn't a good match. She had her own life and her own problems that frankly were a lot more dire than his. But something wouldn't allow him to let her go. She was smart, funny, cute as hell. She apparently struggled with money management, but that was fixable. She didn't deserve to struggle this way. He could help her if he could convince her to stay.

"I'll pick you up," he said. Was he starting to sound desperate?

She looked at him, posture rigid. "We don't even know each other. How do I know you're not a crazy person who murders women and throws them through a wood chipper to fertilize your vines?"

He smiled again. "And how do I know *you're* not unhinged? Who runs to a vineyard in stifling humidity with a backpack full of vending machine cheese?"

She laughed, and the sound warmed him from the inside.

"That's fair. Okay, so it's an equal risk situation here."

Her arms relaxed, and she looked over the vineyard, seemingly making up her mind.

"Why are you offering this after I sweated all over your counter? Don't you see like thirty bachelorette parties a day? You could ask anyone to be your date."

He took another step closer to her. "I told you. I know

what it's like to be where you are. I know how lonely it is. And I really could use your help for the party. You're an artist, right? I bet you're great at creating atmosphere. I can handle the wine, but I'm useless at décor."

Penny jumped up on Rett and licked him full in the face. He laughed and scratched her cheeks. Who cared if dog hair got all over his suit? It would be a reminder of this humid morning even if Jade said no.

"Okay," she said. "We'll do it. Give me your phone."

He bit back the "really?" that had almost come out and handed over his phone. There was time to figure out logistics later. Hopefully she was okay with being picked up after the winery closed. It would be a long night. But he hadn't been sleeping much anyway.

Her phone rang, and she passed his back. "There. Now we have each other's numbers. I'll text you later with details, but I have to get going. It'll take at least an hour to get back to the house, and I have rehearsal dinner duties."

"Where are you staying?"

Jade pointed across the lake. "On the eastern side."

He scoffed. People drove like idiots on the state highway. She would be run over before ever making it to town. "Don't be ridiculous. I'll take you back."

He wouldn't be gone for long. It was probably a twenty-minute round trip. He just needed to run inside and grab his keys.

"That's not necessary. I'm perfectly capable of—"

"Hang out by the truck." He hitched a thumb at the dusty pickup. "I can't have you dying of heatstroke on my property. It's bad for business."

"You really don't have to—"

"Think of your cheese," he called over his shoulder.

Leaving at the beginning of the workday felt wrong.

Customers would arrive any minute. What if something happened? A half dozen scenarios flashed in his mind—broken pipe, shattered case, medical emergency.

Rett sucked down a deep breath. Maybe, just this once, it would be okay. It was only half an hour. And Jade needed him, even if she didn't realize it.

CHAPTER SIX

JADE

Ten minutes later, she was in a truck with a borderline stranger, bumping down the stony driveway. The air conditioning was mercifully on, and it was without a doubt better than sweating her ass off all the way back to the house.

"So," Rett said. "If we're going to do this, we need a plan."

"A plan?"

This was insane. Was she seriously doing this? Fake dating a complete stranger just so she didn't have to face Nate and his judgy family alone?

Penny had chosen the middle seat, with her head propped on Rett's lap. Traitor. Jade was going to have to dip even further into her experience budget to buy him a lint roller.

"Yes," he said. "My parents will ask questions. So we should at least get to know each other."

"That's fair," she said.

"You'll have to show me your art, of course. I'll need to know about your friends, your family. Hobbies and interests. All of that."

"There's not much to tell."

"I find that hard to believe." He took his eyes off the road for a moment and smirked at her.

"Fine, I'll start," he said in response to her silence. "Everett Ignatius Rhodes—"

"*Ignatius*?"

"It means fiery." He glowered. "My mom was really sleep-deprived."

"Fair enough. Go on."

"So. Everett Ignatius Rhodes."

She bit her lip and looked out the window. A name like that belonged in a faraway castle or, at the very least, on a memorial somewhere celebrating a Puritanical town founder.

"Mostly lifelong resident of Hammondsport, graduated from the local high school before getting a master's in business from Cornell—"

Hmmm. An Ivy League guy. He was like a slightly more approachable version of Nate.

"—and an advanced sommelier certificate from the Wine School of Philadelphia."

"There's no way that's a thing," Jade interrupted.

"Which part?"

"The Wine School of Philadelphia?" she raised her eyebrows. "Is that just a euphemism for tailgating outside Lincoln Financial Field?"

Rett frowned and turned on his blinker. "It's one of the most highly respected wine schools in the entire country."

"Sure. Well, in that case I graduated summa cum laude from Fancy Pants Arts Academy and apprenticed under Dr. Robert Ross."

"You're really going to besmirch the good name of American treasure Bob Ross?"

She smiled again. There was a sense of humor beneath that buttoned-up exterior. Who knew?

"You're right," she said. "That was too far. So after obtaining your sommelier certification from that imaginary school, you came back here?"

"I did. My grandmother was sick. She taught me every-thing she knew, left countless notebooks filled with her winemaking notes. She passed away last February."

"I'm so sorry to hear that. And she left the winery to you? Not your parents?"

Rett nodded. His smile was gone. "My dad—Gerald Rhodes, for the record—is really into music. He moved to California to write scores for movies. That's where he met my mom."

"What does your mom do?"

"She's an actress. Teresa Rhodes."

That name sounded familiar. She'd have to Google her later.

"Shortly after they got married," he continued, "my dad realized he wanted to be closer to home. So my mom pivoted to Broadway, and we moved to Hammondsport. They technically stayed until I graduated high school, but my mom was gone a lot. She still took a lot of roles in movies, and I knew she always considered California her real home. They've been there ever since. I spent summers in college here with my grandma learning about wine."

"Wow. And just in case it comes up"—and definitely not because she was being nosy—"the ex?"

His grip tightened on the steering wheel. "Alexa. We met when I was at school in Philly. She moved to Rochester when I got my certificate, and we dated for two and a half years. Now she's dating my older brother."

She grimaced. At least Ashley wasn't her sister.

"Yeah," he said. "We don't talk much."

"I don't blame you. Thank you."

"For what?" He shot her a glance. His brows were still contracted.

"For sharing. It makes me feel a little less weird about the fountain of crazy I spewed all over you. Sorry again for that."

"Don't do that," he said. True to his middle name, fire was in his eyes.

"Do what?" She looked around the interior. She hadn't put her feet on the dash. It was a little late for him to be scolding her on the metric ton of dog fur that was probably stuck to the seat.

"Don't apologize needlessly. Don't make yourself small."

Oh. A thrill ran through her. She had never been one for bossy men—the world had enough of them—but there was something intriguing about being bossed around for her own good.

"It's a pet peeve of mine," he added. "Even if you're just my fake girlfriend, I want you to be completely and unapologetically you."

"S—I was going to say sorry, but I won't. Because you're right. I'm not sorry for talking about my feelings."

"That's right. So we were discussing your tenure at... what was it? Fancy Pants Art Academy?"

She bit her lip. In thirty minutes, she had already shared more with Rett than she had told any of her flings over the past two years. But with the exception of this golden anniversary event that she still wasn't totally sure she was committing to, she'd probably never see him again. So what was the harm in letting him in a little?

"Yeah. My story isn't as cute. I'm a lifelong resident of the greater Manhattan metropolitan area. I grew up in a lower middle-class family in Queens and attended public school through eighth grade. Then I got a scholarship to Rothschild Academy. That's where I met Ashley—the bride—and probably the only reason why I got into NYU."

He let out a low whistle. "NYU? That's a pretty big deal."

She shrugged. "I did the art program. It was great for a while. I was actually pretty successful. I sold almost everything I ever painted while I was there. Even made it onto a few 'thirty under thirty' lists."

He nodded and appeared to be listening intently.

"And then everything fell apart," she said.

"Because of your ex?" he asked quietly.

Jade laughed, a weird reaction for such a serious moment. A weight settled on her chest. She hadn't intended on telling him this. She had certainly never told any of her hookups about the incident. But someone she was truly dating would know.

She took a deep breath. "Because my parents died. It was completely unexpected."

The truck rolled to a stop at an intersection. Rett turned to face her, concern in his eyes. He must really think she was pathetic now.

"I'm so sorry." He reached across the middle seat—or, more accurately, the dog—and gripped her hand. His hand was soft and warm. Comforting. She wasn't usually much of a hand holder, but there was nothing awkward about his embrace.

Another thrill ran through her in spite of the heaviness of the conversation.

"Yeah, it sucked. It was my last Christmas Eve of grad school. They had gone downtown to pick up my favorite cake from this bakery, Crumb and Get It. A drunk driver ran a red light and hit them while they crossed the street."

He blew out a long breath and squeezed her hand before lifting his foot from the brake. The truck inched forward down the highway.

"I know. Didn't know you were getting a three-for-one deal on sob stories today, did you?"

They were in town now, crawling around the village green. There was silence in the truck as they passed another restaurant emanating amazing smells. If only she could hang out here and get to know this adorable little town. But she had to get back to the city. Didn't she?

"So you met the boyfriend in grad school?" he asked.

"Yeah. Nate was studying finance at NYU. We collided while ice skating at Rockefeller Center and started dating the next week." She shifted the collar of her shirt to cover up the tiny ice skate tattoo that commemorated the event. Nate had a matching one. "He really stood by me when my parents died. Helped me deal with the house, the life insurance, the double funeral."

Rett hadn't moved his hand. He squeezed hers again.

The lake sparkled outside the window. She took a deep breath and paused. It had been almost three years since she opened the door to a cop with his hat in his hand, but the memory stung as much as it ever had.

"He met Ashley at the funeral. That day passed in a complete blur. I barely remember anything. But I do remember him laughing when he talked to her. That stuck out to me because, of course, why was he laughing while my parents were dead behind him? I probably should have seen it then, but I was..."

"Distracted?" he offered.

"Yeah." She turned away to look out the window.

"And your other friends?"

"I lost a lot of them in the breakup. Ashley's always stuck

by me. You know, as long as you don't count the part where she fell in love with my boyfriend."

Rett turned up the eastern side of the lake. His brow was furrowed.

"So why do you stay?"

"In the city? I told you, it's where the art world is."

"But you could make art anywhere. And probably cut your rent in half just by leaving city limits."

Jade paused. He had a point. Maybe she had been holding on to a small piece of her original dream with Nate—a New York City power couple who dominated in the art world and in finance.

"Yeah, well. It's the only home I've ever known."

Maybe it was a stupid reason to stay. But the city was also filled with memories of her parents—trips to the zoo, gawking at the exhibitions at the Met, mugs of warm coffee in their favorite cafe.

Rett was silent as the truck shifted up a steep incline.

"Well," he said a minute later, "now that we've covered the basics, we should probably get to the plan. Are plus-ones invited to the rehearsal dinner?"

She shook her head.

He frowned. "So there won't be anyone to take the heat off of you if necessary. But they can't stop me from bringing something to you. Where's it at?"

"Alder and Oak." It had an awfully Manhattan-esque name for a restaurant in a tiny town.

"Great place," he said. "When we get to the house, run inside and grab something for me that you'll need for the rehearsal or the wedding—shoes, earrings, lipstick, whatever."

He was awfully bossy.

"Why, so you can hold it hostage?"

"No, so I can storm in and save the day and bring it to you. They don't need to know the details of why I have them. A new mystery boyfriend is guaranteed to shift the conversation away from your career."

She turned to face him. "Okay, seriously. Why are you doing all this? Is this a fetish thing?"

There was no reason on earth why a man as pants-searingly hot as Rett would be single and ready to take on the role of a lifetime for a girl he just met.

He chuckled. "It's not a fetish. I'm just hoping if I play my role well enough, you'll agree to come back for the anniversary party. If it'll help get my parents off my back, I will happily fake propose to you in the middle of your ex's wedding."

"They must be really bad matchmakers. Oh, it's the next left." She pointed at the driveway flanked by a stone wall.

He slowed down and put his turn signal on. "You have no idea. The last time they came home they brought along a twenty-one-year-old daughter of a business associate. I had to entertain her the whole weekend. Have you hung out with a twenty-one-year-old lately?"

Jade shook her head.

"It was exhausting. She got drunk off of two wine coolers and threw up on my dock."

"Yikes."

They pulled into the circular driveway. Thankfully no one was outside.

"Okay, let me grab something. I'll be right back."

As she moved to open the door, Rett caught her wrist.

Her skin tingled at his touch.

"Wait. One more thing."

"What?" She looked at him expectantly.

He had leaned over Penny, leaving inches between them.

His eyes were meadow green in the dappled sunlight. One forearm was flexed on the steering wheel. His fancy waistcoat lay buttoned over what were probably six-pack abs. Desire stirred deep and hot in her core.

Could they update their agreement to include a friends-with-benefits clause? If he was going to murder her, she might as well die in the throes of passion.

The air between them vibrated with possibility. She tipped toward him, no more than a centimeter.

His phone vibrated in his pocket, and his expression changed. He drew his hand back, her heart falling with the movement. *Obviously he wasn't going in for a kiss, idiot.* She needed to stop thinking with her vagina.

"Don't forget to refrigerate your cheese," he finally said.

Was that really what he had meant to say? It didn't matter. At least she hadn't made a fool of herself. Again. Time to focus and give him a reason to return later on.

"I just remembered something." She unzipped her backpack and dug through it, pushing aside art supplies and a bag of dog treats. Finally, all the way at the bottom, a small Tiffany-blue box appeared.

She pressed it into his hand. "Here. I put them in here for safe keeping. I'm supposed to wear them tomorrow."

He cracked the lid of the box open, then glanced at the house. "Looks like it's going to be a hell of a wedding."

"You have no idea. Don't lose those, okay? Or Ashley might actually murder you."

He shrugged. "She can't marry your ex if she's in prison for manslaughter."

She smiled in spite of herself. "I'll see you later?"

There was a seriousness in his eyes. "I'll be there."

CHAPTER SEVEN

JADE

THE SECOND SHE ENTERED THE PRIVATE DINING ROOM AT Alder and Oak, all her hopes for a drama-free dinner evaporated. She had barely managed to avoid Nate during the rehearsal at Barrington Terrace. He had caught her eye more than once, but she would rather log-roll into the lake than spend a single moment talking to tweedle dick.

And now she was seated directly next to Nate's dad, Reginald. Great.

Her shoulders hunched up as she sat. She should have asked Kenya for a sip from her flask before dinner. But then everyone would have gossiped about how she smelled like the alley behind a bar on Cinco de Mayo.

Dinner began with toasts, each more uncomfortable than the last.

"From the first moment Ashley brought Nathan home, I knew that you two would be together forever." Tracey, a neurosurgeon and dedicated collector of ceramic cats, held her champagne glass aloft, tears in her eyes.

Jade slumped in her seat. When would this night of torture end?

"This union of families is certainly cause for celebration," Reginald said minutes later. "I believe in my bones that the two of you were meant to be."

Jade bit the inside of her cheek. Nate's parents had always been pleasant to her. But they had never once described them as *meant to be*. There had always been a feeling, from their very first meeting, that they were disappointed in Nate's choice. Jade didn't wear the right clothes or have the right career path. Even when she was successful in the art world, her middle-class upbringing was apparently insurmountable for Reginald and Patricia.

"Some of my partners' wives have asked about your latest collection, Jade," Reginald told her through a mouthful of steak.

She picked at the tortellini on her plate. It was delicious, but not enough to keep her from wanting to sprint out of the room.

"Things have been quiet on your website for a while," he added. "You must be working on something big."

"Yes, I'm in the middle of a really unique collection," she said with the best smile she could muster. Unique in that it was completely occupied by blank canvases, but he didn't need to know that.

She pulled her phone out of her purse and fired off a quick SOS to Rett. Would he really follow through on his promise to interrupt the rehearsal dinner to bring her earrings back? He hadn't texted her all day. But he was at work.

"Fabulous. Well, when it's finished, I'm sure they'd love to be the first to know. I'll email you their contact information."

"That's...great."

"Jade, are you seeing anyone?" Tracey suddenly piped up and leaned across the table, broccoli speared on her fork.

What was this, twenty questions day?

"Oh, I—"

"Jade." Someone tapped her shoulder. Her heart lifted an inch, and she turned, half-expecting to find Rett. But no. It was just Nate.

"Yes?"

"I was wondering if I could talk to you for a second."

The word no was on the tip of her tongue. Which was the lesser of two evils—an uncomfortable chat with Nate or being grilled by a bunch of adults who were perpetually disappointed in her?

She glanced across the table at Kenya with a plea in her eye.

Kenya screamed, and the dinner party crashed to a halt.

One of the groomsmen ducked under the table. Camila leapt onto her chair. Everyone else frantically searched the room.

"What? What is it?" Ashley's dad, Frank, had jumped out of his seat with his hand on his hip. Had he really brought a gun to the table? What kind of trouble was he expecting in a pink bed-and-breakfast in the middle of wine country?

"Sorry, I thought I saw a mouse. But I think it was just a shadow."

There was a collective sigh of relief. Several people chuckled.

"Thank you," Jade mouthed across the table. Surely that was enough of a diversion to keep anyone else from asking more questions.

Kenya nodded and raised her glass in a silent toast.

"Jade?"

Oh, for fuck's sake. She whirled around again. Nate was still standing there. Her hand curled into a fist.

"Yes?"

"Can we? Talk?"

She would rather be tossed face-first into a dumpster outside a daycare.

"I really don't think that's appropriate," she said in a low voice.

"Come on. Please?"

He looked sincere. But he had also looked sincere the day he asked her to move in with him.

"What were we talking about? Before the imaginary mouse? Oh, right." Ashley's mom turned back to Jade, a question on her lips.

"Fine," Jade said to Nate. She pushed her chair back and stood up before she could change her mind.

"Maybe outside would be best?" he asked.

"Whatever."

She followed him on a winding path through the dining area and outside. It had started to rain at some point, so they were trapped under the awning. Perfect.

"Sorry. I know my dad can be a lot." He smoothed a hand over his slicked-back hair and set his gaze on her.

Those blue eyes used to make her come undone. Now they just made her want to lace up boxing gloves.

"It's fine. I knew I'd get the third degree all weekend long." She crossed her arms over her chest and stared across the rows of cars. Vehicles zipped by on the highway, but there was no view of the lake from here to soothe her frazzled nerves.

She had been so stupid to agree to this.

"I asked them not to," Nate said.

"Why?"

"Well, I know you've been going through a tough time."

She bit down hard on her tongue. It was either that or she head-butted his dumb ass into the muddy parking lot.

"I don't know what you're talking about. Things are great."

"Come on, Jade. It's me. You don't have to lie. I know you're not seeing anyone, and you haven't painted in years."

Her mouth dropped open. How *dare* he? A molten wave of anger that she had been damming up for the last two years threatened to explode.

"We never even really talked after everything that happened," he continued. "I never had the opportunity to tell you I'm sorry. I just wanted to make sure you're okay."

Was that *pity* in his voice? Oh *hell* no.

At that moment, a pickup truck pulled into the parking lot. It turned into a spot and out jumped Rett.

Thank. God.

"Jade!" he called as he crossed the lot at a jog, cocky smile visible from a mile away. His gaze shifted between her and Nate. "I'm so glad I caught you."

Nate looked instantly annoyed, but Jade barely noticed thanks to the now soaked button-down shirt that clung to— of course—a chiseled set of abs.

Rett darted under the awning. The rain had washed his hair out of its perfectly molded place. It hung in his eyes.

She barely had time to register the deep, hot burn of desire that had flared on his approach before he crushed his mouth to hers. He cradled her head in his hand, gentle but firm. Every cell in her body lit up like Times Square.

Holy hell. All the sloppy make outs in dark clubs in the world couldn't have prepared her for this. If he was a chronic bachelor, who had taught him to kiss like this?

A long, slow pull inside her set her body aflame. His

thumb brushed against her cheek, and her knees trans-formed into Jell-O. His tongue slipped between her parted lips. She snaked a hand around his waist, fisted her hands around his wet shirt. It was everything a kiss was supposed to be—heat, passion, fireworks. The promise of something deeper.

She had never been kissed like this.

It was too bad it was fake.

Nate cleared his throat, and Rett pulled back. Regret set in immediately.

"I thought you might need these," Rett said to her. "They're for tomorrow, right?" He pressed the little blue box into her hand.

Jade blinked. She seemed to have left her brain inside. The ability to form words eluded her.

"Yes," she finally said. "Thank you so much."

"I don't think we've met," Nate said with an expression that suggested someone was spreading manure nearby.

"Nice to meet you," Rett said. "Everett Rhodes." He held a wet hand toward Nate, who took it with narrowed eyes.

"Nathan Astor."

"The groom," Jade blurted out.

Rett's eyes darkened. He was a good two inches taller than Nate. Ha.

Nate flinched and drew his hand back. "Well, I should get back inside. Gotta check in with my beautiful bride."

Ugh.

"I should head out too," Rett said with his eyes on Jade. He turned to look at Nate. "It was nice to meet you. Congrat-ulations, by the way."

"What? Oh, yeah. Thanks," Nate mumbled. As the door slammed shut behind him, a weight lifted from her shoulders.

She clutched Rett's arm. "Thank you so much. Seriously. I was basically a homicide suspect in a room full of detectives in there."

"I'm glad I could help."

He smiled, and for a moment they just stared at each other. Rain pinged off the awning. Petrichor—one of Jade's favorite smells in the world—emanated from the earth. What was that feeling?

A tingling sensation crept up from the base of her spine. Was that her muse? Could it be? A chill hit her that had nothing to do with the night air. Maybe it wasn't just the wine. Maybe there was something here, in the soil or the water. It called to her.

"I guess I should get back in there," she said with a reluctant glance at the door. She could have happily spent the whole night out here, sketchbook in hand as the rain fell.

"You don't want me to come schmooze with the parents? I bet at least one of them is in the wine club."

She smiled. "Let's save it for tomorrow. You're kind of wet."

"I'll have you know I'm way more attractive when I'm wet. Especially to middle-aged women."

Against her will, Jade's eyes traveled down the topography of his torso. His usual fancy suit coat was missing, and the rain made his button-down cling like a second skin. Damn it. Something stirred deep within her.

"Well, maybe I'll hose you down with overpriced champagne at the reception." She took a step back. If she didn't, there was an eighty-five percent chance she was going to jump on him and commit a crime of indecency.

"I'll see you tomorrow then."

Neither one of them moved.

His hair was still hanging in his eyes. He smirked like he could tell what she was thinking. Every cell in her body screamed at her to kiss him again. But there was no one around. Nobody to prove it to. What would be the point?

She tilted her face up to his, and he looked down at her. What was this feeling? A hyperlocalized gravitational storm drawing them together? Did he feel it too?

A peal of laughter rang out inside, and she jumped. The spell was broken.

She smiled nervously and took another step back. If this was just lust, it wasn't a kind she had ever experienced before. She needed to be more careful.

"Right. Tomorrow."

CHAPTER EIGHT

RETT

"You're taking the day off?" Elaine's voice was full of disbelief.

Rett frowned. "Just half of it. I made a promise to someone. Unless you think you can't manage."

As stressful as it would be to leave the winery on a peak day, the idea of disappointing Jade was somehow worse. He had done what he could—the shelves were fully stocked, everything was staged for the day's tastings, all the bills had been paid.

"No, no," she said hurriedly. "I think it's a wonderful idea. We have plenty of people today. Molly and Rob will be in for the afternoon shift. Everything will be fine."

"Great. I'm going to the barn. Call me if you need anything."

Rett ducked out the front door before she could ask any questions. The idea of leaving the winery twisted his stomach. If he wasn't there, anything could happen. But he had made a promise.

He walked through the rows, eyeballing the grapes and

vines. The viticulturist had given the harvest a clean bill of health.

His phone beeped, and his heart skipped a beat. Was it Jade? It wasn't—just Tom with a beer emoji and a question mark—but Rett's thoughts turned to her anyway.

Their kiss was seared into his memory like a scorch mark. He hadn't asked her permission. The kiss was instinctive. As she stood under the awning with the most rigid body posture he had ever seen, something protective deep inside him had taken over. He had claimed her on that stoop.

And it had been incredible. She was soft and warm and tasted like strawberries. Their first contact had been an electric spark, sending shockwaves down his limbs. He had longed to press her against the side of the restaurant, run his hands down the length of her body. Discover what hid under that dress.

But they hadn't discussed physical boundaries. Some kissing was expected in a fake relationship. Would she be open to more?

He hadn't felt a pull like this in eons. The connection was instant, undeniable. It begged to be explored. Jade was smart, funny, beautiful. A little chaotic and disorganized, sure. But that wasn't a deal-breaker. Especially when he counted Penny. But in twenty-four hours, the wedding from hell would be over and they would be on a party bus bound for the city.

Unless he could convince her to stay until the anniversary event.

The doors of the barn creaked as he pushed them open. Maybe he could ask her to consult on a label for the sparkling wine. Their usual ad agency had thrown a tentative one together for him, but for some reason it didn't feel right—maybe because it didn't have an official name yet. This wine was a labor of love decades in the making, and it deserved the perfect label and name.

She had mentioned that money was an issue, so it wouldn't be financially responsible for her to cover her own housing. His house had six bedrooms. She could stay in one of them. He could make a space for her art supplies, set up an easel in the room with the best lighting. That was what artists used, right? It wasn't just in the movies?

And having her under his roof would make it so much easier to coach her on all the things she desperately needed to be coached on. A career change would be infinitely better than becoming homeless. That meant interviewing tips, networking, exploration of transferable skills. And certainly a driver's license. Maybe he could do some reading and see how he might bring back her muse permanently. He didn't put a lot of stock in the idea, but it was worth a shot.

He had whipped countless friends into shape. They always joked that he had been born an adult. Two weeks was plenty of time to set her up for success and send her back out into the world. And in the meantime, maybe she'd be open to friends with benefits.

But he was getting ahead of himself. There was no guarantee she'd stay. She seemed a tad prideful and might take offense to his offers of help. There also wasn't a lot of wiggle room in the winery budget for outside contractors.

The memory of that kiss was outweighing all the logic though. He ached to feel her under his fingertips again, to hold her and shield her from the world that was hell-bent on destroying her.

He wouldn't know until he tried.

CHAPTER NINE

JADE

"Smile!" Cameras flashed as the photographer paced back and forth in front of the group.

"Beautiful. Okay, now bride and groom kiss."

Jade bit back a sigh. Sweat was collecting in a pool on her lower back beneath the world's most non-breathable, satin bridesmaid dress. She wasn't even allowed to sit in it because it would wrinkle immediately.

Every part of the wedding day had already been irritating and performative, and they hadn't even made it down the aisle yet.

In front of her, Nate and Ashley leaned in and kissed. Jade's stomach clenched. Ashley was a picture-perfect bride in the mermaid-style gown and elegant, pearl-studded chignon.

Today was the culmination of the dream her best friend had carefully cultivated since high school. On more than one occasion, Ashley had pulled out her wedding scrapbook during sleepovers and they argued over color schemes, flowers, and DJ set lists. It should have been the most joyous day of her life, but Ashley had been acting on edge all morning long. Was it just nerves?

Frankly, she kind of deserved to be nervous. Even though nothing physical had happened between her and Nate while he was dating Jade, Ashley had still opened her heart to him. An egregious breach of girl code at best.

What would Jade's mom say if she had been around for what happened? Quick to anger, Linda Gardner would have probably written Ashley off immediately and stormed to her parents' penthouse to ream them out.

Jade bit her lip. Her mom wouldn't be at her wedding. She would never have a father-daughter dance. And yet Ashley, who had an emotional affair with Jade's boyfriend, was granted a hundred-thousand-dollar wedding in the Finger Lakes. It figured.

Between takes, Jade glanced down at her chest. The stupid ice skate tattoo remained concealed behind a thick layer of foundation despite the river of sweat dripping into her butt crack. Thank goodness. It was time for the tattoo to go. Not that laser removal was currently in her budget.

At least the view was beautiful. Behind them, the sun glimmered on the surface of the lake. The vineyards on the surrounding banks were a vibrant green. The air was clean and clear, and even the sun didn't seem so bad with the gentle breeze.

The group broke up so the bride and groom could get some pictures on their own.

"Don't sit down," Nate's mother, Patricia, reminded everyone.

Sure, Jade would just stand in these death heels until she passed out. Anything for the bride. Now was as good a time as any to make use of the free champagne and cheese platters in the bridal room.

The air conditioning was a welcome, frosty caress after the humid stickiness of the outdoors. Jade found her champagne glass from earlier and poured a fresh drink.

Just one ceremony, one reception, and one awkward brunch to go. And in the meantime, she'd have the attentions of a suspiciously handsome winemaker to distract herself. She pulled her phone out of her clutch and glanced at it.

Her heart jumped when she saw a message from Rett.

Rett: Just so you know, I'm purposely tying an Eldredge knot to upstage the groom.

What the hell was an Eldredge knot? She turned to Google and admired the intricate knot. Just how deft were those fingers? Maybe tonight she would find out.

Jade: Very nice. I assume you'll be riding in on a white horse with carriage attachment?

Rett: Best I can do is a Palomino and a Radio Flyer wagon.

She smiled. Nate had been a lot of things—charming, for one—but funny wasn't one of them. Not that it mattered. Because she would probably never see Rett again after the winery's anniversary party. Hopefully by then her life would be back on track.

Footsteps clattered down the hallway outside. Oh, hell. Maybe the other bridesmaids had the same idea. She was not in the mood to speak to anyone or catch more sympathetic glances. She scooped a handful of cheese off the plate and darted behind the folding screen in the corner.

The door opened.

"I'm fine. I'll just be a minute."

Shit. It was Ashley. And now she was hiding in the corner with a handful of cheese. Should Jade announce her presence?

"Hi, Dr. Bennett. This is Ashley Moore. I would really appreciate it if you could give me a call back in the next half an hour. It's kind of an emergency."

Jade's ears perked up. Dr. Bennett was the therapist Ashley swore by. Why did she need to talk to her therapist on the happiest day of her life?

A muffled sniffle came from the other side of the folding screen. Her breath caught in her chest. The bride was crying. Comforting her was definitely listed in the official bridesmaid duties.

Resolved to step out and speak to her, she took a step sideways. A triangle of gouda slipped out of her hand and landed on the carpeted floor with a muffled thump.

"Hello?" Ashley's voice was still teary.

Fuck.

"Hey, Ash," Jade said in a way she hoped sounded casual. She inched out from behind the folding screen.

"What were you doing behind the screen?"

"Sorry. I thought the other bridesmaids were coming in. I just wanted a break from all the—you know what? It doesn't matter."

Ashley sniffed again, and tears started streaming down her cheeks. If Jade didn't do something right away, there would be a full-blown makeup emergency.

"Whoa, hey. What's going on?"

"This," Ashley said, gesturing at her. "This is exactly why I'm upset."

Jade glanced down at her bridesmaid dress. It wasn't wrinkled. She hadn't even sat down. What was so distressing about her appearance?

She tossed the handful of mangled cheese back on the plate and came to stand next to her friend.

"Tell me what it is, and I'll fix it. Do you hate my hair? I'll call the stylist back in."

"No." Ashley choked back a sob. "It's not you. Well, it is you. I can't keep this secret anymore."

A secret? That didn't sound good. If Ashley was pregnant, Jade would be honor-bound to slap the champagne out of her hand.

Ashley trained her tear-stained eyes on Jade. She was still lovely, but the makeup artist was definitely going to have to take a second pass at her.

"You have been so kind and understanding during this whole process. If I was in your position, I would have punched me in the face. Maybe even burned my apartment to the ground."

Jade smiled and handed her a tissue. "I told you before. I know what it's like when Nate sets his sights on you. He's like a whirlpool, sucking you in no matter how hard you fight against the current."

"He is. He really is."

This was exactly the type of conversation she had desperately been hoping to avoid. Why were they rehashing all of this when it was old news? And on the day of the wedding, no less?

"I can't take this guilt anymore. We didn't tell you the truth," Ashley said.

The words settled between them like an anvil.

Jade's mouth went dry. "What do you mean?"

"He told you it was just an emotional affair, right? That nothing happened between us physically?"

Ice shot through Jade's veins. She remembered the moment like it was yesterday.

Ashley had fled the apartment, crying. Nate had stayed behind, empty-handed and stone-faced.

"I can't do this," he had said. "I'm so sorry. I fell in love with someone else."

It would have hurt less if he had slapped her. But the only silver lining of the entire interaction was that he had assured her, time after time, that nothing physical had happened between them. It was just emotions that had grown stronger to the point where they couldn't be ignored.

So what the *hell* was Ashley trying to say?

"We lied. We had been hooking up for a month before you were supposed to move in together."

The champagne glass toppled from Jade's hand. Liquid splashed her satin heels.

Finally, she found her voice. "So when I signed the lease, he already knew he wasn't going to move in?"

"No. It happened right after. It was later that night, at my parent's house," Ashley confessed. "You had a headache from the champagne and went to bed early. I stayed to watch the Knicks game because my apartment didn't have cable yet, and Nate decided to stay too. And during the game...he kissed me. And I didn't stop it. I thought it was a fluke, a onetime thing from the high emotions of watching our team score. But it wasn't."

Jade's entire body was pulsating. Desires warred within her. Should she run? Or should she hurl this cheese platter at the two-faced bride like a Frisbee and bitch-slap both of these lying, sadistic assholes into the lake?

Rage was rising in her, hot and dangerous.

"So you let me believe for two years that you got together honorably. And you asked me to be a fucking bridesmaid. In your wedding. To my ex-boyfriend."

Ashley sniffled. "I'm so sorry. The guilt has just been—"

"Stop it."

Ashley faltered. Her cheeks were pink.

"You could have told me the truth at any point in the last two years. Like maybe before I spent a thousand dollars on a stupid bridesmaid dress I'm not even allowed to sit in."

Jade had always been a strong proponent of believing the best in people. But this was a different kind of betrayal. Something inside her snapped.

"And now you're telling me that while I was still in the initial stages of grief from my parents' untimely death, you were fucking my boyfriend."

Ashley burst into tears again.

A pang of guilt hit, but Jade quickly shoved it down. There was no way she was going to feel guilty for this shit.

She reached down and picked up a fresh bottle of champagne in one hand and the cheese plate in the other.

"I hope he never does to you what he did to me. I hope you never know what it's like to have your future planned out, and then be blindsided when everything is ripped away. Good luck."

With that, she crossed the room and kicked the door open. The storm of emotions was about to hit a fever pitch. Did everyone know? Was that why Kenya was so surprised that Jade had agreed to be a bridesmaid? Were they all just sitting around laughing about how pathetic she was and how she had no idea that her best friend had been fucking her boyfriend while her parents were barely cold in the ground?

That was it. She was leaving. She couldn't care less if Ashley's side looked lopsided because she was down a bridesmaid. She didn't deserve a picture-perfect wedding. And neither did Nate.

She rounded a corner and searched the foyer. The

groomsmen were here somewhere. And she had words for them.

Jade stormed out onto the patio. There he was, smoking a cigar and yukking it up with his band of idiots. She slammed the cheese platter on a cocktail table and stormed across the patio.

She was going to punch him. She would rip his tuxedo off and make him eat it. She would hoist him up by his stupid tighty whities until he admitted what he did.

He turned and made eye contact with her. His blue eyes seared into her, and she almost stopped mid-step. But he didn't have that power over her anymore.

"We need to talk," she said.

"Can it wait?" Nate raised an eyebrow and gestured at his surroundings with his cigar hand.

She slapped it out of his hand, and it rolled across the patio. "No. Now. Unless you'd prefer to have this conversation in front of your parents and friends."

"Uh, okay." He ran one hand over his slicked-back hair and followed her around the corner of the building.

"So what's up?" He looked cool and unbothered, as always. It was infuriating.

"Ashley told me the truth."

Nate pulled a flask out of his tux and unscrewed the top. "About what?"

"The fact that you were fucking her for a full month before we were supposed to move in together."

He sighed. "She wasn't supposed to say anything."

She gaped like a goldfish. "Is that seriously all you have to say to me? We were planning to move in together. We signed a lease. And all you can say is she was supposed to hide this from me forever."

"Look, I'm sorry, okay? I know I messed up. You were

just...not yourself anymore. After the funeral and everything. It didn't feel the same."

"Oh, so it's my fault that you can't keep your dick in your pants? I'm *so* sorry for having a hard time after my parents died. Both of them. In the blink of an eye. Of *course* your only choice would be to run headlong into the first vagina you meet. Even if it belonged to my best friend."

"I'm sorry, Jade. I don't know what else to say. When you introduced me to Ashley, something just changed. She gets me."

"I don't need any more apologies from you. You don't even feel anything, do you? At least Ashley felt bad about betraying me. But you? You're irredeemable. I can't believe it's taken me this long to see it."

She ripped the flask out of his hand and debated slamming it into his stupid face. But the Astors were a litigious family, and she couldn't afford a lawyer.

"What's going on over here?"

Jade jumped. Nate's mother, Patricia Astor, rounded the corner.

She sighed when she saw them together. "I knew it was a mistake when Ashley said she was asking you to be a bridesmaid."

Jade blinked. "Why? Because you didn't want a middle-class nobody from Queens in the wedding pictures?"

Patricia scoffed. "Don't be so dramatic. I knew you wouldn't be able to handle the wedding. And frankly we don't need the drama on Nathan's wedding day. It's bad enough that they're getting married here and not at the Ritz." She brushed a piece of lint off his tux.

"Well, I didn't need the drama of your son cheating on me and blowing up my entire life either. So I guess we're even."

"You can go now, dear. We had a spare bridesmaid dress made for Nathan's cousin. We don't need you."

Anger flared in her belly. Were they trying to dismiss her? Fuck that.

"No. I'm staying," Jade said.

"What?" Nate's nostrils flared.

She ripped open the top of the flask and chugged. Whiskey stung her throat. "I spent almost six thousand dollars to be in this stupid wedding. I'm staying. And I'm going to be in all the pictures. And you're going to be reminded of me every day for the rest of your life."

She made steady eye contact with Patricia and pulled out a chair that was probably meant for a parking attendant. She lowered herself down onto the seat, staring Patricia down.

Patricia inhaled sharply.

"Oops." Jade sloshed some whiskey onto her dress.

"Come, Nathan." Patricia put an arm around her son and steered him back to the patio.

In their absence, Jade caught her breath.

A chapter had closed here. It was time to move on. To forget about Nate and the heartbreak that followed in his wake like a thick fog. Despite her adrenaline-induced words, though, she wanted nothing more than to flee.

"Jade?"

If this was someone else coming to confront her, she was going to lose her mind. She whipped around in the chair.

Rett stood there, dressed to the nines and looking like he had just wandered off the set of a GQ photoshoot.

Her lower lip wobbled, and tears pricked her eyes. She had never been good at hiding her feelings. And here they were, ready to spill out all over some guy she had kissed one time.

"What happened?" He took her hand and pulled her up from the chair.

"Well," she said, swiping her free hand under both eyes. "Remember that story I told you that Nate and Ashley fell in love without doing anything physical?"

Rett nodded with a frown.

She took a deep breath and continued. "Turns out it was all bullshit. It shouldn't change anything. It's been two years."

His eyes softened. "But it does. Change things."

She nodded. "I can't believe she lied to me for two years. She was supposed to be my best friend. She was my only friend, really. Everyone else took Nate's side in the breakup. Now I have no one."

The future was looking lonelier and lonelier. But compared to her impending homelessness, that was the least of her problems.

Rett drew her closer. He was warm and strong. The cologne he had picked for the occasion was so much better than the pine bullshit Nate was always wearing.

"A best friend wouldn't have done something like this in the first place," he said.

She grunted.

"So are we leaving?" he asked.

Jade pulled back, but he kept his arm around her.

"No. I did a dumb thing."

He cracked a smile. "Do tell."

She rehashed the story.

He whistled. "I really admire your commitment to the pettiness. I'm not judging, by the way. They earned it."

"You should have seen the way she looked at me. It was exactly what I was afraid of all along. I knew everyone was going to pity me, to whisper behind my back about how my life turned out."

"Hey." Rett held her chin and gently turned her face towards his. "A lioness does not concern herself with the opinion of sheep. They'll get what's coming to them."

She blinked. "Did you just quote a motivational poster at me?"

He chuckled. "Yeah, sorry. What I really wanted to say was 'screw those guys and let's go eat our bodyweight in shrimp cocktail on their dime,' but it felt a little uncouth."

She smiled. "I like uncouth."

"You're in luck. I have it in spades."

Thank god the urge to vomit and/or wail like a banshee had passed. Rett had been her little guiding light, there before she even knew she needed him.

She took a step back. "I understand if you want to leave after hearing all that. Nobody wants to be the arm candy for a professional mess."

He shook his head. "We had an agreement. I'm not going anywhere. Especially not now. Let's go find another bottle of champagne. I think you're going to need it."

CHAPTER TEN

RETT

RETT STOOD IN THE FOYER, HALF-EMPTY BOTTLE OF champagne in one hand and Jade's clutch in the other. She was rolling on the floor, over and over again like a drunk rotisserie chicken.

And frankly, he didn't blame her. He knew all too well what it was like to have someone close utterly betray him. Although a lot of the sting had subsided, he'd never forget that morning.

His heart ached for Jade. While she probably should have suspected from the beginning that it wasn't just an emotional affair, that didn't make the news any less devastating. She deserved better than this.

The door opened, and one of the other bridesmaids—not the rude one from the tasting—walked in. She probably could have crushed his skull with one of her biceps.

"What the hell are you doing? The wedding starts in twenty minutes. Camila will shit an entire duck," the bridesmaid said.

"I'm processing, Kenya," Jade said from the floor. "It turns out Nate screwed Ashley for an entire month before breaking up with me. And then they both lied about it for two years."

Kenya's mouth fell open. "Oh, *hell* no. Give me some of that."

She snatched the champagne from Rett's hand and tossed it back. Then she threw her clutch at him and dropped to her knees. Seconds later, her hands were above her and she was rolling along right next to Jade.

"Who makes bridesmaids wear thousand-dollar satin dresses? I'm so done with them." Kenya rolled over to a potted plant and grabbed a fistful of soil. She sprinkled it on herself before continuing to roll.

"I'm not stopping until every inch of this dress is rumpled. And then I'm going to get obscenely drunk and make a scene. Sorry, Rett," Jade said in his direction.

He smiled. "I'd be happy to help."

He was friendly with the owners of Barrington Terrace. They would definitely give her a pass if he explained the circumstances.

"And then tomorrow," Jade continued from the floor, "I'm never going to think of any of these people again. Except for you, Kenya. I like you."

Kenya stopped and rolled onto her front. Potting soil had created several dirty streaks and splotches on the dress. "Aww. Thanks, Jade. I like you too."

"And then," Jade added, "I'm going to make so many incredible paintings. And one day, Patricia is going to want one of them so badly. And I will make sure every single one of her friends gets to have a Jade Gardner original. But never her."

"What are you doing? Are you insane? Patricia is going to flip out." Another bridesmaid had apparently entered the foyer. Her eyes bulged.

Jade shot a glance over her shoulder. "Good."

The newcomer marched over and grabbed Jade's wrist. "Was this your plan all along? Wait until the wedding and then humiliate Ashley?"

Jade yanked her wrist back. "No, Camila. My original plan was to marry Nate and have his babies. But then he fucked Ashley because I was sad that my parents died."

Camila's thin lips pressed together. "What do you mean?"

Jade relayed the story.

Camila listened intently. At the end, she crossed her arms and glanced out the front doors.

"Well, that certainly explains why Ashley was hiding in the closet and refusing to come out. She kept saying 'what if he does to me what he did to her?'"

"It's going to be a disaster," Kenya said as she climbed to her feet. She smoothed a hair that had escaped from her updo. "Is she coming?"

Camila nodded. "I sent Nate in after her. They're outside now."

Good. Assholes deserved to marry each other. Jade seemed to feel the same way, because she rose to her feet, adjusted her straps, and took her clutch back.

Her eyes blazed when she turned to him. "I'll see you out there."

———

THE SUN BEAT DOWN OVERHEAD, AND RETT SHIFTED uncomfortably in his seat. The air was choked with the scent of the floral arrangements that covered nearly every surface. He was already on his third check-in with Elaine, whose responses were getting shorter and snippier. Everything was fine, or so she said. It was just as well, since he couldn't leave Jade when she was in such a vulnerable state.

A string quartet off to one side of the ceremony site began an instrumental version of Taylor Swift's "Lover." It had been one of Alexa's favorite songs. And here it was again, back to haunt him.

He narrowed his eyes. The groomsmen came down the aisle and lined up at the altar. They all looked a little hungover. Or maybe high? The best man was particularly sweaty and a little pale. Nate looked smug, like he had gotten away with something. If anyone deserved to be punched off the side of this hill and into the brush, it was that douche.

Based on the overly showy dress that was just a shade darker than white, the mother of the groom had just walked by. And from the smell of things, the flower girl had just shat her pants. The bridal party was falling apart at the seams. Good.

Everyone turned as the bridesmaids began to filter in.

Kenya led the charge, smiling coyly as she strutted down the aisle. Her dress was irrevocably wrinkled and soiled, but it almost looked like she was just making a fashion statement. She had taken her hair down, allowing her natural curls to shift in the wind. A couple attendees cocked their heads and whispered among themselves.

There was the rude one, a pinched expression on her face. And then there was Jade.

Her eyes moved over the rows as she walked, brows contorted. Even with the wrinkly dress and disheveled hair, she was breathtaking. She caught his eye, and he smiled.

"You've got this," he mouthed at her.

She smiled and passed by him, taking her place by the altar.

The music stopped, and the doors at the end of the aisle swung shut. The song changed to the bridal march, and everyone stood.

There went the bride, buried in yards of fluffy fabric. There must have been thirty thousand dollars' worth of jewelry on her person if those diamonds were real. She looked happy in spite of everything that had transpired. Apparently her confession had granted her some unearned peace.

Snap. The sound drew Rett's attention back to the altar, where the head of Jade's bouquet looked to have fallen off.

He made eye contact with her and mimed taking a deep breath. She hid the stems behind her back.

"Dearly beloved," the officiant began.

Twenty minutes passed as he expounded on the importance of marriage, love, and kindness. It was sweltering outside. All the attendees looked miserable. Rett checked his phone and email while the man droned on. His mind turned to the party. There was still so much to do—decorations to select, catering to confirm, and time was running out to name the wine. While he enjoyed hosting parties, he didn't have a knack for décor. Hopefully Jade would make good on her promise to help.

He glanced again at the financial projection he had run. His stomach twisted. Would the party and the new wine be enough? Or would he destroy his grandmother's last dream and completely embarrass his family? He had to pull the winery out of its nosedive. Whatever it took.

His gaze shifted back to Jade. Maybe she would be willing to do some kind of promotion for the winery. Or better yet, a paint and sip night? He had hosted one once before, and it had gone reasonably well. But Jade was a respected artist—or at least she had been. Such an event might be beneath her.

This ceremony had lasted a decade at least. He didn't even have the benefit of extra time with Jade during it since she was currently sweating to death while watching her ex marry her best friend. For all the drama of the morning, it was a boring ceremony. They had moved on to some kind of unity ceremony with two glasses of wine.

"As these wines came from two different regions, so did Ashley and Nate," the officiant said. "These grapes were nour-ished by the minerals in the soil and the warmth of the sun, just as you were nurtured by your families and your unique environments. But now, your paths become one. Your—"

The officiant was interrupted by the best man, who apparently lost consciousness. He fell into the back of Nate, who lurched forward and dropped his glass.

Red wine hovered in midair for an instant before splat-tering down the ivory fabric of the wedding dress. It dripped onto the ground, sending streaks down the fabric. Ashley looked like she had just stumbled off the set of a horror movie.

She stared open-mouthed at her dress. Gasps escaped the crowd.

A woman from the audience jumped to her feet and appeared to be checking for a pulse in the unconscious groomsman. The woman in the showy dress joined her.

"You idiot!" she screeched at the groomsman, who was starting to come around. "You've ruined everything."

"Mom," Nate said with a warning in his voice.

"We're going to take a five-minute recess," the officiant announced.

Rett jumped up and hustled to the patio, where large

water dispensers waited. He carried a cup back to the altar and dropped to one knee next to the woman who was still checking vitals. The groomsman was sitting up and appeared no worse for the wear. The bride, on the other hand, was nowhere to be seen.

"Oh, thank you," the woman said when he presented the cup.

"No problem." He stood and winked at Jade before going back to his seat.

It had happened once or twice at his winery too. Hungover bachelorettes on their fourth stop of the day. There was always emergency water at the tasting tables.

When he sat back down, he glanced at Jade. How was she feeling? The idea of standing up with Chris while he married Alexa was enough to make him itch for the punching bag strung up in his gym. But it would never come to that. Alexa would eventually get tired of him, and then she'd be gone for good.

Eventually, the officiant restarted the ceremony. Ashley emerged in yet another white dress, though this one was a lot less complicated-looking. The rings were exchanged, the vows were repeated, and finally, mercifully, everyone stood for the recession.

Rett checked on Jade again. Her eyes were closed, and her shoulders dropped away from her ears. Even in a wrinkled dress, she was a vision.

Was it the catharsis she had been hoping for?

As people drifted away from the ceremony site, he sidled up next to her.

"You did it." He laid a hand gently on her arm. "How does it feel?"

Her eyes snapped open. "Good. I'm kind of glad I stayed.

I never in my wildest daydreams would have imagined this shitstorm of a ceremony."

"It's not often you get to see karma in real time."

"Right. You want to go get drunk and eat a stupid amount of hors d'oeuvres?"

"I'll have a glass, but one of us needs to keep their head above water. Especially since I'm driving you back to—"

She inhaled sharply. "Oh, shit. I didn't even think about the fact that I was supposed to stay overnight and leave with them in the morning. Ashley won't be there, but—"

He shook his head. "We'll leave early and get your things. You can bring them to my house. We'll figure out how to get you home later."

She hesitated, and he almost proposed a different plan. Was he being too forward?

"You know what? Fuck it. That sounds great."

A night alone with Jade? He couldn't imagine a better distraction.

CHAPTER ELEVEN

JADE

"What's your favorite memory of your parents?"

Rett sat cross-legged underneath a table, tuxedo jacket discarded on the floor. He was wearing a waistcoat again, and his white shirt was rolled up to his forearms.

Jade sawed off a bite of prime rib and leaned back thoughtfully while she chewed. They were concealed by a white linen tablecloth that hung to the floor. Music droned in from the ballroom down the hall. They had run off with their dinners and taken refuge in the smaller event room after Patricia elbowed her on her way to the dance floor.

"It's so hard to choose. We didn't have a lot of money, so we never traveled very far outside the city. But once in a while, my mom would take me out of school on a 'mental health break.' We'd take the train into the city and go to museums or head to Coney Island. She was so patient, even when I was a bratty teenager. I hope she knows how much she meant to me."

Was it physically impossible for her to not overshare? Get it together, girl.

Rett leaned over and squeezed her hand. "Trust me, she knows."

Warmth flooded her. It was hard to tell if it was the wine or Rett's strong, comforting presence, but she was feeling a thousand percent more grounded than she had this morning.

"What about you? It sounds like your parents were gone a lot."

He finished his bite before speaking. How civilized. "They were. But I'll never forget the first time I saw my mom onstage on Broadway. She was amazing. She just effortlessly captivated everyone in the room."

She smiled. A late-night Google of his mom the night before had revealed a decades-long career. "Well, it's easy to see where you get your charisma from." Oops, the wine had brought out the flirting. And not even a very skillful attempt.

Take it easy, dumbass. He's only your fictional boyfriend.

"And your dad?" he probed.

"Oh, he was just your classic, salt-of-the-earth kind of guy. He was a truck driver, so he was gone a lot. He loved quietly. Sometimes he'd bring me gifts from places he'd been. A stuffed animal from a truck stop, a weird candy from a small town. He was so proud of me for getting into NYU. Sorry, I feel like I'm talking a lot."

He smiled. "I like hearing your stories. Besides, as your fake boyfriend I'm obligated to obtain an extensive personal history to play the part. Speaking of which, we should probably make our dance floor debut soon."

Jade dropped her napkin onto her lap. Suddenly, the idea of impressing her ex-boyfriend's family with her personal and professional growth wasn't as attractive. She would much rather stay here, under the safety of the tablecloth, with the sexy winemaker and his bedroom eyes.

"I don't know that I need to prove anything to them," she said. "I don't care if Nate's grandpa thinks I'm pathetic, you know? They're not going to be a part of my life anymore."

Rett nodded. "I understand. I just don't want you to have any regrets. One dance? We'll make a big show of it and then get the hell out of here."

She sighed. "Okay, one dance."

He crawled out from under the table. She followed, and he gently tugged her to her feet. Oof. The wine was definitely catching up to her. She stumbled on the hem of her infernal satin dress, and he caught her. For a moment, they stood there in the dark banquet room, staring into each other's eyes.

There it was again—the hint of a tingle at the base of her spine. Shit, all of her art supplies were in her big purse at the house. With the amount of wine in her system, any artistic attempt would probably look more like cave drawings anyway.

"Come on." He led her out the door and into the hallway.

She snuck a look at him. Her head was swimming pleasantly. How was a man like him on the market? Curiosity won out.

"Rett?"

"Hmm?"

"Why are you still single?"

"What do you mean?"

"Come on. You're stupidly hot. And you own your own business. You dress like an adult. Or maybe like a merchant from the early nineteen hundreds."

He cocked a smile but didn't say anything.

"You must get a dozen thirsty bachelorette parties a weekend, and you're polite even when confronted by drunk assholes. How have you not found your soulmate yet?"

He smiled grimly. "I thought I had. But then she found my brother. Since then, I've tried to keep things...less complicated."

"I hear you on that. It's easier to keep people at a distance."

"Is that why you're still single?" he asked as they walked.

Jade sighed. "I have a really unfortunate history of falling in love super quickly and having my heart obliterated."

"How fast are we talking here?"

"Maybe a week for my high school boyfriend. He made me a mix CD," she explained.

Rett raised his eyebrows.

"A few days for my college boyfriend. I found him playing the guitar on the back porch at a house party so it kind of felt 'written in the stars.' Spoiler alert: it was not."

Rett nodded, but had a pinched expression like he was trying not to laugh. "And this idiot?" He gestured towards the ballroom.

"A weekend." He had called her up after the ice skating incident and drawn her into his web almost immediately.

"You weren't exaggerating."

"Nope. So it's a good thing this is temporary or I'd probably be proposing to you tomorrow."

He laughed. "Are you ready?" He paused with one hand on a side entrance to the ballroom.

She nodded. "Let's get it over with."

As they opened the door, the DJ transitioned to "The Way You Look Tonight" by Frank Sinatra.

"Oh man, you are so in luck," he said, dragging her to the dance floor.

"Why?"

"My mom was obsessed with this song. And like the Hollywood socialite she was, she insisted that I take ballroom dance lessons. We're about to impress some old people. Just follow my lead."

Ashley's parents box-stepped by them. Tracey waved cheerily as if she hadn't just resuscitated a groomsman at her daughter's wedding.

Nate and his crew of tuxedo-wearing buffoons were huddled around a table watching something on his phone—probably football. Patricia had taken a break from reaming everyone out to chug some champagne. Ashley was nowhere to be found. Hopefully she was accidentally dipping her reception dress in the toilet.

Rett took Jade's waist and placed her other hand in his. She wasn't a complete klutz, but she had certainly never been a ballroom dancer. With his hand in hers though, she glided across the dance floor, twirling and box-stepping across the polished floor. His hand was warm on her hip, and she followed his gentle guidance like she was reading a book in a language only the two of them understood.

They locked eyes as he shepherded her around the dance floor. She was dimly aware of some of the other attendees looking at them, but their interest didn't matter. Patricia could lob a Molotov cocktail onto the dance floor and Jade wouldn't even notice. All that mattered was this moment, spinning in a wrinkly dress on the arm of a winemaking stud. The first gentleman she'd met in a long time.

Oh, hell. She was romanticizing her life again. Had she learned nothing? If she didn't pump the brakes, she was going to catch feelings for this guy and then have her life ruined again when he didn't need her anymore.

Just as she made a conscious decision to put some

distance between them, the song came to a stop. She breathed a sigh of relief as there was a smattering of applause. She jumped and looked around, but it seemed like everyone was clapping for them. Drunk Jade curtsied and turned back to Rett with the intention of yanking him off the dance floor. They had made their point. And if someone still wanted to accuse her of being pathetic, that was on them.

But the DJ was back with another banger. "At Last" by Etta James melted out of the speakers.

"Oh, I love this song," they said at the same time.

Okay, universe. Relax.

"One more dance?"

She nodded, and they came back together. Closer this time. His grip was lower than the last song, strong fingers brushing the top of her ass beneath the silk dress. Her toes curled.

They swayed together, dangerously close under the flashing lights. He spun her out and locked eyes as he pulled her back.

Maybe it was just the alcohol, but her brain seemed to have shut off entirely. She had never danced like this with anyone, let alone a complete stranger. Grinding in a dimly lit club was one thing, but this was something else. He took charge, effortlessly steering her around. Her fingers itched to pop the buttons on that waistcoat.

As the chorus swelled for the last time, he dipped her so low her breath caught in her chest. There was fire in his eyes as he held her. Slowly, so slowly, he lifted her back up.

The chemistry between them was indescribable. Every atom between them vibrated at a frequency she felt deep in her bones. Something was bound to spontaneously catch on fire. Or at the very least, her nipples would cut straight through this flimsy satin dress.

Her arms wound around his neck, and she nudged herself closer. His face was tipped down to hers, just centimeters away.

"And now please join us in the eastern corner of the ballroom where our bride and groom will cut their cake," the DJ announced.

Stupid cockblocking DJ.

Rett pulled back and smiled. "Ready to go?"

Did he mean ready to leave so they didn't run into anyone at the house? Or ready to rip her dress off in the parking lot? Either way, she would follow him through a tunnel made of barbed wire and scattered Legos.

"Definitely." She barely gave the corner a passing glance on their way to the exit.

Nate smashed a fistful of cake directly in Ashley's face. The crowd chuckled. Jade shook her head and pushed through the doors.

She would probably never see either one of them again. The thought didn't hurt as much as it had that morning.

It was time for a fresh start.

CHAPTER TWELVE

JADE

"So," Rett said over the rumble of the truck, "do you think we pulled it off?"

"Pulled what off?"

Jade's gaze drifted down to his pants. Speaking of things that needed to be pulled off.

"Convincing his family that you're in a happy relationship and your life is super on track?"

"Oh, right." Jade shook her head, trying to clear it, but the day-long alcohol marathon had made everything fuzzy. "Yeah, I think we nailed it. You weren't exaggerating, by the way. You're a really good dancer," she said.

She couldn't stop looking at him, drenched in moonlight. It was like the first time she had laid eyes on an MC Escher lithograph.

"Thank you. It's come in handy before."

"You should consider giving dance lessons at the winery. You would probably get busloads of wealthy elderly women from upscale retirement communities."

"Are you a business consultant in your free time?" He smiled.

"More like an expert-level procrastinator."

Dark trees flitted past the windows. Every few yards, a strip of the dark lake peeked out.

"I can't get over how beautiful it is here."

He glanced at her. "So why don't you stay? At least until the party. If the city hasn't inspired you in two years, what are the odds that will change tomorrow?"

A thrill ran through her belly. Did he want her to stay, or was he just pointing out that doing the same thing over and over again was unlikely to work?

Jade sighed. "I was kind of hoping I would get some huge emotional catharsis from seeing Nate marry someone else."

"And did you?"

She shook her head. "Though to be fair, I wasn't expecting a bonus betrayal on top of the already uncomfortable event. Either way, they're in the past now. And at least he's not dating one of my siblings. Sorry," she said when he flinched.

His grip tightened on the steering wheel. "It's fine. Do you have siblings?"

"No."

"So you're alone now? In the city, I mean."

"Yeah." Alone in the world now that her best friend had accidentally fallen onto her ex's dick and lied about it for two years.

"That sounds lonely. I'm sorry."

She took a deep breath. He was bumming her out, but at least it had managed to smother some of the all-consuming lust. "It really has been."

"Then why not stay? Here in Hammondsport. The leaves are going to start changing any day. Trust me when I say you've never seen anything like it. It might inspire you."

Jade shook her head even though her heart stuttered. Something in this town called to her. But she couldn't afford it.

"I wasn't exaggerating when I said I was broke. I don't have money to rent a place, even for two weeks."

"You could stay with me."

The fire rekindled at the very idea. But playing house with her fake boyfriend was a surefire recipe for disaster.

"No," she said, maybe too quickly. "Sorry. Thank you so much for the offer, seriously. I just know that if I stayed with you, it would be physically impossible for me to not develop feelings for you. And I know that's not what you're looking for. Especially not with a random has-been artist who lives five hours away."

"I think you vastly overestimate my animal magnetism. I work all the time, and my only hobbies are working out and —" He stopped suddenly, like he had almost divulged something. "That's it, really. Bad enough to drive any woman away."

She cracked a smile. "Sounds awful. You're sure you don't mind me staying tonight?"

One night was doable. Tomorrow she would be back in the city where she could buckle down and figure out her next steps.

"I told you, you could stay for two weeks," he said.

She smiled. "You would hate having an artist-in-residence. Paint supplies everywhere. Not to mention a metric ton of dog hair on your furniture."

"I always meant to get a dog. That's why the winery is dog friendly."

"You won't be saying that when you need a three-month supply of lint rollers on hand for all your fancy suits." She poked him. The wine was still coursing merrily through her veins. "Do you dress like this at home too?"

He laughed. "No. The suit thing is a relic from my grandmother's day. She always insisted we wore our Sunday best while in the building."

"Well. I'm sure it's uncomfortable. But you really do wear the hell out of it."

Why was she incapable of shutting her stupid mouth?

"And it's a beautiful way to remember her," she added.

"Thanks," Rett said. "Looks like the coast is clear."

They had finally reached Ashley's parents' house. The circular driveway was thankfully deserted. She should be able to dart in and out and grab Penny. She breathed a sigh of relief.

"I'll come help." He unbuckled his seatbelt.

She put a hand on his chest. She had definitely left the bedroom a disaster, and she had a sneaking suspicion that he kept a very clean home. "No need. I'll only be a second."

She hustled inside like a thief in an art museum. Penny greeted her at the door and proceeded to follow Jade as she darted from room to room, tossing her scattered possessions into the foyer. If she didn't move quickly, someone could come back from the wedding early. And she was not in the mood for another confrontation.

She shouldered the front door open and shoved her possessions outside. Rett jumped out and carried them to the truck.

Finally, Jade had collected all of her things. With Penny's leash in hand, she turned in the foyer and took in the house one last time. A picture of Ashley and her brother caught her eye. She would never see her friend again. And she'd definitely never be in this house again.

Against her wishes, a tear slid down Jade's cheek. She had been running on adrenaline and spite since Ashley had dropped her truth bomb. But now reality was settling in. The two of them had been through so much together. Ashley had stood by her while the other prep school girls had turned their noses up. She had stayed in contact all through college, sent flowers and groceries after Jade's parents had died. They had taken family vacations together and girls' trips to the beach.

And now she was virtually a stranger. Just like Nate. The two of them were gone from her life forever. Now she really had no one.

"Onward and upward," she mumbled to herself and dragged Penny outside.

The ride to Rett's house was quiet.

As they passed through the little town of Hammond-sport, her head was on a swivel. She ached to investigate the restaurants, sit down at the bars, and absorb the local culture. And she would be damned if she didn't sit in that gazebo the next time she was in town.

Maybe, if things were financially better during the anniversary party, she would extend her stay.

"Beautiful town, isn't it?" Rett said.

Penny's chin was propped on his lap again. It was probably better that they had some doggie distance between them.

"It's like a movie set. I keep expecting Chad Michael Murray to wander into frame. Which restaurant is your favorite?"

"It depends what mood I'm in." He came to a stop and looked carefully both ways before turning. "Can't beat Louie's for pizza. The Tavern for Italian or seafood. And if you like breakfast, Margie's Café is unbeatable."

"How's the bagel scene here?"

He turned to her. "Bagel scene? Is that a thing?"

"I take bagels very seriously. Wars are fought over them in the city."

He smiled. "I promise the bagels are great, but there's so much more to experience here. Like eggs benedict that has made grown men weep."

"Grown men? I assume you mean you?"

"I can neither confirm nor deny." Rett turned off the highway and climbed the hill.

Her drunk brain was interpreting everything as sexual. The way his long fingers gripped the steering wheel, the fact that he had discarded his tux jacket for the ride home. *Calm down, you horny idiot.*

Rhodes Vineyard came into view on their left. The sight made her blood pressure inch up. They were almost at his house. What would happen when they got there?

Not that it mattered. She was going home tomorrow anyway. Wasn't she?

Rett turned off on a paved lane marked only by a mailbox and drove toward the lake.

Lust warred with whatever amount of logic was left in her brain. If she didn't find out what was going on under those clothes, she might actually go insane. But what if she made a move and got rejected? This wasn't a random club hookup. And if he kicked her out, she and Penny would have nowhere to go. They would have to walk back to Ashley's parents' house and sleep in the party bus.

"Did your house belong to your grandparents too?"

Nothing killed libido like a dead grandma. Ignoring her raging hormones was almost certainly the safest course of action here.

He nodded. "They left it to me in the will. Kind of a package deal with the winery."

"How kind of them."

When her parents died, Jade had been forced to sell their family home and use the proceeds to pay off debt. Ashley's parents had taken her in until she and Nate signed the lease. No place had ever really been home since.

One bay of a three-door garage opened in front of them. A mammoth structure that looked like a small castle stood to the right. Holy hell. Was that a friggen turret?

The truck slid smoothly inside. A dark SUV was parked in the corner. Penny sat up and immediately crawled across Rett's leg. She shoved her nose against the window and inspected her new surroundings. Hopefully he had Windex, or that would be coming out of the dwindling experience budget too.

Rett jumped out and came around to her side while she fought with her seatbelt. Her fine motor skills were already suffering. He popped her door open and reached across her lap to release her.

"It sticks sometimes," he explained.

He offered his hand, and she took it to jump down. She staggered on her heels, and he steadied her. His touch burned through the thin fabric of her dress. They made eye contact again. Something nameless passed between them, and a shiver racked her body. His hand rose, and her breath caught in her chest. Was he going to tear this stupid dress off right here in the garage? She'd never been banged against a pickup truck.

"I think you have...yep, that's mashed potatoes." He pulled something white from her hair.

"Oh." She was an idiot to think he was interested in her. The kiss from the night before had meant nothing. He had probably learned all kinds of acting tricks from his Holly-wood mom. "Thanks," she added.

"Come on." He led her inside.

Even the mudroom was fancy. Not like golden Dalmatian statues and crystal caviar dishes fancy, but quietly expensive. He put his keys in a dish on a console table and removed his shoes. She bent to do the same, but Penny lunged forward and she was still holding the leash.

She screeched and nearly hurtled to the floor.

"Whoa." He caught her arm.

"Sorry. I can't walk in these things."

"Really? You were dancing in them just fine."

"Well. I wasn't dancing with a golden retriever who's searching for some balls to put in her mouth."

That made two of them.

He chuckled. "Here, let me."

He kneeled and set his nimble fingers to the buckle on her heel strap. His head was basically at vagina level. *Down, girl.*

"You are suspiciously adept at removing women's shoes," she said. "Fetish?"

"Definitely. I have a whole room of severed feet in the basement."

His hand glided up her calf before tugging her shoe off, and she bit her lip as her foot planted on the floor. That amount of calf stroking was not strictly speaking necessary for shoe removal. Was he making a move? Or was her drunk brain just interpreting everything as a green flag?

"You can drop the leash," he said. His green eyes stared up at her as he moved on to the other shoe. "Penny has free rein here."

"Oh. Thank you." She unclipped the dog, and Penny gamboled into the house and disappeared.

Her other shoe came off, and Rett stood. There was a

sparkle of something naughty in his eye as he shot her a half smile before turning away.

Jade took a second to survey her surroundings as he flicked lights on. The kitchen was predictably massive. Was that a pasta arm? Who lived here, Emeril?

It was also shockingly clean for a bachelor pad. Either he had a dedicated housekeeper, or his list of hobbies did not extend beyond cleaning and winemaking.

Jade's apartment, on the other hand, was more...free-spirited. It wouldn't be unusual to find a towel on the floor in the bathroom, or dishes from the night before in the sink. But her apartment was homey, charming, and beautiful in its own way, even when it wasn't surgically clean.

"Your house is beautiful. Very clean for a bachelor. Not a single discarded Solo cup or bong."

He smiled. "Thanks. I have a cleaning service in twice a month. They were just here, so I can't take credit for it."

Thank god. She had already been half worried he was going to make her wear flip-flops in the shower.

"Let me show you to your room."

She put a hand on her rolling suitcase, but he tugged it away from her.

"You're my guest. Come on," he said, wheeling the suitcase through the kitchen. A dining room stood to their right, lined by floor-to-ceiling windows. It was hard to tell in the dark, but the view of the lake must have been spectacular.

Her bare feet padded over the hardwood floors. They passed through an absurd living room—lots of neutral tones, definitely needed more color—with a double-sided fireplace and what looked to be a very nice patio before finding the stairs.

"You don't have to take the stairs."

"Are you going to throw me over your shoulder and

carry me? Is that part of the patented Rhodes Hospitality Fake Girlfriend Package?"

He smiled again. "No." He walked to a bit of molded paneling next to the stairs and pressed a button.

"Your house has an elevator?"

Her apartment building barely even had an elevator. It only worked for one week out of the month if she was lucky. And it was never when she had an armful of groceries.

"I know it's absurd. In my defense, my grandmother had it installed when they both still lived here. My grandfather had mobility issues."

She eyed it suspiciously. "Have you ever been trapped in it?"

"Only twice. And it wasn't for very long."

"Well, then how can I refuse?" She sidled inside. The quarters were cramped with the two of them and her suitcase.

His eyes locked with hers as the elevator inched up. Her cheeks grew hot. Why did he have such an effect on her? Maybe it was just the wine.

The door slid open, and she shuffled out into another hallway. There was a railing next to her with a view of the living room down below. A framed print of an antique-looking wine bottle hung directly in front of her. It was nice, but it had no personality.

"This way," he said, leading her past the loft and down the hall. "You're across from me if you need anything tonight."

He opened a door and turned the lights on. There was a king-sized, four-poster bed with elaborate blue damask drapes.

"I see your grandma decorated this room," she said.

Rett rubbed a hand over the back of his neck. "I haven't

had a chance to do many updates since moving in. But I think you'll be comfortable here."

"Oh, I was not throwing shade on your grandma at all. This room is amazing. I immediately feel eighty percent more royal just by stepping inside. It just definitely wasn't designed by a twenty-nine-year-old straight man."

"Definitely not." He stepped further into the room and reached for another light switch. "You have your own bathroom."

There went her half-formed drunk plan to walk in on him naked. It was for the better.

"I don't know about you, but I could use a shower."

She nodded vehemently. A cold one would be best.

"I'll leave you to it and meet you downstairs when you're done. There's something I want to show you."

What else could possibly be left to show her? An indoor tennis court? A chocolate fountain?

"Sounds great. Thank you so much again for letting me stay here. I honestly think I would have rather slept in the party bus than under Ashley's roof."

"I'm just excited to have a chance to use the guest room. Most of my friends live here so it barely gets used. I'll see you downstairs."

He closed the door behind him and left her in silence. She took a moment to center herself. A cold shower truly was her only option.

The guest bathroom had great bones but was also in need of a slight update. Some navy, maybe. A nice set of pendant lights.

She reached around to her back and groped for the zipper. Shit. It had taken Kenya to zip her into this wretched satin nightmare earlier. Even with years of CrossFit, she couldn't reach the damn thing. She had no option but to ask Rett for help.

"Really, universe?" she muttered to herself as she stepped out of her room and crossed the hallway.

His door wasn't completely closed. She knocked on it, and it drifted open.

He stood across the room with his back to her, and he was shirtless.

He whirled around. A chiseled six pack and biceps for days greeted her. The universe was enjoying her suffering.

"Everything okay?"

"Uh." She seemed to have lost all of her vocabulary. All she could do was stare at this stupidly hot winemaker like a googly-eyed goldfish.

"Do you need help with your dress?"

She snapped her eyes back up to his. "Please. I almost dislocated my shoulder trying to unzip it."

He smiled and crossed the room. Good lord. She spun around and moved her hair out of the way.

As he tugged the zipper down, the straps fell from her shoulders. In an instant, her dress was puddled on the floor.

"Shit, sorry," he said.

"It's okay. Satin's slippery." She stepped out of it and bent to pick it up. Of course she was wearing unflattering undergarments—a nude strapless bra and matching thong.

"Thanks for your help."

She turned to look at him, and his eyes snapped up to meet hers.

"Well, we couldn't have you dislocating an elbow. I imagine you need those for work." As he spoke, he reached a hand out to stroke the offending body part.

Her breath caught in her chest. They were standing half-naked in front of each other, and he was stroking her arm. This had to be a move, right?

She took a step closer to him and looked up at him. Fuck it. She had to shoot her shot. If she didn't, she would regret it every day for the rest of her life.

She had just reached out one hand to plant on his abs when he cocked his head.

"Do you hear that?"

She turned to look over her shoulder. "Oh shit. It's—"

At that moment, Penny, apparently unable to stop her momentum, crashed into her with the force of a furry freight train.

Jade shrieked and hit the carpeted floor with a muffled thump. Every part of her had probably just jiggled like she was an elaborate Jell-O mold from the fifties.

"Zoomies," she whispered. The wind had been completely knocked out of her. Her thigh stung where a shockingly solid doggie skull had collided with her.

Rett's concerned face appeared above hers. Penny popped up next to him, panting happily like she had just hit a zoomies PR. She licked his cheek.

"I'm fine," Jade said, rolling onto her side and clambering to her knees. She reached over and grabbed her dress.

That had surely been a sign from the universe. She was not meant to jump Rett's bones tonight.

"Are you sure? That was a pretty hard fall."

"All good." She crawled into her room and shut the door.

"Fuck," she whispered. She had made a damn fool of herself.

CHAPTER THIRTEEN

RETT

RETT, STILL KNEELING ON THE FLOOR, STARED AT THE CLOSED door. This was definitely the first time this had ever happened to him—a beautiful woman, half-naked in front of him, slide tackled by a golden retriever. If Penny hadn't made an appearance, there was a strong chance he would have tested the waters. He had been seconds from holding Jade's long, lean runner's body. Feeling the quickening of her pulse under his fingers. Pressing her against the wall while he explored every inch.

Their kiss from the rehearsal dinner burned in his mind. Maybe it was just because it had been awhile, but it had been electric, almost earth-shifting. Had Penny saved him from making a mistake?

Beyond the fact that Jade was obviously stunning, even in a rumpled dress, she was resilient, funny, acknowledging of her own flaws, and all-around intriguing.

But she was determined to leave tomorrow, and he wouldn't see her again for two weeks. And after that? Maybe never. Getting romantically or physically involved would be a mistake. Especially with the winery in jeopardy.

Regardless, he couldn't shake off the feeling that she deserved more than this. She had mountains of potential, if only she could unlock it. A few small changes—a driver's license, a fresh resume, some financial literacy classes, a steady job—and she'd be unstoppable. Their relationship would be much better as mentor and mentee, especially at a distance.

Would he be able to ignore that indescribable pull? She'd already been through so much. She deserved love and companionship whether she realized it or not. He couldn't be the one to hurt her again, but maybe he could help her realize what she truly wanted.

His phone beeped on the dresser, and he snapped out of it. It was Elaine, reporting that everything had gone well and the winery was locked down for the night.

His heart stuttered in his chest. In the chaos of the evening, he had somehow forgotten about the winery. He logged in to their accounting software on his phone and checked the deposit. Not terrible, not great. Another luke-warm Saturday.

After a quick shower, he traipsed down the stairs and opened his refrigerator. Apple dumplings—last night's stress bake—stared back at him. He whipped off the cello-phane and popped them in the oven to warm.

The tip-tap of Penny's nails on tile drew his attention, and he turned around. There Jade was, a slightly frayed NYU T-shirt draping down to her butt. Her left arm clutched her right, and she approached slowly.

Penny surged forward and planted her paws on his chest.

"Down, Penny." Jade laughed. "Thank you again for the hospitality. The shower was great. You said you wanted to show me something?"

She was talking fast. Had their half-naked encounter in the hallway rattled her? His eyes drifted down to the hem of her shorts again, then snapped back. He wasn't getting involved.

"Yes. Come with me." He stepped into the hallway and opened the basement door.

She followed him. Was she nervous? Scared? They were barely more than strangers. Maybe a joke would help.

"Before you ask, I'm not bringing you down here to murder you."

"No? It's such a perfect setup. I bet no one could hear me scream."

His dick hardened at the idea of her screaming his name, but he dismissed it immediately. Not the right time, not the right girl. He glanced at her. Well, not *not* the right girl.

They passed the family room and arrived at a bookcase. It was one of the only updates he had made to the house since moving in. With a half smile and an arch of his eyebrow, he pulled on one of the books.

The bookcase swung toward them, and lights flickered on in the room that lay beyond. Penny barked at it and hid behind Jade.

Jade gasped, and his smile grew.

"It's...beautiful." She stepped barefoot onto the brick floor.

He followed her. Her head swiveled as she took in the dozens of bottles in wooden racks. A bar stood at the back, decanter and glassware waiting. A small circular table with four chairs was positioned underneath a rustic-looking chandelier. Bricks arched above them in a curved ceiling.

"It's one of my favorite rooms in the house. Sometimes I come down here just to read and have a glass."

"You read?" She shot a glance over her shoulder.

"When I can."

"Me too. I thought it would help my artist constipation, but instead I just got addicted to Nora Roberts. What's this?" She paused at a bottle in a glass case.

"That's a bottle from the first batch of wine my grandparents ever made."

"Wow," she uttered breathlessly.

"Pick something. We'll have some with dessert."

She straightened and looked at him. "You've done enough for me. You don't need to ply me with wine to convince me to come back for the party."

He shook his head. "That has nothing to do with it. I love to share my love of wine. It's the lifeblood of my family. If you were staying, I'd do a personal tasting for you."

She seemed to deliberate for a moment before pulling a bottle from the wine fridge. A five-year-old Gewurtzraminer. She held it out to him.

"Nice choice." He took it from her and swept his arm toward the exit.

"Was that a test? It felt like a test."

He chuckled. "Not a test. I don't get to entertain very often. Indulge me."

Her gaze moved around the room. "Why not? Are you waiting for a sixteen-person hot tub to be installed?"

"I work a lot."

She made a noise of disapproval as they climbed the stairs. "It seems like a waste to have this amazing house and not have it filled with laughter and good food. And honestly probably a minimum of three dogs."

He frowned.

"Sorry," she said hurriedly, "it's not my place."

"It's not that. That's exactly what my mom says every

time she visits. Except she normally mentions half a dozen grandchildren."

Jade raised her eyebrows. "In this economy? I can see why you want to get them off your back."

In the kitchen, he set the bottle on the kitchen counter and peered into the oven.

"Almost done." He pulled out bowls and glasses.

"Can I help?" she asked.

"No. Sit."

He poured a generous serving of wine into each glass and slid one across the island to her. She perched on a barstool, hair still damp from her shower, looking like she belonged there.

What was she thinking?

"So what smells so good?"

"Apple dumplings. We didn't get to have any wedding cake," he explained.

She tilted her head. "I've never had an apple dumpling. But it smells incredible."

"Just you wait," he said, opening the oven and sliding on a pair of hot mitts.

When he topped the dumpling with ice cream and set the dessert in front of her, her stomach audibly growled.

"Sorry," she said.

"What did I tell you about unnecessary apologies?" he asked as he slid onto the seat next to her.

Pink rushed into her cheeks.

He held his glass up, ignoring the effect her expression had on his manhood. "To new beginnings."

"To new beginnings," she parroted. They clinked and drank.

She closed her eyes like she felt something deep in her

soul. She tipped her chin to the ceiling and cocked her head.

Her eyes snapped open like she could read his thoughts.

"Is your tingle back?" he guessed.

"A little bit."

For some reason, the fact that his wine had the power to return a muse to its artist was intoxicating.

"Try the dumpling." He nudged the bowl toward her.

She dug in and let out a moan. If she didn't stop making sex noises, he was not going to be able to stick to the plan. She was like a work of art herself, and he was having a hard time taking his eyes off her.

"This is incredible. Did you make these, or are they local?"

He hesitated. His baking hobby was not something he shared with the world. "Have you ever tried different kinds of food to fix your block?"

Jade laughed. "I wish I could tell you all the things I've tried to unblock myself. It's part of the reason why I'm so poor now."

His dumpling sat in front of him untouched. "Really? Like what?"

She took a sip of wine, and her body trembled for an instant. "Everything. I mean it. That's been my whole philosophy since my brain shut down. I thought that if I just opened myself to enough new experiences, something would eventually click."

She ticked items off on her fingers. "Cooking lessons, skydiving, every legendary dish from every restaurant in the city. I learned sign language, did polar plunges, took up CrossFit, started running, volunteered at community kitchens, rode roller coasters, took helicopter tours. I did everything short of throwing myself over Niagara Falls in a barrel."

He paused with a bite halfway to his mouth. "When you say you're poor—"

"I mean I'll be homeless in three months."

His stomach clenched. How had she let the reins get so loose over the years? Sure, the winery wasn't thriving, but they weren't on the verge of shutting their doors.

He took a deep breath and searched for the right words. She didn't need more criticism.

"I know I sound like an idiot." That saved him from a response. Her cheeks were pink again. "It wasn't always like this. I was actually making great money while I was in school. But then my parents died, and I had to settle everything with their estate. I used the life insurance to pay off the funerals and the mortgage and my student loans. And of course I thought I was entering into a partnership where expenses would be divided and I would have some breathing room. But then I was totally blindsided and locked into an insanely expensive lease by myself for a year. I moved to a cheaper apartment, but I've been barely treading water ever since."

The right words still evaded him. His heart ached for her. Sure, she had stumbled into a few pitfalls. But she was a good person. He could help her if she'd let him.

"That's why I have to go back," she added, voice barely more than a whisper. "I have to figure out where to go from here."

He laid a hand on her arm, and his skin tingled at the touch. Maybe some honesty would help bridge that gap.

"I think we could help each other," he said gently. "The winery has been...underperforming."

She raised her eyebrows and looked around the kitchen.

"I know it doesn't look like it based on where we're sitting. I'm somewhat of an expert at budgeting, so we've absorbed a lot of hits. But with all the competition in the area, we're not making sales like we used to. People who mean the world to me depend on me for their livelihoods. I need to try some new tactics. If you stayed in town, we could do a joint project. What about a paint and sip night?"

Jade straightened up and looked indignant for a second. Then her shoulders slumped. "I couldn't even lead a paint and sip. We'd all just stare at blank canvases for two hours."

"Why don't you sleep on it?"

"Okay." She climbed to her feet.

She was going to bed already? He hadn't meant right this second. But maybe it was better if she went to bed. Then he wouldn't run the risk of losing control.

She brought her bowl and spoon to the dishwasher and whistled for Penny. She disappeared outside for a moment, then returned.

"Rett?"

He turned to look at her. She had paused with one foot on the stairs.

"Thank you."

"For what?"

"Everything. For coming with me tonight. For dessert. And for believing in me."

She darted up the stairs without waiting for a response.

Warmth coursed through his body. She would see reason in the morning. He was sure of it.

CHAPTER FOURTEEN

JADE

JADE'S EYES SNAPPED OPEN JUST AS THE FIRST STREAKS OF PINK filtered into the room. She bolted upright, startling Penny out of what appeared to be a deep sleep.

What kind of velvet-lined purgatory had she stumbled into? Oh, right. Rett's house. The wedding from hell was finally behind her, but the memory had almost been superseded by the Penny incident.

It was time to go. She had embarrassed herself enough in this town.

Ten minutes later, everything was back in her suitcase and she had sent a text pleading with Kenya to wait. Ashley wouldn't be on the party bus. The cheating twosome were probably already at the airport, headed to their lavish Hawaiian honeymoon. Good riddance. She crept over to the door and pressed her ear against it. Silence.

With any luck, she'd be able to slip out without Rett knowing. Would he even want her to come back for the anniversary party? Another manic pixie wine groupie was sure to stumble into his winery and effortlessly fulfill his wishes. She'd probably never see him again. All she would have left was a memory—a toe-curling kiss in the October humidity and the sweet sting of late-night apple dumplings.

The door creaked open. The whirring sound of a fan came from the door across the hallway, but there was no sign of movement.

She clicked her tongue for Penny and hurried downstairs as quietly as she could with a bulky suitcase and backpack full of wine. She slid her flip-flops on and was just about to head for the front door when the windows in the dining room caught her eye. She stopped in her tracks.

The sun was rising, sending streaks of pink and orange into the powder blue sky. A simple wooden dock stood fifty yards from her. The lake wound away from her like a serpent tinged with gold.

Full-body tingles exploded up and down her arms and legs. Even her scalp was tingling. Her backpack hit the floor with a thump. She dug through it and pulled out emergency art supplies. All she had was a cheap palette of watercolor paint, brushes that were barely fit for a kindergarten class, and a measly stack of cold pressed watercolor paper.

Leaving everything else behind, she pushed her way through the double doors that led to the patio and ran toward the water's edge. She took a couple quick pictures to preserve the scene, then darted down the dock.

Shit, she hadn't brought any cups of water out to rinse the brush. Lake water would have to do. If she didn't capitalize on this sensation right this second, it could slip away for good.

She dropped to her knees and trapped the paper beneath rocks from the shoreline. Her brush dipped into the glass surface of the lake, sending ripples dancing. It had been a long time since she'd used watercolors. But it felt like the perfect medium to capture the sun on the water.

She glided the brush across the page, painting just with the lake water. Dabbing her brush in the yellow pot, she paused for a moment before touching it to the page. A yellow sun blossomed. Next she added tinges of pink, then orange. They bled together, a perfect pastel blanket draping over the verdant hills.

Wind tugged at her hair, and she shivered. But not even six inches of unseasonal snow could have pulled her away from this simple act of creation.

Her brush slid over the paper, bleeding and blending blues, yellow, oranges. Tinges of purple for the fading night. Shadows and deep greens to mark the rows of the vineyard across the lake.

Her heart hammered in her chest. She was right. There was something here—in the soil, the water, the air. The magic of the worn wood beneath her fingertips. The brush moved seemingly of its own accord, rendering her surroundings in miniature.

Finally, her bristles hit the dock. She leaned back on her heels, carefully lifting the page to inspect it.

It was far from perfect. It wasn't the mixed media with a cheeky name and snappy social commentary that had made her semi-famous. But it was a start. And it was so, so much better than nothing.

She laughed out loud, clutching the paper like it was a lifeline.

"I thought you left," Rett said from behind her.

She shrieked, and her grip loosened on the paper. The wind ripped it out of her hands and sent it flying into the lake.

"Wait—were you? Oh shit." In seconds, Rett had ripped off his T-shirt and sweatpants. His footsteps thundered down the short dock, rattling the palette, and he leapt into the water. Small waves lapped at the shore.

He swam for the paper, snatching it from the water and holding it overhead.

"I'm so sorry," he sputtered. "Is it ruined?"

It almost certainly was. Wet-on-wet technique didn't usually mean hurling freshly-painted paper into a lake.

It was a bummer that her first breakthrough in two years had ended up waterlogged and clutched the wrong way in the hands of an untrained person. But it didn't matter. Because if she could do watercolor, maybe she could find her way back.

He slapped the painting onto the dock and swam past it, climbing to his feet on the shoreline. Still dripping, he plodded down the dock and collapsed on his knees next to her.

"Shit. I'm so sorry, Jade."

"It's okay."

"It's not. This was probably a breakthrough for you, and I scared you and made you drop it into the damn lake." He buried his hands in his hair.

"I mean it. It's okay. This wouldn't have been sellable anyway."

Goose bumps rose on his skin. "What do you mean? It's stunning."

"I'm not known for watercolors. I doubt the gallery would have had much interest."

"Who cares what you're known for? It's part of you."

She smiled. "I wish it was as simple as that."

The sun gilded Rett's jawline. He looked like a friggen Adonis contemplating the earth.

Her eyes dipped without permission, taking just a glance at his waterlogged physique. Desire stirred in her again.

What the hell was she going to do? The need to stay was growing by the second. Would the lake grant her another burst of inspiration? But she had next to no money and frankly she didn't know Rett well enough to stay with him for two weeks.

The city was safer.

"Shit. What time is it?" She patted her pockets, but her phone was still in the house.

"About seven twenty."

Kenya would be awake any minute, ready to load up the bus.

"I have to get back. We're scheduled to leave by eight."

"Let me take you back to the city."

She turned to look at him. "You want to take a spontaneous eight-hour round trip? Into downtown Manhattan? Don't you have a winery to open?"

He hesitated, then shook his head. "I need to make it up to you. I wanted to help, not make things harder for you." He gazed at the waterlogged paper.

His fingers landed on her arm again, and a shiver rocked her body. His green eyes were quiet today, serene like the lake behind him. Was she really about to climb into a car with someone she barely knew?

"You really want to take me back to New York?"

"I think I've made it pretty clear that I'd like you to stay here. Look what you've done since you've been here." He pointed at the runny watercolor. "But if you need to go back to the city, that's where I'll take you. Consider transportation a perk of our agreement."

The idea of having another five hours to spend with Rett was very tempting. But how would she fill all those hours of conversation? There was only so much she could word vomit.

His thumb stroked her wrist.

"Let's go to brunch. Then I'll drive you back."

Her stomach growled as if on command. She hadn't even finished the incredible apple dumpling from the night before. Some brunch couldn't hurt. And if it meant avoiding the awkward post-wedding conversation with the other bridesmaids in the party bus, even better.

"Okay. Just brunch."

An hour later, Jade had made her excuses to Kenya, and she and a freshly showered Rett were in his truck.

"You're going to love Margie's," he said. "The food is incredible."

He hadn't opted for a suit today but had still insisted on wearing a button-down with the sleeves rolled up. Was this part of his trick to convince her to stay? How badly did he need an artist-in-residence to do paint and sip?

If she was being honest with herself, she didn't want to leave. But a paint and sip event wouldn't cover even a third of first and last month's rent on a new apartment. There was no choice but to go home to the apartment she was already paying for and look for a new job and place to live.

Rett pulled into a spot on the street and jumped out. Jade fought with her seatbelt again until Rett popped her door open and reached across her. The seatbelt retracted, brushing against her skin as it went. Great, now she was getting turned on by seatbelts.

"I really need to get that fixed," he said as he offered her a hand.

She jumped down, and he steadied her with a hand on one hip. She stepped onto the sidewalk and took in her surroundings. Townspeople waved at each other as they ducked into shops. A group of elderly women power walked through the village green. Glimpses of the lake were just visible beyond the iconic gazebo.

"Come on. I'm sure you're eager to get back." There was a smirk on his face, like he could read her mind.

He led her across the village green to the turquoise building with the yellow door she had spotted on her run. Margie's.

The second Rett opened the door, Jade could have levitated the rest of the way just from the scents drifting towards her. Savory pork and fried hash browns. Buttery muffins and flaky pastries.

She took one step inside and stopped in her tracks. "Holy shit."

"What?" Rett appeared at her shoulder.

She pointed to the far wall with a shaking finger. "That's my painting."

He turned where she pointed. "The muffin?"

Breakfast at Epiphany's, one of Jade's favorite pieces, hung next to a bathroom door. It was an abstract take of a blueberry muffin perched on the railing of the Empire State Building. The crumbs were coarse sand from the beach at Coney Island. The New York skyline sprawled in the background. Newspaper clippings about gentrification and corruption in the police force were papier-mâché'd into the shapes of buildings.

She had painted it the day Nate had told her he loved her for the first time. Was this a sign? She looked for Rett, but he had abandoned her to inspect it.

"There he is," called a woman from behind the counter. Her curly gray hair was swept back into a loose bun. "I was hoping you'd stop in today. Who do you have with you?"

Rett swiveled away from the painting and side-stepped

around one of a dozen tables. He wrapped an arm around Jade and dragged her up to the counter.

A tingle ran up her spine, but then she remembered. Right, the townspeople needed to believe they were dating. His arm was around her for show.

"This is Jade. Jade, meet Margie. The owner."

"It's so nice to meet you." Jade extended a hand over the counter, and Margie shook it. "I actually painted that." She pointed to the muffin.

Margie gasped and splayed a hand over her heart. "You're Jade Gardner?"

"Yeah," Jade said with a silly smile. She was recognized maybe once in a blue moon in the city, and only in the art district.

"Oh my lord," Margie said. She threw a tea towel down on the counter and turned over her shoulder. "Amanda, you're on register."

Margie stepped around the counter and took Jade's hand. "I have two of your paintings. If my house was burning down, I would save them first. I love your work. What in the world are you doing here?"

"I was just here for a wedding. I'm headed back to the city this morning, but Rett insisted on breakfast first."

Margie looked at him like she was impressed. "Well, I'll be. Jade Gardner in my little town. Let me get my phone for a picture." She scurried to the back.

Jade's cheeks grew hot, and she looked around the café. The longest wall was largely bare, a glaring void in the otherwise colorful and playful restaurant. An idea struck.

"Have you ever considered adding a mural?" Jade asked when Margie returned, phone in hand. "I noticed your wall is a little bit bare."

"A mural?" Margie asked thoughtfully. Her eyes moved

to where Jade had indicated. "It hadn't crossed my mind, but now that you point it out, it is a little underwhelming."

"I could paint one for you."

The words were out before she could take them back. What was she thinking? She had never painted a mural before, and the only art she had produced in the last two years was a half-assed sketch of Rett and a waterlogged sunrise.

Rett shot her a look, clearly surprised.

Margie seemed to deliberate for a moment, gray-blue eyes moving over the far wall. After a beat, she spoke.

"You know what? I think a mural is just what this café needs."

Relief flooded Jade. Maybe this would be a step towards digging herself out of her unfortunate hole. Or maybe it would be the final nail in her coffin.

"But you're planning on leaving this morning?" Margie asked.

"That's...negotiable," Jade said.

Rett straightened beside her.

What was she doing? Was she really staying? Where would she live?

Margie smiled. "Good. Come in tomorrow morning and we'll talk terms."

"Sounds great," Rett said before she could take it back.

She would figure it out. She always did.

"It's a deal."

CHAPTER FIFTEEN

"For someone who just single-handedly solved all your own problems and had a 'full-blown mouthgasm' from brunch, you don't seem very happy," Rett said.

Jade bit her lip and looked out the window as they passed the café. They were in the truck on the way to the city, Penny sprawled between them like a sixty-pound, snoring throw blanket. Even though Jade was staying, she needed materials and clothes to make it through the next two weeks.

Her decision to stay had been a surprise, but a welcome one. It would be much easier to coach her when she was physically staying in town. But now they needed to hammer out the details of their arrangement.

"What if I can't do it?" she asked.

"Do what? The mural?"

"Yeah. I don't want to disappoint Margie."

"You won't. You were just painting this morning."

"That might have been a fluke. And I told you, it's not my usual art. That's what she wants—the bold, fun Jade who throws feathers and glitter on a hot pink mess and calls it

'Tuesdays at the Horny Ram.' What if I can't remember how to be that person anymore?"

Rett pulled up at a red light and turned to her. She looked at him. The sun shone punishingly bright, illuminating the dust motes and dog hair swirling in the cabin. The air conditioning blew her hair away from her face. God, she was beautiful.

"You're an artist in your bones. I know you'll find your way."

Her cheeks flushed. "Oh," she said, shooting up in her seat as they moved through the intersection. She pointed out the window at a grocery store in the distance. "We need snacks."

"Snacks? We just had brunch."

She slid her heart-shaped sunglasses down the bridge of her nose. The strap on her overall-short things slipped off her shoulder.

"We can't have a road trip without snacks. There are rules."

"You have a lot of convictions about road trip etiquette for someone who doesn't have a driver's license."

She nudged him. "Listen here, Mr. Three-Piece Suit. Snacks and playlists or a handful of carefully curated podcast episodes are required. I don't make the rules."

"Fine. But we're not going to that grocery store."

She peered at it. "Why? Is it owned by a rival vintner?"

He cracked a smile, then shook his head. "No. It's the price gouging. Nine dollars for a bottle of ketchup. Thirty dollars for two chicken breasts. It would be cheaper to buy a plot of land and all the tools and materials necessary to become a farmer than it would be to do your weekly shopping there."

She settled back into her seat. "Damn. Okay, well, I'm

sure we'll pass a gas station or something. I'll get to work on the playlist in the meantime." She pulled out her phone. "What kind of music do you like?"

"Depends on the time of year and my mood. I've been in a nineties summer hits rut for weeks."

She reached over and touched his arm. "I love nineties summer bops. Say no more."

In no time, their nearly five-hour journey was punctuated by a well-rounded representation of nineties artists. Sugar Ray crooned as they rolled into the town of Bath.

Rett glanced in the rearview mirror. He couldn't see Hammondsport from here, let alone his winery. But even though he owed this trip to Jade after ruining her painting, the thought of stepping away from the winery for a full day brought a dim feeling of panic. Anything could happen, and he wouldn't be able to do anything about it from five hours away.

"So we should probably talk about the terms of our agreement," Jade piped up.

His attention snapped back to the present. Elaine was capable. Everything would be fine. And he would check in every hour.

"Did you draw up a contract before bed?" he teased.

"No, I'm just thinking. If we really want to sell this lie, we're going to have to put the work in and spend at least a little time together while I'm here in town. Your parents still have friends here, I'm sure. If they ask them about me at your event, we'll be exposed right away if we've never been seen together and know nothing about each other."

She had a point.

"So what do you suggest?" he asked.

"Public dates. Town events, festivals, dinners out, canoodling in the gazebo. I'll visit you at the winery. You can stop in at the café. We'll have to take a lot of pictures and put them up in your house and office."

"Did you just say 'canoodling in the gazebo'?"

She threw her hands in the air. "It was just an example."

"You sound suspiciously well-informed for someone who's never fake dated anyone."

"I've read a lot of romance novels in the past two years, okay? Trust me. We should discuss boundaries."

"Boundaries?"

"Even in a fake relationship they're important. Based on our earlier conversations, I would assume you would prefer that catching feelings is a boundary. The affection is just for show—when the party is over, we're both free and clear."

"Right," he said. Thankfully she understood the situation. He should have thought of a fake girlfriend years ago.

"Okay, great." She pulled up her notepad on her phone and began a list. "So criteria number one—no feelings. I might need some help with this one. If you could routinely insult me and remind me of your unredeeming qualities, that'll really help."

"Where do I start? Emotionally unavailable, baggage the size of Mount Everest."

She put on a shocked face. "Same."

"Nice."

They fist bumped.

"Number two—no outside entanglements or situation-ships for the duration of the trial. If someone sees you hooking up with someone else while fake dating me, it'll destroy your reputation."

"This will probably shock you, but the dating pool in Hammondsport is exceedingly small."

"I'm just saying. I'm sure you get a lot of tipsy hotties in the winery."

His gaze drifted down to her outfit again. Overalls, but in the form of shorts. How did one even take them off? Now that she was staying, maybe she would be interested in exploring the physical connection between them. He had a deep feeling that this attraction wasn't just one-sided.

Fuck it. It was about time he did something impulsive for once.

"Fair enough. I do have a question."

She lifted her gaze from her phone. "Go on."

"We should probably address the elephant in the room."

She straightened up in her seat. "Which is?"

"The insane sexual tension between us."

Her cheeks flushed. "Ah. So you noticed that."

"If Penny hadn't crashed into you last night, I would have dragged you into the shower with me. So we need to talk about it. What's off limits?"

"Well," she said, "I, for one, have no problem separating sex from feelings."

Blood rushed south. How illegal was sex on the side of the road?

"Same. So there's really no reason why this can't be more of a friends-with-benefits situation."

"Exactly," she said. "So on the outside, we're in love. And on the inside we're—"

"Enjoying each other's company."

"Then it's decided," she said. "Criteria number three—friends with benefits. We should probably make a subsection for dealing with PDA. What's your comfort level like?"

"I think we'll need some at least to sell the story. But what do you think?"

She nodded, and there was a glint in her eye. "I'm not opposed to a little public declaration. A hand on the small of my back, a quick kiss when the mood strikes. Holding hands in front of the neighborhood busybodies."

"As long as we're not being chased by anything."

She stared at him. "Is that likely to happen?"

"You should see the groundhogs we get in the vineyard."

She made a note in her phone. "Oh, what will you tell your family after the event? When I'm gone?"

He hesitated. "The truth. That you're an incredibly talented artist who needed to go back to New York to chase your dreams."

"If it helps, I could stage a very public breakup."

"I don't think that will be necessary. I'll just put in a couple weeks of dramatic moping. It'll get the point across."

"Fair enough. Well, while we're talking about sex, let's make it as un-sexy as possible so I don't spend the next three-and-a-half hours thinking about jumping on you and committing a traffic crime."

His lips pressed together. "Go on."

"First, I have an IUD, but condoms are a must. It's nonnegotiable. I don't need to accidentally bring a child—no matter how perfect their genetic makeup and bone structure would be—into this world when I can barely afford my rent."

"Got it. I'll pick up a box when we do our snack run."

"Second," she said, "there will be foreplay. I spent too many years of my life faking orgasms with a warm-blooded jackhammer. I will coach you until you get it right. And don't worry," she added with a hand on his thigh. "I'm a very enthusiastic giver as well as a receiver."

The leather creaked beneath his palms on the steering wheel, and his pants stretched a bit tighter than they had moments before. "I thought we were supposed to be making this un-sexy."

"Right. Sorry." She withdrew her hand.

"So," she said after a moment passed. "What are your expectations of me? How can I best wow your parents? I'll need to do some research, I'm sure."

"For starters, I would appreciate it if you could name drop Rhodes Vineyard when you describe the circumstances of your remarkable comeback in your next big interview."

"Obviously," she said. "What else?"

"Reconsider the paint and sip night. You could also help with some things for the party. I'll pay you as an independent contractor—I can't afford to pay you what you're worth, though."

"Something's better than nothing. We'll talk about it." Her expression was cloudy in the reflection of the window.

"Also, I always want you to be yourself," he began. "But historically speaking, my parents will ask for your top three favorite musical scores and Hollywood actors."

"Got it. I'll look into it. I think we've made great progress today. Any other boundaries I should note?"

"Open communication and truth always."

"Definitely. Is it super tacky if I request a case of wine for my services?"

"I'll send you home with two."

"Deal."

She extended a hand over the dog, and he shook it, cementing whatever the next two weeks would bring.

CHAPTER SIXTEEN

RETT

Jade paused at her front door, keys in hand. "You don't have to come in. It's not...what you're used to," she said with a glance over her shoulder.

He frowned at her. What did she think he was, a member of the royal family?

"I went to college. I've lived in small apartments before. Besides, this is your own home. I live in my grandma's house. How embarrassing is that?"

She cracked a small smile and unlocked the door. It opened and instantly blinded them with afternoon sunshine.

He followed her and hefted her tote bag inside. Penny torpedoed past them, nearly knocking him headlong into the entryway.

Jade's head swung from left to right. She was clearly self-conscious having someone else in her space.

"Make yourself at home. I'll try to be quick. Do you want some water?"

"I'm fine."

There wasn't any reason to be embarrassed about her

apartment. It was a standard New York studio brightened substantially by a bright orange couch and magenta accent wall. His toes sank into a rug that looked just like a patch of moss on a forest floor. A pile of colorful throw blankets waited in a wicker basket next to the couch, and the appliances in the kitchen were a shade of mint. It was cozy. Much homier than his place.

He strode over to the easel that clutched a blank canvas. Art supplies were organized neatly in a three-tier cart next to it. He inspected them and took pictures of the brands. Just in case she agreed to the paint and sip night.

While she climbed a small spiral staircase that must have led to a sleeping loft, he cracked a smile at the cross-stitch mounted next to the window that read "Eat a Dick" in flowing script. A painting hung above the couch. He had Googled some of her past work but seeing it in person was something else.

Gray clouds and raindrops came to life, practically dripping onto a red umbrella that covered two adults each holding the hand of a child. He almost reached out to see if it was actually wet. A sign that read "Bronx Zoo" hovered above them.

"This is beautiful," he said without turning to look for her.

Footsteps rang on the staircase.

"Oh. Thank you. It's a memory."

"Your parents?"

She sidled up next to him and stuffed her hands in her pockets. "Yeah. I painted it the week after they died. My dad was gone a lot, so this was a special day. We practically had the zoo to ourselves because of the rain."

"I think they'd be really proud of you."

She cocked an eyebrow. "Ah yes, I'm sure all parents

hope that their children will be nearly bankrupt and on the brink of homelessness at twenty-six."

He turned to her and put his hand on her shoulder. Her blue eyes were watery as she stared back at him, and he caught a tear with his thumb as it slid down her cheek.

"You will never be homeless. If the worst happens, you can come back to Hammondsport. We take care of our own."

His pulse quickened at the thought of Jade settling down in town. Not that he was rooting for her to lose her apartment. Or looking for a real relationship.

She stepped out from under his arms and turned toward her windows. She took a deep breath and closed her eyes. "I'm sorry. I'm usually a lot better at looking on the sunny side of things. This week has just been...a lot."

"What have I told you about unnecessary apologies?"

"You're right. I'm going through some shit, so chill, okay?" She crossed her arms and stared defiantly at Rett.

He smiled and almost moved forward to kiss her. But it wasn't the right moment.

"That's better. How can I help?"

"Mind taking this to the car?" She nudged a weekender bag toward him. "I have to pack up Penny's things. She's very particular."

He nodded. "Did you pack something for the party?"

She tossed her hair over her shoulder and turned to look back at him. "Of course. I went Old Hollywood glam."

"Perfect." He picked up her bag and headed for the truck.

———

An hour later, Rett stood in front of a display of primers. He glanced at his watch. At this rate, they definitely wouldn't make it back before closing time at the winery. Jade had insisted that they visit her usual paint store before heading back, and it was becoming an unexpectedly irritating adventure.

He thrust his phone at her. "Financial literacy lesson number one. Do not buy the same product in the city that you can get from Home Depot for thirty dollars cheaper."

She pouted. "But I prefer to support small businesses."

Frustration prickled under his skin. This was basically budgeting 101. "That is a relic from another time when you didn't have to worry about money. For now, you can only get the absolute musts here. Everything else—primer, equipment, brushes—"

She gasped. "How dare you accuse brushes of not being in the 'absolute must' category."

He sighed. "Fine. I'm not an artist. But I'll tell you right now we will not be buying stirring sticks and paint tray liners here. A piece of plastic is a piece of plastic."

"Just so I'm understanding everything properly, my time is worth nothing and it's more financially responsible to leave the city and drive five hours out of the way to save two dollars on painter's tape?"

"I only said that because we're going that direction anyway." Rett's voice rose.

A shopkeeper in a brown smock appeared. "Aww. How long have you guys been married?" she asked.

"We're not married," they responded in tandem, both glaring at each other.

"My mistake. Can I take anything up to the counter for you?"

Jade huffed, then hefted everything out of her cart

except for paintbrushes, a rainbow of different mural paints, and matte wall varnish.

"I have to put these back. But you can take these up. Thanks."

The shopkeeper wheeled the remainder of the supplies away. Jade's expression was cloudy as she forcefully shoved paint tray liners back into their place on the shelf. It was worth it, though. He had probably just saved her upwards of $200.

His phone buzzed in his pocket, and he pulled it out. Shit. It was Elaine.

"Hello?"

"Hi, boss. Everything is okay, I just needed to let you know one teensy thing."

His stomach contorted.

"What is it?" he asked flatly. He knew something would go wrong. He shouldn't have left.

"Since you were gone, Rob led the afternoon tour," she said hesitantly.

"Yes?"

"And while they were in the barn, one of the customers knocked over a case. We lost all twelve of the bottles."

He inhaled sharply. One case wasn't great, but they had had worse mishaps.

"It seems he was overserved before arriving," she explained.

"Okay, well, thank you for letting me know."

"There's one other thing. It was a case of the sparkling."

He pinched the bridge of his nose. Fuck. He only had two cases allotted for the party. Now fifty percent of it was gone. And he didn't even know if it was any good.

A hand landed on his arm, and he almost jerked away. Jade looked at him with concern in her eyes.

"Is everyone okay? Glass cleaned up?" he asked.

"Yes, everything's fine. For what it's worth, it smelled great."

He let out a humorless laugh. "I'll stop in when I get back to town."

"All right, boss. Sorry again."

"It's fine." He hung up the phone and wiped a hand over his face. This was what he got for taking his hands off the wheel.

"Is everything okay?"

He moved through the aisles to the register. "It's fine. We just lost an entire case of sparkling wine."

Jade pulled her wallet out as the cashier scanned her items. "Sparkling? I don't remember seeing that on your tasting menu."

"It's new. It was my grandmother's dream. She died before she could start a test batch."

She squeezed his arm. "That sucks."

"It was also my plan to reinvigorate the business. Sparkling is a different beast, and not many of the wineries in this area offer it. And now half the test batch is gone."

She paid and seemed to consider the news in silence. As they hit the sidewalk, she piped up.

"You know, this might actually be a good thing."

He raised his eyebrows. "How?"

"Scarcity, Mr. Finance. On the occasions that I produced just one painting, the value sometimes tripled. By destroying half your product, you've significantly increased the value of the remaining half."

"That's assuming it's any good."

She glared at him. "Don't be modest. Every wine I've tried is incredible. It brought back my muse tingle."

"That's because we use tried-and-true methods. Barring

a bad harvest, it guarantees good results. But sparkling is an entirely new territory. There's no precedent for me to follow. It's a brand-new technique. It's been an expensive endeavor, and I'm not sure that it's going to pay off."

And if it failed, disaster would follow. He would have to cut hours, raise prices, and do a hundred other things that would impact the livelihoods of people he cared about. There was no one to blame but himself.

They piled the supplies into the truck and buckled their seatbelts.

"I would be more than happy to be your impartial sparkling guinea pig. So you don't have to risk your friends or employees lying to you."

"Thank you. I might take you up on it. Want to hit a drive-thru? I have to get back."

He had to make sure the glass was cleaned up properly. The last thing he needed was a shard stuck in a customer's foot. Tomorrow would be a long day. And he still needed to budget time to start Project Jade. They had a lot of work to do in two weeks.

"Sure. There's a great taco place four blocks that way." She pointed north, and he inched into the road.

"What are you doing tomorrow?" Rett asked.

"Prepping the mural space."

"Café closes at two. After that?"

"I...don't know."

"Come to the winery. I'll give you a private tasting. On the house, so you don't have to touch your experience budget. Consider it part of your training for the anniversary party."

She seemed to consider for a moment. "Fine. But I'm bringing backpack cheese."

He shook his head. "We have backpack cheese. We're

going to do it right. And who knows? Maybe it'll unlock something in you."

"You have a deal."

"Where are you staying tonight, by the way? You know you're welcome to stay with me."

Jade froze for a moment. "At Ashley's parents' house," she said quickly. "I think it's the least that family can do."

"Okay. I'll drop you off."

CHAPTER SEVENTEEN

JADE

RETT'S TAILLIGHTS FADED INTO THE DISTANCE. THE RETURN trip had been quieter, and despite the verbal foreplay, he had left without even a kiss on the cheek. What more did she have to do, gelatinize some chardonnay into the shape of edible panties?

It was hard not to be disappointed, but he was clearly distracted. They had pulled over twice on the way home so he could chat with someone from the winery on the phone and review some work-related documents.

He worked too much, and he definitely seemed to struggle when he wasn't in control. But the promise of tomorrow hung in the air. Maybe she could teach him how to let go. Just a little.

And more importantly, tomorrow was the first day of the official re-launch of her career. She needed some rest. And maybe some Tums.

She whirled around and took in the house in front of her. Penny whined at her side. Okay, so she hadn't technically asked permission to stay here. But everyone had left that morning, and it made no sense to leave a perfectly good house vacant. The Moores had never sprung for a security system, so they would never know. She slipped around the side of the house and grabbed the spare key from beneath a flower pot.

Inside, sad, taxidermized animals greeted her. She left her bags next to the stairs and strode deeper into the house, on the hunt for antacids. Penny followed close behind.

Headlights flashed across the windows, and a car pulled into the circular driveway out front. She stopped in her tracks. Holy shit. Was that Ashley's parents?

"Fuck fuck fuck," she whisper-shouted. She threw open the door to the basement and ushered Penny down the stairs before whipping her bags down. She closed it behind her just as the front door creaked open.

It was dark. Boxes were stacked haphazardly all over. All it would take was one thwap of Penny's tail to announce their presence. Mr. Moore was a dedicated gun enthusiast and would undoubtedly shoot her dead on the spot. She sheltered deeper into the basement, heart hammering in her ears.

She needed to leave. But where would she go? A rental was out of the question. She had watched more than her fair share of crime shows in the last two years, and the truth was she didn't know Rett well enough to stay with him for two weeks. The only other person she knew in town was Margie.

"I'm so glad we decided to stay," a voice said faintly above her. That was definitely Tracey, Ashley's mom.

"It's been too long. This place really needs a reno," said a male voice that could have only been Frank.

Jade swept the room, heart in her throat. She needed to get out of here before they caught her lurking in the base-ment and shot her—or worse, told Ashley and Nate about it. But how?

A sliding door caught her eye. Thank god it was a walk-out. Hefting Penny through a standard window well wouldn't have been easy.

She scanned the room and spotted a hiking backpack that was partially illuminated by moonlight. She yanked it towards her and dug through it. A sleeping bag was rolled beneath, and there were poles and a large piece of canvas that must have been a tent. That settled it. She would camp somewhere. She'd never done it before, but how hard could it be? It might even be nice. Something to put on her experience list.

She put the backpack on and carefully opened the door. Penny rushed out and nearly pulled her arm out of the socket.

"Did you hear something?" came a muffled voice from the house.

Panic flared in her chest. Jade slid the door closed and made a run for it. Between her heavy bag and the bulky pack, there had never been a less stealthy getaway. Penny galloped happily along next to her, apparently not recognizing the urgency of the situation.

Jade rushed into the woods and paused for a deep breath. Seconds ticked by. Silence. They weren't coming after her.

She and Penny made it to the road and hurried past the house. Jade's heart rate slowed as they headed towards town. She pulled out her phone and searched for the nearest campsite. It was a three-mile walk from town, but sort of doable with a price tag of fifty dollars a day.

Her experience budget would be completely slashed for next month, but hopefully she wouldn't need it anyway.

Shit, what would she do with Penny while she was at the café? She couldn't leave her at the campsite. She could be stolen or eaten by bears or get loose and find another family to love.

Before she could think better of it, she fired off a text to Rett asking if she could leave Penny in the winery while she was working. He sent a thumbs-up emoji and reported that he would drop her paint supplies off at the café in the morning and pick up Penny.

Relief flooded her. All she had to do was assemble a tent and survive the night. How hard could that be?

———

Caw.

Jade sat bolt upright in the tent, sleeping bag clinging to her like a weird, squishy exoskeleton. She clutched a flashlight she had found in the hiking backpack and listened. Was that a twig cracking?

It was so quiet here in the country that every sound was like a gunshot. She had slept for maybe ten minutes, and that was after fighting with the tent for two straight hours. It sagged a bit in the middle, but so far it had protected them from the light drizzle that was coming down.

Her stomach growled, and Penny's head perked up. There hadn't been time to scrounge up food for herself. The nearest gas station was another mile away, and frankly she was exhausted after being in a car for almost ten hours. Penny was fed, and that was what mattered most.

She peeked through a gap in the zipper but couldn't spot anything beyond the dark row of trees. There could have been thirty bears with chainsaws back there and she'd be none the wiser.

Penny nosed her arm, looking thoroughly unconcerned, and Jade drew her close. They would be fine. They just had to make it through the night. And then thirteen more nights. It had better be worth it.

Three hours later, Jade woke to a rustling sound. Something draped heavily across her, and she screamed and hurled her flashlight. Penny panicked and charged toward what used to be the exit only to crash into floppy canvas.

Jade thrashed her way to the zippered compartment, and the two of them crawled out onto the wet ground. She rested on her hands and knees for a moment and groaned. Drizzle pelted her back and neck.

This had to be rock bottom. Eight-year-old girls could assemble tents and survive a night outdoors. Entire organizations were founded on it. So why couldn't she last five minutes? Had city life made her soft?

A dog tongue on her cheek startled her out of introspection. There was no use in feeling sorry for herself. She glanced at her watch. It was almost five a.m. As good a time as any to make her way back to town.

The collapsed tent stared back at her. She would have to deal with it after the café closed. No one was going to steal a tent, right? But what about her bag? Everything she needed for the next two weeks was in there.

She looked around, taking in the dark shapes of trees. She couldn't risk the bag going missing. She'd have to hide it somehow.

The tree nearest her—an oak, maybe?—had low branches. Maybe she could scramble up there and tuck it someplace out of sight.

With the bag secure in a disposable poncho from the hiking backpack, she slung it over her shoulder and tested her weight on the lowest branch before beginning to climb. Hopefully no one else at the campsite was up yet. The bag would be her secret.

This wasn't so bad. It was almost invigorating. Maybe when she got back to the city she would take up tree-climbing. As she hit the midpoint of the tree, two thick branches appeared that looked like they could support some weight. She clung to the wet base of the tree with one arm while removing her bag. She situated it on the branches and jiggled them. They didn't budge.

Perfect. No one would spot her bag up here behind the thick curtain of leaves. It was totally sustainable and not at all insane to do this every morning for the next two weeks. All she needed was—

Fuck.

Her foot slipped off the branch, and her stomach lurched. Her skin scraped against the rough bark of the tree, and there was a brief feeling of weightlessness. A scream tore from her throat, and she threw out her arm to break her fall.

Thump. She lay on a carpet of leaves, shoulder stinging and wrist throbbing. The wind was knocked out of her. Penny came over and frantically licked her face.

Oh, hell. Had she broken something? Her shirt was torn where it had scratched against the trunk, and her cheek stung. But at least her bag had stayed up.

She flexed her fingers, and pain shot through her wrist. Fuck. This was her painting hand. Now what?

CHAPTER EIGHTEEN

JADE

A GASP ROUSED JADE FROM SLEEP.

"Jade? What happened to you?" A warm presence settled next to her.

Jade and Penny had briefly fallen asleep beneath the awning of the café. The inky darkness of night was receding, replaced by a deep purple with pink edges.

Margie stared back at her, concern in her eyes.

Jade sat up and smoothed her hair back. "Sorry, I just wanted to make sure I was here on time."

It was mostly true.

"Come inside," Margie ordered.

"Oh, I have Penny with me. Rett is supposed to—"

A full-body shiver shook her. Her clothes were still soaked, and the wind cut straight through them.

"Never mind that, she can stay in the back until he gets here."

Keys jingled as Margie unlocked the bright yellow door, and Jade climbed to her feet. Okay, her wrist was definitely swollen. But everything was probably fine. She could paint through the pain.

Margie ushered her inside. She whipped a blanket off a couch by the window and wrapped it around Jade.

"Oh, I don't want to make it—"

"Sweetheart," Margie interrupted. "Where were you last night?"

Jade hesitated. Something in those deep brown eyes compelled her to tell the truth. "I was...camping."

Margie raised her eyebrows. "Have you ever camped before?"

"Well, no."

Margie shook her head. "Why didn't you stay with Rett? Or at a hotel?"

Jade's shoulders slumped. Maybe it was best to be honest. She explained the entire situation minus her agreement with Rett.

Margie crossed her arms and looked sternly at Jade. "That settles it. You're staying in my guest house."

"Oh, I couldn't."

"Nonsense. I will not have one of my contracted employees falling out of trees and walking six miles in the rain. Consider housing part of our contract." She swept her gaze over Jade from top to bottom. "And food while you're here working. You look like you need a hot meal."

Jade bit her lip. She hadn't expected such an outpouring of kindness. If she had fallen asleep under an awning in New York, the business owner probably would have chased her off with a broom. But Margie had opened her home to her without hesitation. She was either insane or incredibly kind.

"I have a bike you can borrow too. Sit," Margie said. She pointed to a table.

Jade obeyed without comment. Some of the paintings had come off the wall, and Margie had cleared a space. Her stomach twisted. Would she be able to create something to fill that space? What would Margie even want?

The heavenly scent of coffee spiced the air. A minute later, a steaming mug landed in front of Jade.

"Let's chat about the mural before everyone gets here." Margie took the seat across from her.

"Of course." Jade sat up straight and grasped the mug between her hands. Pain shot through her wrist, and it was definitely swollen now that she could see it clearly. Shit. Maybe she could paint with her non-dominant hand?

"I would love an encapsulation of the town," Margie said. She put her hands in the air like she could see it already.

Jade froze. What the hell did that mean?

"Hammondsport is such a unique place. The people are so kind, the history so rich."

She gestured widely, and Jade took in the model airplane that dangled above the register and the Keuka Lake silhouette on the bathroom door.

"It's impossible not to love. And I would really love to see it on my wall every day."

"So you just want me to paint the town?" Jade clarified.

Margie shook her head. "No."

She swiveled and pointed at *Breakfast at Epiphany's.* "When I look at that painting, I can *feel* New York. I want you to paint a feeling. I want my customers to feel the town when they look at it."

"Okay," Jade said slowly. Just how the hell was she supposed to manage that? And with an injured wrist, no less.

Just another impossible task for her To Do list.

———

"WHAT THE HELL HAPPENED TO YOU?"

Jade jumped. She had been staring at the wall, willing it to show her exactly what Margie wanted. What if she couldn't give her what she asked? How was she supposed to evoke a feeling?

Rett stared at her, a bouquet of sunflowers clutched in one hand. Her heart jumped for a second, and her mood immediately shifted. Oh, right. They were supposed to be fake dating.

The café had opened, and a table of elderly women gawked at them. What was this, some kind of busybody quilting circle?

"Morning." Jade rose to her feet. She sidled over to him and kissed him on the cheek. He smelled like sandalwood and soap. The energy emanating from the busybody table was palpable.

Rett's energy, meanwhile, was rigid. He tossed the bouquet on Jade's table and pulled her closer. His thumb scraped over her cheek.

"Did this happen at the house?"

"Not exactly." She stepped away to escape his unnerving gaze, but he grabbed her injured wrist. She inhaled sharply and snatched it back.

"What happened?" he asked again, voice hard.

"I fell out of a tree. Wait—"

Rett picked her up and hefted her over his shoulder. The bell on the door clanged as he carried her out onto the sidewalk.

"Put me down," she yelled at his back. She had an unimpeded view of his ass from here, and it wasn't helping her focus.

"No." He pulled his phone out and held it to his ear, still walking.

"Hey," he said to someone. "I need you to meet me at your office. Yes. Thanks."

He slid it back in his pocket. "What were you thinking, climbing a tree in the rain? If this was part of your experience crusade—"

"You thought throwing myself out of a tree was an experience I decided I needed to have?" she said to his back.

"I don't know how your mind works," he said.

"Obviously not."

This was ridiculous. She didn't have any time to waste. She needed to figure out how to encapsulate an entire town or her rebirth as an artist would go up in flames.

"Morning, Rett. Everything okay?" an unseen person asked.

"We're doing great, Ted. Save me a scone, okay?" Rett's voice rumbled in his chest like a bass drum.

"Put me down," she said firmly.

"No. You need medical attention."

"No, I don't."

"I saw you flinch when I touched your wrist. Is that your painting hand?"

"Maybe," she admitted.

He stopped in the middle of the sidewalk, sighed, then continued on.

"My legs aren't broken," she added.

He ignored her. "Why were you climbing a tree?"

"I was hiding a bag."

He stopped again. "Is this a social media thing?"

"No," she said indignantly. "I just didn't want it to get stolen while I was working."

"Why would somebody break into a random vacation home to steal your bag?"

Jade didn't respond.

"Jade."

"Yes?" Her head began to throb from being upside down.

He lowered her to the ground and gently held her arms. His green eyes burned into her. "Where were you last night?"

"I was at a campsite, okay? Are you happy, Detective Kidnapper?"

"Why—"

She explained everything. Honesty was technically in their fake relationship bylaws, so she owed him the truth. When she was done, he closed his eyes and massaged his temples.

"That's it. You're staying with me," he announced.

"No, I'm not."

How many times did she need to tell him that she didn't know him well enough? Every true crime story started with a charismatic stranger.

"You can't stay at the campsite. It was freezing last night. You're—"

"What's going on?" a new voice interrupted.

Jade whirled around and came face-to-face with a stunning woman in a white coat. A colorful dress in a funky pattern lurked beneath. Her red lipstick matched the frames over her eyes.

"Thanks for coming," Rett said as the newcomer unlocked the door.

Jade took a step back and read the sign on the building: Braeburn Family Medicine.

"Cindy, this is Jade."

Cindy stuck her hand out, and Jade shook it, then flinched. Pain flashed in her wrist.

"Oh. I see." Cindy peered at Jade's wrist. "What happened?"

Rett glanced at his watch. "I have to go. Take care of her, please. Send me the bill."

Jade spluttered, but Rett silenced her with a kiss. His mouth was warm and hard against hers. She froze and nearly shoved him away, but tingles exploded up and down her spine. Damn it, muse tingle. Always the worst timing.

And with that, he was gone.

Cindy's eyes were wide, and there was a small smile on her face. "Please tell me this was a sex injury."

Jade's mouth froze in an O of surprise.

"I'm just kidding," Cindy said. "Come with me."

She led her to an exam room and did a quick set of vitals.

"So, how did this happen?" she asked as she gingerly turned Jade's wrist over.

Jade explained the bare minimum.

Cindy looked a little suspicious but refrained from commenting. "Okay. I don't think anything's broken, but let's get a set of X-rays to be sure."

Relief struck like a blanket fresh out of the dryer. "You don't have to do that."

"As your doctor today, I kind of have to." She ushered Jade down a hallway to a room marked Radiology.

"So how do you and Rett know each other?" Cindy asked. "I almost fell out of my chair when he told me he was escorting someone to a wedding. I'm not exaggerating when I say it's been over a year since he's taken a day off work."

"We met at the winery. I was on a bachelorette trip and one of the attendees insulted his wine. Which was ridiculous."

"Right? It's the best," Cindy said. "Turn your hand this way."

She manipulated Jade's hand on the table, then lowered

a machine over it. She left the room while the X-ray was taken and came back a minute later.

"Not broken. But I bet it hurts."

Jade nodded.

"Ibuprofen or Tylenol as needed and ice for fifteen to twenty minutes at a time," Cindy instructed. "With rest, it should look better in the next two days. If it doesn't, stop back in."

"Thank you. I have my insurance card in here somewhere—oh, wait. My purse is back at the café. Rett didn't give me a lot of time to prepare."

Cindy waved a hand. "You don't need it. This one's on the house. I rarely get to use the X-ray machine, so it was a good refresher for me."

Jade squirmed. Was this town's entire economy just run on kindness? It felt a tad irresponsible, even to her.

"But anyway, I'm not surprised about Rett. When he has something in mind, it has to be taken care of immediately."

"How do you know him?"

"I've known him since middle school," Cindy said with a smile. "We used to date, but we very quickly realized we're better off as friends."

"Oh." Of course he would have been interested in Cindy. She was smart, kind, and gorgeous. The two of them probably would have made children so beautiful it would have hurt to look at them.

Cindy got up, and Jade followed her back to the lobby.

"So, are you staying in town?"

"For a little while. I'm doing a mural for the café."

Cindy's gaze drifted to her wrist. "I hope you didn't promise delivery in the next two days."

"No. Just before Rett's anniversary party."

"Good. You'll be fine. Come see me again if you're not."

"Thank you so much again. Are you sure I can't pay you?"

"I'm sure." Cindy's eyes lit up. "Hey, the boys usually play poker the second Wednesday of the month. It's like the one social thing Rett still commits to. Do you want to come over for a girls' night in? We usually do dinner and cocktails and engage in some career or book chat. Maybe some idle town gossip."

Jade paused. If she went, she would be perpetuating the fake relationship narrative and blatantly lying to Cindy, who seemed by all accounts to be a lovely, warm, genuine person. It hadn't seemed so bad to lie to Rett's family for just one day. But these were his close friends. She resolved to talk to him about it before the evening—surely if they were best friends, they would be able to let them in on the secret.

"I'd love to come. Thank you so much for inviting me."

"Here, put your number in. I'll text you the address." Cindy handed over her phone.

Jade entered her number and handed it back. Even though this whole situation was temporary, the prospect of new female friends warmed her soul.

Cindy tucked her phone away. "Awesome. I'm so excited. With you, there's just four of us. Do you have any dietary restrictions? It's my turn to cook."

Jade shook her head. "How do you feel about dogs? I have a golden retriever who's kind of my ride-or-die slash emotional support fur baby."

"Um, I love dogs. Bring her. We have a big, dopey pit bull named Branson and a fenced-in backyard." She glanced at her watch. "Crap, I have to get some charting done before my eight o'clock. We'll see you on Wednesday."

"Can't wait." Jade waved as she left. Had she just made a new friend?

CHAPTER NINETEEN

RETT

RETT SLAMMED AN EASEL INTO THE GROUND AND RIPPED OPEN the tape on a package. Penny pounced on it.

His phone beeped, and he checked the message.

> Cindy: I can't tell you that. HIPAA, dummy.
> Ask her yourself.

The *audacity*. What kind of person was so afraid to accept help that she stole camping equipment, walked miles in the rain, and fell out of a damn tree while hiding a bag that no one would have taken in the first place?

His heart had plummeted when he saw the state of her. Scratches, bruises, hollow eyes presumably from staying up all night. He had meant to wish her luck on her first day, maybe show her off a little to the town. Instead, he had been forced to introduce her to Cindy before he was ready.

He was going to have words with Jade when he picked her up later.

A cart laden with painting supplies bumped over the grass. He arranged them around the easel with more force than was necessary. *Crack.* A plastic rinse cup lay in two pieces.

He took a step back and inhaled deeply. There was no use in being mad at her. She hadn't had anyone to rely on in years. Why would she want to live in a stranger's house?

But they weren't really strangers. What about him was so untrustworthy?

An image of that smug motherfucker Nate looking at Jade on the porch appeared in his mind. Cheated on her before the grass was even growing on her parents graves. No wonder she had trouble trusting people.

These one night stands weren't serving her anymore. Loneliness radiated from her. She was clearly a monogamy girl, a believer in true love. She wouldn't truly be her authentic self until she opened her mind to the possibility of partnership again. Friends with benefits wasn't going to cut it. She needed the full girlfriend experience to remind her. He added it to his running mental list before turning back to the task at hand.

The easel was set up on the winery's most beautiful vista —the spot where he had planned to propose to Alexa, in fact. If the view could unblock Jade, maybe she wouldn't have to consider a new career. But he was prepared for the alternative. Especially if she had just done permanent damage to her painting hand.

And that didn't even cover the host of other issues— budget revamp, networking, and of course, getting a driver's license.

The stone wall of the winery caught his eye. How was he supposed to focus on business when mentoring Jade was a whole business itself?

———

All the anger fell out of his sails when he opened the café door. Jade, still scratched to hell and looking even more frazzled than that morning, was seated at a table in the corner. She stared at a blank sketch pad in front of her, eyebrows drawn together.

He put a gentle hand on her shoulder, and she jumped.

"Is it two o'clock already?" she asked.

He nodded. "How's the wrist?"

"Not broken. You didn't have to come get me."

"With your luck, you probably would have gotten run over on your way to the winery."

She cracked a small smile. "You're not wrong."

He picked up her sunflowers and offered his hand. She took it and stood.

"I would like to revisit our discussion on your living arrangements," he said.

Nailed it. He hadn't shouted even once.

"There's no need. Margie kind of bullied me into staying at her guest house."

He instantly deflated. "Oh. Good."

He had almost been looking forward to convincing her to stay with him. But it was better this way. It was only two weeks. Having her under his roof could have made things complicated.

"Was Penny okay today?"

She had peed on the welcome mat and knocked over a display of wine-themed oven mitts in the gift shop, but it could have been worse.

"Of course. But I'm sure she's eager to see you. Shall we?"

He offered his arm, and she took it.

"See you later, sweetheart. I'll leave the keys under the mat," Margie called as they left.

"Are you okay?" Rett asked when they reached the sidewalk.

"I'm fine," she said, but her expression told a different tale.

He pulled her around in front of him. He brushed a thumb over the cut on her cheek.

"Tell me what's going on."

She turned to look at the café. "What if I can't do it?"

"Do what? The mural?"

She nodded. "Margie wants me to 'encapsulate a feeling' about the town. How am I supposed to do that?"

He held on to her arms. Her skin was so soft. And what was that smell? Vanilla?

She shivered under his grip.

"You can do this. But I don't think you'll find what you're looking for by staring at a blank sketchpad for six hours. You need to go outside and explore. Sit in the gazebo. Attend a festival. Do some *Gilmore Girls* shit."

She laughed, and the sound was like music. The light was back in her eyes. A bit of color had rushed into her cheeks.

Before he could stop himself, he dipped his mouth to hers. She froze for a second, then pressed herself close to him. Her arms snaked around him, and her heat washed over him. When he opened his mouth, she mirrored the movement. She tasted even better than she looked. His finger slipped beneath the hem of her T-shirt.

There weren't words to describe the feel of her wrapped around him. It was like the first sunrise after weeks of overcast skies. The smell of a fresh harvest.

Crash. They sprang apart and Rett put himself between her and the sudden sound.

A mail carrier was sprawled on the asphalt, bike with a bent-rimmed tire lying next to him. Damn it, Tom.

Jade gasped and sprinted across the street to him without bothering to look both ways.

"Oh my god. Are you okay?" She dropped onto her knees beside Tom.

He sat up and looked at them. "Well fuck me dead," he said, his Australian accent even stronger than normal. "Never in my wildest daydreams did I think I'd come upon Everett Rhodes pashing in the square. I'm Tom." He extended a hand to Jade.

"Jade." She took his hand and shook it. "Are you sure you're okay?"

He shrugged. "Eh, she'll be apples. This why you didn't want to slap the bag last night?" He eyed Rett while pointing his chin at Jade.

Rett shook his head. "As a winery owner, drinking boxed wine would be equivalent to committing treason."

Tom scoffed. "Fine. We'll crack a couple coldies at poker, then. Cheers."

He hefted his bike onto the grass of the town square and set off with his mail pouch on foot.

"He's just going to leave his bike there?" Jade asked.

"Yeah. That's Cindy's husband, by the way."

She shook her head thoughtfully as if it had just answered a question. "If we were in the city, that bike would already be in a different borough."

"This isn't the city. Which is why you don't need to hide your bag in a tree. That's our first stop, by the way."

The flush on her cheeks had grown stronger. "Okay. Let's go."

"IN HERE."

Two hours later, bag rescued from the tree, he led Jade through a set of doors at the back of the tasting room. Nerves rippled in his stomach. Apart from his contractor and employees, no one had seen this room yet. It was another attempt at bringing them back out of obscurity.

They emerged into a room that felt like it came straight from the 1920s. A crystal chandelier dangled overhead, casting a soft glow on the dramatic, dimpled leather sofa that sat before the front windows. A long oak bar stood to their right, barstools nestled beneath.

Leather armchairs flanked a small table in the corner, built-in bookshelves laden with antique-looking bottles lining the window behind them. A long, peacock-blue velvet booth stretched nearly the full length of the longest wall, paired with small cocktail tables and upholstered chairs.

She gripped Rett's arm. "Is this a speakeasy?"

He nodded. "It's a new addition. I designed it myself. I thought it might draw more people in during the winter. It's something else I'm hoping to reveal during the anniversary party."

"I love it here." Jade sank onto the brown leather sofa. Penny jumped up next to her. "This is heaven."

Warmth sprouted inside him. With any luck, the renovation of an old storage room wouldn't have been a complete waste of time.

"Let me grab the tasting supplies. I'll be right back."

When he returned with an art déco-themed bar cart minutes later, Jade was staring into the crackling fire.

"Where would you like me?" she asked.

His gaze moved to the bear-skin rug on the floor. An image of Jade completely naked and staring into his eyes while the fire crackled sprang into his mind.

"Where would you be most comfortable?" He took a step closer to her. His eyes dipped down to the red sundress she had put on after they'd retrieved her bag. It would take nothing for him to trail his hand up her thigh, find out what she was wearing underneath.

A laugh rang out in the tasting room, and he blinked. There were a dozen customers on the other side of the wall. This was supposed to be business—step one in empowering Jade. That was what was important. If her muse came back, she could be leading a paint and sip by the weekend.

As if she could read his mind, Jade slunk off to the least sexy corner of the room. She sat in an armchair and looked at him expectantly.

"I'm ready. Gimme the spiel."

He cracked a smile and launched into a story of how the vines of this particular grape came to be grown in the fertile soils of Keuka Lake.

She nodded along and raised the glass to her nose. The wine sloshed in the glass as she swirled it around.

Rett watched as she raised it to her lips. She moaned, and a warm, invigorating tension flooded his body.

"I'm not going to be able to concentrate if you keep responding like that," he said before he could think better of it.

Her eyes snapped open. "Sorry. I'll keep it PG."

He shoved the plate towards her, eyes glued to her. "Try it with the smoked sausage."

She obliged.

"This reserve Blaufränkisch was aged for about twenty-four months in old French oak."

"Forgive my ignorance," she said after swallowing. "But I thought it was hard to grow red grapes in this climate."

"It's doable. If you know what you're doing." He took a sip of wine and chased it with a slice of sausage.

"Then you must really know what you're doing," she said after another sip.

"You have no idea."

She shifted in her armchair, causing a small farting noise.

"That was the chair," she clarified.

"Sure." He winked.

The dog ambled up and laid her snoot on Jade's leg, then whined.

Jade sighed. "Penny would like some cheese."

"Oh." Rett stood up. "I almost forgot. The best part of the VIP tasting is that there's a separate one for dogs."

"What does that mean?"

"It means," he said, striding over to the cart, "that Penny gets to sample the finest local organic dog treats while we have wine."

"That's a really nice idea."

He tapped a knuckle on his temple. "Told you I know what I'm doing."

"Well, I admire your confidence. With any luck, maybe some will rub off on me."

He certainly wanted to rub something on her.

The rest of the tasting passed uneventfully. Rett guided her through a series of reds and whites, cheeses and chocolates.

"That was incredible. Oops. I appear to be a bit tipsy," she said as she stood and staggered into the table.

Shit. He had pulled out their best lineup in the hopes that one of them would be the key to unlocking her for good. Maybe he had overdone it. But they wouldn't know until they tried.

"Maybe it's time for a walk. I can give you that tour we talked about."

"Let's go." She found the nearest door handle and pulled.

"That's an emergency exit," he said with a chuckle.

"You're an emergency exit," she muttered as she crossed to the other side of the room.

CHAPTER TWENTY

JADE

"So what did you think of the tasting?" Rett said from Jade's right, Penny's leash wrapped around his wrist. Her nails tip-tapped down the walkway toward the vineyard.

"It was amazing."

She meant it. Every wine was perfect in its own way. Bold, fruit-forward, aromatic. The cheese was a step up from backpack cheese. It was so good that even the pain in her wrist had dulled.

"You don't think it was missing anything?"

"Aside from the sparkling wine that I'm not allowed to taste?" she said.

"Fair enough. Soon. How are you feeling?" He came to stand next to her. Penny planted next to them.

"Perfectly fine."

"Tingly?" he probed.

She looked down at her hands. "To be honest, most of my body is feeling tingly, but I'm having trouble differentiating between booze tingles and potential muse action."

"Come with me." He led her past the building and over a

charming stamped-concrete patio where chairs were stacked on top of tables.

"Aren't you going to tell me about these vines?" she asked, poking the grape nearest her. "Not much of a tour so far."

"Sure. These were some of the first vines my grandparents planted when they moved here," he said over his shoulder. "They're the fourth oldest pinot vines in the country."

Penny ran ahead, frantically sniffing the rows. She would have green feet for a week.

"Wow," Jade said. She paused to turn around and take in the acres of lush greenery and vines. It was stunning.

"Where did you say we were going?" She stumbled into a post.

"Just a little bit further."

"Fair enough." It must have been a special spot.

She snuck a look at him as they climbed a hill. He was in yet another three-piece suit. Would she ever find out what was underneath them? At what point was the whole friends-with-benefits part kicking in, anyway?

The heat was amping up outside. Humidity settled heavily in her lungs.

"Here." Rett led her into a clearing on the top of the ridge.

She gasped. An easel and stool were set up alongside two cocktail tables full of art supplies.

"I don't know if any of this will speak to you, but I thought maybe it was worth a shot after you painted that sunrise."

Her lip quivered.

"This is the most picturesque spot on the vineyard," he explained. "I hope it helps."

Jade rushed in and threw her arms around him. She had

been hoping for an elaborate, sexy picnic away from prying eyes. But this was somehow even better.

"Thank you," she said, voice muffled by his suit.

"I know you can do it. I'm sorry if the wine is interfering."

She pulled back and shook her head. "I used to paint drunk once in a while. It's what inspired *U Up?* and *Pizza Town, Two A.M.* back before I met Nate. Maybe it'll help me get out of my own head."

He squeezed her arm. "I'll take Penny for a walk. We'll meet you back down at the winery when you're ready. No rush. I mean it. I don't care if you stay out here till midnight."

In seconds, Rett and Penny were headed back down the slope toward the vineyard. Jade turned to the blank canvas clipped to the easel. She approached it cautiously, as if it might scream at her.

Universal primed, medium grain linen on a stretched canvas. Several more were stacked on one of the tables.

Tupperware containers overflowed with products. Oil pastels, six different sets of brushes, acrylic paints, pencils, wax, feathers, glitter, twigs, dried vines, newspaper, powders, gouache, even a stray bottle of wine. Virtually everything she could have wanted in her dream studio was spread in front of her. How much had he spent on all of this? And what would he expect in repayment?

The least she could do was commit to the paint and sip night.

She lifted her face to the sun and basked in its warmth like a drunk lizard. The cloying humidity wasn't ideal for paint drying conditions, but maybe that was okay for today. This was just practice.

She dabbed a layer of glue on the canvas and quickly set

to work. Sticks broken to varying lengths were pressed into the canvas for texture. As it dried, she lifted the wine bottle and dug through one of the totes. The vineyard and the lake were a stunning mix of browns, blues, and greens, layer after layer of color.

She turned the bottle on its side and squirted small puddles of acrylic paint onto it. When the glue was dry, she pressed the bottle onto the page and carefully rolled it back and forth, leaving a gap for the dirt road that split the property. The colors bled together, creating a serene scene.

It didn't look like much—a blue-green mess on a canvas. But there was a whisper of something there. She set it aside to dry and pulled out another canvas, then closed her eyes and took a moment to still her mind.

Penny's adorable form floated in, running full-tilt between two vineyard rows. Jade's eyes snapped open, and she picked up the nearest pencil. After roughly sketching Penny in, she prepared a palette in a rainbow of colors. She set to work bringing it to life with yellows and greens. Shades of brown for her haunches. Robin's egg blue for the sky. A shiny black nose and a perfectly pink tongue.

It was the first time she had ever tried to capture Penny in any medium beyond the probable two thousand-plus pictures in her camera roll.

Like the experimental landscape, it was far from perfect. It didn't sing to her in the way that many of her pre-breakup paintings did. But there was something purposeful and meaningful here. Penny had been her reason to get out of bed every day for the last two years. Her furry and faithful companion, always there to drop a slobbery tennis ball in her lap when it felt like things were getting to be too much.

Setting Penny to the side, she came back to the first painting. She added in powdery white clouds and bursts of purple, and just the corner of the stone-covered tasting room. Before she could stop herself, the shape of a man leading a vaguely yellow dog-like creature up the dirt path added itself in. It was abstract, unclear. But there was feeling in it.

Gradually, the fog of alcohol lifted. And still she painted. She pulled out the next blank canvas and just threw paint and feathers at it. It was hot pink and lime green and tempestuously loud, like her apartment back home.

"Hey," a familiar voice said. "Just me. I thought you might be getting hungry."

Rett rounded the corner of a row with a picnic basket in hand.

Jade jumped in front of her canvas and threw her arms out like a teenage boy blocking a laptop screen.

"Oh, god," he said.

"I know. I'm sorry. I was in the zone. I'll clean it up."

"No, I don't care about the stuff on the ground. You just kind of look like you got shot by a unicorn."

She glanced down at herself. Apparently she had been unknowingly wiping her hands on her dress.

"Shit." She giggled and slapped a hand to her mouth to stifle it. "I can't go back in there looking like this."

"Well, there's always my house. Walking distance."

She debated for a moment before tossing a brush into the water cup.

"Race you." With that, she took off downhill, beelining for the crest of the roof that was barely visible between the dense trees.

"Wait!"

She smiled and glanced over her shoulder.

Rett was full-on smiling, dragged through the vineyard

by Penny's exuberant tugging. The picnic basket hung from his other hand.

With a quick glance at the highway, she dashed across and kept going. It felt so good to run. Her hair streamed behind her in the wind. She stepped onto Rett's driveway and sped up, bolting down the lane until she rounded the house.

The shadows had grown long. She had been painting longer than she realized.

Dashing through the side yard, she didn't stop until she hit the dock. The sundress skated down her goosebump-covered skin and fell to the worn boards.

By the time Rett rounded the corner of the house, she stood in the late afternoon sunshine in her bra and panties. With a calculated glance at Rett, she slowly shed those too, then ran down the short dock, leaping into the water before she could change her mind.

The chill of the water hit her like a fist. She broke through the surface, sputtering and gasping.

"Holy shit, it's so cold." In seconds, her nipples had pebbled with the strength of diamonds.

"I could have told you that," Rett said with a mischievous grin. He set the picnic basket on the dock. His fingers went straight to the buttons on his waistcoat.

She was ready to climb out and find a warm shower, but if stiff-nippling it for a few more minutes meant that would shortly be joined by a naked Rett, she would tread water until Halloween.

"I'm surprised you're joining me." She hopped in place for warmth, just enough for the swell of her breasts to tease the water line.

Rett tossed his suit jacket and waistcoat to the dock.

"I'm trying to take your advice to heart," he said as his pants puddled to the ground. "Have more fun."

"Skinny-dipping on a Monday definitely qualifies." She kicked off the rocky bottom and floated onto her back. Dappled sunlight shone through the trees on the shoreline. The mixture of the frigid water and the warm, humid air was strangely invigorating.

Boat motors whirred somewhere in the distance.

Something crashed into the water next to her. She straightened up and whirled around, but it was just Penny. A tennis ball was clamped in her mouth.

Okay, if the dog was invited, sexy things definitely weren't on his mind. It was just as well. She wrestled the ball from Penny's mouth and threw it back to Rett. Penny doggie paddled back to the dock and climbed up. With a mighty shake, she relinquished what had to be a half ton of water.

Jade shrieked and ducked underwater as Penny and Rett cannon-balled in.

"She's definitely a lake dog," he said as he wrestled the ball from her mouth. The water brushed the bottom of his ribcage. Had he taken his boxers off before climbing in?

Jade glanced surreptitiously at the pile of clothes on the dock, but it was hard to tell.

"That does explain why she always tried to leap into the reservoir in Central Park during our runs."

Penny ambled her way back onto the dock, clearly having the time of her life. It was going to take forever to get her dried off.

"You have some paint on your neck." He pointed to her left side.

"Oh, here?" She rubbed at the spot indicated.

"Lower. Here, let me help." He swam toward her with long, confident strokes.

He slipped one hand behind her neck and cradled her head while he rubbed with the other. It was impossibly sensual. Her toes curled on the lake floor, probably digging up decades of silt. Could he feel how fast her pulse was hammering?

"Your heart's beating a little fast," he said softly.

Damn it.

"Probably something to do with being in constant fight-or-flight mode from this arctic water," she mumbled over numb lips.

"Maybe I can help." He closed the gap between them. The steel of his abs pressed against her.

Finally.

She shivered, and his arms drew around her like a protective shroud. Where did he find time to work out between running a winery and being a professional financial stick-in-the-mud? His biceps were the size of cantaloupes.

Since the two of them were already pressed against each other, she drew her arms around his neck. "I'm just going to say this once. Your ex was an idiot."

A wry smile appeared, crow's feet crinkling at the corners of his green eyes.

"What makes you say that?"

"I've only known you for a handful of days. And in that time you've repeatedly shown up for me. You saved me from abject humiliation at the wedding. You drove me into the city, introduced me to someone who has the power to change my future. Supported my weird artistic journey of self-reclamation. I'm paying you back for those supplies, by the way."

"No, you're not. They were a gift."

"Yeah, to your fake girlfriend. They definitely exceed the

threshold for appropriate gifting."

His grip on her tightened. "I'm just trying to set you up for success. Speaking of which, we really should set up a time to look at your budget."

She shot him a dirty look. "You really want to talk budgets right now?"

His gaze drifted down. "Not particularly."

His hands slid lower, gripping her thighs and lifting her from the rocky floor. He wrapped her legs around his waist and glided his hands over the curve of her ass, settling on her lower back.

"Would I be out of line if I suggested adding a skinny-dipping practice kiss to your calendar?" she asked. "We want to be sure we're comfortable with each other if we end up having to perform in public."

"Let me pencil it in."

His mouth claimed hers. Her back arched and she pressed herself even tighter against him.

She trembled under the brush of his fingers over her spine. His hands slipped between them, coming up to cup her breasts. He squeezed, and it stole the breath from her.

Holding on to his neck with one hand, she reached beneath her with the other and groped blindly under the water. His erection was rigid under her touch.

Rett gasped against her lips. She pumped and stroked, ran his head experimentally over her folds.

His hand slipped between her legs and was a second from exploring deeper when a speed boat roared into view.

"Rett!" someone called.

Jade gasped and relinquished her death grip on his waist. She fell into the water and dipped below the surface. When she surfaced, she ducked behind him.

"Hey, Shirley," he called sheepishly. "What brings you over on this fine day?"

"Well, I was just about to drop a bag of apples on your dock and call it a day. I had no idea I would be...interrupting. You're usually still at work."

He chuckled. "Yeah, well. This one thinks I work too much." He reached back and dragged Jade out from behind him. "Right, honey?"

"Hi," Jade said, one hand strapped over her chest like a fleshy bra.

Shirley was a squat older woman, mid-60s, with kind brown eyes and a face filled with laugh lines. She was beautiful.

"You've got something green in your ear, dear," Shirley said, moving her sun hat to gesture to the affected part.

"Must be paint," Rett said affectionately. "Jade's an amazing artist. She's doing a mural for Margie's Café, you know."

Shirley whistled through her teeth. "I'll have to come take a gander. You kids take care," she said with a wave.

"Just checking," Jade said after Shirley handed over a bag of apples and roared off in her boat. "Is this town populated entirely by some kind of cockblocking purity cult?"

"To be fair, we were naked in a public waterway."

She sighed heavily. She was so close to finding out what it would be like to get him in bed. A lake bed maybe, but a bed nonetheless.

A phone buzzed from the pile of clothes on the dock, and Rett's expression instantly changed. His eyebrows contracted, and he took a step toward the shore.

"I have to get back to work," he said. "Let me grab you a towel."

A protest was on her tongue, but she swallowed it. Clearly he wasn't feeling it like she was. It figured.

CHAPTER TWENTY-ONE

JADE

Gravel crunched under Jade's feet. A charming cottage came into view, stone-fronted with ivy climbing the side. A few yards away, a catamaran bobbed in the lake.

The tingling was back again, just a little bit. She had never imagined living anywhere other than the concrete jungle of New York. But there was something so quaint and perfect about this tiny lakeside cottage. And it was all hers for two weeks. It was a sizable step up from a dilapidated tent in the middle of a field.

Penny pulled the leash from Jade's hand and began sniffing—and peeing on—her new surroundings. Rett had dropped her off before heading back to the winery.

Their interaction earlier had left her feeling all weird and prickly inside. There had been fire in her veins when he pressed against her in the lake. A kind of lust she had never experienced during one of her sweaty club hookups. She craved the feel of him against her, inside her. But despite all his talk about friends with benefits, he hadn't really moved the needle. Maybe he was having second thoughts?

"Yoo-hoo, Jade!" A screen door slammed, and Margie

came bustling out of the main house fifty yards away. Something furry and striped was draped over her shoulders.

"Are you sure about this?" Jade asked as Margie approached. She gestured at the cottage.

"Yes," Margie said firmly. "It's been awhile since I had a guest. I think I'll enjoy having someone else nearby."

"I can't thank you enough."

"I don't want to hear another word about it," Margie said. "Let me give you a quick tour and I'll get out of your hair."

Penny darted over to greet Margie and then froze. She growled softly, staring at the furry stripes on Margie's shoulder. Jade picked up her leash. The last thing she needed was for her dog to attack Margie's cat. Or fur stole. Whatever it was.

Margie opened the front door of the guest house, and Jade followed her inside. It was charmingly rustic. Rough-hewn boards came together to make the pointed ceiling of the foyer. A pottery wheel stood by the window. Floorboards creaked underfoot as they went deeper. A small living room with a TV and cozy stone fireplace stood to their right, while a kitchen with shabby chic green cabinets and white appliances gleamed to their left.

"It's beautiful." Jade hefted her bag into the foyer.

"Thank you. I hope you'll be comfortable here." Margie started to leave, then stopped. "Also, there's a bike on the porch. I want you to use it. It's not safe to walk on these roads."

The furry mass on her shoulder made a chittering sound, and Jade jumped.

"Oh, this is Steven. He's an indoor-outdoor raccoon, so don't be alarmed if you see him around at night."

"And he's...domesticated?" Jade regarded him warily. She had seen more than one rabid raccoon in Queens.

"One hundred percent," Margie said with a smile. "The bedroom's through there, bathroom over there." She indicated two separate doors. "If you think of anything you need, just give me a holler."

With a squeeze of Jade's hand, Margie left. It couldn't have been more different from her apartment in the city. But strangely enough, it felt like home. It was easy to imagine waking up here every morning, greeting the morning sun on the lake, and darting out the door for a run.

Jade shook a couple ibuprofen out of a bottle in her bag and headed to the kitchen in search of ice. While her wrist looked better than it had this morning, the impromptu painting session in the vineyard had brought a new wave of pain.

She caught a glimpse of herself in a mirror and gasped. Following her dip in the lake, she was indistinguishable from a drowned rat. Scratched cheeks, pale as a beluga whale. No wonder Rett had left. She needed a shower before tackling anything else.

An hour later, she curled up in the armchair next to the gas fireplace she had finally figured out how to operate. A notepad was open on her lap, full of research on hosting a paint and sip night. Since Rett was so pathological about working, it might be the only way she got to spend some time with him.

She sent him a link to an article.

> Jade: Thursday? We'll need to meet to chat about what supplies we need.

Minutes passed, but there was no response. Something about that shattered case of sparkling wine seemed to have broken him. It was just as well. The more time he spent at work, the less likely she was to fall in love with him. Or be murdered by him. It was too early to tell.

She set her notepad down and Googled the vineyard. Their Yelp page came up. Her heart jumped into her throat. How the hell did they only have three-and-a-half stars? The wine was incredible, the staff was friendly and professional.

She scrolled through until she found the one-star reviews. All of them but two had been left on the same day. Either Rett had tremendously dropped the ball that day or someone had a vendetta against him.

"Worst wine I've ever had in my life." Jade shook her head. Whoever Lexi D was, she better hope Jade never ran into her.

She strolled to the window and looked across the lake. He was over there somewhere, probably spiraling about something. He really needed to have more fun.

She turned away and shook her head. She needed to worry less about the hot-and-cold vintner and more about her future. While she had produced something today, it wasn't anything sellable. There was a long way to go.

Shit, what had happened to those paintings anyway? Hopefully Rett had put them somewhere safe. She wasn't about to text him to find out.

She turned her attention to studying for her driver's license exam and was immersed in dull facts about school buses when a message from Rett came through.

Rett: Let's have dinner tomorrow. Bring your current budget and a full financial accounting. Savings, checking, retirement, investments, any passive income.

Jade: Do you really think I'd be here if I had a passive income?

Great. More homework.

She Googled budgeting for beginners. Thirty minutes later, a distressing financial reckoning was laid out in front of her.

Even lowering her biggest monthly expense—rent—wasn't going to be simple. Finding a new apartment meant first and last month's rent plus security deposit, and possibly roommates. Finding a place that accepted large dogs was going to be a nightmare. Her fortress of solitude would be gone.

Even moving into the more affordable boroughs wasn't necessarily the answer. Rent appeared to be at an all-time high.

But if she moved away from the city, public transportation became sparser. And she didn't have a driver's license. Or a car. Her only real choices were to suck it up and find a place in Brooklyn with three roommates, or look around the country for a walkable/bike-friendly neighborhood with everything she needed.

On a whim, she went to a real estate website and searched for apartments in Hammondsport. Her mouth dropped open. She could save two fricken thousand dollars a month and give Penny her own bedroom if she decided to move here. But moving here would make no sense. If she couldn't paint anymore, she would have no income. And what was the job market like in a tiny-ass town like Hammondsport? What would she do, work three part-time jobs to make ends meet?

There was no future here, and having constant exposure to Rett wasn't going to help anything. Maybe there were similar neighborhoods on neighboring lakes? Seneca, maybe?

"Fuck." She slammed her laptop shut and pushed it away from her.

There was no easy answer. It was going to take a lot of quick soul-searching. Her future security rested on her ability to reclaim her artistic identity. Maybe spending some time alone in town tomorrow after her shift at the café would help.

CHAPTER TWENTY-TWO

RETT

RETT ROLLED HIS SHOULDERS BACK WHEN HE PULLED INTO Margie's driveway. It had been a long day at the winery. Todd had called off with a bout of man-flu, and Rett had taken over his tastings. He had run straight to the bank with a deposit and barely had time to go home and laminate some dough for tomorrow morning's sticky buns.

The front door of the cottage opened, and Jade smiled at him. She wore an orange top and high-waisted jeans. It looked incredible on her but would have looked even better piled on the floor.

He needed to stick to the plan, but she was making it impossible.

He handed over a bouquet of goldenrod and lavender asters.

"For you."

Penny immediately planted her paws on his torso and panted happily in his face.

"They're beautiful," Jade said. "You know there's no one here to prove anything to, right? Margie went to her bridge club."

"I don't need a reason to give a beautiful woman flowers," he said with one eyebrow cocked.

She smiled. "Come in while I get these in some water."

A mess of loose papers on the kitchen table caught his attention.

"You've been busy," he said.

"For your information, I was doing my homework."

Jade put the flowers in one of the many vases scattered around the guest cottage and topped it off with water. Then she made a face and fished out a handful of papers from the pile on the table.

"I hope wherever we're going is cheap. Some of us are on a fixed income."

"I'm paying," he said firmly. "I have a gift card."

She scoffed. "Fine." Her eyes screwed up, and she took a step closer. "What's on your ear?"

His hands flew defensively to his head. It wouldn't be the first time cork shavings had hitched a ride. He drew his hands away and found some flour. He had gotten a bit aggressive in the kitchen before leaving.

"Just some dust," he said.

She gave him an odd look, then turned to Penny. "Bye, sweetheart," she said with a kiss on her furry nose.

Rett added a couple enthusiastic pats, and then they climbed in his truck. An alternative radio station played quietly in the background as they descended the hill into town. His hand found hers in the glow of the dash lights. Her hand was small and warm.

"How's the wrist?" he asked.

"Better today," she said. "Not that I needed it since I painted exactly nothing today. I did get everything sanded and primed, though. Where are we going, anyway?"

"The Tavern. Our reservations aren't for another twenty

minutes. I thought we could walk around and see if that helps your mural decision."

"Thank you. That sounds really nice."

Once he had parked downtown, they prowled the streets. Most of the shops and bakeries had closed down for the day, but maybe some personal history would help.

"Tom projectile vomited into that bush after playing slap the bag the first time I met him." He pointed to a bush on the edge of the square.

"What exactly *is* slap the bag?" she asked.

"No one really knows. It's sort of a drinking game. That's how we met. I walked into Cindy's parents' house for her graduation party, and Tom ran up to me in an Australian flag-themed shirt while holding a sack of red liquid."

"So you slapped his bag and you've been best friends ever since?"

"Basically."

"What a meet-cute." She bumped Rett with her hip.

He had forgotten how nice it was to have a little companionship. A beautiful woman on his arm. Clever conversation. Someone to introduce to the town he loved so much.

He pointed out more special spots, including the site of his senior prank where several classmates had ridden their lawn mowers to school.

"Come on," he said. "Time for dinner."

They walked into the Tavern, and the hostess greeted Rett by name. In no time, they were seated at their table with a tantalizing menu spread in front of them.

"Any suggestions?" Jade asked.

"The surf and turf is amazing, but I would go to war for the French onion soup."

She cast an eye down the menu and shifted in her seat.

"You look distressed."

She glanced up. "I'm aware that I'm not an expert on this subject, but it seems awfully financially irresponsible to spend a week's worth of grocery money on one meal."

He leaned forward. "Occasional splurges are allowed. And remember, it's on me. Don't make me order for you."

She picked the menu back up. "Fine. If we're going this hard on a Tuesday, what does that mean for our next date?"

"Oh, we're going to Applebee's."

"Good. I love mozzarella sticks."

As soon as they'd ordered, she dug around in her purse.

"So," she said, removing a half dozen sheets of paper, "down to business."

From the corner of his eye, Rett spotted Glenda, a notorious town gossip and old friend of his parents.

"Hang on." He picked up Jade's hand and pressed a kiss to it. Frankly he would have rather kissed her face, but probably would have knocked the table over.

Jade's cheeks grew pink. "What was that for?"

"The woman at your three o'clock is on the guest list for the party. She's also old friends with my parents."

"Got it. Let me deploy some footsie." Her wedge found his wingtip.

"Perfect," he said. "Now let's take a look." He flipped through the papers in front of him. It was by far the messiest financial accounting he had ever seen. "You know, I was kind of hoping for a spreadsheet."

"I'm an artist, not an accountant."

It was probably better to keep his comments to himself. He perused the papers for a few minutes before shuffling them into a neat stack and folding his hands together.

It wasn't good. If anything, she had underexaggerated.

"So. You're twenty-six and have no retirement savings, no equity, no investments, and no predictable income."

Jade folded her arms. "This is starting to sound like a conversation that ends in a screaming match. Do I seriously not get any credit for paying off my student loans?"

He threw up his hands. "The fact that you don't have any other debt is great. But your bank account is running on fumes and rent in the city is astronomical. It's not good."

"I know. I'm researching rent prices in the outer boroughs."

"Good. When is your lease up?"

"End of December," she said hesitantly. "I gave the super my sob story and got him to give me a six-month lease."

He bit the inside of his cheek. Her lease was up in two months and she hadn't found a new place to live? She didn't need his criticism, but it was damned hard to keep his mouth shut.

"Change is scary. But the good part is I think you have transferable skills. I prepared a list of career suggestions." He pulled out the document he had typed up earlier. "Do you have any interest in graphic design?"

"It's not something I've ever gravitated towards, but I'd be willing to try."

"That would be a great solution, and it can even be temporary if your muse comes back for good and things go back to normal. What kind of computer do you have?"

"A ten-year-old Mac I got for high school graduation."

Rett shook his head. There was enough wiggle room in the budget for an upgrade. "We're getting you a new one. You won't be able to freelance with a ten-year-old computer on its last legs. Second," he said louder to cover the series of splutters she had just released, "I know you're busy with the mural right now. But if it helps your portfolio, I would love for you to design a label for my new line of sparkling wines. If I haven't destroyed my grandmother's legacy and shamed my entire family with a faulty product, anyway."

She narrowed her eyes. "Stop it. There is no way you made a crappy product. Did you try it today?"

"Well, no."

"We're opening a bottle on the next date night. No discussion."

He nodded. It was probably time to stop avoiding it.

"And you're not buying me a laptop. I have—"

"You have nothing. I am buying you a laptop. Consider it a contractor perk for working on the new label. And the paint and sip. Let's talk about that."

She straightened. "Great. I have some thoughts."

Ten minutes later, they had a supply list, theme, and a date. He had done it once before and it had been lucrative. It should be a boon for both of them.

"Anything else?" Jade asked. "I don't suppose you prepared some literature about selling a spare kidney on the black market?"

"You're going to have to make immediate cuts. No more CrossFit and you definitely need to cancel HBO."

She pouted.

"I did have one other question," he said. "You use a gallery to sell your paintings?"

"Yes."

"Why? I imagine they take a large chunk of your earnings?"

She leaned back in her chair. "They do, but it's a necessary evil. They get the art into the right hands."

"But theoretically if your muse came back, you could direct sell your own art? Online or to previous customers?"

"Sure, if I wanted to burn a bridge."

"Okay. Well, maybe we can revisit that idea if your muse

comes back. I'll help you with your resume later. Down the road once you get a job we can start talking about your investments and retirement savings."

"Thank you," she mumbled.

There was silence for a beat.

"You think I'm a project," she accused.

Rett frowned. What was she, a mind-reader? Project was too harsh, though. "No, I think you're a work in progress. As are all of us. Me especially."

She sat back and folded her hands in her lap. "You are. You live in your grandma's house, and you've made next to no effort to personalize it or make it feel like home to you. Why?"

This wasn't supposed to turn into an interrogation. He sloshed the ice in the bottom of his drink. "It doesn't really feel like mine. It doesn't feel like I've earned it."

"Ah. Impostor syndrome. It gets us all."

"What do you mean?"

"Maybe you were handed some opportunities that other people weren't. But your wine is incredible. You put in the work. You went to school, became a sommelier, learned everything you could about the craft. You're so worried about honoring her legacy and her memory that you've forgotten that she left the business to you for a reason. She trusts you."

"And if I mess it all up?"

They were already approaching a tipping point. If he didn't figure out a way to cut costs or bring in a fresh influx of cash by the end of the year, big changes were coming. And Grandmother Rhodes would never forgive him.

Jade reached across the table and took his hand. "You're not going to mess this up. In the incredibly unlikely event that your batch failed, you don't need to release it at the party. We'll hide it in the basement, pretend it never existed, and you can try again."

"It was her dream," he said.

"And what's *your* dream?"

Her question stopped him mid-sip. He had been so fixated on the success of the winery ever since his grandmother's death that he had never stopped to ask himself if it was enough.

The winery brought him purpose. Joy, even. There was nothing like the satisfaction of a perfectly fermented batch enjoyed on the porch at sunset. But was that all he wanted from this life? Fitting himself into someone else's dream?

"I'm...not really sure."

"Well," Jade said as a waitress set a plate in front of her. "Lucky for you, I'm the queen of dreaming. That's *your* homework for next week. I'll get my stupid driver's license, pick a new career, and find somewhere to move, but *you* have to figure out what you want out of this life."

"Deal."

CHAPTER TWENTY-THREE

JADE

WHEN THE CAFÉ LIGHTS TURNED OFF, JADE RAISED HER HEAD. She had been so engrossed in another sketch idea that she hadn't even noticed the passage of time. Her stomach grumbled. Margie had surprised her with a request to join her for a late lunch.

"Ready, sweetheart?" Margie had loosed her gray hair from its net, and she had a sunflower-shaped pocketbook slung over one shoulder.

"Sure." Jade flipped her book shut.

She cast a wary glance at the wall that was still completely blank. If Margie had opinions about the delay, she didn't share them.

"Why don't we leave the bike?" Margie asked. "You could ride with me. I'm sure Rett will pick it up later. Will you see him tonight?"

Jade nodded. He was dropping her off at Cindy's on his way to poker.

Margie was silent as they climbed into her Toyota Camry. A pair of dog tags hung from the rearview mirror.

The name Stoneroad was barely visible. A tiny sunflower joined them.

"Were these your husband's?" Jade gestured to the tags.

Margie nodded.

"How did you meet?"

"The army," Margie said. "I was a culinary specialist. David was a combat engineer with an insatiable sweet tooth. There's a picture in the glove box."

Jade opened the glove box, and a picture frame with two people slid out. "Oh, wow." Margie had been a certified babe, with wavy brown hair down to her waist. Her husband had the jawline of an A-list actor and a smirk that suggested he knew it.

Jade smiled. "He is so incredibly handsome. How did you know he was the one?"

Margie put her turn signal on and waited for a car to pass. There was a small smile on her face. "He felt like home. He was wildly charming, of course. But that wasn't it. When I was with him, I felt safe. During the dinner rush, no matter how frazzled I was, I could look up and find him in the crowd. And it was like everything else just melted away."

"That's beautiful," Jade said softly.

Margie turned to her with a question in her eyes, but she thankfully didn't ask it. She had probably just opened up a direct line to some Rett questions that didn't have answers.

Even their budget date the night before—which had ended with a kiss on the cheek as he jetted off to the winery—had been fraught with feeling. It felt more like a mentorship than a date (even a fake one). But there was no denying the chemistry between them. Being in limbo was driving her insane.

"How long have you lived here?" Jade asked.

"Oh, since we were discharged. This was David's hometown. I wanted to see the world, but he wanted to be close to family. I didn't have roots the same way he did. My parents rolled around the country in a Volkswagen van. They were musicians."

"How did you compromise on Hammondsport?"

Margie smiled wistfully. "He brought me home to meet his parents, and it was right in the middle of fall. It's virtually impossible not to fall in love with this place. Even if you don't drink wine."

"I can see that."

They rolled down the driveway and pulled into Margie's spot.

"How long has it been since he passed?" Jade asked quietly.

"Six years, four months, and nineteen days. I miss him terribly."

Jade reached over and squeezed Margie's hand. "I bet he's insanely proud of you. For your strength and resilience. And for your bangin' French toast."

Margie let out a full-body chuckle. "You know, I think he is. Come on, love. You get Penny and I'll get the picnic basket. I'll meet you on the deck."

Minutes later, Jade and Penny traipsed up the stairs to the deck that reached out over the water. A rope covered the entrance to a slide that twisted down and disappeared at the lip of the lake. Unlit tiki torches stood sentry at the railing, and a gas firepit stood in the middle of an assortment of mismatched chairs.

Margie emerged moments later with a pitcher of tea and a picnic basket.

"Nothing fancy today. Just some sandwiches and an assortment of cheeses."

"That sounds perfect. Thank you so much for having me

over."

"I've been meaning to do it since you got here. I'm so honored that you decided to stay here in our little town."

"I'm really happy to be here."

Jade turned to take in the hills and the fresh air. Even if her entire relationship was a lie, her love for this town was quickly becoming an uncontestable truth. Somehow, some-way, she would find a way to come back every fall. Even if she had to hitchhike from the city.

Margie set down a stack of plates, and Jade jumped up. She carefully set the table and poured glasses of tea.

"These look amazing. What is this, buffalo chicken?"

"I might have commandeered some leftovers from the café," Margie said with a conspiratorial wink. "There's a caprese one too."

Penny leapt up into the chair next to Jade.

"Penny, down," Jade commanded.

Margie laughed and clapped her hands. "It's okay. She can stay. Does she like cheese?"

The only thing Penny loved more than Jade was cheese. Her ears perked up like she had just been promised an all-expenses-paid vacation.

"Definitely," Jade said.

Margie whipped a piece across the table, and Penny snatched it from the air.

Jade swallowed an (incredible) bite of a caprese sand-wich. "Did you and David ever have children?"

"Oh, dozens," Margie said.

Jade's eyes bugged out.

"Foster children," Margie clarified with a smile. "We tried to have our own, but it just never worked out. The science wasn't as good in those days. But we were still able to have quite the legacy. Most of the kids still keep in touch. A couple of them bring their families over for Christmas."

"That's beautiful. I often wished I had siblings. My parents always said I was all they needed, but I think they couldn't afford more."

"Do you want children someday?" Margie asked. "I know Rett does."

Jade choked on a crumb, and Margie hammered her on the back.

If he wanted kids, why was he shying away from romantic entanglement so hard?

"Uh, we haven't had that discussion. I don't think I'll have an answer to that question until I know *my* future, let alone our future. Raising a baby in a studio apartment wouldn't be ideal."

"Hammondsport's a great place to raise a family," Margie said pointedly, staring at Jade over the rim of her glass.

"I'm sure. Here, let me take care of the dishes." Jade sprang to her feet and picked up their plates and glasses.

"Thank you, dear. The kitchen is inside to the right. Be sure to take a peek at the art over the fireplace in the living room," Margie said.

Jade slid open the glass door with her elbow and stepped inside. Margie's interior was lovely—eclectic furniture in vibrant hues. To her right was a dining room with lake views and mismatched chairs around a butcher-block table. To her left, a vaulted ceiling stood tall above a bright blue couch and yellow coffee table. Sunflower artwork bloomed on the right wall, while above the fireplace was something that made Jade catch her breath.

Better (Date) Than Never, one of Jade's favorite pieces, hung over the fireplace. Brushed metal clock gears hovered over a scene of a couple huddled around a dinner table.

Glimmering shards of broken glass made up the wine in their glasses. The woman's dress was spray-painted lace. Jade had painted it after her first date with Nate. He had been twenty minutes late and she had nearly left. In hindsight, she definitely should have.

With one last glance at her painting, Jade hustled into the kitchen and washed the dishes. When she emerged onto the deck, Margie turned to her with a smile.

"How about we take the boat out?"

Cheese for lunch *and* a free boat ride? It was Jade's lucky day.

After some finagling, she, Margie, and Penny had climbed aboard the pontoon boat. Penny sat happily on the padded seat, two tennis balls shoved in her mouth and sun shining on her honey-colored fur.

The boat rumbled beneath them as Margie guided it away from the dock. She had wrapped her hair into a long, colorful scarf and donned a pair of sunglasses. "What was it like to see your painting again?"

"I'm so glad it found a home with you. I painted that when I was in grad school."

"I saw it in a gallery in Midtown and I swear it just called to me," Margie said fondly. "It reminded me so much of dates with my David. It hung in the café for a while, but I eventually brought it home."

"I don't usually get to see them again after they leave the nest," Jade said. "Thank you for showing it to me."

"Never doubt yourself, love."

Margie cranked the throttle, and soon they were flying north toward the bluff. Wind whipped through Jade's hair while sun warmed her skin. She closed her eyes and soaked it in. The roar of the boat, the spray of lake water on her cheeks.

Eventually, Margie lowered the speed to a crawl. They were approaching a small inlet.

"A family of herons used to nest here. They're probably gone, but it's a blissful place to read a book. Or go fishing, if you're my husband."

Jade smiled fondly. "I never did much fishing in the city. Maybe with my dad a couple of times."

Margie glanced at her. "You plan to go back to the city after your time here?"

"I have to. But I've been so grateful for my time here."

Even though she'd only been here for a week, this town and its people had become almost as important to her as her own home.

"It woke up something that I thought was gone for good," she added. "Now I need to figure out if I can go back to being who I was."

"Do you want to be who you were?"

The word "yes" was on the tip of Jade's tongue, but she paused. Was that still true?

"I don't know if I can go back to being exactly who I was —the carefree girl with two parents, a steady boyfriend, and a bright future. She's gone."

"Not gone," Margie said. "Maybe just different. Different doesn't have to be a bad thing."

Silence settled around them as Margie navigated the inlet.

"You know, I'm something of an artist myself," Margie said.

"Yes, I've seen your pottery," Jade said. "It's stunning."

"Thank you. I didn't pull out my wheel for a long time after my David passed. A long time. It felt like all the color had just drained out of the world and there wasn't anything beautiful left."

A pang hit Jade's heart. She had felt the same way after that devastating day. Her entire family unit, gone in an instant while Christmas music played hauntingly in the background.

"So what made the difference for you? How did you recapture your magic?"

Margie gestured broadly. "This place. My friends. The community. They healed me from the inside out. They organized meal trains kept me company even when I didn't want it. Even though giving up living in an RV and traveling the country full-time felt like saying goodbye to a dream at the time, that compromise has made all the difference here in my golden years." She looked fondly at the green hills. "I don't regret it for a second."

"Is that what keeps you here now?"

Margie nodded. "It's home. And for the record, we still did our share of traveling, but there truly is nothing like home."

Jade stood at the railing and contemplated the tiny, peaceful inlet. Maybe there was some wiggle room in her definition of home.

CHAPTER TWENTY-FOUR

RETT

"Have you given any more thought to my financial plan?" Rett asked.

Penny had adopted her usual space, sleeping in the middle seat between them. They were on their way to Tom and Cindy's for girls/poker night. A vase of purple flowers—a hostess gift, Jade had said—sat in the cupholder.

"Yes," she muttered. "I've already cancelled all of my extraneous subscription services and everything else that brings me joy. CrossFit will now have to be done illegally in the middle of the night, probably at a train yard or dock where I'll be murdered."

"I'm proud of you. I know it's not easy to cut back. That reminds me, do you run?"

She brushed her hair over one bare shoulder. She had put on a tight white shirt with no bra, which was making it very hard to concentrate.

"Almost every day," Jade said. "Why do you ask?"

"Saturday is the town's annual Pie-K and harvest festival. It would be good for us to make an appearance if you're up for it."

She lifted her chin. "Will there be backpack cheese?"

"If by backpack cheese you mean at least four artisanal cheese makers, twelve wineries, and many local artists, then yes."

"Consider it on my calendar."

"Good. We should talk about what we're telling Tom and Cindy about us."

"It's probably easier to be honest, right? Your friends aren't going to rat you out to your parents," she said.

"Agreed. Why are you mad at me, by the way?"

Something had clearly been bubbling just beneath the surface all evening.

She jumped. "What do you mean?"

He rolled to a stop at a traffic light and stroked a finger between her eyebrows. "You've had this line ever since I picked you up. What's going on?"

She sighed and looked out the window. "Have you changed your mind about our friends-with-benefits arrangement?"

He frowned. "Of course not. Why?"

"You turned me down at the lake the other day. And then after our date last night, you kissed me on the cheek like we were courting in the 1800s."

"I didn't turn you down," he said. What the hell was she talking about?

She squirmed in her seat. "My hand was on your dick, and you told me you needed to get back to the winery. It felt like a rejection. Like after getting to know me better the attraction just evaporated for you."

Rett took a hard right and pulled into a parking lot by the lake. A full moon shone brightly above them.

He turned to look at her.

"I've been a little in my head. But trust me when I say—"

He paused to trail a hand up her thigh. "I am very attracted to you."

Moonlight illuminated half her face. There was still a sadness there, and he hated himself for putting the thought in her head. Any other time he would have just given into temptation. Why did things feel so different with Jade?

"I also want our first time to be momentous. Incredible," he explained. "Not a frigid bang on a splintered dock. You deserve more. From me, and from anyone you get involved with."

She turned to look away, but he gently turned her to face him.

"You're enough, Jade. More than enough. And I'm going to prove it to you on our next date. How about Friday after closing?"

He tipped her chin up and pressed his lips to hers. A shiver shot through his body, followed by a wash of heat. There was a long, slow pull in his stomach as she opened her mouth and let him in.

Penny had apparently decided that was enough and catapulted herself into the backseat. Rett dragged Jade to him, burying his hand in her hair. Strands slipped between his fingers as he plundered her mouth with his tongue.

Her fingers splayed across his chest. Could she feel his heartbeat? It was stuttering along at an unprecedented pace.

He had just meant to show her his attraction was genuine. But now it would take an earthquake to tear them apart.

She climbed on top of him, and her pelvis ground onto his. His hands moved from her back to her front and began a slow ascent to cup those infuriatingly distracting breasts. She gasped and arched her back. Her body responded to him like a finely tuned instrument.

He had never been this hard in his life.

He tugged the neck of her shirt down and took her nipple between his teeth. Her whole body shuddered like a plane battered by turbulence. She reached between his legs and groped over the layer of denim.

Suddenly, something rapped at the driver's side window. Jade gasped and scrambled away from him.

He bit back a sigh. He was going to have to go around all night with a halfie.

A light flashed over the steamy window as she fixed her shirt. Rett adjusted himself and calmly put the window down.

A stern-looking cop with a beer belly appeared, flashlight in one hand. When he saw Rett, his expression changed instantly.

"Rett?" he asked, visibly surprised.

"Hey, Scooter. Slow night?"

"Sorry, man." Scooter clicked off his flashlight and leaned on Rett's window. "There was a complaint. I thought I was about to prevent a teenage pregnancy."

"No teenagers here," Jade said with a smile. She leaned over Rett and shook the cop's hand. "I don't think we've met. I'm Jade."

"My name's Pete, but everyone calls me Scooter."

"Any particular reason?" She cocked her head.

"In high school, he rode down the hill on Route 54 on two scooters before crashing through a plate-glass window," Rett explained.

Scooter tutted. "That's why all these are fake." He tapped his top row of teeth. "Hey, listen," he said to Rett. "I don't mean to be a buzzkill. I'm all kinds of excited to see you getting back out there. But maybe in the future, try not to do it at a public park that's closed. It's kind of illegal."

"It was my fault," Jade said. "I got carried away."

"I don't blame you, miss. He's a good-looking fella." He mussed Rett's hair, then drew back. "You all skedaddle and have a safe night."

"Thank you, officer," Jade called as he left.

"Now you've done it," Rett said.

"Done what?"

"Scooter is married to Hammondsport's biggest gossip. We'll be the talk of the town by morning."

"Whoops. Well, poker night awaits." Jade smoothed her hair back and smiled. Her perma-frown was gone. It felt better than it should have to see her smile again.

———

"In here!" Cindy's voice called when they arrived five minutes later.

Music thumped from the kitchen. Rett guided Jade with a hand on the curve of her back. They passed a small office on the right before continuing down the hallway to a lake-themed living room with luxurious furniture and vaulted ceilings. Rett gently nudged her to the right.

Cindy and Tom were in the open-concept kitchen, wearing matching aprons and dancing to The Killers.

"Oh, I love this song!" Jade dropped Rett's hand and rushed in, fist pumping and hopping to "Mr. Brightside" until the song came to an end. Even Penny joined in, dancing on her back legs and doing a couple turns. Branson came to investigate.

Rett stood at the kitchen island. The wild, bra-less dancing was not helping the pants situation.

"I'm so happy you're here!" Cindy said breathlessly,

pulling Jade in for a hug. She lowered the volume on the music.

"Excellent dancing." Tom offered a fist bump.

Jade happily accepted. "It smells amazing in here. Oh, here." She retrieved the flowers from Rett and presented them to Cindy.

"These are gorgeous. Thank you so much. I hope you like lasagna." Cindy carefully set the flowers so they were exactly in the middle of the spotless island.

"I *love* lasagna," Jade said.

"Speaking of love, we have to talk to you guys about something," Rett said.

Tom dropped the spatula he was holding. It clattered to the floor. "You're getting mazzed! Of course I'll be your best man!"

He rushed Jade for a hug.

"Mazzed?" she mouthed to Rett over Tom's shoulder.

"We're not getting married," Rett clarified.

"Oh." Tom took a step back, clearly disappointed.

"Kind of the opposite, in fact."

"So you're breaking up?" Cindy looked at them with concern.

"No," Rett said. "This is all fake." He gestured between the two of them.

Cindy's face changed from concerned to interested. She walked over to a bottle of wine and plunged a corkscrew into it.

"Right. Rett helped me out by pretending to be my date for my ex-boyfriend's wedding last weekend. And I'm helping him by pretending to be his date for the anniversary party next weekend."

"We wanted to be transparent. I know I can trust you to

keep it under wraps around my parents. You know how they can be."

Cindy nodded and poured wine into two glasses. She handed one to Jade. "So all of this is fake. There are no feelings involved."

"Correct," Rett said.

Cindy looked between the two of them with her eyes narrowed. She and Tom exchanged a glance. "Well. That's disappointing."

Rett clapped his hands. "Now that that's out of the way, we're leaving. I'll bring Tom back and pick you up."

Jade shook her head. "You don't have to. I'm sure Penny and I can walk."

"In those shoes?" He stared pointedly at her feet, which seemed to be encased in some kind of torture device.

"Fair enough. Thank you." She leaned in for a hug, and the smell of her perfume gave him half a mind to drag her back out to the truck.

With one hand on her waist, he tipped her chin up to kiss her. An action that felt almost automatic. Her cheeks flushed.

"For practice," he announced to the room. "I'll see you later."

Cindy's eyes narrowed again. "Apron," she called to Tom, who had disappeared down the hallway.

"Crikey. I nearly forgot." He reappeared and ditched his apron in a closet. "Bye, love," he said to Cindy.

Rett waved, and they left. It was a relief to have Tom and Cindy in on the secret.

"So," Tom said the second they sat down in the truck. "Why are you just fake dating her, mate? She seems great."

Rett sighed. Why did they have to talk about this? Couldn't Tom just be happy that his best friend had stumbled into a friends-with-benefits situationship with a smoking hot artist?

"She's only here for two weeks," he said. "I can't get involved."

Tom tsked. "You're already involved."

CHAPTER TWENTY-FIVE

JADE

"Thanks for being cool with everything," Jade said. She took a swig of wine, then glanced at the bottle. One of Rett's. Of course.

Cindy peered into the oven, then shut the door. "I will admit, I am disappointed that this wasn't real. He's been alone for so long. But Rett's a grown man. He can do whatever he wants. Even be an idiot."

Jade smiled. "He really came through for me. I'm just trying to return the favor."

Cindy slid onto a barstool and picked up her wineglass. She took a long sip. "So there are really no feelings involved in this...entanglement? Only Rett answered before."

Jade plopped her glass down on the island and hitched herself onto the stool next to Cindy. "Just a warning, I'm about to be very frank."

"I wouldn't have it any other way. Cheers." Cindy held her glass out, and they clinked.

"So it's the weirdest thing. We set up a friends-with-benefits agreement while I'm here. No feelings, just fun. But he also won't sleep with me."

"Huh?" Cindy's face scrunched up.

"I know. He wants to wait until our next date and keeps saying I 'deserve more.' And then he's doing all this stuff for me, like driving me places and giving me budgeting advice and setting up an outdoor studio. It's very mixed messaging."

Cindy sighed. "Honestly, that sounds like him. He thinks he has to take responsibility for everything and always tries to prop his friends up for success. He helped Elena study for her NCLEX and played prosecution for Gemma. He even let me excise some of his moles for practice."

"Oh."

So he wasn't doing this for her out of interest. It was just a force of habit.

There was a knock at the door.

Cindy hopped up. "That'll be Gemma and Elena."

Cindy ran for the front door, and Jade followed hesitantly behind her.

"Hey, Gem."

A buxom redhead bustled inside, laden with shopping bags. She couldn't have been more than five two. "I'm so glad we're doing this tonight. I had the worst day in court."

"Let me guess." Cindy collected two grocery bags from Gemma. "That douche nozzle Damian Jones."

"That suit-wearing fuck tried to sneak in evidence that wasn't provided in discovery. Again. I cannot for the life of me figure out why he thinks the rules don't apply to him. Even the judge was annoyed. Who's this?"

Gemma seemed to have suddenly realized that there was an unfamiliar person in the foyer.

"This is Jade. Rett's Jade," Cindy said.

Gemma's eyes grew wide. "Holy shit. I never thought I'd live to see the day." She reached out one hand.

Jade shook it and fought the urge to wince. Gemma had a grip like a pair of pliers.

"To be fair," she said, "you still haven't seen the day. I'm just helping Rett distract his parents from matchmaking."

"Really? That's disappointing."

"Tell me about it," Cindy said.

Time to change the subject.

"Whoever Damian is, he sounds like a dick." Jade took another shopping bag from Gemma and peeked inside. A half gallon of what appeared to be local apple cider was nestled inside with a bottle of top-shelf tequila.

"Oh, honey. You have no idea," Gemma said.

"Are you a defense attorney?" Jade asked.

"She's a public defender. Let's stop standing in the foyer like a bunch of weirdos," Cindy said. They side-stepped the dogs, who were currently playing tug, and followed her back to the kitchen.

"Public defense is such a noble calling," Jade said.

Gemma paused. "My dad was wrongfully incarcerated for most of my childhood for a crime he didn't commit. We couldn't afford a great lawyer. I wanted to prevent that from happening to as many families as possible."

A pang hit Jade's heart as she unpacked the grocery bag.

"Cute tattoo," Gemma said. Jade looked down. Her off-the-shoulder top had left her stupid ice skate tattoo completely exposed.

"Ah. Thanks. My ex has a matching one. His wedding this past weekend is what brought me to town."

"Oof," Gemma said. "Let me make a round of apple cider margaritas. I need to hear this story."

"She might not be comfortable telling it," Cindy said pointedly.

"Shit, sorry," Gemma said. "I forget sometimes that not everyone copes by bitching."

"It's fine, I'm only like eighty-five percent still traumatized. I'm happy to tell the story. After a margarita."

"You're my kind of girl. I can tell."

Warmth engulfed Jade as she watched Cindy rip open a bag of frozen garlic bread while Gemma pulled out a cutting board.

It had been so long since she had been surrounded by strong women supporting each other. It was like a comforting, feminine hug.

There was another knock at the front door.

"I'll get it." Jade hopped down from the barstool and walked back down the hallway.

She opened the door to find a woman with dark hair and strong eyebrows, clad in a pair of dark jeans and a bright yellow sweater.

"You must be Elena." Jade extended her hand.

"Yes. And you are...?"

"Jade."

Elena's eyes swept over her. "You look like an artist."

"Oh. Thank you, I think."

"Trust me, it's a compliment. So you're the girl to finally nail down Everett Rhodes."

Jade shook her head. "We're just friends. With benefits. Sort of. But don't tell his parents that. If they ask, we're in love."

Elena left her flip-flops by the door. "Another situationship. Hola, chicas," she called out. "What's on the menu tonight?"

"Apple cider margaritas." Gemma brandished a bag of limes.

"You're really going to bastardize my culture like that?"

Gemma stared at Elena as she lit a cinnamon stick on fire. "It's fall."

"That's fair," Elena conceded. "I want the first one. I had to help extract something from a patient's rectum today."

"Uh oh," Cindy said. "Another Coke bottle?"

"Worse. A Honeycrisp apple."

Jade grimaced. "How festive."

"If I had a dollar for every time I fell on a Honeycrisp apple in the shower," Cindy said pensively.

Elena snorted.

"How can I help?" Jade asked.

Cindy waved a hot pad at her. "Just sit. You're a guest."

Gemma passed out margaritas. Smoking cinnamon sticks and springs of rosemary protruded from the rims.

"Uh, I'm going to have to retire in shame because you're clearly the real artist here," Jade said with an appreciative whiff.

"I will hire you to follow me around and compliment me all day," Gemma said.

Jade smiled and took a sip of the margarita. Not too sweet, and not too sweaty-tasting from the tequila. It didn't give her a tingle, but with any luck, it would give her the fortitude to tell the entire humiliating story.

"So," Cindy said, pulling a bubbling pan of lasagna from the oven. "The tattoo."

"Right. It all started in grad school."

———

AN HOUR LATER, THE GIRLS SPRAWLED AROUND THE DINING room table.

Penny and Branson were passed out on the living room floor, exhausted from a rousing game of tug.

"I'm sorry," Gemma said. "I'm still stuck on the fact that both of them lied to your face for two years. And she was supposed to be your best friend."

Jade picked up her margarita glass only to find it empty. "Yeah. The last time I checked, 'screw your best friend's boyfriend five seconds after her parents died' was not included in the girl code."

The other girls cringed.

"Sorry. Too far with the morbid humor?" Jade asked.

Cindy reached over and patted her on the hand. "You cope however you need to. I'm sorry everyone in your life is such an asshole."

Elena leaned forward. "Sorry. I have to ask. What is Rett like in bed?" She held two fingers out in front of her and started indicating various lengths.

Gemma threw a balled-up napkin, which hit Elena in the face. "He's our friend. That's such a weird question."

Elena threw it back at her. "Come on, like you haven't been curious?"

Jade cleared her throat. "Sadly, I have no answers. Yet."

"Really? Because I heard from Betty Lou that Scooter caught you guys in a...compromising position," Elena said with eyebrows raised.

That had been all of two hours ago. Just how quickly did news travel in this town?

"He's insisting on taking me on a real date first."

"The fucking nerve of that guy," Gemma said.

"I know. So what about you guys? Boyfriends? Girlfriends? Life partners with surprisingly realistic robots?"

"Tragically single," Elena said with one end of the cinnamon stick in her mouth. "I don't know if you've noticed, but the dating pool around here isn't huge."

"Yeah. Same here," Gemma said. "Even Cindy had to

import hers. Besides, I work too much to make a relationship work."

Jade nodded. "Rett did mention the dating pool was an issue. You've never thought about leaving?"

"Nah. I landed here after law school and never looked back. It's small, but it's home," Gemma said.

"My family lives here," Elena explained. "I take care of my abuela most weekends."

"I can see why you stay," Jade said.

Cindy locked eyes with her. "But you live in the city?"

"Yeah. For now. In addition to having terrible taste in men, I have also somehow completely mismanaged my life savings and am now in danger of becoming homeless in the next few months."

Elena's mouth formed an O.

"Why don't you just move here?" Gemma asked. "I'm sure Rett would let you move in. His house is so big that he probably wouldn't even notice you were there."

"We haven't even known each other for a full week," Jade said. "For all I know, he could be a serial killer."

Cindy shook her head. "I've known him forever. He doesn't have the stomach for it."

"Still," Gemma said, "rent has to be cheaper here than in the city."

"Sure," Jade said, "but how's the job market here? If I never get my ability to paint back, I'm going to have to pivot and learn a new skill set. I don't have the temperament for customer service, nor the long-term memory required to be a waitress. And then what happens if this friends-with-benefits situation implodes and then I have to dodge him around town for a year?"

"You make some valid points." Gemma pressed her fingertips together. "But if you moved here, you would never be alone. You would have us. Regardless of your involvement with Rett."

Jane's bottom lip quivered. The apple cider margaritas had made her a tad emotional.

"Agreed." Cindy reached across the table and grabbed her hand. Gemma and Elena reached over too.

"Hey." Gemma shot up like she had just had a brilliant idea. "Are you still doing the thing you talked about? Trying to knock the artist block out of yourself with experiences?"

Jade nodded. "When I can afford to."

Gemma jumped to her feet. "Let those dogs go pee. We're on a mission."

Cindy groaned. "Why do I feel like this is going to end poorly? Also, none of us can drive."

"We don't need to drive. But we do need inflatables."

Elena narrowed her eyes. "Are you suggesting...?"

"Yes. It's been years. We have a sacrosanct duty to introduce Jade to the semi-annual ABB challenge."

"We usually do it in July. It's October."

"All the more reason it'll help. Come on. I think I still have some in my car."

"ABB?" Jade whispered to Cindy.

"Anything but a boat," Cindy replied.

––––––––

Twenty minutes later, Jade crept down Water Street in a borrowed bikini and pair of shorts, arm wrapped around the neck of an inflatable unicorn. She clutched a paddle in the other hand.

"Are you sure we're not going to get arrested?"

There was no way she'd be able to make bail. Prison

would be real rock bottom. Maybe they would at least allow her to have watercolors?

Gemma scoffed and turned partway around. An inflatable flamingo was propped over her shoulder. "Scooter owes me. I already gave him a heads-up. It's fine."

Elena turned, and her paddle almost thwacked Cindy. "Sorry. So basically, Jade, we put in at the boat launch and flail our way across Depot Park to the inlet. Whoever wins gets a prize."

Cindy eyed Jade's torso. "I don't know, girls. I don't like my odds against Jade. Your delts are insane. Do you do CrossFit?"

"I used to," Jade muttered.

They had reached the boat launch.

"All right, ladies," Gemma said. "Single file."

Cindy sighed and traipsed into the water with the help of an inflatable llama and a paddle. Apparently it was some kind of lake-life prerequisite that everyone carried emergency lake supplies in their car—inflatables, paddles, swimming suits.

Jade rarely had the opportunity to swim. In fact, if she fell in the water, there was a better than average chance that she would drown. But at least then her problems would be over.

Yikes. She made a mental note to look up a gratitude meditation before bed and put the thought behind her.

Jade followed Cindy into the frigid water. "Oh, god. This is so cold."

Elena was behind Jade with a mean-looking peacock. "Come on, you blandengues. Live a little."

Gemma brought up the rear, laughing maniacally.

Unable to help herself, Jade burst out laughing too. What a sight they would have made to anyone driving by.

"Everyone mount your floaties," Gemma commanded.

Jade slung one leg over her unicorn and almost flipped into the water. Eventually, she settled on her knees in the middle. It was still cold, but not unmanageable.

"Ready. Set. *Go.*"

At Cindy's words, they plunged their paddles into the water. Jade bumped into Gemma's flamingo. Cindy's paddle slapped the back of her unicorn. Jade drove her paddle deeper and soared ahead.

There was something absurd about riding a unicorn across a lake under a star-strewn sky. But it was also amazing. The muddy scent of the lake mingled with the chemical stink of plastic. Strength rippled in her arms as she thrust the paddle into the water on one side, then the other. Dollops of lake water landed on the floaty.

Shit. She didn't exactly know where she was going. Something about a pier at the beach? But surely the other girls would call out to her when they hit the finish line.

She risked a look behind her. Elena and Cindy were screeching and shoving each other's floaties with their paddles. Gemma was a few yards behind Jade, face set in determination.

Jade had never been incredibly competitive. But she really needed a win. She set her eyes on the horizon and focused on her breath. She drove the paddle in again and again, relishing in the feeling of gliding across the smooth surface of the lake. An owl hooted somewhere in the darkness. Crickets called in a chorus around them.

Shit, this was farther than it looked. Her arms burned. She stole another glance behind her. Gemma was still hot on her heels, face red and breathing heavily.

Oh, there was the inlet. That hadn't been far from the

beach when she and Rett had almost committed a crime of indecency. She must be over halfway now.

"Is this it?" Jade called over her shoulder. In the distance, a wooden expanse stretched out into the lake.

"That's it. You better watch your back," Gemma called. "I'm coming for you."

Jade glanced farther behind them. Elena was in last place. Her thick brown hair hung wetly around her shoulders. Cindy's white teeth were practically gleaming in the dark.

Gemma was gaining on her. Jade whirled back around. Her arms were burning, but the end was in sight. Her heart was lighter than it had been in months. Years, maybe. Who knew that crawling across the lake with an assortment of zoo animals was exactly what she needed?

As they approached the dock, human-like figures appeared. She squinted but couldn't quite make them out. Apparently they would be ruining someone's late-night fishing expedition.

"There they are," someone called from the dock. The sound carried across the expanse.

Shit. Were they about to get kidnapped? Her arms were too sore to fend off attackers. A swift kick would have to suffice.

Flashlight beams clicked on and illuminated the space between Jade and the dock.

"Yeah, get her," an unfamiliar voice said in the darkness.

CHAPTER TWENTY-SIX

RETT

"AND IN FIRST PLACE WE HAVE JADE STRADDLING A UNICORN," Tom's Australian accent announced.

"Tom?" Cindy called out.

Rett shook his head. It had been a couple years since the last ABB event. Normally the men would have participated too, but apparently they hadn't been invited.

"Followed directly by the feisty Gemma, charging into battle astride a large pink flamingo. They're neck and neck, ladies and gents," Tom continued.

Jade was only feet from the dock, but Gemma was right behind her. With a final push, the unicorn bumped into the dock to a chorus of cheers.

"That's my girl," Rett said. He reached down and plucked Jade from the raft. She swayed on her feet and he put an arm around her to steady her.

"Damn it!" Gemma called from behind her. "I was so close."

"Second time today you were close," Damian said from the end of the dock.

"What the hell are you doing here, Jones?" There was vitriol in Gemma's voice.

The sniping at each other was starting early, apparently.

Tom cleared his throat. "Damian joined poker night. Don't worry, I took a lot of his money."

"You were amazing," Rett said to Jade. He swooped down and gave her a kiss. "Here." He handed over a sweatshirt and a pair of sweatpants. "Thought you might be cold."

There was a strange sense of pride in his chest. She had looked so confident, so capable gliding over the surface of the lake. Now they just needed to channel that energy to the rest of her life.

"Thank you. I thought you guys were here to murder us." Jade took the pants and climbed into them. She rolled the waistband three times, but the legs were still too long.

Rett chuckled.

"Here." Damian had dropped down onto one knee and reached toward Gemma. She slapped his hand away and paddled toward the shore. He laughed.

"Come on," he said, rising to his feet. "You can't take it personally. It's just work."

"Maybe to you," Gemma said. "But that's my client's life. His livelihood. And you think you're immune to all the rules."

"I can't help that someone presented me with evidence in the middle of court."

"And I can't help my foot smashing into your balls the second I get out of this goddamn flamingo."

"They hooked up once," Rett whispered in Jade's ear. "It didn't end well."

"How did you guys know we were down here?" she asked.

"Cindy texted Tom. You know, in case all of you disappeared."

"Nice. I should probably stop Gemma from murdering Damian."

Jade bustled off to the end of the dock, flip-flops smacking off the wood. She must have given up on the torture devices. She pulled Gemma to shore.

"Don't murder him now," Jade said. "You can murder him later. In court. With words."

Gemma shot daggers down the dock.

Cindy and Elena arrived, cackling in the darkness.

"I hate you." Elena slapped Cindy's llama. "I'm freezing."

Jade tugged the sweatshirt off and helped Elena clamber onto the dock. "Here."

"Oh, bless you." Still shivering, Elena tugged it on.

Tom pulled Cindy up and dipped her, greeting her with a head-turner of a kiss.

"Care for a ride back?" Rett asked the crowd. He really needed to check on his dough and go over the accounts before bed.

"Not if *he's* going to be in the car," Gemma said.

Damian threw his hands up. "I drove myself. I'll see you later this week." He backed away like he was expecting her to backhand him with her paddle. Knowing Gemma, it was possible.

"You can ride in the bed if you promise not to tell Scooter," Rett announced.

Five minutes later, Rett and Tom were in the cab of the truck while Jade, Cindy, Elena, and Gemma sprawled in the bed. He glanced in the rearview mirror. Jade was turned toward him, but her face was tipped up to the stars. The wind tangled her hair, and she looked like a goddess embracing the power of the moon.

Something flickered in his guts, and he tore his eyes away from the rearview. They only had two weeks. He couldn't get involved. But part of him wanted to.

————

"Thanks for dropping me off. Here." Jade wriggled out of the borrowed sweatpants and folded them neatly on the dashboard. She was still wearing Cindy's bikini.

They were sitting outside her cottage. Margie had left a light on, but Steven the raccoon was nowhere to be seen.

"No problem."

For a moment, they just stared at each other. The memory of their tryst in the truck mere hours before was on his mind. If Scooter hadn't interrupted, Rett probably would have lost control and taken her right there.

He wanted her in his bed more than he'd ever wanted another woman. Maybe it was just all this buildup. Or maybe it was the dimple in her right cheek, the softness in her eyes. As satisfying as it would be to trail his hands down those beautiful curves and find out what she tasted like, she deserved their first time to be special, meaningful, reminiscent of what she could have if she opened herself to relationships again. Sex was worlds different when you connected on more than a surface level. It was part of fixing her up, and he couldn't let his selfish impulses derail it. She deserved better.

"See you tomorrow?" he asked. The reception for paint and sip had been very enthusiastic.

She nodded. "I'll come early to set up."

"Did I tell you we sold out?"

She balked. "Already?"

He nodded. Almost all the tickets were bought by his

friends and fellow business owners in town, but she didn't need to know that.

Her face went pale. "Well. I'd better make sure it doesn't turn out to be a disaster, then."

He leaned in. "It won't be."

"What if it's just stick figures?"

"Then I'll pour more wine until people don't notice."

"That sounds uneth—"

She was silenced by Rett crushing his mouth to hers. Penny grumbled and jumped to the back seat again.

Jade released her seatbelt and crawled on her knees over to him. He pulled her on top of him and yanked on the bikini string until it released. Her warm, soft breasts tumbled into his hands, and her nipples hardened in response.

She arched her back and tipped her head up, providing an unimpeded view of the curve of her neck and a moon-light-dappled collarbone.

She was so beautiful. His hands trailed down and cupped her ass. Everything in him was screaming to take her here, now. Date be damned.

His hand slid forward to her bikini bottoms. He had one finger inside the waistband when she drew back.

"It's not Friday," she chastised.

Son of a bitch. He knew he was going to pay for that suggestion.

"You're the one who insisted," she said with a devilish smile. She slid off him and re-strung the bikini around her neck.

"Maybe there's some wiggle room in this verbal contract." He reached for her.

She shook her head. "You're the one who set the terms. I would hate for you to go against your convictions at the first sign of temptation. I'm going to go paint. Night," she said. With that, she hopped out of the truck without a backward glance.

He sat for a moment and watched her close the door to the cottage behind her.

He was in trouble.

CHAPTER TWENTY-SEVEN

JADE

Jade closed the door behind her and set her keys on the console table. She stretched her arms overhead, luxuriating in the tension that would surely mean sore muscles tomorrow.

The easel set up by the window caught her eye. A small tingle sent sparks up her spine. It might have had something to do with Rett, which was problematic.

She grabbed a palette, then dabbed acrylic paints across it in a semi-circle. With brushes fresh from the drying rack, she perched on a stool in front of the blank canvas. She closed her eyes for a moment, reveling in the sensation of gliding across the dark lake, new friends in her wake.

She opened her eyes and dabbed a brush into the black. Long strokes across the canvas, marking the hills on each side. Dabs for trees, dashes of deep blue sky behind the branches that—in her imagination at least—swayed in the darkness.

A moon rose, sending a light trail down the center of the painting. She fiddled with the grass in the foreground. When she had done as much as she could, she stepped away. There was no sense in tinkering too much. There was more to come, but this layer had to dry. Movement outside the window caught her eye. Steven the raccoon waddled past her cottage.

She shed the bikini and pulled on her comfiest pair of sweatpants and a long-sleeved shirt. From the fridge, she pulled a bag of cheese sticks and a bundle of grapes.

She upended a bucket by the door and spread the food on a gingham napkin. Steven deserved a nice snack. The night air was cool as she settled into an Adirondack chair on the front porch. There was an excellent chance that, once again, this painting wouldn't be sellable. It might just be shitty. Shitty and nostalgic. But this lake—this town—had given back to her something she hadn't seen in two years.

Before Hammondsport, she would squirt some paint onto a palette and stare at a blank canvas. It mocked her, gaping at her like a black hole. Even if she touched a brush to the canvas, it immediately felt wrong. But here, her soul was relaxed. She allowed herself to experiment, to create, without judgment.

Hopefully it would translate onto the wall at Margie's.

———

THE NEXT MORNING, JADE BREEZED THROUGH HER MORNING run—as much as she could with a side stitch undoubtedly brought on by too many apple cider margaritas the night before—and pedaled into town with a happy heart.

Apart from her abject anxiety about the mural, something else had been swirling in her brain. Rett had asked her to design a label for the new line, and she had stayed up too late perusing designs online. Something told her an ordinary, scripted-font label or sketched bird wasn't going to cut it. She needed to find a picture of Rett's grandmother.

But first, she needed to *encapsulate a feeling*. After locking her bike on the rack outside the café, she took a deep breath, appreciating for the millionth time how clear the air was and how bright the sunshine. It was cooler today, with crisp notes of fall on the wind.

A store down the block had crates of apples stacked on the sidewalk. The smell was intoxicating, and she couldn't stop herself from buying half a bushel. If only she could paint a smell.

A church that looked like it had come straight from a movie lot stood on one side of the street. Crisscrossing sidewalks intersected at a gazebo with benches scattered all over.

She sat down at the gazebo for a moment and just breathed in the town. People passed by on foot. Many were clearly from out of town—dressed extra warm and huddling in the square around a phone, pointing in different directions. Others were locals, greeting each other with warm smiles and pleasantries.

It couldn't have been more different from the city. There was an absence of urgency. People lifted their heads to say hello. There wasn't a pair of earbuds in sight.

A tingle hit her spine, and her breath caught in her chest. Could it be? She pulled out her sketchbook again and dug around in her purse until she found a pack of colored pencils. The lines of the buildings in front of her slowly took shape. There was the steeple of the church, the sunflower on the logo of Margie's Café. Weathered brick and curving paths. Bins overflowing with apples and bulbous lights on lampposts. Sprawling green hills with pops of yellow and red.

A few minutes later, she snapped out of her trance and pulled back to look at it. It wasn't done, and it definitely wasn't perfect. But something about it resonated within her.

She hurried into the café with her sketchbook before she lost the feeling.

"Morning, Margie," she called.

Margie waved from behind the counter.

"Hi, Jade," Alex, one of the servers, called.

She waved back at him. Was this what it was like to live in a small town? Everyone knew your name and had a smile for you?

"Good morning, ladies," she said as she passed the table of busybodies.

"Hello, Jade," one of them said enthusiastically. "Hey, listen. You wouldn't have an interest in joining our book club, would you? We usually read romance and meet once a month."

She sighed. "I would love to, but I'm only in town to do the mural." She gestured at the blank wall.

"And for Rett, of course," another one said, staring over the rim of her bifocals.

"Right, of course. But we're just getting to know each other. It's a little soon for me to be putting down roots when he could get sick of me tomorrow."

The second woman shook her head fervently. "He won't. I can tell. That boy has a spring in his step that's been missing for years."

Oh, good. More guilt.

"I think he's just excited about the new product he's unveiling at his party." Maybe some gossip would throw them off the scent. "Speaking of which, would any of you happen to have a picture of Rett's grandmother?"

"Why, sure," a third woman said. "Valentina used to be

in our book club too, you know. I'll bring it in tomorrow if you'll be here."

"That would be wonderful. I better get to work."

"What does she want a picture of Valentina for?" the first woman called loudly.

"Hush, Ethel. It's none of our business," another said.

Jade smiled and confronted the blank wall of endless possibility in front of her. Minutes later, earbuds in and bopping to No Doubt, she studied her sketchbook.

Someone swooped in and kissed her on the cheek, and she almost punched them in the throat. Rett stood next to her, smiling a devilish grin.

"Rude," she said, yanking her earbuds out. "You scared the crap out of me."

"Sorry. I couldn't resist. Payback for last night."

She couldn't help but smile. "Oh, so you're mad about me following your misguided rules?"

He leaned in to kiss her again, this time just below the earlobe. Tingles shot through her hands and feet. "We'll see if you still think they're misguided Friday night."

She poked him in the chest. "Not fair. You're distracting me at work. Don't make me sic Margie on you."

"Sketching out the mural?" He leaned over, one hand on the back of her chair. It was a little possessive, but nice.

"Yeah. Margie's been hesitant to give me feedback. Would you mind taking a look?" She handed her sketchbook over to him. He wasn't one to mince words, so any opinion he doled out would at least be honest.

He straightened up and flipped through several pages.

"These are good. You've pulled a lot of pieces of town history in."

"But you don't have a preference?"

He tilted his head. "It's hard to say. Wait, what's this one?"

Jade straightened up and peeked over the edge of the tablet. "Oh, shit."

She had completely forgotten about the half-finished sketch she had made during her disastrous first wine tasting at Rhodes Vineyard. It was sloppy and embarrassing and frankly a little creepy since she had drawn it before ever speaking to him.

She went to snatch it back, but he lifted it out of reach.

"Is this...me?" He pointed to the side profile of a man hefting wine bottles onto shelves.

She stood and yanked it from his hands. "It might be. You weren't supposed to see that. I forgot it was in there."

"You forgot? How old is the sketch?"

"It's from the day we met, if you must know." She slapped the sketchbook on the table and pinned it under her purse. "I told you your wine inspired me. I looked around for something to sketch and you just happened to be the closest object."

He narrowed his eyes, but they were lit with amusement. "I was twenty yards away from you in a different room, though."

"I'm not going to dignify that with a response."

"You thought I was handsome. Admit it."

Jade crossed her arms. "I thought it would be an interesting study of the human form."

"Whatever you say." The infuriating grin was back. He planted another palpitation-inducing kiss on her.

At the busybody table, a fork clattered to a plate.

"Maybe we should re-read *Fifty Shades of Grey* for book club," one woman said.

"For the fourth time, Jeanette?" another woman asked.

"Breakfast to go, Romeo?" Margie called from behind the counter.

Rett tore his eyes from Jade for a minute to smile and nod. "The usual, please. Thanks, Margie."

"What's your usual?" Jade said with a smile.

"Chicken sausage and egg white breakfast burrito," he replied. "Margie's homemade salsa is incredible."

"That sounds amazing."

"Make it two, Margie," Rett called over his shoulder.

Jade's phone beeped, and she glanced at the screen. Weird. It was a message from Kenya.

Kenya: You didn't hear this from me. Ash just texted from Hawaii. Apparently she and Nate got in a gigantic fight. He went down to the bar and never came back that night. Turns out he slept with a resort waitress. Anyway, she said he left and she's looking up divorce lawyers.

Jade's mouth fell open. The marriage that she had spent so much time, energy, and

money mentally and physically preparing for had dissolved within a freaking week?

"Are you *kidding* me?" she yelled at her phone.

"What's wrong?" Rett frowned.

She shoved the phone at him. The wheels of justice had turned more quickly than she had ever imagined. What kind of person was Nate to sleep with someone else on his own freakin' honeymoon while his brand-new wife was upstairs? The fucking *audacity* of this man.

How had she never seen this side of him? Was it always there, buried beneath the glitz and glamour of long weekends in the Catskills and dinners in trendy, impossible-to-get-into restaurants? Was Ashley really the first person he had cheated on her with?

She had trusted him implicitly, never glancing at his phone when he was out of the room or sifting through Instagram DMs. She had accepted his love for her at face value only to be blindsided in the worst way.

Rett handed the phone back with a dark expression.

As much as Nate's betrayal had hurt and even quite possibly ruined her career as an artist, at least she had never married the bastard. She deserved better. And she would find it.

CHAPTER TWENTY-EIGHT

RETT

THE LAST OF THE CHAIRS HIT THE HARDWOOD FLOOR WITH A *thunk.* Now he remembered why he had never scheduled another paint and sip. The setup and teardown was a giant pain in the ass. Hours that should be spent going over things for the party the following weekend were instead spent lugging dusty easels out of the barn and all the way to the tasting room. But it would be worth it to help Jade.

He flexed his fingers and surveyed the space. They had managed to clear the tasting tables away and fit twenty workstations in their place. At $50 a pop, they had grossed $1,000. He had tried to give her all of it, but she had insisted on splitting the proceeds evenly. It definitely wasn't life-changing money, but hopefully it helped her a little.

Across the room, Jade was securing canvases on the easels he had just set up. Elaine said something to her, and she laughed. She wore a rust-colored sweater and jeans that she had spent a full ten minutes de-furring upon arrival.

She didn't look any worse for wear after the news broke about Nate. She wouldn't get involved with him now that he was single again, would she? The very thought raised his hackles.

There had been a moment—nothing but a moment—after Alexa had dumped him when he'd contemplated rekindling things. It had been their first Christmas broken up, and everyone had gathered at a rented house in Aspen for the holiday.

Their hands had closed over the punch ladle at the same time. A look had passed between them. Something had felt unfinished. Alexa, who had been several cups of punch deep, had looked at him with clear meaning in her eyes and walked purposefully into the empty basement.

He had walked over as if in a dream and had one hand on the knob before snapping out of it. Maybe his brother was a cheater. But he wasn't. He had almost let the call of the familiar compromise everything he believed in.

But Jade wasn't weak. She hadn't even given up on her dream despite overwhelming evidence that she needed to move on.

Her question from earlier drifted to the front of his periphery. What *was* his dream?

Ever since his grandmother died, he had been laser-focused on the success of the winery. He had given everything he had to this place, and still they were just treading water. Did he even deserve a dream when he couldn't succeed with a business someone had hand-delivered to him?

That wasn't to say that the winery wasn't a dream itself. There was such beauty in the claret color of a fresh batch, a sense of pride from watching people enjoy the literal fruits of his labor. Every day had something amazing in it.

The tray of pastries on the far wall caught his eye. He had stayed up for hours the night before, perfecting each gold-dusted macaron. There was something deeply pleasurable about fiddling with a recipe until he got it exactly right. Baking was a lot like winemaking. It was science.

But baking wasn't a dream. The Finger Lakes were lousy with bakeries. There was no market for a new one. Besides, he couldn't very well betray the existing patisseries in Hammondsport. Ted would never shake his hand again if he bought the business next door and started hocking croissant fraises.

"I thought I was supposed to be the one freaking out." Jade's voice snapped him back to reality.

"I was just thinking about my homework," he said with a smile.

"Good. I look forward to a full report. I've been doing mine too. Did you know that you can make a right turn at a red light?"

"Sure. Unless you're in the city," he said.

She frowned. "Shit."

"How are you feeling about tonight?" He ran a hand down her arm. A flush instantly crept into her cheeks.

"I think it'll be fine. I practiced at home—uh, at Margie's." She showed him a picture of a canvas with pumpkins beneath fall leaves.

"It looks great. You can do this."

She gave him a flat smile like she didn't really believe him.

"Do you want a glass before everyone gets here?" he asked.

"Yes," she said immediately.

As soon as he poured her a glass, the front door opened and in walked the book club. He barely had a second to enjoy the way Jade's eyes closed at her first sip, like she was tasting with her full body.

"Ladies," he said. "Welcome. I hope you're ready to paint."

Jeanette wandered up and squinted at the bottles of wine on display. Mildred swiveled until she found Jade, then she whispered something to Ethel. As suspected, they were here primarily to spy.

Rett poured Jeanette a glass of semi-dry Riesling while Ethel and Mildred approached Jade. Ethel handed something off to Jade, but he couldn't quite hear what they were saying. Probably interrogating her. It wouldn't be the first time they had meddled in his love life—or lack of one.

More people trickled in until all twenty seats were filled. When everyone's glass was full, Rett strode to the front of the room. Jade's shoulders shook. He stood beside her and put one arm around her.

The book club straightened up and leaned forward.

"Thank you all for coming tonight." He glanced around the room. There were a handful of unfamiliar faces, but most of the attendees were townspeople and local business owners. An old friend who carried his wines at their charming string of bed-and-breakfasts in Seneca winked at him.

Hmm. That would be a good opportunity for Jade to practice networking. He filed the idea in the back of his mind and continued.

"For those of you who haven't met her yet, this is Jade. She's a remarkably accomplished young artist from Manhattan, and she also has amazing taste in wine."

A couple people laughed.

"Let's make her feel welcome." He clapped and applause broke out.

Ethel put her fingers to her mouth and whistled. Her dentures shot out and bounced off the canvas.

"Take it away," he whispered in Jade's ear. With one last squeeze of her arm, he left her to sink or swim.

———

AND SWIM SHE DID. BEAUTIFULLY. THOUGH HER MOVEMENTS had been halting and unsure when she first stood in front of the group, within minutes, she'd settled into her role as teacher and the paintbrush moved like it was a part of her. Every swipe of color brought her closer to her dream of returning to the art world. It was exactly what they both wanted. So why did the thought of her returning to the city churn his stomach?

An hour later, Jade put down her brush. "And there you have it—a fall pumpkin patch. Thank you all so much for coming tonight. Don't forget to leave a review for Rhodes Vineyard on Yelp before you leave."

Rett tilted his head. A prickle of irritation flared. Why the hell was she pushing Yelp reviews? That wasn't one of his core goals this quarter. In fact, he barely ever checked the winery's online reputation. Word of mouth was a much more powerful tool.

"Any questions?" Jade asked.

Jeanette's hand shot into the air, and Jade hopped down from her stool to help her. A couple people came over for a refill while their canvases dried. When everyone seemed satisfied, he ducked out from behind the counter and strode over to Jade.

"It's time to practice your networking skills," he said with a hand on her arm.

"What?" she asked.

"Firm handshake, look him in the eyes, ask about his bed-and-breakfast business."

"But—"

He steered her in front of his friend. "Vince! It's been awhile. This is Jade."

"So nice to meet you." She extended a hand to Vince and shook it firmly. Good girl.

"Rett said you're in the hospitality industry," she continued. "It must be a busy time of year for you."

Someone rang the bell at the counter, and Rett turned toward it. As he bagged up a few bottles for a customer, he caught a glimpse of Jade pointing at something on Vince's painting. It seemed to be going well. Maybe she didn't need as much help as he thought.

Eventually, people took their canvases and began to trickle out.

"Bye, Rett. Let's do this once a month," Mildred called on her way out. "I want to paint a library next time."

He smiled, but he didn't really feel it. There wouldn't be a next time.

He busied himself by packing up the easels and dragging them across the vineyard five at a time. When he came back from his final trip, Jade lifted her head.

"I did it," she said.

"I knew you could. You didn't tell me you have a natural talent for schmoozing."

"How do you think I got into my gallery when I was twenty years old?" she asked. "I'm not entirely hopeless. Just mostly hopeless."

"Not hopeless," he said sternly. "By the way, why were you asking people to leave Yelp reviews?"

"Have you not looked at the reviews of the winery online?"

He shook his head. The winery was critically acclaimed by some of the finest sommeliers in the world. What did he care what some people with too much time and internet access had to say?

She typed something on her phone. "I was asking for reviews to counteract all the bad ones. I don't know what happened two Februaries ago, but people were *pissed*. You might not want to see these."

He held his hand out, and she gave him the phone. There were a handful of one-star reviews, all left in the same couple of days. A few people criticized the wine while others complained about the "surly and unprofessional vintner."

The date jumped out—February 17th. The week after his grandmother had passed, and his first week in charge of the winery. Flames of anger kindled.

"These really dragged down your average," Jade said. "You're at three point five stars. When I'm looking for someplace new to go, I avoid anything that's less than four stars," she explained. "I think this is part of the winery's problem. Do you have any idea what happened?"

Who the hell was comfortable criticizing a grieving man? Let alone on the internet for everyone to see? No wonder the winery was suffering. Was he supposed to sling chardonnay with a smile when they had just buried the matriarch of his family?

He huffed a frustrated sigh. "My grandmother died the week before."

"Oh." She bit her lip and tucked her phone away. "Well, if we can incentivize people to leave reviews after their tastings, I really think we could drive your average back up. Maybe if you offered a ten percent discount with proof of a review?"

"I don't need advice on how to run my business," he snapped before he could stop himself.

She shrunk back like he had shouted at her. Regret hit

him instantly, but before he could take a breath to apologize, she waved a hand in the air like it wasn't a big deal.

"You're right. It's not my place. Well. All the supplies are packed up," she reported. "Any chance you want to hang out? You can quiz me on street signs or talk to me about dividends."

Rett hesitated, a yes on his lips.

There was a final portion of his unspoken dream, one he had given up on when Alexa left. A wife, a family, someone to share this life with. He had pushed it to the back of his mind for years now. But something about Jade had brought it back to the forefront.

It still didn't matter though. All of this was temporary. And if he couldn't pull the winery out of its flatline, how could he support a family? If he didn't find a way to boost sales, his grandmother's legacy would be tarnished forever and his parents—and his brother—would never let him forget it.

"I'd love to. But I have a lot of work to finish up."

"Oh. Okay." Her face fell for a second, then was replaced by a neutral expression. "Are we still on for tomorrow?"

"Yes. That reminds me." He ducked behind the counter and pulled out a gift bag. He handed it to her. "Don't open this until you get back to Margie's."

"Mysterious. I like it." Her smile was back. "I'll see you tomorrow."

She left before he could offer a ride home.

Tomorrow night, he would remind her what she deserved. With any luck, she would steer clear of Nates in the future.

CHAPTER TWENTY-NINE

JADE

JADE BRUSHED A COAT OF MASCARA OVER HER EYELASHES. Another full day of staring paralyzed at a blank wall in the café had passed. Anxiety was setting in. Her sketchbook was full of half-assed ideas, but none of them seemed right. This wasn't some ordinary painting that Margie could just take down and put in storage when it fell out of fashion. This mural could very well stand until the building was one day taken down to the studs. The pressure was cripplingly high.

She thought this little town had given something back to her. And in a way, it had. She could sketch again, even paint a little. But the real magic was still missing.

Rett's gift bag from the night before caught her eye. She had been slightly miffed after he snapped at her and hadn't opened it as instructed. She hefted it onto the counter. Why was it so heavy?

Inside was a laptop and a tablet. Anger flared like someone had just dropped a match at a gas station. What the hell was he doing, buying her expensive electronics? She didn't need his help.

She grabbed her phone with a mind to cancel for

tonight. Penny whined from her position curled up at Jade's feet. Something about her soulful eyes froze her on the spot. Jade paused and took a deep breath.

Penny was right. This was her past trauma coming out. Rett was not Nate. This wasn't some flashy gift meant to control her or enhance her public image like the Hermes bag Nate insisted she carry during her photo shoot for *Painter's Brush* magazine. The one she later sold to cover a couple months of rent.

Rett had never given her a reason not to trust him. He had done nothing but help her since the day of her apology.

She opened his contact and typed out a message.

> Jade: Thank you for the gift. I'd like to pay you back, but it might be awhile.

A few minutes later, her phone dinged.

> Rett: There's nothing to pay back. It's an investment from someone who believes in you. Are you wearing the last gift?

She glanced down at the electronics. Unless he wanted her to fashion a dress out of an iPad box as some sort of creative exercise, there wasn't anything to wear. She dug through the bag and found another parcel wrapped in tissue paper. She yanked it out and unfolded it. A lacy bra and panty set in a deep eggplant color slipped into her hands.

A thrill ran through her belly at the thought of him discovering it, peeling away the layers of clothing until only this gift separated them. What would his hands feel like as they raked over her flesh? Would he be rough? Gentle? Domineering?

She put it on and flittered around the kitchen.

Gravel crunched outside, signaling his arrival. A tingle ran down her spine, and she turned and threw her sketchbook into her oversized studded tote. Just in case.

She blew out another long, slow breath. Why was she so nervous? This wasn't even a real date. It was a façade. She could have explosive diarrhea the entire time and it wouldn't even matter. The stakes could not have been lower.

But when she opened the door and saw Rett standing there in a suit jacket, with slicked-back hair, and holding yet another bouquet, the nerves multiplied.

"Hi," she said, almost tripping over her overnight bag as she backed up. He hadn't explicitly stated that she was staying over, but she believed in being prepared.

Penny immediately descended on him, pressing a slobbery tennis ball into his side until he plucked it from her mouth and bounced it across the floor.

When Penny vacated, Rett handed Jade the bouquet and leaned in for a kiss that left her lips burning.

"I'm running out of vases, you know."

He raised an eyebrow. "You live in a pottery shed."

"That doesn't mean I can just start shoving flowers in things all loosey-goosey."

He cracked a smile.

"Sorry. Thank you. They're beautiful."

"You're beautiful." He held her at arm's length and looked her up and down.

Butterflies danced in her stomach. His gaze was long and slow, like he was trying to memorize everything about her. For a fake boyfriend, he lent a lot of intensity to the role.

"You're looking pretty handsome yourself." She tugged at a button on his shirt and let her hand trail to belt level.

"Are you wearing my gift?" he asked.

"I might be. Will I need it?"

"Oh. You'll need it. Did you pack an overnight bag?"

"Is it incredibly presumptuous of me to say yes?"

"On the contrary, it would have been rude if you hadn't."

Her insides might as well have been in a paint mixer. "Great. And what am I doing with Penny?"

"We'll drop her off at home. Uh, my house." A slight flush crept into his cheeks. Interesting. She had never seen him flustered before. Maybe he was a little nervous too. It had probably just been awhile since his last date.

"Perfect. Come on, sweet girl," she called to the dog.

Penny rocketed out from behind the couch, three tennis balls in her mouth.

"Are dogs allowed in the 5k tomorrow?" Jade asked as she packed up the dog's things.

"Can she run that far?"

She scoffed. "She's practically a triathlon competitor. She's definitely in better shape than I am."

"I doubt that," Rett said.

Jade turned to him, and his eyes snapped up from her ass-region to her face-region. He winked and picked up her overnight bag. "Ready?"

She nodded, and they left, locking the door behind them.

———

"Oh, pull over." She craned her neck. A lemonade stand had just come into view.

"Why?" He looked her up and down like he was expecting to find a sniper's red dot.

She gestured out the window at the two children manning the booth. "'Cause dreams."

He obligingly pulled the truck over, and Jade hopped out. She had a special soft spot for child entrepreneurs.

"Hi, guys," she said.

The two kids straightened. "Customers." A boy nudged the little girl next to him. "How can we help you?" he asked in what sounded to be his best customer service voice. Adorable.

"What do you have?"

"We have lemonade, iced tea, and apple cider."

"Ooh. I'll take two apple ciders, please."

"Coming right up. The cups." He nudged the little girl with his elbow.

In seconds, two slightly sticky cups of apple cider were waiting for her on the table.

"How much?"

"Two dollars," the little boy said. He sounded unsure.

She slid a ten across the counter. "Thanks, guys. Have a good night!"

"Your change," the little girl called.

"I don't need it. Thanks."

Rett was waiting for her with a smile. He opened the door and helped her climb in. By some miracle, she didn't slosh apple cider all over the truck.

"Here. Best apple cider in Steuben County," she said when he slid back into the driver's seat.

"Cheers," he said, and they clinked paper cups.

She pulled a face. "Wow, that is...warm."

Rett snorted. "And just slightly alcoholic. Do you think they found it on the side of the road?"

"Definitely. Or maybe the trunk of an abandoned car?" She rolled her window down and dumped the rest out.

Rett did the same, then reached over Penny to put his hand on her thigh.

"What? You look like you have something to say," she said.

"You know how we were talking about wise financial decisions?" A tight smile was on his face like he was suppressing a laugh. His eyes shone in the fading light.

"Listen, they were kids, okay?"

"And you're on the verge of homelessness. Maybe let's try to rein in the spending on backpack cheese and roadside hooch."

She poked him. "I will give up my apartment before I give up backpack cheese."

"Well, at least you have your priorities in order."

She snort laughed, then clapped a hand over her mouth. "Sorry, I think that apple cider might have given me some kind of exotic infection."

"Same. Maybe we should skip the date."

"Don't you dare. Explosive diarrhea be damned. You've made me wait this long. If you don't shiver my timbers tonight, I'm going to tell your parents we're not that serious and I've caught you looking at pictures of twenty-one-year-old actresses on Instagram."

"Did you say shiver your timbers?" Amusement sparkled in his eyes again.

"Yeah. What, you've never heard of pirate foreplay? You naïve vanilla waffle cone."

"Do you always insult people so much during first dates?"

"I could say the same to you. I think you've called me a poor dummy about thirty-seven times since you picked me up."

"You're not a poor dummy," he said defensively.

"Mmhmm," Jade said noncommittally. "So, Vanilla. Tell me what's on the agenda for this date?"

"It's a surprise."

She stared at him. "That's all I get? It's a surprise?"

"Yes."

"Well, am I dressed appropriately? These suede boots are not built for nighttime hiking."

"No nighttime hiking."

"Great. So we've eliminated one of several thousand possibilities. All right, I'm prepared to be wowed."

Jade didn't mind a good surprise. Nate had often pulled them off. It was one of his few redeeming qualities, though in hindsight they were usually just bait for his Instagram. She sat back in her seat and buried a hand in Penny's floof. At least they were almost at Rett's.

"I forgot to tell you," he said. "The winery added a booth at the festival tomorrow, and my usual employees can't run it, so I'll have to take you home after the 5k."

"Are you kidding me right now? You're going to deprive me of my first Finger Lakes fall festival? No way. I'm obviously going to help you with the booth. No arguments," she said with a pointed finger. "It'll be great for our cover story for the town to see two lovebirds running the booth. And I'm sure you can give me a crash course on whatever your mobile POS system looks like."

"You have a point. I'll get you a T-shirt."

"And a bandana for Penny."

"Obviously."

He turned into his driveway and they crawled down the lane. It was shaping up to be a beautiful night. The sky was missing its usual scatter of clouds, and the sun and moon both hung low on the horizon. It was warmer than she had expected.

"Wait for me," he said sternly as he pulled to a stop in

front of his house. "I don't want you to break your ankle in those boots. A trip to the ER is not on the agenda."

"Fine," she said with a smile. In seconds, he had opened her door and helped her down. He lingered a bit on the descent, far slower than he needed to. Her body slid down his, the hem of her skirt sliding up a little.

With her boots on, she was significantly closer to his height. Their lips were just a breath apart.

"Thank you," she said in a whisper.

"You're wel—"

Jade's arm nearly separated from her body as Penny tore off across the front yard. Rett caught her, and she managed to hold on to the leash. Penny came to a halt and looked disapprovingly over her shoulder.

"Are you okay?"

"I'm fine. Told you she can't be trusted off-leash. She's one errant rabbit away from ending up in Newfoundland."

He opened the front door, and Penny dragged Jade inside.

Jade unclipped the leash and took off her shoes before following Penny deeper into the house. The kitchen smelled tantalizingly of vanilla and almond. Maybe they weren't leaving at all? That would certainly make seducing him easier.

She followed the tip-tap of Penny's nails into the kitchen, where a brand-new set of dog bowls waited. Penny lapped loudly. A small tote with toys was next to them.

"I thought you didn't have any pets," Jade said over her shoulder.

"I don't."

"So you just went out and bought dog toys and bowls? We could have just used a cereal bowl."

"I told you, I want her to be comfortable while we're gone."

"About that. She won't destroy anything, but she will almost certainly jump on your furniture while we're gone."

"As she should."

Jade raised her eyebrows. "This couch probably cost more than my apartment."

"And it should be used." He glanced at his watch. "We better get going."

"Okay. Bye, sweet pea." She bent down and pressed a kiss to Penny's furry face.

Penny immediately dove into the toy bin and came up with a tennis ball. She trotted over to the living room and hopped onto the couch, looking very pleased with herself.

Rett fiddled with the remote on the TV for a moment until a YouTube video of birds appeared. Penny sat straight up and tilted her head. He gave her a pat and then turned to Jade.

"Ready?" he asked.

She nodded and started to follow him. She cast a glance over her shoulder at Penny, who was happily sitting on the couch that probably cost $15,000. Her heart skipped a beat.

Rett was generous to a fault, sure. But he had picked up dog toys and equipment for a couple hours' absence. Things were starting to feel a little...not fake.

She was reading too much into it. He was just being nice. This didn't mean he was getting attached, or that feelings were surfacing. And maybe spending time with Penny had made him decide that he wanted to get a dog once Jade was out of his life. Even if Jade wasn't the kind of girl you fell in love with, Penny definitely was.

"You seem quieter than usual," Rett said after they climbed back into the truck.

She had never been good at covering up her emotions. "Oh, I was just disappointed that I didn't find the source of the incredible smell coming from your kitchen."

"Later," he said with a smoldering glance. His hand rested on her thigh, and his pinky brushed the bare skin an inch underneath her skirt.

All worries promptly fell out of her head. Tonight was the night. Finally. All she had to do was make it through whatever incredibly thoughtful and romantic evening Rett had planned, and then she could finally, *finally* experience the full package.

In the past, her one-night stands had always scratched that itch and provided mental clarity, an inner peace, and a readiness to move on. It would be a relief to find the same sensation after being relentlessly teased by Rett for the past week. She was starting to confuse hormones with feelings. Sleeping with him would help realign her priorities. She would be set free.

She inched slightly closer to him, and he smiled as he swung the truck around. His hand slid a centimeter higher.

"There's a little bit of a drive. But it should be a nice night. We'll be up a bit late, though."

"I'm fine with staying up late."

She usually got up before the sun, but one late night wouldn't kill her.

They trundled up the road, and Rett noted points of interest along their route. They passed wineries, breweries, shops, and châteaus. The view was stunning. Sunset was approaching, elongating the shadows of the trees.

Finally, they pulled to a stop along a random road.

"Where are we?" She looked around, but didn't see anything familiar.

"You'll see." He hopped out and came around to her door.

He helped her down in that same infuriatingly slow way, bodies brushing against each other and strength rippling in his forearms.

Screw it. She leaned in and kissed him, pressing every part of her body she could against him. His hands snaked around her waist, and he pulled her in even tighter. Heat formed between them like a geyser had opened up in the inch of earth that separated them.

Their tongues danced, and his grip tightened for a moment. Then he pulled back.

Jade frowned. Her body called out for his in a way she had never experienced. It was equally as spiritual as it was physical. So why the hell did he insist on constantly holding her at arm's length?

"Later," he said with that infuriating grin. His hand found hers, and he tugged her down the road on foot.

She looked to the left and right, lips still throbbing from their kiss. There was nothing around, not even a stray house or mailbox. So where was he taking her?

An iron gate appeared out of nowhere, and Rett led her through it and down a rocky incline. A magnificent stone chapel appeared in front of them.

She stopped in her tracks. He turned to look at her.

"It's beautiful," she whispered. What she would have given for her oil paints and a few more hours of natural light.

"It's the first stop on our Artist Constipation Elimination Date," he said in a low voice.

Jade pulled her phone out of her purse and swung it around, capturing as many pictures as she could. Eventually, she took his hand again and allowed him to pilot her around.

He spoke about the history of the chapel and the family who owned it. They had once been some of the most prolific wine producers in the United States.

A view of the lake over a stone wall nearly stole her breath away. Trees in hues of orange and red crisscrossed the vista.

"Rett."

"Hmm?"

"Stand there." She pointed to an outcropping. "Next to the arch."

"Okay," he said slowly.

"Face the lake," she said.

He obligingly turned around, propping his hands on the low wall and looking out over the lake.

It was almost too perfect.

"Stay. Please."

She took another picture before pulling her sketchbook out and setting to work. Deep shading for the shadows under the stone arches. Bricks of varying age and material. The curve of Rett's deltoids beneath his collared shirt.

"I should have brought your oil paints along," he said.

"Shh."

In minutes, she was done.

"Can you move up there next?" She gestured to a wall that overlooked a curving stone staircase with a wrought iron handrail.

"One more pose. Then you have to come upstairs and see the sunset with me," he said sternly. But he smiled as he stood at the wall, staring off into the distance.

Leaves fell softly to the stone pavement. Rolling hills

dotted with vineyards and dense clumps of trees stood on the opposite shore.

One series of moody pictures and one sketch later, Jade flipped back and forth and looked at her handiwork. It wasn't like anything else she had ever created. But there was something beautiful about these sketches.

"Come on, we're losing the light."

She jumped up the stairs as quickly as she could, and he led her up another set to the top of a bell tower.

"Oh, wow," she said. The lake spread out before them, tinged pink with the dying light.

"Take a picture with me," he said. He pulled out his phone.

"Is this part of the ruse?" She snuggled in under his arm, which he draped over her shoulders. It was warm and comforting. If she closed her eyes, she could almost pretend it was real.

"Maybe. But I also just think it'll be a nice picture."

He snapped a couple selfies, then they turned back to the majesty of the sunset. They stood side by side, hands brushing against each other as they stood on the tower. The sun had almost disappeared, no more than a brilliant speck on the horizon. Deep blues set in all around them, blending with the pinks and oranges of sunset.

His hand brushed hers once more. He had turned to look at her, and there was something different in his eyes. Almost like he was seeing her for the first time. Her heart staggered in her chest again, and she reached over to take his hand. They stood together, fingers intertwined, and watched until the light faded.

CHAPTER THIRTY

RETT

"This is wild," Jade said in the complete darkness.

Rett squinted in her general direction. Although he could hear with unusual accuracy the scraping of forks on plates and water glasses being refilled, he couldn't see a damn thing.

"I hope it helps. Shit."

Clang. Something metallic clattered to the floor.

"Are you throwing your cutlery on the floor? Our poor waiter has enough stuff to do without constantly replacing your knife," she said with a giggle.

Her foot found his under the table. They were at Blackout, a restaurant in a nearby town where visually impaired waitstaff served dinner in the dark.

"Your red, ma'am," someone said in the darkness. *Clunk.* Something heavy and glass landed on the table.

"And your white, sir." There was another clunk. "You'll find them to the right of your plate. I suggest reaching carefully...and I'll bring you another knife."

A few seconds passed, and Jade moaned across the table. "Oh, god, this is good."

At least the deep oblivion of the restaurant made it harder to see the pants tent he was pitching. Stealth boner.

"Of course it's good. It's a Rhodes."

"And how's yours? The chardonnay?"

He raised his glass and inhaled. A good bouquet—oaky, rich. A hint of vanilla.

He took a sip, and the crisp acidity hit his tongue. The darkness had leant an unusual potency to his ability to taste. Hmm. Maybe he should offer wine tastings in the dark.

"Not bad," he admitted. "Not as good as ours, though. And twice the price."

"Are you perpetually worried that you're going to find another winery that outperforms yours?"

"A good vintner is always worried about performance."

"In wine or in the bedroom?"

He choked on a sip of chardonnay and coughed. His nostrils burned. "Both."

The night had finally arrived. With any luck, the date would remind Jade that she deserved so much more than she currently allowed herself to have. And, selfishly, he couldn't wait to uncover the gift he had gotten her.

Snatches of conversations drifted in all around them—someone to their right was about to buy a boat, while another voice whispered about a coworker's secret affair.

Their starter arrived, a palate-tingling mix of spicy, sweet, and savory. He stared into the darkness. Would the food help? If she could reclaim her muse, she could live anywhere. Somewhere with a lower cost of living. Some-where like Hammondsport, even. Not that he wanted her to move here. Did he?

"Did you give any thought to your homework assign-ment?" an unseen Jade asked.

He knew this conversation was coming, and yet he still

wasn't prepared to answer. "I did. I have a lot of half-assed ideas about the business. The only one I've ever brought to fruition was the speakeasy."

"Which is amazing, for the record."

"I like to think so. But as for the big dream...I'm just not sure. My priority right now has to be fixing the winery. I don't have a lot of time for dreaming."

"Dreaming is free," she reminded him. "I find it hard to believe that six-year-old Rett was sitting in first grade being like 'boy, I can't wait to make a nice red blend when I get older' while everyone else was talking about being a doctor or a firefighter."

His fingers tightened around his fork. "There was one other dream."

"Do you feel comfortable sharing it?" she asked after a full thirty-second pause. Her voice was gentle, hesitant. She probably thought he was about to confess to being an aspiring serial killer.

"I haven't told anyone about it. Not since—"

"Twatty McCheaterFace?"

"Right."

Her foot bumped against his under the table. "You know I would never tell anyone. All secrets are strictly protected under the Fake Relationship Clause."

His heart beat uncomfortably fast. "I wanted to be a baker."

Since he couldn't see Jade's face, he had no idea how she reacted to the news. He plunged onward.

"I was really close to going to pastry arts school instead of business school. My parents convinced me not to, so I gave up that dream. But I never gave up baking."

Her voice was soft. "You made those apple dumplings, didn't you?"

"I did. And the ice cream."

"Rett." Something clanged on the table, then she gripped his hand. Her touch was like velvet. "They were incredible. No offense, but this is the opposite of a problem."

"It's not like I can do anything about it. My focus needs to be on the winery."

"Sure, but you're the boss. You could do a special menu with wine and pastry pairings. Baking classes. Hell, just sell some baked goods in a case at your register."

"It's not that easy. That would mean a different license and all kinds of changes."

She squeezed him again. "Respectfully, I'm hearing a lot of excuses. I'm sorry that it's so hard to be good at so many things. But you are in a position to do something about it."

"That's not all, though. Wine has kind of become my new dream. I love it and I wouldn't want to abandon it."

"Okay, so why don't you outsource some of the winery grunt work and focus on the parts you love best? That would give you more time. If you needed the extra money, you could probably sell some of your grandma's crazy furniture."

He tugged at his collar. The thought of publicly offering his baking made him deeply uncomfortable. The wine was one thing—it was proven, practically a chemistry experiment in a bottle. But the baking was his special secret, and his creations were far from perfect.

"We should be talking about you. You're the one in crisis here."

"Yes, thank you for reminding me."

"Are you feeling inspired? Did this help?"

There was a beat of silence. "I was really hoping it would."

Damn.

"Well, there's always tomorrow."

They chatted through their entrees—prime rib and garlic mashed potatoes with apple chutney for Jade, blackened ahi tuna and fall vegetables for him. The fish was tender and smoky with a hint of spice, and the vegetables had a crisp snap. It was delicious, but nothing was about to distract him from the fact that in one hour, he'd be uncorking the first bottle of sparkling wine.

If it was terrible, his financial investment was worthless. He'd either have to try again or give up and sell the equipment. Admit defeat. Find another path forward.

"Hey," Jade said in the darkness.

"Hmm?"

"You can do this." Her hand landed on his, soft and invisible.

He squinted in her direction. Could she see him spiraling? Shouldn't he be reassuring her that everything was going to be fine?

"Your energy is super intense right now," she said gently. "Do you want to go so we can try it?"

"I think so," he admitted. "I'm sorry."

She cleared her throat. "What do you always say to me about unnecessary apologies?"

"This was a necessary one. I didn't mean to make this about me."

"It's fine. Your anxiety makes me feel a little more normal. Let's go."

After some fumbling in the dark, they exited the restaurant and took the road south toward Hammondsport. Jade held his free hand but her worry line was back. Now he had ruined her night with his nerves.

Maybe it had been a mistake to tie the wine to this date.

He should have just tried it by himself. But for some reason, he wanted her to be there.

After a quick stop to let Penny out—thankfully she hadn't eaten the couch—Rett crawled up the driveway to the winery.

He turned the truck off, and they sat outside in silence.

"Do you need a pep talk?" she asked.

He straightened his shoulders. "I'm sure everything's fine."

She turned his face so he had to look at her. "You are a gifted winemaker. Whatever is in that bottle won't change that. And you know what else? Nothing is ever promised. Tomorrow isn't guaranteed. Seize this moment. Pop that cork. Bake your desserts proudly. Have sex with the weird artist from Manhattan."

A startled laugh burst out of him.

He smiled and put his hand on her knee. She took his hand and slid it up her thigh. His pinky slipped back under the hem of her skirt. Heat radiated off her. Suddenly, he wasn't so nervous.

He jumped out of the truck and opened her door for her. When he helped her out this time, he pressed her back against the door of the truck. He stared into her eyes for a moment before leaning in and kissing her deeply.

She opened her mouth and let him in, gripping the sides of his shirt and pulling him in tighter. Her leg drifted upward and he caught it, sliding his hand around to grip her ass. His fingers brushed against lace.

He had never experienced a week like this before. Endless mental and physical foreplay with no release. It was going to be all he could do to not come the second she touched him.

With a deep, shuddering breath, he pulled back.

"Soon," he said breathlessly.

She pouted. "I'm not exaggerating when I say my blue ovaries and I will murder you."

"It'll be worth the wait. I hope."

First, the wine. Then he could concentrate on every beautiful inch of that skin.

They walked hand-in-hand down the brick walkway and into the winery. He unlocked the door and held it open for her to enter, then guided her through the storeroom to the stairs.

They emerged on the roof, and he swiveled to take in her reaction.

Her mouth dropped open. Lights were strung up over a cocktail table set for two. The neck of a bottle stuck out of an ice bucket. And on the other side of the roof, a projector screen was set up in front of a pile of pillows and blankets.

"This is amazing." She bent over to inspect the pile of blankets.

He flushed with pleasure. With any luck, a date like this would help her remember her worth. She desired and deserved love. Any man would be crazy not to sign up for the job.

But the scene wasn't perfect yet. He strode over to the cocktail table and flipped open a Tupperware container. He set a series of small desserts on some plates while he gave her a moment to take it all in.

The unmarked bottle stared back at him, full of promise.

Or maybe failure.

No pressure.

He took a deep breath.

Jade was still inspecting the rooftop as he twisted the cork until it popped. She turned at the sound and came to stand next to him. Her gaze was soft, her demeanor gentle as he poured two glasses.

She took it from him carefully. "No matter what happens, everything is going to be okay. And for what it's worth, I think your grandmother would be incredibly proud of all your efforts."

He squeezed her free hand. "Let's hope so."

She held her glass up. "To you, Everett Ignatius Rhodes. Thank you for everything."

"And to you, Jade—" Shit. What was her middle name? They hadn't covered that yet.

"Alexandria," she prompted.

"Right. And to you, Jade Alexandria Gardner. Thank you for helping me remember that there's more to life than work."

They clinked glasses, then both ducked their heads to inhale the aroma.

"Doesn't smell like vinegar," she said.

"That's comforting."

The bouquet was delicate and fragrant—raspberry, vanilla, and a hint of grilled bread. There was a good number of bubbles, and they were minuscule.

With eyes on each other, they raised their glasses and took a sip. Effervescence rolled over his tongue, bringing with it an acidic sting of green apple and a refreshing finish of lemon.

It was good. Maybe better than good.

Relief flooded him, and he nearly sank to his knees. It hadn't all been for nothing. Maybe it wasn't the best sparkling wine in the world, but it was damn good for a first try.

Would it be enough to turn things around?

CHAPTER THIRTY-ONE

JADE

Lightning rushed down her spine.

"Rett," she said.

"Yeah?"

"It's so good."

He took another sip, then set his glass on the table. He turned back to her with serious eyes. Slowly, a smile spread across his face.

"It's good," he repeated.

"Fuck that. It's amazing." She set her glass on the table and gripped his arms. "I know I'm not a sommelier, but that's a damn good bottle. You did it."

"I did it," he said, looking back at the bottle as if expecting it to disappear.

"And this was your first attempt. Just imagine the possibilities."

"I did it," he repeated.

"You did it."

She jumped into his arms and wrapped her legs around him. He greeted her with a hard kiss, remnants of champagne flavors on his tongue. One hand buried itself in her hair while the other slipped beneath her skirt to hold her up. Her heart thumped erratically. Was it finally time, or was he going to tell her she had to eat dessert first?

She ground against him, eliciting a soft moan. Every part of her body was tense and primed, like she was at the starting line of a sprint.

She unwound her legs and dropped to the ground. His suit coat slid off and puddled on the floor. Her fingers gripped his shirt as she slowly, carefully undid the buttons. She ducked her head and kissed her way down his neck and chest, enjoying the quiver of his muscles beneath her touch. The sting of salt hit her tongue as she teased each ab.

She looked up at him and made steady eye contact as she undid the buckle of his belt. She whipped it to the side like a cowgirl withdrawing a lasso. On her knees, she slowly undid the button and glided the zipper down. His pants fell to his ankles.

Oh, he was a boxer briefs guy. His eyes bored into hers as she released him from the cotton confines. The force of his spring nearly nailed her in the chin.

"Concussion by erection" had not been on her bingo card, but there were worse ways to go.

The earthy scent of sandalwood was all that separated them. He inhaled sharply when she trailed her tongue down his full length, teasing and tasting the velvety flesh. His head fell back, and he gripped her shoulders so hard she suddenly realized what it was like to be the bar in her barre classes back home.

Oh no, he wasn't going to be a head-shover, was he? She knew he was too good to be true.

But he didn't. Ragged breaths tore through him as she took him into her mouth, slowly at first, then faster. She pumped with one hand while raking the other down his exposed torso. He tensed beneath her touch.

This was it. It was finally happening.

But after a minute, he took a step back and separated himself from her.

She looked up at him again, a question in her eyes. The tension that had been building since the first time she saw him unaware in his bedroom was reaching a fever pitch.

He dragged her to her feet and stepped out of his pants. He kicked them across the roof, then took her hand, leading her to the cocktail table. Was he really going to make her sit down and eat dessert?

He hesitated for a split second with his hand on the tablecloth.

"Wait. Don't sacrifice the desserts." She swooped in and moved the glasses and plates out of the way. Throwing it all on the ground would have been mega hot, but there was no sense in wasting a drop of that sparkling wine. She didn't even have time to turn around before he grabbed her by the hips and set her roughly on the table.

The cool night air wicked at the sweat on her neck, and she shivered. With her eyes on him, she slid her sweater up and over her head, then winced when a loop got stuck on her oversized earring. He deftly released her and planted his body against hers, flesh against flesh.

His mouth met hers, still tasting of faint notes of raspberries. Every cell in her body lit up like a neon sign. It was like two elements meeting, fire crashing against water. But instead of extinguishing, the fire burned hotter.

He pulled back, and his eyes raked over her body. She spread her legs, resting a boot on each chair. His eyes were darker, more dangerous than she had seen. Did he like the lingerie?

He slid a hand around her back and released the hooks of her bra. Her breasts tumbled from the cups, and he took her into his mouth. Heat washed over her.

This time there was no cockblocking cop, no nosy neighbor. There was just the two of them and the ceiling of stars twinkling above.

She released a moan and arched her back. His beard tickled her skin as his head dipped lower and lower, savoring each inch of flesh.

This was so much better than a clumsy, tipsy hookup after a sweaty night in a club.

His hands glided up her thighs, and he shoved her skirt higher up her hips. He took a moment to simply look at her, thumbs swirling in half-circles closer and closer to the source of her heat.

She arched her back again, dying for his touch. She was going to go insane waiting for contact.

Finally, he slid the thin layer of lace to the side. He glided a finger over her folds. There would be scorch marks on the table.

Then he ducked his head. His tongue probed her with long, slow licks.

Her heart galloped. She threw her head back and fought for breath. Was she hearing colors? What the hell was happening to her body?

His thumbs spread her apart, and he found her clit like she had hand-drawn him a map. Under the quick flicks of his tongue, her entire body went rigid on the table.

Showers of sparks made their way up and down her body as he licked and sucked. Was this what an exorcism felt like?

Harder and faster he pushed her. A mountain was building beneath her. She might not have even been on the same planet anymore. There was just the two of them and the stars, a different plane of existence.

A finger slipped inside her, and that was enough to break her. She shattered over the peak, her body convulsing and twitching.

He plucked her from the table and gathered her into his arms, which was helpful since there was a zero percent chance that her legs were currently working. He carried her across the roof and set her gently down onto the pile of pillows.

"All good?" he asked breathlessly, kneeling next to her.

She flashed him a weak thumbs-up.

"I'll give you a minute. But only a minute, because this is torture."

He leaned over, and his mouth moved to her neck. She slid a hand down his torso and grabbed ahold of him. Still hard as ever.

He moved down and took a nipple into his mouth, gently clamping down with his teeth. Holy hell. A flicker of pain was followed by pleasure building in her again like a runaway freight train.

Maybe it was the straight week of foreplay. But the connection between them was electric, alive. All-consuming. Had she ever experienced this, even with Nate?

"I don't need a minute," she said.

He disappeared from her side and crossed the roof to his pants. She stared as he rolled a condom on, then stalked back to her.

He hiked her legs up and settled between them. The lace panties slid down her legs and off.

"Are you sure?" he asked in a low voice.

"Please." Ugh, she had never begged for sex. But if she

didn't feel him inside her in the next thirty seconds, she might actually explode and die.

He hovered at her entrance, trailing himself over her. She appreciated foreplay as much as the next girl, but it was go time. She planted her hands on his hips and pulled him toward her.

In a swift movement, he entered.

She gasped. Even though she had never been more turned on in her entire life, her body hadn't been quite prepared for that girth.

There was concern in his eyes, and he froze. "Did I hurt you?"

"No." She gripped his hips and pulled him in deeper, until he was completely buried in her.

They stayed like that for a moment, something indescribable passing between them. For a second, she felt more whole than she had in two years. Fulfilled, cared for. And painfully aroused.

The spell blurred at the edges like a hazy watercolor, and he glided in and out. Pressure was building again. She yanked him down to kiss him, desperate to be as close as possible.

The strength of his thrusts grew until they were inching across the blankets.

Breaths tore from her lips, and her fingers twisted in her hair as he propelled her closer and closer. Her eyes went shut, and his free hand drifted to her cheek.

"Look at me, Jade. I want to see you feel everything."

Her eyes snapped open, and he stared hungrily back at her. That wasn't something you would usually say to a casual hookup or even a friend with benefits. The lines were blurring. Did he feel it too?

There was no time to dissect what was going on in the present moment. All she could do was feel.

She lifted her hips, rocking with him as he thrust deeper and deeper. His thumb slid over her lips, and she clutched at his back. She was probably leaving Catwoman-level scratch marks down his spine as she fought for control.

His hand slid down her torso until he found her center again. His thumb traced circles over her, and everything in her threatened to explode.

"God, you're beautiful."

Her whole body tensed. His did too. With a final thrust, release engulfed her like a detonation. He lowered himself onto his forearms, still buried in her. Her arms fell limply around him as her legs shook like a leaf in a hurricane. She might never recover from this.

Dropping his mouth to hers, he kissed her softly, tenderly, still pulsating inside her. She gripped him for a final time, and he broke apart with a nip to her bottom lip.

He lowered himself to the pillows and lay next to her, tugging her over so she rested on her side. She placed a hand on his chest, and his glided to settle on her hip.

Sex when you actually cared about your partner was different. Worlds different. She had almost forgotten.

"How am I supposed to go back to meaningless hookups now that I know what's waiting for me in the realm of friends with benefits?"

"Well, it's only a five-hour drive," Rett said softly.

Five hours. They might as well have been on opposite sides of the country. Anxiety flared in her chest. Maybe some more sparkling wine would help take her mind off that fact.

She sat up, and he looked at her. "More wine?"

"Definitely. I'll get the dessert."

CHAPTER THIRTY-TWO

JADE

"I still can't get over how good this is," Jade said as she sampled a fresh glass of sparkling wine.

Every part of her body was at peace—except for her mind, maybe.

"It's not bad," Rett conceded. "But it could be better."

She nudged him under the comforter. "You're selling yourself short, Mr. Perfectionist. Are we ready to name the wine?"

He nodded and stared pensively at the sky.

"Did you already have some ideas?"

"A few. None of them felt quite right. For our basic line, we just go with whatever varietal is in the bottle. But for the special batches, we usually go for something vague and serious-sounding. Autumn Splendor Select, Golden Harvest Reserve, that kind of thing."

"Autumn Splendor Select?" Jade asked. "You know that abbreviation spells 'ass,' right?"

Rett stared at her for a moment and seemed to be thinking hard. "Shit."

A smile spread across her face. "It's still better than all

the bird-themed ones I tasted while I was here. If I never again have one more Ruby-Crested Sparkler or Whistling Warbler Chardonnay, it'll be too soon."

"Well, you can see why the name thing is so important. And I left less than a week to figure it out. How irresponsible," he muttered.

Jade snorted. "Sorry. It's just nice to not be the irresponsible one for once." She took a bite out of the remaining mini cheesecake on her plate and flopped back onto the pillows, luxuriating in the caress of the blanket against her bare skin.

"My god, this is so good. It's really annoying that you're so good at everything. Also, you're way overthinking this name thing."

"What do you mean? It's hopefully going to be a permanent part of our offerings. I have to take it seriously."

"The answer is right in front of you." She sat up and jabbed a finger down the driveway where the winery's welcome sign was partially visible.

He turned toward her, brows furrowed. His gaze dipped temporarily to her chest, then corrected to her face. He may have been a businessman and hell of a baker, but he clearly wasn't used to thinking outside the box.

She smiled. "Your wine should be called Valentina. After your grandmother."

He sat up and picked up the bottle, rolled it in his hand. "Valentina," he repeated, like he was trying it on for size.

"It's your homage to her. No offense to Ass Select or Gasoline-Infused Elegance or whatever you wanted to call it, but this wine is called Valentina. I won't be convinced otherwise."

"It's perfect." He sat the bottle down and leaned back into the pillows, ghost of a smile on his face. He rolled over and turned to her, brushed a hair out of her face. "Thank you."

"You're welcome. And I'll take care of the label design."

"I shouldn't have asked you to do that. You have enough on your plate." His grumpy expression was back.

"Consider it an investment," she said and booped him on the nose.

His hand slipped around her back and he gathered her close. It was hard to tell which was more intoxicating—the wine on his lips or the gentle give of his flesh against hers. His fingers skated up her skin, leaving behind a trail of goose bumps.

He leaned in and pressed a tender kiss to her lips.

Her heart staggered as she returned his embrace, pushing her bare torso into his. The sex had been mind-blowing. Probably the best she had ever had. But the post-orgasm clarity she'd banked on had never come. And now she was helping him create a permanent piece of his business.

He insisted everything was fake. Nothing beyond a mutually beneficial friendship. But these tender, post-coital kisses? They didn't feel fake or temporary. And the look in his eyes when she named his wine? There was a flicker of something deeper there. Wasn't there?

Maybe she was doing what she always did—romanticizing and idealizing. Misreading the signals. There was probably a dog hair in his eye. He had said in no uncertain terms that he didn't want a relationship. But didn't he deserve a partnership, even if it wasn't with her? Life was too short to be bitter, scared, and alone. Work wasn't going to take care of him when he was old. The vineyard couldn't take him on memorable trips and build a life with him. Let alone start a family like Margie said he wanted.

She pulled back with half a mind to tell him her thoughts. But something in the burning intensity of those green eyes made her swallow her words.

A fall wind whipped across the rooftop, pebbling her nipples.

Maybe the post-orgasm clarity had never come because she hadn't been in charge. She had been a pillow princess, lying back and allowing him to ravage her. Maybe she just needed one more solid bang.

She closed her eyes and kissed him again, harder this time. His tongue slipped into her mouth, gently probing.

She rolled him onto his back, then climbed on top. Desire was building in her again. Was their insane connection a fluke? Maybe the romantic date and seven straight days of psychological foreplay had clouded her experience. There was only one way to find out. Sweeping her hair to one side, she dipped her head to kiss his neck. She licked and sucked, determined to give him something to remember her by.

"Again?" His eyebrows were raised.

His hands slid up and down her back, eventually clamping on her ass. One slipped around her front to tease her, stroking and fondling. A moan escaped, and she bit her lip. She lowered herself to find him hard between her legs.

"Again." She ground against him, releasing a gasp from between those infuriating lips. For one wildly irresponsible moment, she debated throwing caution to the wind and lowering down, taking him in until he filled every emptiness in her. But that was how people got pregnant.

"You don't happen to have another...?" She rolled her hips against him again.

He moved her over and threw the covers off, sprinting

across the roof. He came back with protection and moved to push her onto her back.

She shook her head. "My turn."

He obediently sank back into the mountain of pillows. She climbed aboard and took him inside her.

They both gasped. They were like two puzzle pieces who had met at long last even though they had been joined barely twenty minutes before. He filled her from within, sending a shower of sparks from her head to her toes.

His skin was damp beneath hers. They locked eyes as she gyrated on top. He was completely at her mercy, powerless beneath her strong and capable body. He bit his bottom lip, and she was nearly undone.

Maybe she should switch to reverse cowgirl. Less chance of feelings that way. But she wanted to see him, study his reactions, watch as she shifted her pressure or gripped him tighter.

He yanked her down on top of him and raised his hips. There was a hunger in his kiss. His fingertips pressed into her hard enough to leave bruises.

But she didn't care. She wanted more—*needed* more.

He moved with her in perfect sync. She pulled back, and their eyes locked.

How was she ever going to come back from this? Her heart stuttered in her chest. She averted her eyes and focused on the irresistible sensation building inside her. They crashed together again and again, harder and faster than the last time. Friction whipped her into a frenzy. Her hands clawed the blankets beneath them.

Finally, they shuddered over the peak together, liquid heat washing over her and sending her body into a quivering mess. She collapsed onto him, a sheen of sweat between them as she pressed her ear to his chest.

His heart thumped beneath her, strong and fast. He wrapped his arms around her, hands tangling in her hair. Shuddering breaths escaped as their heart rates fell.

Eventually, she rolled off him.

He faced her. "You're extraordinary."

Her face grew hot. What was it about Rett that turned her into a blushing schoolgirl? Was it those devastating good looks or the way those fierce green eyes penetrated her right to her core? Maybe it was his open appreciation of her body now that he had finally lifted the temporary sex ban. The way he took in each part of her like she was crafted by a master sculptor.

Or maybe it had just been awhile since he'd gotten laid and he was grateful for whatever scraps she threw to him.

Oh, right. She should probably say something back. "Thanks. You too. I should probably go pee. UTIs and all that."

Was it her imagination, or did he look a little bit sad when she yanked on her sweater and underwear and traipsed down the stairs?

There was no time to worry about that. She padded barefoot over the floorboards and ducked into the bathroom. She splashed water on her face and stared into the mirror. Her face was flushed, but her posture was relaxed. She kind of looked like she had just left a spa day.

The second bang hadn't relieved the encroaching thoughts. Now she was more confused than ever.

The chemistry between them was electric. Undeniable. She had felt it the second she walked into the winery at the bachelorette party. He noticed things, cataloguing likes and preferences and always brought a thoughtful gesture. He listened, cared, was willing to provide solutions when asked. He would be the perfect husband to someone someday.

But she didn't have time to wait around for him to decide he was open to the possibility of love. There was nothing she could do or say to make him fall in love with her. And besides, what if they did end up together? He would always prioritize work. He had basically said it himself. It would never work between them, and she needed to accept that. He needed a responsible, financially savvy partner, not a free-spirited artist with no family who had wasted two years of her life mourning Nate the concussed fucking papaya.

Her only choice was to get through this week with as much of her dignity left as possible. She would repay her debt to him, paint the mural, and go back to the city. That was the only solution. There was no future here. Was there?

She did her business, then headed back up to the rooftop.

The projector was on, and a movie was paused.

"Is this—"

"*Eternal Sunshine of the Spotless Mind*? Maybe," Rett said from the floor.

"That's my favorite movie."

"I know."

"How did you know that?"

"I read an interview you did with *Artist's Weekly* a few years ago. I planned to seduce you during the movie. But apparently I couldn't wait." He held out his arms.

She dropped to her knees and crawled across the blankets to settle on his chest. His hand curled around her waist. Warmth surrounded her like a cocoon.

"Do you always do a deep dive like this on your dates?" She yawned and snuggled in closer.

"No," he said quietly.

What the hell was she supposed to do with that information?

AN EAR-SHATTERING POP SPLIT THE AIR.

Jade leapt out of the tangle of blankets, heart hammering in her chest. A flock of birds took flight, frantically fleeing as the sound echoed off the hills behind them.

The sun had just risen, sending streaks of pink and gold into the sky. Had she not been in the midst of fearing for her life, the view would have been unparalleled.

"What the hell was that? A gun? Are we being attacked?"

She scanned the horizon, but nothing was amiss.

Rett rolled over and cracked one eye open. "Bird cannon."

"A what?" She clasped a hand over her staggering heart. An image of a soldier loading sparrows into a Civil War-era cannon filled her mind.

He sighed and sat up. The blankets fell around his waist, exposing his defined pecs and abs. Desire stirred in her despite the threat of danger.

"A bird cannon. They get shot off at periodic intervals during harvest time. Keeps the birds from eating the grapes."

"Oh." She collapsed back onto the blanket. "Well, now I feel like an idiot."

Rett joined her on the blanket. His eyes were already closed. "Don't. Can't imagine you have many of those in the city."

"Hey." Jade nudged him. "Don't we have to get ready for a 5k?"

He sat up again. "Shit. You're right. And Penny."

"I'll make you breakfast. Come on." She reached down and pulled him up.

"Wait," she said as he bent down to grab his abandoned pants. "Can I just—"

His eyes snapped up to meet hers. "No, you're not taking a picture of me naked on the roof of my business."

"What if I let you put pants on? Please?"

He sighed and turned to her. "Will this help with a painting?"

"Maybe," she said. And if not, it would definitely give her something to remember him by.

"Fine." He rolled his eyes and put his pants on.

"Okay, now just turn halfway towards me. Too far. Just enough to get the sun on those abs."

He raised an eyebrow as he followed her directions.

"Perfect. Now stare out over the land. Remember, this is your kingdom." She lifted her phone and took in as many details as she could. The crisp feel of the air, the glimmer of dew that lay on everything.

Lust engulfed her again. God, he was beautiful. Those thick, dark eyelashes that were always wasted on men. The strength rippling in his triceps as he gripped the railing.

Not now, vagina. There was a 5k to run and a booth to manage.

She captured several pictures from different angles. Hopefully there would be enough to translate this into a painting later.

"Can we go now?"

"Fine, fine."

Leaving the blankets and remnants of dessert behind, Rett grabbed her hand and tugged her down the stairs.

"We'll have to get you a T-shirt," he said, still shirtless. "There's some in the gift shop."

They opened the door to the tasting room, and there was

a scream followed by a crash. Rett leapt in front of Jade, shielding her with his body.

She peered around him. "Elaine?"

"Oh, no. I'm so sorry." Rett bent down and helped the woman up. She looked shaken.

"No, no. *I'm* sorry," she said. "I didn't realize you were here. I just came in early to grab some inventory so the booth was ready for you after the race."

"Thank you so much," he said earnestly. "Oh, I have something for you to take home."

He disappeared into the storeroom, leaving Jade and Elaine staring awkwardly at each other.

"Beautiful morning," Jade said.

"Absolutely. Great day for a festival." Elaine smiled warmly. She glanced at the door to the storeroom, which had swung shut behind Rett. She dropped her voice. "You know, I'm really glad you came here. I haven't seen Rett like this in years."

Heat crept into Jade's cheeks again. Elaine needed to believe this was real. Getting caught was actually probably best-case scenario for the ruse.

"I'm glad too," she said, just as Rett nudged his way back through the door.

"Glad about what?" he asked, carrying another unmarked bottle.

"Nothing," both women said.

"Is that what I think it is?" Elaine peered at the bottle.

"It is. And it's good."

"It's amazing, actually," Jade interjected.

Elaine danced on the spot and flung her arms around Rett. "Oh, Rett. She would be so proud of you. Not just because of this. But because of the man you turned out to be. It's so good to see you moving forward, capturing your dreams. Opening your heart again."

He cleared his throat. "Yes, well. Enjoy the wine. We had better get going."

He strode over to a stand with T-shirts in different sizes and plucked out two matching ones. He tossed one to Jade.

She caught it with one hand. "So nice to see you again, Elaine. Hey, what day are we starting setup for the party?"

"Decorations are coming on Thursday."

"Perfect. I'll be here to help with setup and prep work."

Elaine squeezed her hand.

Rett shook his head. "Come on," he said to Jade.

"Bye," she said over her shoulder.

"You don't need to help with the party," he said as soon as the door shut behind them. "I don't want to interfere with your mural time."

Jade laughed. "Margie kicks me out of the café every day at two. What else am I supposed to do?"

"Study for your driver's test? Find a new place to live? Practice with your paints?" he suggested.

"None of that will help you convince your parents you're seeing someone," she reminded him. "If I clock face time with your employees, friends, and the townspeople, they'll be more likely to have a favorable impression of me. It's not enough for them to know I exist. They should like me."

She paused to gauge his reaction. Did he still feel the same way about their initial plan?

"You have a point," he said as they crossed the parking lot to the truck. "As long as it doesn't interfere with your studies."

"Yes, Father," she said mockingly. "If only they would allow women into the university instead of forcing me into a lifetime of feminine hobbies of needlepoint and embroidery."

"Get in the truck," he ordered, but he was smiling.

CHAPTER THIRTY-THREE

RETT

AN HOUR LATER, THEY ROLLED INTO TOWN WITH PENNY panting happily between them. The town square was decorated top to bottom with pennant banners, booths, and buckets full of vibrant fall flowers. A sign over Shethar Street proudly proclaimed Hammondsport Fall Festival.

Rett couldn't take his eyes off Jade as they walked from the parking lot. Sunshine brought out a copper glint in her hair. Her lips were a distraction, her eyes a labyrinth.

Last night had been amazing. They had come together like they had known each other for eons. She had deftly and methodically lit every cell in his body on fire. It had been worth every painful second of waiting.

Something felt different this morning. They only had a week left to explore each other. And she still had a lot of learning to do before he set her loose. The date had failed to awaken her spark, so they needed to talk more seriously about alternate careers.

Graphic design was the easy choice for her. With a handful of à la carte classes, she would be a master in no time. With a refresher on interview skills and a new resume, she would be unstoppable.

And then there was the fact that graphic design could be done anywhere. She could even stay here, if she wanted. But that would complicate things.

Besides, she wanted to go back to the city. That had always been her plan. It was home for her. So why did the idea of watching her leave put his stomach in knots?

"Do you run often?" Jade asked as they approached the registration booth.

He almost jumped at the question. "Not really. I mostly lift weights."

"So no cardio?" She raised her eyebrows.

"A little boxing here and there. But not much."

Her lips pressed together like she was suppressing a smile. "And you thought you'd just wake up and run three miles with no training or conditioning?" she asked carefully.

His arms crossed over his chest. He was in great shape. He did strength training almost every day. "Sure. How hard can it be?"

"I'm sure you're right," she said.

They walked up to the registration counter and secured their numbers.

"Allow me." He brushed her ponytail out of the way and slid a hand under the back of her T-shirt. In seconds, the number was safety pinned to her back. He finished with a quick kiss on her neck. She smelled like sunshine.

Cindy rushed over with Tom in tow. "I'm so glad you guys are running. How did you convince Rett?"

Jade hugged Cindy. "Believe it or not, it was his idea."

Cindy snorted. "Oh, this should be good."

Why was everyone so convinced he was going to die running three measly miles?

"Are Gemma and Elena coming?" Jade asked.

"Not for the race. Elena's working and Gemma's prepping for a case. But we might see them later."

"Great. Should we get lined up?"

Twenty minutes later, Rett pulled to a stop and bent at the waist. He clutched at his side and took short, shallow breaths. Had he been stabbed on the track and just not noticed? It had only been half a mile. This pain wasn't normal.

"All right, mate?" Tom and the apple-shaped hat he had donned for the occasion bobbed into view.

"Am I dying?" Rett asked Cindy. "It feels like I'm dying."

Penny looked up at him with concern.

"You're not dying," Cindy said. "It's a side stitch. Why did you think you could run three miles with absolutely no training? We're not eighteen anymore. Our bodies don't work like they used to."

"Why don't you guys keep going?" Jade said. "I'll walk with Rett until he feels better."

"I don't need to walk," he insisted. He was about to set off again when Jade hooked his arm.

Cindy nodded. "Sounds good. I'll save you a piece of strawberry rhubarb for the end."

"Cheers," Tom said, and off they went.

"Here." Jade pulled a Gatorade from her belt bag. "Let's pull over for a second."

He left the track and leaned against a tree. "You're not even winded."

She put a hand on his arm. "Cardio's a different beast. Running requires training."

A child who must have been seven or eight ran past them, clutching what looked to be a Game Boy in front of his face.

Rett shook his head and panted. "You think that kid trained extensively for this?"

"Children don't count. They're an exception to most exercise rules."

Penny curled up on one of his feet and looked up at him. He scratched her behind the ears, still bent over.

"Side stitch?" Jade asked gently.

He nodded.

"Take some deep breaths, okay? Which side is it on?"

He pointed to his right side.

"Okay. Raise your left arm." She guided his arm into the air. "Now lean towards the pain."

She pressed on his upper body, and he leaned obediently.

"Great. Deep breaths."

He begrudgingly followed her advice. He was a master of discipline. So why the hell couldn't he run?

He glanced at Jade, who was neither wheezing nor struggling. There was kindness in her eyes, but also a sparkle of amusement.

His phone buzzed, and he glanced at it expecting a teasing text from Tom. Instead, a far worse surprise waited: his brother was coming to the party. And that meant Alexa would surely be joining him.

He straightened, stomach in a hard knot. "Let's go."

He set off at a jog again, and Jade joined him.

"You know," she said gently, "it's probably just dehydration. We polished off that bottle of sparkling last night without a water nightcap. It's a rookie mistake."

Dehydration. Of course. Not the inevitable aging and failing of his body. A mile later, the deep burn in his chest had grown almost unbearable. Ragged breaths tore through him.

He couldn't control his own body, and he couldn't control the winery's flatlining. He couldn't even keep his long-term girlfriend from falling in love with his jackass of a brother. His attempts to help Jade would probably fail too. They only had a week left together. What was it about him that was so innately destined for failure?

His pace quickened. Maybe if he just pushed hard enough, he could outrun everything. The stabbing pain worsened, and he pressed his hand to it.

"Why don't we take a walking break?" Jade asked gently. "Penny would love the sniffing time."

Rett nodded. "For Penny."

Fuck.

Their pace slowed to a walk, and she wound her fingers through his.

"Are you okay?" she asked in a low voice.

"I'm fine."

"Your vibe is super intense for someone who knocked their first attempt at sparkling wine out of the park."

Penny paused her tree-sniffing duties to nose his hand.

He grunted.

"Party stress?"

He nodded. "My brother is coming."

The words were out before he could second-guess them. What was it about her that pried the truth from him?

Jade stood tall. "Your brother the girlfriend-stealer?"

"The only one I have," he muttered.

"Shit." She tugged Penny away from a jogger. "I'm happy to spill wine on him. Or your ex. Or I could propose to you in front of everyone and totally upstage him."

He cracked a smile against his will.

"Why did you invite him?" she asked.

"If I hadn't, my parents would have. I didn't want to rock the boat."

"You don't owe him anything just because you share DNA."

"Maybe not. But if I have a family someday, I don't want family gatherings to be awkward."

She frowned. "You're a better person than me. I would have dumped gasoline on that bridge, tossed a match, and never looked back."

"Weren't you just in your ex-boyfriend's wedding?"

She faltered. "You have a point. Regardless, don't let him steal your joy. This is *your* day. Your triumph. And if he tries to ruin it, I will at minimum fill his pockets with Penny's poop."

He squeezed her hand. Jade was like sunshine—bright, brilliant, nurturing. Even facing his brother and his ex sounded more tolerable with her at his side.

But it was only for another week. Then she would be back in the city, chasing her dreams. The reality of the timeline stirred something in him.

He pulled her roughly to him and pressed his lips to hers. She froze for an instant, then relaxed under his grip. Salt stung his lips. His heart rate, which had slowed down during their walk, ticked back up.

"Yoo-hoo!" someone called.

They broke apart. Jade looked a little dazed, and her cheeks were flushed. She glanced behind them.

"Hi, Margie," she said with a smile.

Margie, decked out in tie-dyed sweatbands and followed by the book club, waved at them.

"I'm glad to see you safe, sweetheart. I was worried when you didn't come home last night."

"Sorry about that. I was—uh—"

"She was with me." Rett winked. "I wouldn't expect to see her tonight either."

"Oh, to be young and in love," Margie said. "You kids have fun. I'll stop by the booth later."

The book club passed by with merry waves.

"Now this is just embarrassing." He gestured down the hill where Mildred power walked in a purple leotard.

"Slow and steady," Jade said. "Come on, let's walk the rest of the way. I don't want to be super sweaty for our shift at the booth."

"If that's what you want," he said, lacing his fingers through hers again.

Together, they set off for the finish line.

CHAPTER THIRTY-FOUR

JADE

Jade held a tray with sample cups as Rett schmoozed with his patrons. Even though he had been panting and dying not half an hour before, he had recovered with ease. His presence was warm and comforting, and it was easy to see how he made each person feel welcome as they approached the booth.

Older women giggled when Rett demanded to see their ID before they could sample the wine. He crouched down when children approached, handing out lollipops and asking about their hobbies. It never felt forced or performative.

Bottles disappeared by the case. Men and women alike listened with rapt attention as Rett explained the wine-making process and difference between varietals. His intense vibe from earlier was gone, replaced by the calm, collected Rett she usually saw. He was in his element, and he was amazing.

Oh, no. Feelings. *Danger! Danger!* She needed to get out before she witnessed something that tipped her over that precipice.

"I'm just going to stretch my legs," she announced.

The sample tray banged onto the table as she rushed away from the scene. When she was a good twenty feet away, she took a deep breath to clear her head.

This was not a time for feelings. Rett had been crystal clear about the terms of their relationship. There was an agreement in place. There was no future here. Falling for him was not an option.

She had no passion for budgeting, no driver's license. She lacked the stamina to hold down an office job. Rett was a workaholic who excelled at everything...except maybe running. He was confident, charismatic, strong, generous. He probably expected a partner who was at least not on the verge of homelessness. They were just too different. It would never work.

She scanned the festival. Booth runners greeted customers like old friends. The smell of pie was everywhere —warm notes of cinnamon and apples, buttery crust, and rich blueberries.

Heart still beating uncomfortably fast, she beelined it in no particular direction and came to a stop in front of a booth with spun glass figurines. Pieces twirled in the light breeze, casting rainbows onto the ground.

She reached out to touch one, then snatched her hand back. She didn't have money for beautiful trinkets. She barely had money to eat.

"Jade?" a female voice called out to her.

She whirled around, probably looking like a still-sweaty madwoman.

Cindy, who had smoothed her hair back into a sleek topknot and changed into a white coat, waved at her from a booth. A banner flapped in the breeze. It read *Braeburn Family Medicine—Free Mole Checks.*

Jade scrambled over.

"Are you okay? You look flustered."

Jade glanced to the right and left, but no one was looking at them.

"I messed up," she admitted.

Cindy turned to the woman in scrubs next to her. She pulled cash out of her purse and handed it over. "Brooke, would you mind running over to Ted's booth and picking up a couple slices of apple cake? I think Tom's going to need it later."

Brooke disappeared into the throng, and Jade stepped closer.

"What's going on?" Cindy's brows drew together.

"You remember the whole fake relationship thing?" Jade asked with a glance at Rett's booth. His eyes were on her.

"It's hard to forget," Cindy said.

"Well, it's still fake for Rett. But I think I'm having feelings."

Cindy took a step back and sat on a pub chair. She took a long sip from a metal water bottle, looking almost amused. "You mean spending time with a handsome and thoughtful eligible bachelor and pretending to be in love led to feelings? Who could have predicted this?"

Jade shot her a dirty look. "You're not helping."

"I'm sorry." The water bottle hit the table with a clunk. "This is what I was worried about. I don't want to see you get hurt. Either of you. Rett's been out of touch with his emotions for so long, I don't think he knows how they work anymore."

Jade leaned against the booth. "I'm so stupid. I know myself. I fall in love easily—way too easily." She relayed the mixed CD and guitar-playing incidents.

Cindy cringed.

"I can't be trusted. That's why I've been keeping everyone at a distance for over two years. One-night stands, meaningless flings. There was no danger of getting attached. It was the only way to keep myself safe. But I fucked up. I let Rett in. And the worst part about it is he's been so clear with the terms from the very beginning. It's all fake. To him."

"I don't mean to interrupt this realization for you," Cindy said slowly. "But there's some guy behind you staring you down."

Jade whirled around. If there was a creeper trying to get in on their conversation, she was going to set them straight. But what she saw stopped her in her tracks.

"Nate?" Her lips stumbled over the word.

What. The. Fuck.

There he was. The ex-boyfriend who had cheated on her and lied about it for who knew how long. Cheating with Ashley was painful enough, but how many others had there been?

He slunk up to her, clad in aviators and a pink Vineyard Vines polo.

She crossed her arms over her chest. What the *hell* was he doing here?

"Hey," he said in a low voice. "Can we talk?"

Her mouth fell open, but nothing came out.

Cindy cleared her throat, and Jade found her voice.

"No."

"Come on. I just want to apologize. I know I did a shitty thing."

"A shitty thing?" A bitter laugh escaped her lips. "Are you kidding me right now?" She punctuated the sentence with a pointed finger. "My parents' bodies were barely in the ground, and you were screwing my best friend behind my back. And then you had the audacity to lie about it to my face and pretend like nothing happened between you two. How many other girls were there, Nate?"

"None. I promise," he said. He took his sunglasses off and slid them into the neck of his polo. He reached for her hand, and she slapped it away.

"Your promises mean nothing."

"I'm sorry, Jade. The guilt's been eating me alive. Ashley too. We had a huge fight. We should never have been together. I know what I've done to you. Done to your life. You were this amazing, gifted painter. And look where you ended up." He gestured at the fall festival. "Some Podunk-ass town surrounded by nobodies. This isn't where you belong."

She reeled like he had slapped her. Her hands curled into fists. She was going to drown him in this Podunk-ass lake. Someone put a hand on her arm and she whirled around. Cindy. She shook her off.

Cindy sighed, and a first aid kit hit the booth with a *thwack*.

"Why the fuck are you here?" Jade said to Nate.

"I told you, I want to apologize."

"No, you don't." A realization shattered over her like a glass window in a hailstorm. "You're here because you're jealous. You saw me with Rett and couldn't handle the idea of me preferring someone else to pining over your shitty memory. I only have value to you when another man is interested."

Her voice was basically at shouting level, but she couldn't stop herself.

"And I'm sorry, but where's your wife? The girl that you fell so madly in love with that you 'had no choice' but to crush my heart and leave me in an apartment I couldn't afford by myself?"

"We never should have gotten married. I never should have left you. I had what I wanted, I was just too blind to see it."

"You're despicable. You always want what you can't have. The second you nailed Ashley down, you got bored and slept with someone else. And you will keep doing the same thing because it's all you've ever known. I'm not an idiot."

"Come on, Jade," he said in a softer voice. "I know you don't love him. I know you've been going from guy to guy, chasing after what we had. But you haven't found it. Because you're meant to be with me."

He tugged down the neck of his polo, where a matching ice skate tattoo lurked beneath his collarbone.

She was numb. She was going to carve this tattoo out of her body like a cancerous tumor. Forget laser removal.

"You don't know *anything* about me."

He took a step closer. "I know you're a city girl. You need the lights, the action. You're not going to find your muse here. When we were together, you painted something new every day. *I* was your muse. Can't you see that? I can give it back to you, Jade. Let me help. Let me take you home."

What the hell was this? Some kind of ego trip? Was he getting off on the idea of being her inspiration? Maybe that was part of his problem with Ashley. She was poised to become a brilliant doctor in addition to a shitty friend. Ashley didn't *need* him. Nate had always had a deep desire to be needed.

But he wasn't Jade's problem anymore either. And she sure as hell didn't need him.

He reached for her again, but a large shadow moved in front of her.

"Jade doesn't want you here. It's time for you to leave."

Even with moderate sweat stains and baggy athletic

shorts, Everett Rhodes was a commanding presence. There was danger in his voice. A thrill ran through her.

Jade peeked around him in time to see Nate take stock. Did he just stand up a little straighter to try to close the distance between their heights? Pathetic.

At some point, Margie, the book club, and a large number of people she recognized from the café had crowded around. Margie came to stand beside her with a protective hand on her shoulder. Ethel had produced a pair of knitting needles and was holding them menacingly in Nate's direction.

Was an *Anchorman*-style rumble about to go down at this picturesque fall festival?

"Why don't you make me?" Nate lunged toward Rett but stopped before making contact.

Rett didn't flinch, though he did curl one hand into a fist.

Jade gripped Rett's arm. "Don't take the bait. He will sue you."

Scooter the cop sauntered into view. "What seems to be the trouble here?"

"This is a public event. I'm allowed to be here."

The entitlement in Nate's voice would have been detectable from the opposite shore of the twenty-mile-long lake.

Scooter looked at Rett, who shook his head.

"No, you're not," Scooter said. "Now I suggest you leave the premises. Unless you'd rather leave in handcuffs."

"This is discrimination," Nate announced to the crowd. "You're all witnesses."

"The last time I checked, 'Douchebag Status' was not a protected class in the state of New York."

That was Gemma, who had come to stand next to Cindy.

Nate tried to juke around Rett, but he blocked him.

"Jade," he said, barely visible peeking over Rett's shoulder. "I know you don't want this—whatever this is—with this guy, or with the others. I know it's not serious. You want a relationship. You want love. And you had that with me. You could have it again. We could have a future together. You need me."

Jade's fingers clenched tightly. "And you think I'm going to find what I'm looking for with you, a cheating fuckboy with less remorse than your average serial killer?"

"Come on," Nate called. "You know we belong together. You're not like other girls, Jade. You're different—alive, colorful, wild. We would be unstoppable together. Come with me. Let's go home." He extended a hand toward her.

Rett's shoulders tensed.

It would take fifteen spiral-bound notebooks to unpack all the insanity in his last comment.

"Let's get something straight here." Jade stepped out from behind Rett and drew herself up to her full height.

"First of all, I'm *exactly* like other girls. Women are powerful, beautiful, wonderful beings who have had to deal with toxic men like you pitting us against each other for our entire lives." She took a step closer to him, filled with a deep rage.

"You use people. You chew them up and spit them out when they don't serve you anymore, or when the interest fades away. Even Ashley, who's about to be a whole-ass doctor. Nothing and no one will ever be enough for you. I realize that now."

She took another step. Rett's hand landed on her shoulder, and she dropped her pointy rage finger.

"Even if I've forgotten it at some point in the past two years, I am smart. I'm capable. I'm worthy of love, of partnership. But I don't want any of those things with you. And

I definitely don't *need* you. Now get the fuck out of my town before I shatter a wine bottle over your over-inflated head."

"She's threatening me. You all heard it," Nate said to the crowd.

"Anyone hear Jade say something?" Scooter asked.

Ted from the bakery shook his head. "Not a word. You might need to get your hearing checked, son."

Others in the crowd shook their heads too.

"I didn't hear anything," Elena said, pushing her way into the circle. She must have finished up her shift at the hospital.

Nate took a step back, eyes darting from one side of the crowd to the other. "She doesn't love you," he said, one shaking finger pointed to Rett. "You'll see."

Scooter pulled his baton from his utility belt.

Nate eyed it up and took a step back, then another, before he dove through the crowd and beelined for the lake.

"And stay out!" Scooter called after him.

The crowd dispersed. Rett stared off in the direction that Nate left as if to make sure the scoundrel never returned.

Margie came up to Jade and clasped her cheeks in both hands. "You all right, sweet pea?"

Jade nodded. The adrenaline was starting to wear off. And she had just aired her dirty laundry to the entire town.

"I can't believe he had the nerve to show up here," she muttered.

"Well, you'd be a hard one to let go," Margie said with a pointed glance at Rett. He didn't seem to notice as he was still scanning the crowd.

"Speaking of which," she continued, "did I hear you call this place 'your town'? Does that mean you're thinking about staying?"

Rett stopped his scanning and turned around. Their eyes locked.

Jade hesitated. If she was being honest with herself, she had seen a glimmer of a different life here, full of possibility.

It would be insane to uproot her entire life and move to a tiny town five hours away. She couldn't give up the only home she had ever known to chase some belief that there was magic and promise in this glacier-carved lake. Hammondsport didn't have Michelin-star restaurants or world-renowned art museums. There was no Broadway, no subway, no real public transportation to speak of.

And yet, it could be beautiful. The entire town had just rallied around her when her evil ex-boyfriend rolled into town. They knew her name, greeted her on the street. There could be a yard for Penny. Backpack cheese and wine. Real friends. A book club. She could leave the anonymity of the city behind and become a part of something that was technically smaller, but bigger and richer in so many important ways. A place where she truly belonged.

And of course, Hammondsport had Rett. But what if he didn't want her to stay? Or if she did stay, but he didn't want to be with her? Could she live in the same town as him and watch as he fell in love with someone else?

Their agreement was always meant to be temporary. But the last few days hadn't felt temporary. They felt like a calling.

Shit. She should probably say something.

Jade deflated. "I don't know. Nothing is set in stone."

"Well," Margie said with a sad smile. "The guest house is yours for as long as you want it. I'd love to have you long-term. We always have room for another server at the café if you need to start over."

"Thank you, Margie." Jade squeezed her hand.

Margie was so similar to her mom. Truly kind, generous to a fault. Willing to bend over backward for someone in need, even if they were just the random artist behind their favorite muffin painting. She was remarkable.

Rett slid a hand around her waist and pulled her in. She leaned her head on his shoulder. The confrontation had taken a lot out of her.

"I have an idea," he announced.

"Hmm?" she asked.

"Why don't we pack up early?" He turned to the crowd of friends around them. Damian and Tom had appeared out of nowhere. "I'll get the grill out. We can do a cookout at my place like we used to."

Jade straightened up. Had Mr. Workaholic just suggested closing up shop early?

Cindy's eyes sparkled. "Absolutely. We'll get the meat."

"I've got buns and condiments," Damian chimed in.

Elena bit her lip. "I should really get back to my abuela."

"Bring her," Rett said. "I've got a whole case of that pinot she likes."

"Sold. I'll bring my abuela and some street corn salad." Elena set off like she was on a mission.

Tom came up to Rett and grabbed him by the face. He kissed him full on the mouth before announcing, "We're slapping the bag tonight, mate."

"No way," Rett said with a chuckle.

"Yes, we are," Tom said. "Relax, I'll put it in the esky." He pointed at the cooler. "I'm not an animal."

"So what do we bring?" Jade said to Rett as Tom disappeared in the direction of home.

"Sides," he said.

"You're not worried about getting back to the winery?"

He shook his head. "I think the crew can handle it. Most

of the foot traffic is down here anyway. Don't make me second-guess it."

"No, no," she said hurriedly. "Let's go."

They packed the remainder of the wine into the truck. Silence fell as they buckled their seatbelts. How would she even begin to unpack what had just happened?

"I'm sorry about the Nate thing," she said.

Maybe that was what had temporarily rendered him speechless.

He narrowed his eyes. "You're apologizing again."

Shit.

"Right—uh, never mind. Events transpired today, and I won't apologize for them because they weren't my fault."

"Exactly. It's not like you asked him to come."

She considered the ripples on the water as they rounded the tip of the lake. "I would have sooner invited my Great-Aunt Mildred who was notorious for turning a day trip into a month-long stay."

Rett smiled. "As annoying as it was to see your ex-boyfriend today, I was really glad to hear some of the things you said to him."

"What do you mean? I mostly just threatened him with violence."

"You said you were worthy of love and partnership. That's what I wanted for you to remember."

"Well, you've ruined one-night stands for me. Now I want a relationship again. Do you know how much harder that's going to make my life?"

"It's what you deserve," he said quietly.

"A difficult life?" She raised an eyebrow.

"No. Love."

Her heart staggered in her chest. He wasn't saying what she thought he was saying. Was he?

CHAPTER THIRTY-FIVE

JADE

"Damn it, Penny!" Jade called after the dog.

Penny zoomed away, hotdog waggling from one corner of her mouth.

Rett turned away from the grill. "It's fine. We have plenty more."

He was wearing a Kiss the Cook apron, which Tom seemed to have taken as an open-ended invitation.

Jade raised an eyebrow. "You say that now, but when she has catastrophic gas later you're going to change your tune."

She took the platter and moved it to the picnic table where it would hopefully be out of reach.

"Sorry we're late," Elena called. She and an older woman appeared around the side of the house. "Abuela insisted on defrosting some arepas."

She dropped a Ziplock bag on the table and helped her grandmother sit in the lounger Rett had parked at the head of the table.

Jade rushed over with a pitcher of iced tea and a fresh glass.

"Jade, this is my grandmother, Antonia."

Jade shook her hand. "Hola, Antonia. Soy Jade."

Antonia smiled. "Encantada!"

Tom leapt out of his Adirondack chair. A bag of wine was slung around his shoulders like a travel pillow. "Antonia!" He removed the bag and held it high. "Slap the bag. Er—what was it again, Cindy?"

Cindy joined him and drew Elena's grandmother into a tight hug. "Golpea la bolsa."

Antonia giggled and opened her mouth. Tom stood next to her and opened the spigot. She gulped for a few seconds, then reached over and slapped the bag. Everyone cheered. Tom set the bladder of probably lukewarm wine on the picnic table in front of her and bowed.

"So how does this work?" Jade asked.

"Antonia is now the keeper of the bag. She decides who drinks next."

Oof. Jade definitely should have packed some Tums. She topped off Antonia's glass of iced tea and hustled back to the grill before she could be named the next victim.

"I didn't know you spoke Spanish," Rett said. He opened the lid of the grill and carefully inspected the burger patties inside before flipping them.

Jade took the spatula from him. "I am a woman of many mysteries."

And by mysteries, she meant she had leaned heavily on language learning apps during her two-year artistry hiatus.

"I'll clean these and bring them back," she said. "Will you make sure Penny doesn't steal anything else?"

"Of course." He leaned down and pressed a gentle kiss to her lips. Her heart staggered, and a stupid smile spread over her face.

Shit. Feelings. She needed to think of his negatives.

What were they again? Emotionally unavailable. Workaholic. Family baggage.

It wasn't helping.

Should she talk to Rett about it? But what if he shut her down and made things awkward and she lost the last week she was meant to have with him?

She scurried away in the hopes of leaving the thoughts behind. She couldn't be falling in love with him. They had barely known each other more than a week.

Get it together, Jade. She was doing the same shit she always did, falling head over heels for someone she barely knew. Though he hadn't explicitly said it, Rett could very well be hung up on his ex. He hadn't made any effort to find love again after the breakup. He wasn't willing to open his heart.

No matter what her idiot brain was telling her, she didn't have a place here. She needed to focus on her career and the mural. She washed and dried the spatula, then cast a glance around his massive house. Maybe she'd stumble upon a deal-breaker.

A painting caught her eye. She strode over to the hallway between the living room and the stairs to the basement. The last time she was here, she swore this spot on the wall had been occupied by a generic piece of Hobby Lobby art. Now, however, her painting of Penny frolicking in the vineyard hung in its place.

Fuck.

What did it mean that he had chosen to display it?

It would force him to think about Jade and Penny every time he walked by. Did he want that? Maybe he was good at dissociating and would be able to think of it objectively. Just a cute dog in a vineyard. Nothing painful or meaningful attached to it.

Uproarious laughter trickled in from outside, and she jumped. There was no need to figure out the emotional significance of a breakthrough painting hanging in Rett's house right now. She needed to get the damn spatula outside before the burgers transformed into charcoal.

She hustled onto the patio to see Rett kneeling in the grass next to Antonia. She held the bag at shoulder height and laughed as liquid dribbled into his mouth. He rose to his feet with a triumphant fist pump and slapped the bag. Antonia clapped her hands delightedly when he took it from her.

He turned, still holding the bag. His eyes zeroed in on Jade. He pointed at her.

"No way." She held her hands up in front of her like she was reasoning with a madman. "I'm wielding the spatula."

Chugging bottom-shelf wine was a surefire way to spend all of Sunday stranded in bed.

"Come on." His eyebrows waggled. "I have ibuprofen."

She smiled. "Fine."

She set the spatula down, then lifted her head. Rett opened the spout.

"Chug, chug, chug," everyone chanted behind her.

A very warm chardonnay washed down her throat. It tasted like undergrad. Her shoulders hunched up, and she did a full-body shudder. He finally closed the tap, and she wiped her mouth on her T-shirt. There was definitely some chardonnay in her bra. Between that and the 5k and the shouting match with Nate, she desperately needed a shower. Maybe she could convince Rett to follow her in when everyone left.

Rett raised his eyebrows.

"Oh, right." She slapped the bag, and everyone cheered.

"As the keeper of the bag, I'm giving it a mandatory ten-minute rest in the freezer. Lukewarm white wine is a crime against humanity."

"She's right," Rett added.

Everyone else grumbled but didn't argue when she disappeared through the back door. She plopped the bag in the freezer before coming back out.

"Let's eat," Rett announced, setting platters on the picnic table.

Everyone gathered around. Jade carefully assembled a burger on one of Antonia's arepas, and it was basically a flavor explosion in her mouth. Her head swam pleasantly from the crappy wine.

Next to her, Rett stood up. He lifted his glass. Oh, shit. Aside from a handful of picnics at Flushing Meadows Park, she didn't have a lot of experience at barbecues. Did toasts normally happen?

"I just wanted to say a couple of things while everyone was here," he began. "I know I haven't been incredibly present over the last couple of years. It's probably been what, two years since we last had a cookout?"

Gemma nodded.

"Right. I really buried myself in work when my grandmother passed. Taking over the winery felt like an impossible, all-encompassing task. But I think I'm starting to see the other side." He glanced down at Jade with a smile, and a thrill ran through her.

"I appreciate all of you for sticking with me. I don't know that I deserve it, but I'm really grateful for all your friendships."

"You're right, mate. You don't deserve us," Tom announced. Cindy smacked him. "But we love you anyway," he added.

"To us." Rett raised his glass.

"To us," they all parroted.

"And to Jade because she's the one who reminded you there's more to life than work," Elena announced loudly.

Jade smiled, and the others toasted to her.

As they ate, conversation ebbed and flowed like the current of the lake behind them.

"So then," Cindy said in the middle of a lengthy soliloquy, "Rett was never one to turn down a dare, right?"

Gemma nodded enthusiastically.

Rett planted a hand over his face. "Do we have to tell this story in front of Antonia?"

"Yes." Cindy patted the bag of wine, of which she had recently become the keeper. "So when Tony Bianchi dared him to strip naked and run down Market Street at four in the morning, he just ripped all his clothes off and took off. Until he got cocky, turned to look over his shoulder, and ran headlong into a parked police car."

"And that is the story of how my mom had to fly back from Hollywood and attend several fundraising events for the local police force in order to save my juvenile criminal record," Rett said. "She still talks about it."

"Gemma," Cindy said with a strong, pointed finger. "Slap the bag."

"Ugh, fine." Her gaze drifted in the direction of Damian, who had driven his boat over shortly after everyone arrived.

He took a long sip of the pinot noir Rett had brought out and raised his eyes over the rim of the glass. Gemma went pink and turned away from him. These two were clearly destined to marry each other—or kill each other.

Once dinner was over, Jade and Rett cleared the plates and piled them in the dishwasher.

"So you're a streaker?" She shot a look back over her shoulder at him as she tossed dishes in.

"I'm afraid I've had to retire my public birthday suit."

"That's too bad. I could really use another rooftop rendezvous."

"It doesn't count as public nudity if it's on your own property. Probably," he said with a puzzled expression.

She smiled. She was really going to miss this place.

He looked over her shoulder. "You're quite possibly the worst dishwasher loader I have ever encountered."

Jade spluttered. "What do you mean? All the dishes are in there."

It wasn't like she had thrown them in a flat pile.

"Sure, but there's no system. You have dinner plates next to dessert plates. Salad forks in the same compartment as dinner forks."

"What does it matter if they all get clean?"

Rett leaned over and started rearranging. "It makes the unloading process less efficient."

"I'm starting to realize why you're still single. Pick your battles, buttface."

"Did you just call me buttface?"

"I'm sorry, where are my manners? Should I have called you His Royal Highness, Prince of Correct Dishwasher Loading? Keeper of Pristine Wine Goblets? Micromanager of Cleanliness? The Third?"

He straightened up and grabbed her around the hips. She squealed but couldn't get away. He pressed her against the refrigerator and kissed her. The stainless steel was cool on her back. As caked in sweat and dried bottom-shelf chardonnay as she was, her body ached for Rett.

He pulled away, and they looked at each other. Heat bounced between them, reverberating like a nuclear reactor. The connection between them was more than physical. It was astral, spiritual. A communion of souls. In short, she was screwed.

She slipped out from under his arms and darted for the door. "We should really get back to your guests."

The sun had dipped low on the horizon. Shadows stretched across the patio.

Everyone had relocated to the firepit. Penny was sitting in Damian's lap, panting directly into his face. The bag of wine now sat on the table next to him. Tom loaded logs into the firepit while performing some sort of elaborate dance.

Rett squeezed her hand, and they took a seat.

Cindy straightened and came to sit in the chair next to Jade. She leaned in close. "We never got to finish our conversation from earlier. Did you want to take a walk?"

"That would be great." Jade stood. "Rett, will you watch Penny, please? We'll be right back."

He accepted, and she and Cindy walked toward the driveway.

"So," Cindy said the second they were hidden by the side of the house. "You accidentally caught feelings."

"I can't help it," Jade insisted. "It's this stupid, beautiful town. You tell me how I'm supposed to avoid getting attached to someone when this is the background of our fake relationship."

She pointed behind them, where the golden rays of the setting sun caressed the lake. It might as well have been a postcard.

"So what now? Did you tell him?" Cindy asked.

Jade threw her hands up. "Of course I didn't tell him. He doesn't want this."

"How do you know he doesn't want this if you haven't talked to him about it?"

"He said it himself. He doesn't have time for a relation-ship. He's so fixated on work—"

"For the record," Cindy interrupted, "I have never seen him take this much time off of work. Ever."

"He probably just can't resist a damsel in distress. And I am the most distressed," Jade said quietly. "Every part of my life is up in the air right now. Do I move to the Bronx? Do I find a new career? How am I going to finish this mural?"

"Easy. Move to Hammondsport, be my office manager, paint some airplanes and wine bottles on the wall. Boom, done."

Jade looked at her. "You've seen how badly I have mismanaged my own life. I would burn your clinic to the ground."

Cindy grunted noncommittally. "I still think you should move here. No matter what, you'd have us."

"And what if Rett falls in love with someone else and I'm right back to square one? Broken-hearted and completely unable to paint again?"

Cindy shook her head. "You didn't lose your ability to paint because of that twenty-four-karat dildo. You lost it because you had two horrible traumas back-to-back. A man does not control your ability to create. You just have to get out of your own way."

Jade paused. Cindy had a point. While Rett had been the subject of her first breakthrough sketch, it hadn't been because Jade was in love with him. Maybe time had finally started to heal the wounds. But even so, she didn't have time to dawdle and see if her dabbling would turn back into the art that had made her semi-famous.

"Besides," Cindy said, "don't people say that the greatest art comes from a place of suffering? I would bet anything there's a whole MOMA exhibit barely dammed up in there." She poked Jade in the chest.

Jade heaved a sigh. "I don't know what to do. I wish my mom was here. She always had the best advice."

"I think she'd want you to be brave. Take him on a date. Talk to him. Then you can figure out everything else."

"Fine," Jade muttered.

Thirty minutes later, they strolled back to a dark house. Everyone was gone but Tom and Rett.

They looked up like they had been caught stealing something.

"What's going on, boys?" Cindy asked.

"Nothing," they said simultaneously.

"Sure. Come on, get the esky," Cindy said. "We need to get home and let Branson out."

She leaned over and hugged Jade. When she pulled back, Jade's heart was full. This is what she had been missing for so long—friendship. And Cindy had given it to her willingly, openly, even though she knew her time here was temporary.

Tom hugged Jade too, then they left.

Jade collapsed onto Rett's lap and slung her arm over his shoulders. Penny settled at their feet.

His expression was still cloudy. "You were gone for a while. Is everything okay?"

"Yeah, we were just chatting. I'm taking you on a date tomorrow."

He seemed to debate for a moment "After closing."

"Fine. Now how about a shower?"

Rett stood up, Jade clasped in his arms. "Thank god. I've never felt so disgusting in my life."

"And you drank warm chardonnay from a bag."

He looked up at the sky as if expecting to see a disapproving celestial grandmother above him. "Don't remind me."

CHAPTER THIRTY-SIX

RETT

"Thanks for visiting Rhodes Vineyard." Rett waved as a customer left with a case of wine.

He buffed the countertop with a cloth and glanced into the tasting room. Elaine was serving a pinot to a table of six. Jade sat with Penny in the corner of the room. She was frowning at something on the new laptop, glass of red virtually untouched next to it. Hopefully she was studying for her learner's permit.

Penny lifted her hand and nosed Jade, who snapped to attention. She secured the leash on Penny and led her outside with a wink at Rett. Jade lifted her face to the sun and stretched like she was drinking it in. She was a master of soaking in a moment.

Tom's words from the day before filtered back in. While the girls were taking a walk, Tom had confronted him about why exactly he was letting Jade leave.

His heart faltered. She was supposed to leave on Sunday. One week left. There would be no more dates, no more mind-blowing sex, no more elaborate attempts to thwart her painter's block.

More than anything, he would miss her companionship. As chaotic as she could be, her presence was like a glass of champagne for his soul. She was kind, beautiful, optimistic, sexy as hell. The city didn't deserve her, damn it. She couldn't leave. Hammondsport was her home. He could feel it in his bones.

But how was he supposed to convince her? She had been hell-bent on going back to the city, and it had taken a lot of convincing for her to stay the two weeks before the party. And what if she went back and met someone else? He wouldn't stand for it.

"What's wrong? It kind of looks like you're trying to buff your way to the floor."

Rett jumped and dropped his cloth. Unbeknownst to him, Jade and Penny had snuck back in. She studied his face, frowning.

"Nothing. Just thinking about the party," he lied.

"But you're still committing to drinks and dinner tonight," she said with a look. It wasn't a question.

"Yes. As soon as we're closed." He crossed his heart. The end-of-day could wait till the morning.

"Good." She leaned across the counter and kissed him before retreating back to her table.

The tasting group dispersed and filtered into the gift shop, a welcome distraction.

He needed to see if her feelings had changed. Communication and truth-telling had been one of the rules of their agreement, after all. There was no sense in pretending like their fake relationship wasn't starting to feel real.

Two weeks wasn't enough time. He wanted—needed—more. He resolved to talk to her about it and went back to work.

"WHERE ARE WE GOING?" RETT FROWNED. JADE WAS BEING very cagey and was giving him directions. They were headed east, in the direction of Seneca Lake.

"So grumpy." She poked him in the cheek. "You'll find out when we get there." With a smile, she went back to staring out the window.

Hammondsport was at its most spectacular. The fall foliage was at its peak. Explosions of red and yellow dotted the hills. The air was cool and crisp.

"Fine. But you *will* answer traffic questions on the way. Tuesday will be here before you know it."

"Do your worst."

The truck crawled to a stop. "What does a double yellow line on the road mean?"

"No passing in either lane."

"Good. Can we make a U-turn at this red light?"

"I think it's fine as long as there isn't a sign prohibiting it? And we're in the leftmost lane?"

Rett nodded. "I'm taking you for your first drive when you get your permit."

In the interest of not acquiring traffic tickets she couldn't afford, they had decided to table driving lessons until her permit was in hand.

"I'm sure you'll be too busy with party preparations. Besides, Margie already offered."

He looked at her. "Margie has more fender benders than anyone in the tristate area. She's not qualified to teach someone to drive a bumper car."

Jade snorted. "Sorry. I mean—I'm not sorry," she said when she saw the look he shot her.

He nodded and continued driving. Finally, they arrived

at their destination. Solera Taphouse, a hole-in-the-wall with the best cocktails and food this side of the lake. He had stopped going sometime after the breakup with Alexa. It was bad enough having his friends and family grilling him about his feelings, let alone his favorite barkeep.

"I haven't been here in forever," he said softly.

"Cindy said it used to be your favorite." Jade hopped out of the truck, and he hesitated. Did Charlie still work here? Would he remember him?

It was exactly the same as he had left it. Scrappy, clean, and with the intoxicating scent of caramelized onions drifting out.

They ducked inside the building to find a charming, rustic atmosphere. Roughly hewn boards lined the walls and floors, and a handsome bar stretched the full length of the room. A tap menu was handwritten in chalk.

"Well as I live and breathe." The gentleman behind the bar, a thirty-something in a flannel shirt and baseball cap, put a hand to his chest. "Is that Everett Rhodes darkening my doorstep?"

"Hey, Charlie." Rett pulled out a barstool and gestured for Jade to sit.

She climbed up and perused the menu.

"It's good to see you again. Where have you been?"

"Busy with the vineyard," Rett replied. "How are you? How about the locals?"

"Oh, just fine. Hey, do you remember that time that guy came in with a crossbow strapped to his back?"

"Of course." Rett leaned forward intently.

"He came back. Now he has a crossbow-wielding wife and baby."

"No." Rett slapped the bar. Good for him.

"I swear on my deceased Aunt Norma. May she rest in

peace. Anyway, when are you going to introduce me to your lady friend?"

"This is Jade," Rett said with a note of pride in his voice.

His anxiety had evaporated. It felt so good to be back in the warm little bar. A spicy note of buffalo chicken dip mingled with the sharp scent of whiskey a stranger nursed two stools down. And Jade had planned it all for him. He was supposed to be showing her what he loved about the Finger Lakes. Instead, she had cared enough to resurrect an old favorite that he had all but forgotten. And it felt like home. *She* felt like home.

"You are the most beautiful creature to have walked in here today," Charlie said to Jade. "Except maybe for the dachshund I saw earlier."

"Oh, well, in that there's no contest," Jade said with a smile.

"What can I get you folks? The usual?"

Rett nodded. Of course Charlie remembered. He had a memory like a steel trap.

"And for you, ma'am?"

"I'll have the special," Jade said.

"Spicy bourbon pumpkin smash? Nice choice. It's made with local pumpkin."

"There's nothing I love more than a local pumpkin."

Charlie left to make their drinks, and Jade leaned over.

"So what's your usual?" There was a sparkle of amusement in her eyes.

"An old-fashioned."

"You are such an old man."

He glowered, but reached over to stroke her knee under the bar. Pink crept into her cheeks.

"I'm a man of simple pleasures. I have another question for you."

"No more traffic questions. I'm ready."

He cleared his throat. "If your house was on fire and you could only take three things with you, what would they be?"

She pressed her lips together. "Penny, obviously. There's a photo album of my parents and me from when I was growing up. And I have a special set of brushes that my mom got me for my high school graduation."

"Not that beautiful painting of the zoo?"

She shook her head. "I would still have the memory. What about you?"

Shit. He hadn't been expecting a reciprocal question. Alexa had never asked many.

"To be honest, I'm not sure. Probably my fireproof safe. It has my passport and deed to the house in it."

"That's cheating. Too many objects."

"Fine. I have a Playbill from the first Broadway musical I ever saw my mom in. It was *Chicago*. She was incredible."

She smiled and leaned closer to him.

"And I have a notebook with handwritten notes on wine-making from my grandmother. That would definitely need to be saved. And then there's the painting hanging in the downstairs hallway."

"Which one?"

"Your painting of Penny in the vineyard, of course."

He hadn't been able to help himself. When he had collected the slew of paintings she attempted after their tasting, the one with Penny had called to him. She had captured everything so effortlessly. It would have a permanent place on his wall as long as she didn't ask for it back.

She smiled. "I don't remember giving you permission to steal it."

"I will trade you one case of rosé for it. It's already on the wall."

"Two cases," she countered. "Do you know what my paintings used to be worth?"

"Not as much as they should be," he said smoothly.

Drinks landed in front of them, and Jade brandished her credit card before Rett had the opportunity to.

"Ha," she said triumphantly as Charlie ran it through their POS system.

"Two cases," Rett agreed.

She took a sip of her drink. "Charlie, this is so good."

"I'm telling ya, it's the local pumpkins."

Bourbon washed over his tongue as he took a sip of the old-fashioned in front of him. It was perfect, as always.

"Any tingles?" Rett asked as Charlie walked away. He needed to talk to her about their relationship. This would be the ideal place to do it—away from the prying eyes of the book club—but something kept holding him back.

"Nah. It's damn good, though." She set it on a coaster and turned to him. She slid her hand into his. "Thank you."

"For what?"

"You have really, profoundly changed my life. I will forever be grateful for the day that Blake Chan grievously offended you."

Rett smiled. He had almost forgotten their first meeting.

"I know I told you this before, but I felt something the day we came here. I thought maybe it was just the change of scenery, the promise of closing a painful chapter in my life. But is it crazy to think that maybe I was *meant* to come here? My mom always talked about taking a trip to the Finger Lakes. She had a whole dream board and everything. She loved wine and would occasionally spring for a good bottle. We were supposed to go as a graduation gift. Not here," she said, waving a hand toward the parking lot. "But Seneca. It was one of the reasons why I felt I had to see it. Let me show you a picture."

She pulled her phone out and navigated to a picture—she and her parents crowded around a table. There was a sumptuous-looking cake with "21" written in candles, and a bottle of wine that looked strangely familiar.

He frowned and ducked his head closer to the screen. Could it be? He pinched his fingers and zoomed in before sitting up triumphantly. Even though the bottle was partially turned away from the camera, the label was undeniable.

"That's one of my bottles."

"What?" Jade leaned in. "Holy shit." The look on her face suggested she had just had a major revelation. Hopefully one that resulted in her staying in town.

"Your mom really did have good taste," he said with a nudge. "And by the way, I don't think it's crazy. I feel the same pull. It's one of the reasons why I've never left for more than a few months. It's home."

"Home," she echoed. Her voice was soft.

There it was. The perfect segue. Now all he had to do was—

"We should go." She jumped up from her seat and tossed the rest of her drink back.

He blinked in surprise. "Oh. Okay."

"We still have to go to the store. Come on." She tugged him back to the car.

When they emerged from the superstore an hour later, they were laden with bags of groceries—which Rett had insisted on paying for—and some mood-setting décor. Tapered candles, cloth napkins.

"I don't want to hear any moping if your dessert doesn't

turn out. There was no reason to choose such a complicated dish," Jade said as he pointed the truck toward home.

They had decided to tag team dinner—she would make the entrée, and he would make the dessert. It was going to give him a chance to try out that Baked Alaska recipe from the *New York Times*.

He straightened up and looked at her. "Baked Alaska is not that complicated."

She shot him a dirty look. "Going forward, let's assume that anything that you have to set on fire counts as complicated. And did we really need to make the ice cream and the cake from scratch? We'll be at this all night."

"That's the plan," he said, and his hand slipped between her thighs. "It seems like we might have some downtime," he said quietly. "You know, while dinner's in the oven and the cake is cooling."

"Indeed," she said.

His fingers slid higher, brushing gently over the lace fabric of her underwear. "There are a couple of really special bottles in the wine cellar I'd love to sample."

Jade raised her eyebrows. "Another private wine tasting? Last time, I almost ripped the clothes from your body and mounted you on the bar. Are you sure you want to risk that? I can't think of a reason we would need to practice fake bar-humping."

"Maybe there doesn't need to be a reason. We could just see where the evening takes us."

At some point in the preparations, he would find the time to talk to her about staying. He had to.

CHAPTER THIRTY-SEVEN

JADE

WHEN RETT CAME UPSTAIRS WITH A BOTTLE OF WINE, cooking was already underway. Ground beef and onions were sizzling in a frying pan. Minced garlic was waiting on a cutting board. And Jade stood in the midst of it all, naked except for the apron she had borrowed from Rett. Well, and the pair of four-inch stilettos she had snuck into her purse.

He stopped in his tracks.

"Good evening," she said smoothly before turning around to separate the beef.

In a second, he was behind her. His hands slid around her hips.

She turned around and brandished the spatula. "Not yet," she said firmly.

"What? Why?" His hands hadn't moved.

"Remember the evening of torture you had in store for me before you'd finally consent to touching my body?"

"I don't think a thoughtful date and careful wooing count as torture."

"It. Was. Torture." She punctuated each word with a

poke in his chest. "And now it's your turn to wait. Go make your ice cream."

He frowned at her but reluctantly withdrew his hands. "For the record, I do not approve."

"Remind me to play the world's smallest violin for you." She turned back to her beef. Ha. It served him right.

There was something so freeing about moving around the kitchen, fall air blowing in from the sliding door she had cracked open. Rett's long glances as he whisked eggs and carefully measured sugar. The scrape of fabric against her bare nipples. As long as she managed to not burn them on the frying pan, the evening was looking good.

Rett baked like a scientist. She half-expected him to pull out some beakers and goggles. He crouched down at eye level to measure liquids, carefully spooned and leveled his dry ingredients.

Jade, on the other hand, measured with her heart. How much of a difference could there be between four and six cloves of garlic?

"Excuse me," she said, brushing past him to open the freezer door. With heels on, she was only a couple of inches shorter than him. When she retrieved a bag of frozen vegetables, he grabbed her hand and pulled her roughly to him, then pressed her against the refrigerator.

The frigid stainless steel pressing into her spine elicited a shiver. He did not relent, opting instead to lean in and kiss her, trapping her against the fridge with his hips. Her lips parted, and he plundered her mouth with a fury.

Heat welled deep inside her, and she couldn't stop herself from reaching for him. The bag of vegetables fell to the floor. Screw dinner.

His hands were back too, palms skating along the curve of her ass and coming up to skim the side of her breast. A thumb rolled over her nipple and was nearly enough to bring her to her knees.

Her desire to make him suffer was quickly being outstripped by her desire to let the shepherd's pie go to hell and have her way with him right there against the refrigerator.

"Sorry," he said, breaking away and releasing her. "Just needed to get the heavy cream."

"Did you find it behind my tonsils?" Even though he had moved away, her hands were curled into claws and the rest of her body was on high alert.

"No." He opened the fridge door and peered inside. "There it is."

He went back to measuring like nothing had happened. The *audacity*.

She took a beat, then bent down to retrieve the vegetables. Thankfully the bag hadn't exploded. Although chasing down all the bits of carrots and peas while on her knees would have made a nice show for Rett, she really was starting to get hungry.

She shot a glance at him out of the corner of her eye as she dumped the vegetables into the skillet. His eyes were on her, and he was smirking. She made steady eye contact and tugged the apron to the middle so that her breasts were significantly more exposed.

His eyes darkened. She triumphantly went back to stirring the contents of the skillet. That would teach him to try to seduce her. She was in charge tonight, damn it. No matter what her vagina was trying to tell her.

"Excuse me," Rett echoed. "Just need to get something out of this cabinet."

In a second, he had come to a knee and planted himself

between her legs. His hands guided her knees apart as she stood at the stove.

A retort was on her tongue. But then he touched her. First with his fingers, gently trailing between her folds. Softly teasing, gently caressing.

Her toes curled in her stilettos. The spatula clattered into the spoon rest. She was completely at his mercy.

When his fingers were replaced by a tongue, her knees buckled. She barely had time to move the pan off the burner before the first orgasm rocked her from head to toe. When she could breathe again, she pulled his face toward her until he was looking at her.

Those big green eyes, like a glimpse into a meadow she desperately wanted to paint. Something ancient and powerful unfurled deep within her like a coiled snake.

She dragged him over to the couch and threw him back onto the pillows. Slowly, deliberately, she released the tie on the apron until it fell to the floor.

His eyes raked over her body, and he reached for her. She climbed over his muscular thighs and straddled his hips. She tipped his chin up so he had to look at her.

Eternity shone back at her through those eyes. In an instant, she could see their future. A beautiful fall wedding at the vineyard. Penny chasing a gaggle of giggling dark-haired children across the front lawn.

Her own studio on the village green next door to Margie's Café. Weekly dinner with Cindy and Tom. Morning runs and steamy afternoons with Rett. Gray-haired and knobble-knuckled, rocking together on the back porch overlooking the lake. It would be beautiful. She could feel it in her bones. Maybe she could pretend that this was all within her grasp. Just for tonight.

He pulled her roughly toward him until her lips banged against his, rough and desperate.

Her hands glided to his shirt collar, then his buttons. One by one they slipped away, revealing a hint of chest hair and his chiseled physique. Her hands traced his chest, determined to memorize every curve, every follicle.

No matter what happened between them, she would remember this for the rest of her life.

His shirt fell to his side, and her mouth moved to his neck. She ground against him, and his hands came around to her back. They caressed her bare skin, drawing a full-body shiver from deep within her.

They pulled back to look at each other for a moment. His eyes spoke volumes. Like, a full set of encyclopedias. But what were they saying? He was looking at her in a way he never had. A way that *no one* ever had.

Oh, hell. She was so screwed.

Determined to ignore the danger that was looking more and more inevitable, she closed her eyes and dove back in, more forceful this time. Their breaths met each other between parted lips. She ripped his belt off and his hips lifted. Pants hit the floor.

He moved to get up, but she pushed him back onto the couch. His boxers went next, sliding over his knees to join the jeans around his ankles. With her eyes on him, she lifted her pelvis and teased herself over him, running his head over her entrance. Her hand slipped between them and closed over him. After a couple of long strokes, she guided him to her and lowered herself down.

A deep sigh burst forth from Rett's lips. She raised and lowered experimentally, marveling at how he filled her every emptiness. Her muscles twitched and expanded to accommodate him.

Slowly, she rocked.

His hands fell limply to his sides. She shifted forward, and he kissed her breasts tenderly.

Her head arched back as her body screamed with sensation. She slid her knees closer together and hovered again, raising and lowering, thighs burning with the effort.

His hands cupped her, supported her as she moved—slow at first, then faster.

She glided up and down, tension radiating inside her. He leaned forward to meet her, pressing his lips against her breastbone.

They were both getting close. His fingertips pressed into her, his breath in ragged gasps.

Their eyes locked again. She wanted to look away, but she couldn't. They watched each other experience every sensation. Every thrust. Pleasure and desperation were in his eyes.

Finally, they exploded together like a cork releasing from a bottle. Rett fell back onto the couch and pulled her down with him.

Still joined, she rested on his chest. She fought to catch her breath as he twitched inside her.

She stayed there, in a cocoon of heat and arms, until their heart rates dropped. He stroked her hair and kissed her behind the ear. Goose bumps sprouted on her skin.

She turned to him, memorizing every inch of his face—the strong jaw beneath a trimmed beard, the vibrant green eyes, the slope of his nose and strength of his eyebrows.

She recognized this feeling. Love. It had been conspicuously absent from her life since Nate had shattered her heart into a thousand pieces. But here it was, all but sewn to her chest.

Fuck. Despite all her careful preparation, she was so

screwed. Danger pulsated in the half-light around them. She might as well have been a freight train on an unstoppable path to heartbreak. There was no turning back. The brake lines had been cut. A head-on collision was coming.

Just as despair was setting in, lightning bolts shot up and down her arms and legs. She stared at them, half-expecting to see scorch marks. What the hell was happening? Her body hummed like she was made out of a trillion pieces of star dust. Something inside her awakened, soared. She itched for her paint set, but she wasn't about to interrupt what could be her last date with Rett. Especially if she accidentally blurted something out and ruined everything.

Seriously, muse? It chose *now* to come back, when she was on the brink of heartache again? Was it really back, or was it just the ghost of the sensation reminding her of everything she had lost?

"Holy fucking shit." Her head popped up, and in a second she had leapt off him.

"What?" His sleepy joy had been replaced with borderline panic.

"You didn't wear a condom." She stared down at herself, half-expecting to see a baby bump sprouting.

That had always been a hard boundary for her. She hadn't even allowed Nate through the pearly gates without a raincoat.

"Oh, shit. I didn't even think—I'm sorry. Fuck. But you're on birth control?"

"Sure, I have an IUD, but there is no way I'm leaving the next twenty years of my future up to one not completely foolproof birth control method. Put some clothes on. We're going back to Target."

Rett grabbed her arm. "Are you sure? The odds of a successful pregnancy have to be incredibly low."

"Are you kidding me? Look at you. Your sperm probably have drill bits for heads and the power to manifest an egg straight out of my ovaries."

"I just meant I know emergency contraception can be hard on your body. You know if something happened, I would always take care of you. And the baby."

His hand drifted to her abdomen.

"Are you insane? You want to try to figure out co-parenting when we live five hours away from each other? I'm sorry," she said before he could say anything. "But if we leave this up to chance, I will fixate on it. I've never let anyone do that. Ever."

"Not even the asshole?"

She shook her head.

His eyes were soft again, and he reached for her. She pulled back. Why was he willing to tie himself to her for the next two decades?

She had always been a bit of a free spirit, as evidenced by her current financial situation. But contraception was never something she had taken lightly. So why had she just thrown caution to the wind? At no point had the idea even occurred to her. She could only focus on the warmth of his breath on her cheek, the sensation of him inside her.

Her heart stuttered in her chest. She was so stupid. Falling in love with some random guy in the Finger Lakes. What was she thinking?

Her gaze fell back on him. But the problem was, he wasn't just some guy. He was kind, careful, whip-smart. So handsome that it almost hurt to look at him. And they had less than a week left together. Unless he wanted her to stay too. Her mom's voice echoed in her mind. Tomorrow was never guaranteed. She needed to woman up and talk to him about it. After the great birth control crisis was resolved.

He cleared his throat and started buttoning his shirt. "I'm sorry for putting you at risk," he said softly. "Let's go."

CHAPTER THIRTY-EIGHT

JADE

Two hours later, Jade and Rett were flat on their backs on the rug in the basement, discarded plates with remnants of shepherd's pie on the side table behind them. A fire crackled, warming their toes.

Jade was tucked into the crook of Rett's arm. Target had been closed, but emergency birth control had been secured from a vending machine at a local college, and so far hadn't resulted in any painful symptoms.

"I'm sorry if I freaked you out after the incident." Rett's deep voice rumbled in his chest.

She lifted her head. "It's fine. It was kind of you to consider the effect the Plan B might have on my body."

"It's stupid," he said. "But even as guarded as I've been with my heart, I've always wanted to be a dad."

She propped her head in her hand and looked at him. "And you thought a great place to start your brood might be with your fake girlfriend who's only here for another week?"

His entire body tensed up. There was a hesitancy in his eyes. After a pause that felt like a millennium, he spoke. "What if I don't want just one more week?"

Holy shit.

She sat up. "What do you mean? You want me to come back for the holidays?"

"No. Well, yes, but—" He stopped and seemed to search for the right words. "Don't tell me you can't feel this." He grabbed her hand and put it on his chest. His heart was galloping.

Was he really saying what she thought he was saying?

"I don't want to drive you away, but I need you to know the truth." His hand closed over hers, and she shivered. "This isn't fake anymore. At least not for me," he said. "I want you to stay, Jade. I know we've only known each other for a week, and it's insane to ask you to move away from the only home you've ever known. But I'm not ready to say goodbye. The thought of you going back to the city and meeting someone else..."

He looked down at her hand for a moment and rubbed her fingers. "I think I would lose my fucking mind. We could really have something incredible if we give ourselves enough time to explore it. It's okay if you don't feel the same way. I just needed you to know."

The mental images she had been desperately driving out of her memory returned. Weekly dinners with Tom and Cindy. Christmas morning at Margie's. Penny living her best life on a boat. Rett coming up behind her to slide his arms around her swollen belly while an unseen foot tapped her from the inside.

She looked at him, and she saw forever. Home. A sensation that had been completely foreign to her since the day that officer had knocked on her door.

"I want to stay." The words were out before she could take them back. It was exhilarating, vindicating, terrifying. Like she had just confessed to a murder.

Rett smiled, and joy shone out from those infuriating eyes.

"You want to stay?" he asked.

"Yes. There's a lot to figure out—"

He silenced her with a tender kiss. Unlike their feral lovemaking earlier, this time he held her like she was made of glass.

"We'll worry about that later," he said when he pulled away. "For now, this is enough."

"This is enough," she repeated. The overwhelming weight of terror was being replaced by something else. The air was full of possibility.

Her heart was galloping. But she barely noticed. Her body was buzzing from head to toe like she had been dipped in a vat of liquid gold laced with Novocain. She was alive, flowers in every color bursting forth from her skin.

She gripped his hands.

"Rett."

"Yes?" He looked concerned.

"I need to paint."

"Come with me."

He led her to a room she hadn't yet visited on the far side of the house. It must have been his home gym at one point. Some dumbbells and weights were piled in one corner of the room, but in front of the window were two easels, a massive pile of canvases, and a workbench littered with all the different paints and tools of creation he had acquired.

"How did you—"

"I wanted to have something put together just in case. Do you think it's back?"

Her eyes fell on his, but her fingers itched to touch paint. "I think it is."

She threw herself on him and kissed him hard. He held onto her a beat longer after she pulled back.

For a second, they just looked at each other. She had so much to be grateful for. So much to thank this grumpy, practical, winemaking sex god for. Coming to the stupid, ill-fated wedding had completely changed the trajectory of her life.

Now she just needed to see if she still had it in her.

"Thank you," she said.

"Go." He pointed at the canvas.

Jade considered the tools in front of her. She grabbed the easiest thing—acrylic paint—and placed dots on a palette. There was no plan in her head, no blossoming internal picture. Instead, she trusted her intuition and picked up a brush.

Brushstrokes skimmed across the page. Red, then yellow, then orange. The colors of Hammondsport blossomed on the canvas. In the midst of it all was the stone chapel, standing sentry on the hill.

Visions poured out of her, guiding her hands. She wasn't in charge anymore as they glided over the surface, adding a brick here, a falling leaf there. A blue sky with a bright sun, tinges of green still lingering on some trees.

She barely glanced at it before running across the room and propping it against the wall.

Rett appeared silently beside her with a series of water glasses. She could have kissed him, but there wasn't time. She dunked her brushes and picked up a new palette. More green in this one, with pops of turquoise and yellow.

Before she knew what she was doing, she had rendered Margie's Café in miniature. It joined the chapel against the wall. Next came Cindy and Tom's house with a manicured lawn and fiery maple tree.

Her hand cramped, and she flexed her fingers while

staring at her creations. The story of the past week was spreading out in front of her. But she wasn't done.

She closed her eyes and conjured up an image of Rhodes Vineyard. A deep sense of calm filled her, and she went back to the paints. Lush green vines. Rough-cut stone, a stamped-concrete patio. Two people in the front window —Elaine and Todd. The cars of her new friends in the parking lot.

Next was an abstract painting, a tipped-over wine bottle bleeding words written in glitter. A rumpled satin bridesmaid dress on the floor.

A couple hiding under a tablecloth, sawing away at prime rib, upended bottles of champagne scattered between them. The same couple under a spotlight on a dance floor, staring longingly into each other's eyes.

The familiarity sent shivers down her spine, and she pivoted. A cocktail table under a starry sky, corner of a pile of blankets just visible in the background. Her tiny cottage on the water. The sun on Margie's face. A couple sitting on the hood of Rett's slightly beat-up truck.

Painting after painting escaped her fingertips. Watercolor, acrylic, mixed media. She was the Taylor Swift of art, internalizing her unique experiences and turning them into something beautiful.

She ran out to the lake shore at one point and gathered rocks. She hot glued them to the canvas and painted a dreamy blue lake in the background.

Even Steven the elusive raccoon scored his own portrait. As she considered the next canvas, she closed her eyes and envisioned Rett. His mischievous smile when he was about to deliver a thoughtful gift. Those emerald green eyes looking up at her in disbelief as he looked over her financials.

Shockwaves coursed up and down her arms. Portrait after portrait joined the ones on the floor—Rett in the speakeasy, on the balcony at the chapel, driving with one hand while the other rested on her knee.

Even intimate moments bloomed onto the canvases— the two of them under the stars on a tangle of white blankets. Pressed together in a mirrored lake, a breath apart.

Eventually, a sunbeam startled her out of her trance. She blinked at the sudden light. Holy hell. She had painted all night long. Everything that had been trapped inside her for the last two years had come bursting out. Her brush landed in a clean cup—somehow, they kept appearing all night.

She glanced behind her. Rett was curled up on the floor, fast asleep. Materials spread out around him—paper plates for makeshift palettes, a stack of clean glasses. Her heart almost split in two.

He had given her everything, believed in her even at her most fragile and reprehensible. No matter what she had felt about herself over the past two years, Rett, it seemed, had believed in her implicitly. Why else would he have had a stack of thirty canvases waiting in his gym?

She took a step back and looked at her creations. The walls were lined with imprints of her trip. The people and places who had made such an impact on her in such a short time.

And sprinkled amongst those memories were ones that went farther back. Ones she had been unwilling or unable to confront since Nate had left her. Many were autobiographical, some were just depictions of feelings. There was a woman sitting on the floor with her head in her hands, surrounded by darkness. Red words crackled out of the inky black around her. Failure. Orphan. Bankrupt. Decay.

One was a scene from her childhood that she had all but

forgotten. It had come to her as if in a dream. She had snuck out of her bedroom on Christmas Eve when she was supposed to be sleeping to look for Santa. Instead she had found her parents, sitting close together on their outdated plaid couch, glasses of wine in hand while a cozy fire crackled in the hearth in front of them. A Christmas tree strung with multicolored lights sparkled in the corner of the room, and a row of handmade stockings hung above the fire.

There was just one depiction of what was supposed to be her apartment with Nate in New York. A gleaming kitchen with a single dilapidated cardboard box. The word Future was written on it in Sharpie. It was on its side with a pair of ice skates spilling out. A burning dollar was barely visible floating outside the window.

While getting over him was part of her breakthrough, Nate didn't deserve any of her energy. And maybe he never had.

Jade closed her eyes and reached her fingertips up to the ceiling. She took in a series of deep, almost sensual breaths. Her body still tingled, but it had slowed to an ebb. There was a weariness in her bones like she had just run a marathon.

She looked behind her again at the sleeping form of Rett. There was still some fear in her heart. A hesitancy. She was opening herself up to getting hurt again. But Rett was worth the risk. And something deep inside her told her that no matter what happened, this time the muse was here to stay. No man and no tragedy would ever take it from her again.

The paintings stared back at her. Would they sell? A couple resembled her old work—loud, exciting, sometimes confusing depictions. But most were memories, landscapes, deeply personal and meaningful flickers of time. And some she already knew were going to be gifts. Margie needed the painting of the café. Margie—oh, shit. She needed to get to work.

She crossed the room to Rett and dropped to her knees. She hesitated, one hand outstretched. He had done so much for her. Her unseen assistant, he had freshened her rinse cups all night long. She shouldn't wake him. It wasn't that far from his house to town. She could walk it.

But as the thought crossed her mind, his eye cracked open.

"Hey." He yawned.

"Hey," she echoed with a smile. She brushed some hair out of his eyes.

"You painted."

"I did. A lot. I actually ran out of canvas. But don't worry, I did stop myself before I moved on to your wall."

He smiled. "You could have painted my wall. It'd give me something to look at while I'm doing my squats."

"Well, maybe during another visit. Thank you so much, for everything. The supplies, for helping me through my breakthrough. But most of all for believing in me."

"Of course I did. I believed in you from the moment I met you. Well, maybe the second moment I met you."

She smiled again. "That's fair. I am so sorry to ask you this. But I have to get to the café. I think I'm finally ready to do the mural and my bike isn't here. Do you think you could—"

"Of course." He popped off the floor before she could finish her sentence. "Give me ten minutes to shower and make a coffee and I'll get you there."

"I'll make the coffee," she said.

He leaned in for a gentle kiss and disappeared. Her heart thudded in her chest as she watched him walk away.

Her muse was back. The proof was spread all around her. Would the gallery take them? There was only one way to find out. She pulled out her phone and typed a hasty email with a few pictures attached. She pressed send before she could change her mind and bustled into the kitchen. There was coffee to make, a mural to paint, and a move to plan.

It was a brand-new day.

CHAPTER THIRTY-NINE

JADE

"Oh, honey," a voice behind her said.

Jade jumped like a bomb had gone off. Her paintbrush clattered to the floor, which she had thankfully covered in a drop cloth earlier.

"It's stunning." Margie put a hand on her arm. "I knew you could do it."

"Well, it's not finished yet," Jade said, surveying the scene in front of her. There were still at minimum two days of work ahead of her on the mural—layering, detail work, final adjustments. But her success in painting hadn't been limited to the small scale of canvas.

In front of her, a massive mural splayed over the café wall. A quaint scene played out—harvest festival banners hung from the trees. Gingham tablecloths covered the picnic tables at the lakeside park, strands of Edison bulbs shone against the magnificent sunset that settled over the crooked lake.

The library towered above the scene. Townspeople were sprinkled over the sidewalks and village green. There was Ted the baker, muffin in hand. Margie was closing up the café, partially obscuring the sunflower on her door. She looked over her shoulder and smiled at someone—David, her deceased husband, who Jade had rendered from the memory of the picture in Margie's glovebox.

Cindy and Tom walked toward the lake, bag of wine barely visible slung over Tom's shoulder. Gemma descended the steps of the courthouse, yammering into a cell phone, while Elena waved down the block, stooped grandmother at her side.

And there, crowded together on the dock, were Jade, Rett, and Penny. A little piece of them would live on forever, even if it was just in the acrylic world she had created.

"I think it's just about perfect. We're closing up, honey. Why don't you get cleaned up and I'll give you a ride home?"

Jade blinked wearily. The day was catching up with her. "Speaking of home. You know how you offered me the guest house? In case I decided to stay?"

A small smile appeared on Margie's face. "Mmhmm."

"We'll have to talk about rent. I was thinking starting in January?"

Margie laughed delightedly and pulled her in for a hug. "You decided to stay?"

Jade nodded. "Rett and I talked about it. We want to see where things go. And I love it here." She gestured to the mural. "It's home."

Home. The reality was setting in. This wasn't just some bachelorette jaunt to the Finger Lakes anymore. She had finally found the place where she belonged.

Margie wiped a tear away and took a step back. "Well, I'm honored to be your new neighbor. We'll talk about rent later."

Jade smiled. "Let me just rinse these brushes and get everything covered up and I'll get out of your hair."

She ran a hand over her eyes. They burned, and rubbing them was like sandpaper. Her phone beeped, and she glanced at it.

Rett: How did it go?

Her heart warmed. He had remembered to check on her at closing time even though he was probably in the middle of doing setup for the party. She glanced behind her at Margie, who had turned back to the mural with her hand pressed to her lips. Her eyes were glued to the tiny David.

Jade: Good. I think anyway. How is setup going?

Rett: Only seven or eight disasters so far. Do we really need unbroken glassware? People can just drink straight out of the bottle, right?

Jade grimaced. It was time to make good on her promise to help with the party. She would just steal a cup—or gallon—of coffee and head over to the vineyard. But first she had to pick up Penny the furry menace and her study materials for her learner's permit.

After an exhausting hour towing Penny in a bike trailer, she rolled to a stop at the rack outside Rhodes Vineyard. Covered in sweat and legs burning, she secured the bike and looped Penny's leash around her wrist.

Boom.

The bird cannon went off, and Penny panicked.

Jade cried out as Penny bolted for the nearest cover—the bed of Rett's truck.

"Penny! Knock it off!" She didn't have the energy to wrangle the startled retriever. But Penny, who had not biked six miles of hills, was more than equipped to drag her mom across the parking lot.

She leapt into the back of Rett's truck and crouched down, quivering.

"What's going on?" Rett called.

Jade turned. He was walking toward them, sleeves of his button-down rolled up to expose his forearms. Even though she was delirious from lack of sleep and probably looked like she had just crawled out of a swimming pool, something in her stirred at the sight of him. Not even just lust. Full-on, heart-staggering love.

Rett, on the other hand, looked none the worse for wear. How was it possible that he looked like he had just wandered off the set of a photoshoot for *Vintner Monthly*?

"I thought maybe you could use some help. Apparently Penny had other plans." She gestured to the dog, who was still hiding in the truck bed.

He pulled something out of his pocket and waggled it in Penny's direction. She approached cautiously, like she expected the treat to explode. Finally, after two more Milk Bones, she jumped down.

"Let's get her inside before the cannon goes off again," he said with a glance at his watch.

He slung an arm over Jade's shoulder and pulled her in for a kiss.

"I'm so proud of you. I went home and looked at your paintings over lunch. They're incredible."

Her cheeks grew hot. "They still need some touch-ups.

But it was nice to finally feel it again. Maybe everything's not lost."

"Have you talked to the gallery?"

She shook her head. "I emailed my rep, but she hasn't responded." Her insides twisted again. She hadn't heard from them for a year. They had moved on to other artists who weren't constipated. But there was no harm in trying.

He squeezed her shoulder. "Don't worry. They'll respond. And if they don't, I'll just buy them all."

"Ha-ha. You couldn't afford me," she said breezily and entered through the door he held open for her. It was a lie. But the support was nice.

The winery was warm and welcoming as always. A small fire crackled in the hearth. Three groups were in the tasting room, rapt with attention as Elaine, her husband, and someone she hadn't met yet explained the complexities of what they were tasting.

Another half dozen people were in the gift shop, perusing shelves and clutching bottles.

"Busy day," she remarked.

"Yeah. It's made it difficult to take stock of what we have and still need for the party."

"Well, you're in luck. I know absolutely nothing about throwing parties beyond the odd birthday, but I'm here to help. And you can pay me in sexual favors," she said in a low voice.

A grin spread across his face. "Don't tempt me. Did you really ride your bike all the way here?"

She nodded. "What can I say? When there's a dude in distress, I must assist."

"But you didn't sleep all night."

"Neither did you."

"I had a cat nap, thank you very much. If I can't persuade you to go back home and get some rest, come with me to the storeroom."

"Can I drop something off in your employee fridge first? I know how you feel about under-refrigerated backpack cheese."

He laughed and led the way. With the cheese safely stored, he led her down into the basement of the winery. They walked past towering crates of bestselling bottles to a door at the back of the room.

"Is this your office?" She stepped inside the dimly lit room. An outdated computer stood on a desk with a blotter covered in neat handwriting.

"I could use your help, actually. I can set up for an event just fine—"

"Really? Didn't you mention that all of your glasses were smashed?"

"Well, besides that. I can set up an event, but I can't make it glamorous. I would really benefit from an artist's opinion. I have a catalogue from the event planning company. They need to know about décor by tomorrow."

"Why didn't you say so? Let me at it."

She collapsed into the chair behind Rett's desk and picked up the catalogue. "What's our budget and the guest list like?" she asked.

"Three thousand for décor. Food's already set. That much I could handle. I'm only expecting about two hundred people."

Jade balked. *Only* two hundred people? How did he even know two hundred people? She lived in one of the biggest cities in the country and was barely on a first-name basis with more than ten people.

"Perfect." She picked up a highlighter and began perusing. Penny curled up at her feet, and Rett went off, presumably to fret about something else.

She marked off items from the event planning company. Sparkly gold tablecloths, loud feather-centric centerpieces, bejeweled bottle sleeves, and antique-looking glassware. An art deco archway. Gold, glam, and pearls everywhere. After a few cuts, she calculated her total.

Boom, totally glamorous *and* slightly under budget. She stood up to find Rett, and Penny followed like a shadow. He was nowhere to be found. Probably schmoozing with the customers.

She trudged up the stairs and through the back room. No sign of him. She pushed through the doorway into the gift shop.

There he was, chatting with two customers. But something wasn't right. His arms were crossed, and his body was tense.

Instantly, she went on high alert. Was someone being rude? She would summon her inner New Yorker and toss the troublemaker out of the building.

She looked at Elaine, who seemed similarly uncomfortable. Even the cashier behind the register looked wary. Who or what were these new arrivals? Business inspectors? The Health Department, maybe?

She stepped closer. They appeared to be a couple. The woman was blonde, tall, rail-thin, and dressed like she was a personal assistant to Lisa Vanderpump. She had a fresh blowout and her shoes would have broken Jade's ankles.

And then there was the man. Something about him looked familiar. She narrowed her eyes. Holy shit. He looked just like a slightly older Rett. The same green eyes and skin tone. Rett was a little bit taller, but he certainly didn't have the air of superiority that seemed to waft off the other man like a toxic fog.

Was *this* the girlfriend-stealing brother? She straightened her shoulders and marched toward them.

CHAPTER FORTY

RETT

"You want to stay at the house?" Rett clarified.

"If it's not too much trouble," Alexa simpered.

"I forgot how the hotels fill up here in the fall," Chris said. "You don't mind, do you?"

Oh, he very much minded. Having his brother and his cheating ex under his roof? He'd rather be drowned in a vat of bottom-shelf merlot. But he could only imagine what his parents would say if he turned his own brother out into the cold.

Nails scrabbled over the hardwood behind him, and he turned to spot Penny and Jade. Thank god. Jade's eyebrows were drawn together and her mouth was scrunched up.

"There you are," he said to her. He held out his arm, and she slid into his side like she had been specifically made to fit there.

Alexa went rigid, and her smile was frozen in place as she took in Jade and her paint-splattered overalls.

Penny, who had historically jumped on every new person she had encountered in the last week, cowered behind Jade.

"This is Chris. My brother."

"Nice to meet you. I'm Jade." She reached over and shook his hand.

Chris flinched, and Rett suppressed a smile. He could feel the tension wafting off Jade.

"And this is Alexa," he said flatly.

"Hi," Jade said, administering what looked to be another very firm handshake.

Alexa flexed her fingers when they broke apart. Good.

"What brings you two to town?" Jade asked.

"We thought we'd come up early for the party. Spend some time with my little bro," Chris said. He jokingly punched Rett in the chest.

"They were hoping to stay at the house," Rett said to Jade.

"Your house?" Her grip tightened on his arm.

He nodded. If he didn't relax his jaw, he was going to crack a molar.

"Rett was coming to my place anyway tonight, so you'll have the place to yourselves," Jade said smoothly.

That was definitely not something they had discussed, but she had gifted him with an out. He drew her in a centimeter tighter. Anything to avoid having to listen to his brother hump his ex-girlfriend through the wall.

"Don't worry, we won't be in your space too much. We're going to do some wine tours while we're here." Chris said. "But maybe Alexa and I could make dinner for you tomorrow?"

"Sounds great." Rett said with a forced smile. That wasn't going to be torture at all. "Well, we'd better get back to party planning. The spare key is where it always was."

"Thanks, man." Chris took Alexa's hand, and they walked out the front door.

Jade whirled around. "Did you know they were coming early?"

"No." If he had, he would have boarded up every window and door on the property.

Jade glowered out the window as Chris and Alexa departed. "You say the word, and I will make them believe in their bones that your grandmother is haunting that house. They will run screaming for the hills before morning."

He sighed. "It's not worth it. They've never had much of a concept for boundaries."

"I'm so sorry. It must be awful to see them together."

"Nothing you don't already know about from first-hand experience." He turned away from the window.

"Come stay with me tonight. At Margie's. Or let me come over and have extremely loud sex with you. They shouldn't be in your safe space because they were too dumb to book a hotel."

His hand found hers. "Let's go to Margie's—or I guess we should call it your place now."

She smiled. "That's right. Are you sure you're okay?"

"I'm fine." He turned back to the wine crate that was sitting on the floor and began shoving bottles onto shelves with gusto.

"I picked out your décor," she said gently.

"That's great. Thank you."

"I have something that might help distract you," she said. "Let me just get the laptop."

She disappeared for a moment, and he went down the row of wines until all the labels were perfectly centered. This, at least, was something he could control.

"Here." Jade's voice startled him.

She held the computer in his direction. Onscreen, a wine bottle label in a striking art déco style stared back at him. And there in the center was a picture of his grand-mother he had never seen. Valentina was written in script font above. His grandmother would have absolutely loved it.

In spite of the shitstorm that had just occurred, his heart grew in his chest.

"It's perfect. I love it. Thank you."

She stood on her tiptoes and pressed a kiss to his cheek. "Do you need some space?"

She read him like the well-worn takeout menu for the Tavern that was stuck to his fridge. "I think I do. Let me give you a ride."

She took a step back and slung her backpack over her shoulders. "It's okay. I could use the fresh air. I'll see you tonight if you decide you're still comfortable coming over."

She picked up Penny's leash and started for the door, then turned back.

"It's going to be okay," she said before turning away and hustling outside.

———

WHEN HE POPPED THE DOOR OF HER COTTAGE OPEN THAT night, Jade screamed and flung a kitchen towel at him.

"A kitchen towel? That's your grand plan to defend your-self?" His leather overnight bag hit the floor. "I thought you were a hardened city girl."

After Jade left, he had buried himself in party prepara-tions until every detail was covered. He might not have been able to control his family members, but he sure as hell was going to make this party a success. He had to, espe-cially now that he and Jade might actually have a future together.

"For your information, I would have fashioned it into a

garotte and murdered you with it had you been an actual intruder."

"My mistake." He shut the door behind him and stepped into the kitchen. Penny trotted up to him and planted her paws on his chest, breathing heavily into his face until he petted her.

He wasn't going to be great company tonight. Seeing Chris and Alexa together earlier had knocked something in his brain loose. The second he saw her, all he could think about was throwing open the door to the guest bedroom in his old apartment and finding her tangled in Chris's sheets. It had been two years, but he still remembered the crimson color of her bra on the floor.

The casserole dish of shepherd's pie hit the counter with a clunk, joined by the leftovers of Baked Alaska.

"Thank you for bringing food." Jade swooped in and snaked her arms around his neck. Her lips pressed to his, bringing with them the taste of chardonnay.

"I'm surprised to see you already," she said when she pulled back.

"I got everything done that I needed to."

"Great. You got the decorations ordered and everything?"

He nodded. "They'll deliver everything on Thursday to give us time to set up."

"I'm happy to help with setup. The mural should be done by then."

The mural. He almost slapped himself in the face. He had been so caught up in his own drama that he hadn't even congratulated her on her incredible breakthrough.

"That's right. It sounds like you made real progress today. I can't wait to see it. I'm sure it's incredible."

"I don't know about incredible, but it's at least a slight improvement on a totally blank wall. Hungry?"

"Very." He helped her shuffle some portions of shepherd's pie into bowls. They stood in silence as they rotated in the microwave. For someone who claimed she didn't cook, the meal had been delicious.

"Are you okay? Relatively speaking?" she asked.

"I'm fine," he said.

"I'm not trying to patronize you. But I want you to know that it's okay to not be okay." She sidled up next to him and slipped a hand around his biceps. He didn't turn to face her. "The first couple of times I saw Nate with Ashley it almost broke me. I didn't know if I wanted to murder them both or just run away and hide in a Mexican restaurant somewhere."

Rett sank onto a barstool but said nothing. What was there to say? Alexa and Chris's abrupt appearance had reminded him that he had never been good enough? He was always going to be second fiddle to his brother, even in his parents' eyes? Even though Chris had a gambling problem, Rett would inexplicably never measure up.

And there was still the very real possibility that the family legacy would crash and burn under Rett's watch. That, at least, was a fair criticism.

Jade set a steaming plate and a glass of wine in front of him.

He lifted the glass to his nose reflexively, then set it back down.

"It needs to rest," he said when he noticed her gaze.

"Of course. That wine must be exhausted from carrying the crushing weight of all this silence."

He sighed. "I'm sorry. I have a hard time talking about it."

"I know. It's okay. I'm worried about you, though. There's been a night and day difference in you from before your brother got here and after."

"I hate that it has this effect on me," Rett said vehemently. "It's been two years. I should be over this."

"A betrayal of that magnitude is not something you just get over," she said quietly. "It takes time. And a lot of wine. Even an adopted dog in my case."

"I wish it was that easy. He's going to be in my life forever. He's my brother."

She put another plate into the microwave. "Yeah, that definitely complicates things. They don't live around here, though?"

He shook his head. "In the city."

"Good. That'll make it harder for them to drop in unexpectedly in the future."

Silence stretched between them as they ate. An internal alarm went off, and he downed his glass in a couple of gulps.

"Did they teach that tasting method at sommelier school?" she asked with a smile.

"No, that was all undergrad." He managed to smile in return.

There was no point in endlessly ruminating on Chris leeching off him yet again. If he knew his brother, dinner tomorrow was going to involve either a request for money or an outlandish business proposition. Even though the vineyard had been left to Rett, Chris couldn't help but try to insert himself every time trouble brewed. It was exhausting.

But at least Jade would be with him. She, at least, seemed to believe that he was enough.

She finished her glass and clapped her hands. "Okay. I

was hoping I wouldn't have to do this, but I think you need it."

"Need what?"

She opened a kitchen cabinet and started pulling out baking ingredients. A minute later, she pushed a set of ramekins across the kitchen island.

"Stress bake me a chocolate soufflé."

"A soufflé? I've never attempted one. I don't even have a recipe."

His phone chimed.

"Now you do. No excuses. Go."

"I doubt Margie keeps a double boiler in her guest house."

She leaned across the counter and looked him dead in the eyes. "If I can attend my ex-boyfriend's wedding, recapture my muse, paint a gigantic mural, and try to get a driver's license a decade later than most people, you can make a soufflé."

"Fair enough," he said. He loosened his collar and rolled up his sleeves. Maybe a new challenge would be enough to pull him out of this rut.

Baking gave him such peace. It was a delicate science, just like winemaking. But unlike wine, he didn't have to stare at a barrel for a year before discovering the outcome.

One heavy-handed measurement could ruin the whole thing, especially with something as finnicky as a soufflé. But there was something invigorating about the challenge.

Jade tapped away on her new laptop as he chopped chocolate and whisked yolks. She already knew him so well. Ninety percent of the people in his life had no idea that he even baked, but she could tell when he needed it to distract him.

And she was staying. A world of possibility had opened.

What would their future together look like? Would she get tired of him when she realized his sixty-hour work weeks were not an exaggeration?

The winery drifted into his mind. It really was a lot of work. Beyond the actual winemaking, most of it wasn't something that required him specifically. Even his grandmother had outsourced most of the administrative stuff, so why was he so insistent on doing everything himself?

Jade's suggestion about outsourcing some of the grunt work was interesting, but not the most fiscally responsible choice he could make. What would he even do with the extra time?

His gaze drifted back to her. She was sitting at the island in silence, brows furrowed in concentration. There was his answer. As Jade had pointed out time and time again, tomorrow was never a guarantee. Maybe it was time he loosened the reins a little. If he could pull the winery out of its flatline with the help of the sparkling wine, anyway.

An hour later, he carefully cracked open the oven door. From his periphery, he spotted Jade sitting up and leaning forward expectantly.

The baking sheet screeched against the oven rack as he withdrew the soufflés. They had risen like a dream. They were gorgeous. They were stunning. They were—

"Shit."

Flat as fuck. They had plummeted almost as quickly as his hopes and dreams. Well, not all of them.

Jade cringed like she was expecting a bomb to go off. They looked at each other, and he burst into laughter. She laughed, then clapped a hand over her mouth.

"I'm sure they still taste amazing," she said gently.

"I can think of something that tastes better," he said. He

left the soufflés on a cooling rack, grabbed her hand, and pulled her into the bedroom.

CHAPTER FORTY-ONE

JADE

"I can't believe it," Jade whispered, turning the card over in her hand. The afternoon light caught the gloss on her picture.

Her very first learner's permit. It felt like holding a tangible piece of freedom. She had to fight the urge to waggle it in a sixteen-year-old's face on her way out.

"First try too," Rett said from the driver's seat. They were traversing the pothole-riddled road away from the DMV. "Very impressive."

"I kind of feel sixteen again. Like I want to do something irresponsible."

He shot her some side-eye.

She snorted. "Don't worry. I'm not going to crash my first time behind the wheel. I meant irresponsible as in drink too much and yell at someone."

Something about this dinner with Rett's brother felt overwhelmingly icky.

"Well, you're in luck. Because this dinner party is going to be a nightmare."

She reached across the seat and laid a hand on his knee. Tension radiated off him.

"It's okay to say no," she said softly. "Sharing parents doesn't make him family."

He shook his head. "My grandmother would want us to be on speaking terms."

"Respectfully, your grandmother is gone. And you're allowed to hold boundaries against toxic people. You don't owe them anything. Not even your presence at some suspicious-ass dinner."

He glanced at her. "What makes you think it's suspicious?"

She raised her eyebrows. "Why show up to a party four days early and uninvited?"

Rett stared straight ahead as they drove down the road. "Your instincts are dead-on. My brother has a gambling habit."

"Aha!" She pointed at him like she'd caught him in a lie. "I knew it. Do you think he's going to ask for money?"

"Probably. Which I don't have."

She sat back in her seat. "It'll be a cold day in hell before I let him take advantage of you and everything you've worked for. Remember that."

"How could I forget?"

They settled into silence as they drove south. He was kind of ruining her post-learner's permit high. She glanced again at the small rectangle in her hand. It felt like a beginning. A world of possibilities opened up. Once she saved enough for a car, she could travel the country in search of inspiration. Not to mention go to Target whenever she wanted.

The sun was shifting lower, sending long shadows across

the vineyards that crawled by the window. The hills were alive with red and yellow leaves.

She pulled the mirror down and glanced at it. Her hair was up, a couple of tendrils framing her face. The neckline of her vibrant orange romper was visible, hovering just below the copper statement necklace she had picked up from a street artist in Greenwich Village. The romper was stretchy enough to allow her to kick some meddling brother ass if needed.

When the truck passed through the town square, Margie's Café caught her eye. Rett hadn't been in yet and therefore hadn't seen the mural. What would he say when he saw it? How would he react to seeing them immortalized together on the dock, Penny between them?

A jazz quartet played in the gazebo on the town green. Ethel waved merrily from a lawn chair, and Jade reflexively waved back. Her neighbors never waved at her in the city. She was on the cusp of starting a completely new life, a giant leap that could go horribly wrong. Her mom would have been proud.

When they pulled into Rett's driveway, his brow furrowed. A red Corvette was parked haphazardly in front of two of the garage bays. He turned the truck off and hopped out.

Jade freed herself, but Rett met her at her door before she could jump to the ground. He lifted her down slowly, and it was like he was seeing her for the first time all evening.

A genuine smile formed by the time her heels hit the asphalt. "You look beautiful," he said.

"Really?" She glanced down at her outfit. "I have a feeling this outfit will cause a stir. It's not very Vineyard Vines."

"It's perfect." He took her hand and pulled her toward the house.

She eyed the entrance like it was the Doors of Durin. What fresh hell waited for them inside? Rett opened the front door, and a medley of scents reached her nose.

They entered the kitchen, and Chris turned around.

"Hey," he said with a warm smile. He was wearing Rett's apron, and he crossed the distance between them in seconds. He offered a firm handshake to both of them. Apparently the Rhodes family weren't huggers.

"Come in, come in." Chris swept a hand toward the long dining room table.

Rett and Jade exchanged a glance. If he had a thought about what it was like to be invited into his own home, he didn't share it.

Alexa appeared, dressed primly in a white cashmere sweater dress with a cowl neck. It clung to her athletic frame. Two bottles of wine dangled by their necks from her hands.

"Oh, hello," she said brightly.

"Alexa," Rett said. It was more of a grunt than a greeting. Jade squeezed his hand.

What was it like to have the woman he could have married in the home they would have shared?

Jade cast an eye around the house. Things were definitely messier than they had left them. A bag of trash stood by the garage door. Plates and glasses were piled on the end tables in the living room.

Alexa's smile faltered, and she turned away from them to set the wine on the counter. She aimlessly opened drawers, fighting with one that wouldn't shut as silverware jingled inside.

Rett took a seat at the dining room table and watched

with crossed arms as the dynamic duo attempted to function in his kitchen. Jade smirked. At least he wasn't letting them off too easy.

"How's business?" Rett said to his brother, who had seemingly joined the hunt for a corkscrew.

"Oh, it's great. I sold a pair of brownstones earlier this month."

Rett's posture straightened a little. "That's good to hear. And you, Alexa?"

"It's going really well. I'm on track to hit \$500k in sales this year. These semaglutide injections really sell themselves."

Rett turned to Jade. "Alexa is in pharmaceutical sales."

Of course she was a pharma girl.

"I thought I'd check in with Cindy while we're here. We just added this new burn cream, but it kind of seems like she's been dodging my calls. I guess I'll just stop in at the clinic tomorrow and see if she's around."

Jade suppressed a smile. Something told her Cindy wouldn't buy into Alexa's burn cream if the entire town caught fire.

"What is it you do for work, Jade?" Alexa asked with a smile.

"I'm an artist." For the first time in two years, the words almost felt true.

Rett squeezed her hand under the table.

"Oh, wow. What's your medium?" Alexa asked. She turned the full force of her blue eyes on Jade, and it was easy to see how Rett had been dazzled into dating her.

"Paint, mostly. Mixed media."

"How amazing. I'd love to see some of your work."

Jade smiled. Alexa was definitely a schmoozer. It was a

good thing Jade wasn't an endocrinologist or she probably would have left dinner with an armful of dubious samples.

"Mom's gonna love you," Chris said. He had finally located a corkscrew and driven it into a bottle of red. "She loves the artsy types."

Alexa shot him a disgruntled look.

"Well, let's hope so. What's for dinner?" Jade said with as much enthusiasm as she could muster.

"Prime rib, garlic mashed potatoes, and delicata squash," Chris said. He stirred something on the stove.

Rett and Jade exchanged another glance. There hadn't been an excess of dirty dishes in the kitchen. The oven was on, but there was no boiling pot of water, no potato masher in the sink. The very same meal had been the weekly special at the Tavern only days ago. Surely his brother wasn't trying to pass off a restaurant's offering as a home-cooked meal, though. That would be insane.

"Sounds delicious. Thank you," she said as Chris passed her a glass of wine. She took a hearty sip. At least the wine was good. Warmth ran through her, and she closed her eyes to savor it.

"This is so good." She lifted her glass at Rett.

He sniffed, then took a sip. "Funny story about this batch," he said.

His eyes lit up like he was about to tell a swashbuckling tale of how he had single-handedly dredged it up from a merchant ship on the bottom of the ocean.

Jade couldn't take her eyes off him. As he explained in detail how the unseasonably warm weather and a slight tweak to the bottling process had affected that particular batch, he finally looked and sounded like himself.

A genuine smile crept over her face as she listened to

Rett's explanation. There was such nuance in winemaking. Such artistry. And made by such capable hands.

"Fascinating," Alexa said when Rett finished, but her expression was glazed.

"Can we help?" Rett asked. He nodded toward the kitchen.

"Oh, no," Chris said. "You relax. We wanted to do something special for you. It's been so long since we were all together."

"Probably since Grandmother's funeral," Rett said.

Chris nodded. His expression darkened almost imperceptibly. "And the will reading, of course."

Jade narrowed her eyes. There was definitely some bullshit going on here. But exactly what it was remained to be seen. She scanned the house again and spotted a laptop on the coffee table in the living room. This was all a setup. She could feel it.

She glanced back at Chris. He definitely wanted something from Rett. He didn't look like he needed money. But the best grifters never did.

"And where do you guys live?" Jade asked.

"Midtown." Alexa drained her wineglass and poured another. Unfortunately, the universe didn't see fit for it to spill down her dress. "I travel a lot for work, though. I'm in Boston next week."

"Sounds very exciting," Jade said.

"It's such a great career. Business is booming, and I get to meet so many new people."

Jade smiled. It sounded exhausting. She pulled out her phone and saw a message from Cindy. She had shared the story of Alexa and Chris's reappearance in the group chat.

Cindy: How's it going?

Jade sent a poop emoji and slid her phone back into her bag.

By the time dinner was actually plated and on the table, the atmosphere had relaxed. The frost between Rett and Alexa had melted a bit, and Chris had taken over the majority of conversation.

As they scraped the last bit of the—admittedly delicious—food from their plates, Chris was on his third retelling of a memory from a family vacation. A New York accent seemed to become stronger with each subsequent glass of wine.

"And then," he said, face slightly red. He had had most of the second bottle of wine himself. "The wave just absolutely wrecked Rett. I'm talkin' obliterated."

Alexa laughed.

"That sounds awful," Jade said, turning to Rett. "Were you okay?"

He nodded. "It's all part of the learning experience. I still surf every time we head west."

"Do you do much surfing, Chris?" Jade asked pointedly. So far, most of his charming family anecdotes had highlighted embarrassing moments for Rett. Her hackles had been raised and she wouldn't hesitate to go for the jugular the second things inevitably went south.

"Nah," he said after another gulp of wine. "Not many waves in New York. But you know that. Where do you live, again?"

"Midtown. For now," she said. "I'm moving at the beginning of next year."

Chris slapped the table, rattling the dishes. "No way. We should meet up for brunch sometime."

"Sounds fun," she said with false cheer. She would rather have an intimate dinner with a pack of wolverines than this grifter.

Alexa set her sights on Rett. "Rett, I was wondering if we could talk before dessert. Briefly. Maybe out on the patio?" Her tone was casual, but it seemed like a calculated move. Why was she trying to get him away from the rest of them?

Jade's hand curled into a fist at her side.

Rett stiffened again. "Sure," he said. He finished his wine and dropped the glass on the table.

He stood, and they disappeared through the patio doors.

CHAPTER FORTY-TWO

RETT

RETT CROSSED HIS ARMS AND STARED AT THE WOMAN WHO had dropkicked him in the heart. There was a time when he would have done anything to get her back. He'd had their entire future planned out. Marriage in two years, kids in five. He knew her favorite band, her Taco Bell order, her ring size. But in this moment, she might as well have been a stranger.

"Thank you for agreeing to talk," Alexa said.

He stared back at her and said nothing.

"I just wanted to apologize." Her cheeks had turned pink. "For everything that happened between us—and the way it all went down."

"It was a long time ago," he said flatly. He turned to look over her shoulder, where the lake lapped at the edge of the dock. Maybe it was time he got a boat. Even if its only purpose was to be an emergency escape for stupid conversations like this one.

"Still. It was unkind and inappropriate."

He raised his eyebrows and barely bit back a laugh.

"Sleeping with my brother in my own apartment? Inappropriate?"

"I'm really sorry," Alexa continued. "I don't want you to think that what we had didn't mean anything. You were an amazing boyfriend."

"Not as amazing as Chris, apparently."

"I wish I could explain." Her voice was softer now. "We were just drawn to each other."

His eyes narrowed. If he wasn't mistaken, that was the same bullshit excuse Nate had given Jade. Alexa was trying to butter him up for something. It was about time he found out what.

"But that doesn't excuse the way I ended things." She was clearly flustered, uncharacteristically stumbling over her words. Good.

In their relationship, he had forgiven too easily, too quickly. But he didn't owe her anything anymore.

"Good talk. I'm going to check on Jade."

He walked off without another word. Finally, an apology. Two years too late. It didn't give him any sense of satisfaction.

When he arrived inside, Jade was nowhere to be found.

Chris looked up from digging in a messenger bag. "She went to the basement."

Rett thundered down the stairs. As he entered the gym, Jade whirled around. A tear was rolling down her cheek.

"What happened? Did Chris say something to you?"

If he had, he would end him. Blood be damned.

She wiped the tear away and straightened. "No. It's nothing. The gallery just emailed me back. She said they're nice, but they can't sell landscapes."

His shoulders slumped. "I'm so sorry."

He held his arms open, and she rushed into them. They

held each other for a moment, blocking out everything else. What fools they were to not see the beauty in front of them.

"For what it's worth, they don't deserve you. We'll figure something out," he said, breathing in the honeysuckle scent of her hair.

She pulled back and squared her shoulders. "I think I already have. But we'll talk about it tomorrow. Do you think you can take a couple hours off?"

He hesitated. The day would be consumed with party prep. But Jade needed him. He could make up the hours later.

"Of course. Whatever you need."

Her gaze moved to the ceiling. "I feel like your brother's up to something."

"Oh, he's definitely up to something. Should we go find out what it is and get it over with?" He offered her an arm, and she took it.

The door upstairs popped open. "Quick question. Where is your fire extinguisher?" Chris shouted down the stairwell.

The piercing wail of a smoke detector screeched in the background.

"Jesus Christ." Rett gathered the nearest five canvases and stormed up the stairs, Jade right behind.

Smoke burned his nostrils when they entered. Something on the stove was on fire. He opened the front door and carefully set the paintings in the front seat of his truck, then ran for the fire extinguisher. In seconds, his previously spotless kitchen was covered in white foam.

"Sorry about that," Chris said. He scraped the contents of the dish into the trash.

Rett grunted and coughed on the smoke. Was it not

enough that Chris had seduced his girlfriend? Did he need to destroy their family home too?

Jade stood by the open patio door, wafting smoke out with a kitchen towel. She shook her head at him. It was a good thing they had left Penny at the cottage.

If he didn't get these people out of his house, he was going to lose his mind.

"What's that?" Rett pointed at the living room. Chris's laptop was open, and what appeared to be a PowerPoint was displayed on the TV.

"Oh, I just had some ideas for the vineyard and thought we could talk about it."

Rett cocked his head. "Surely the real estate market is keeping you too busy to worry about what I'm doing all the way out here."

Chris's face was turning red. "I just thought you could use some help. Mom and Dad said the winery is struggling."

Jade took a step toward Chris, hand clenched in a fist, but Rett cut her off with a look. As much as he would have loved to let her pound his brother to a pulp, Chris was not above pressing charges.

She cleared her throat. "How about I work on cleaning up while you two talk? No sense in wasting a perfectly good —and casual—PowerPoint." Her tone was like the tip of a blade.

"This isn't your mess to clean up," Rett said. He picked up his glass of wine—which had miraculously remained unscathed—and tugged Jade into the living room and onto the couch.

"Thanks for being willing to hear me out," Chris said. He stood awkwardly in front of the TV, beads of sweat on his brow. Smoke was still thick in the air.

Alexa took a seat next to him in an armchair, apparently

unbothered by the fact that she had nearly burned his house down.

The chances of them offering a solution that would magically solve the winery's problems were less than zero. But if he didn't let Chris go through his spiel, his parents would never let him hear the end of it.

"So," Chris said, suddenly producing a clicker. "What I wanted to discuss with you was the prospect of bringing in some outside help. If we bring in outside grapes or outside wines for a blend, we could amp up production by twenty-five percent starting at the beginning of the fiscal year."

Outside grapes? Seriously? For fifty years, every grape in every bottle had been cultivated in this area code.

A bar graph appeared onscreen. Rett's shoulders tensed.

Jade plucked the wineglass from his hand and set it on the end table amidst the trash Alexa and Chris had left. He hadn't even noticed how tightly he was holding it.

"What vineyard?" Rett asked.

Chris fumbled. "It's a small one. Goat's Bollocks Vineyard. They're outside of Trenton. Massive chunk of land, lot of grapes."

Trenton? He had to be joking.

Rett took a deep breath and leaned forward. "Do you know what makes Rhodes Vineyard so unique, Chris?"

"The wine?" Chris asked rather than answered.

"Sure. But do you know why? I'm sure you did some research before coming to me with these ideas."

"The dirt," Chris offered.

"The Finger Lakes create a microclimate," Rett began. He went on to describe retreating glaciers and their effect on the soil, growing seasons, winter damage, slopes, and drainage.

Chris's eyes were glazed over. Alexa was struggling to

focus. Even her customer service smile slipped a bit by the end of the tirade.

"So all of these elements come together to make flavorful, unique wines. Do you know what this region in New Jersey is known for lacking?"

Chris shrugged.

"Adequate drainage. This leads to overblown fruit, diseases, mold growth. You're trying to sell me on subpar grapes. Why?"

"I told you. I'm trying to help amp up production and cut down on costs."

"And what's your role in all this? What do you gain?"

"Well, as the liaison between suppliers, usually there's a fee—"

There it was. As suspected, he came under the guise of offering help, but he was really here to line his own pockets.

"So you need money. Again."

"That's not why—" Chris began.

"What happened?" Rett prompted when Chris's scarlet face turned purple. "I assume there was another bet that went wrong."

"No, I—" Chris began again, but Alexa silenced him with a look. Her expression had soured like someone had forced her to eat the dessert she decimated.

"It was supposed to be a sure thing," Chris muttered. "Beauchamp had it in the bag. But then he tore his ACL."

Jade swore and went to get up, but Rett tugged her gently back down.

"I'm not an ATM. You never paid me back last time, and that's part of the reason why the winery is where it is today. That money was slated for upgrades. You told me you could double it. So where is it?"

"I don't have it, okay?" Chris threw the clicker onto the

couch. It bounced off and hit the floor with a thunk. He pointed at Rett with a shaking finger.

"You're so fucking selfish. I'm the oldest brother. This should have all gone to *me*. But no, grandma gave it to Rett the Golden Boy."

Rett stared at him. "This isn't Downton Abbey. You're not owed anything just because you're older than me. You don't even like wine."

"I love wine."

"Really? What's terroir?"

"*What's terroir*?" Chris mimicked in a high-pitched voice. "Pack your bag, Lexi," he yelled. "We're leaving."

"Finally," Jade muttered.

As Chris and Alexa stomped up the stairs, Jade gasped. "What's Alexa's last name?"

Of all the topics in the world, she wanted to keep discussing his ex-girlfriend?

"Dumont," he said.

"Does she have a friend named Shelby? Or Sheldon, maybe?"

"Yes," he said slowly.

She pulled out her phone and frantically tapped at the screen. She shoved it in his face. "That drug-peddling internet troll. She's LexiD from the mean Yelp reviews. And these must be her friends."

Rett stared at the series of one-star reviews, all from the same day. He assumed a group had had a lackluster tasting. But it was a hell of a lot more likely that Alexa and her friends had left them after the will reading.

"Did she dump you because she thought your brother was inheriting the vineyard and the house?" Jade whispered.

"No, that would be insane—" he began, but Jade had already rushed up the stairs.

He dashed after her, but she was already yelling at Chris and Alexa.

"Delete your review," she said in a voice he had never heard from her before. Gone was the relaxed, fun Jade. This was City Jade, and she looked ready to throw down.

Alexa straightened up, pair of jeans in one hand and a suitcase open on the bed. "I don't know what you're talking about."

"Then how did you know I was talking to you?"

Alexa went pink again. "I'm not taking it down."

Jade took a step into the room, and Alexa flinched. Chris stepped in front of her.

"There are people—real people—who work at the winery and depend on Rett for their livelihood. You're hurting them more than you're punishing Rett. I know you must be a good person, because Rett wouldn't have dated you if you weren't. Do the right thing. Take the review down. In front of me. Right now."

"Even if I did know my password—"

"You know it. And I'm going to sit right here until you delete it." Jade juked around Chris and perched on the end of the bed. She looked calmly at Alexa.

Alexa let out a frustrated noise and pulled her phone out. She scrolled for a while, then turned her phone to Jade. "There, see?" She swiped a finger. "It's gone."

Jade hopped up. "Thank you for doing the right thing. I look forward to seeing you guys at the party." She grabbed Rett's hand and pulled him out of the room and back down the stairs.

"You didn't have to do that," he said.

No one had ever gone to bat for him the way she just had. His parents had pretended like Rett and Alexa had never dated.

"Yes, I did. She doesn't get to ruin your life twice."

"She didn't ruin my life."

"What do you mean?"

"If she hadn't fucked my brother, I never would have met you."

A small smile appeared. "That was almost adorable." She leaned in for a kiss. This one was sweet, tender. Warmth spread to his fingers and toes.

He held her for an extra second. "Do you want to get out of here? Maybe take a drive?"

"You mean me?"

"Yeah. You're legal now. Let's drive over to the winery parking lot. You shouldn't be able to do too much damage there."

CHAPTER FORTY-THREE

JADE

"Whoops," Jade said for the fifteenth time that hour as gravel spun beneath the tires of Rett's truck.

"You know, I thought this would be less aggravating than dinner with my brother. Now I'm not so sure."

"Hey." She swatted him. "I'm doing my best. This is the first time I've ever been behind the wheel. And your gas is so touchy. Are you sure that's normal?"

He glowered at her, but he still looked like a weight had been lifted off him. "Let's try parking one more time. Reverse," he prompted.

"I still don't understand why you don't have a backup camera."

"Backup cameras make you lazy."

"No, they keep you from running over children."

"Do you normally see many children in the parking lot of a winery that's been closed for two hours?" He raised his eyebrows.

"You're impossible," she said with a frown. "By the way, have you been doing your homework?"

He looked blankly back at her.

Jade wound her arm around Rett's headrest as she backed up. "Your dream? Don't think I've forgotten. Now that I'm staying, I won't rest until you figure out what you really want."

Anything to distract her from the disaster that had just happened and the disaster that was likely to happen tomorrow.

"Let's revisit this after we see how the party goes. I won't have time for dreams if I have to start cutting my employees' hours."

With her foot on the brake, Jade stretched her arms. They were sore from holding herself up during their amorous escapade the night before. Almost as sore as they had been after a CrossFit session.

An idea struck her, and she almost gasped. CrossFit. One of the other regulars she was friendly with, Lindon, was a food and wine critic for the *New York Times*. What were the odds that he was free to come to the Finger Lakes this weekend? Maybe she could bribe him with a painting. She resolved to text him the moment she got back to Margie's. There was no point in saying anything to Rett until it was a done deal.

"Fine," she said. She turned the truck toward the exit and started descending the driveway.

"Hey," he said. "Where are we going?"

"To get Penny."

"And you're going to drive there?"

"Of course." She shot him a derisive look, then sat up straight, hands at exactly ten and two.

"And what will you do if we encounter a deer?"

"Brake, then befriend it and teach it to help with laundry."

"Very funny."

———

"Thank you for coming with me."

The truck rumbled outside Burdett Bed and Breakfast. Sunshine streamed through the window, illuminating doggie nose smudges. Hopefully she hadn't gotten too much dog hair on her.

Rett leaned over, one hand on the wheel. "You're going to kill it. You already met him. Just remember: smile, firm handshake, create a little sense of urgency. Say you're talking to other B&Bs. Which is true. You're going to love Avery over at Glouchester Castle."

She took a deep breath and hugged the repurposed pizza box holder to her chest. Inside were six canvases she was about to show to Vince, the B&B owner she had met at paint and sip. Inside were the dreamy fall landscapes the gallery had rejected. If anyone was going to buy them, it was someone who lived here and loved the area the way she did.

The truck door creaked as she hopped out and hustled into the building before she could convince herself not to. She had been through much worse. She could convince one measly business owner to buy her paintings.

After a couple of tense minutes in the lounge, Vince wandered out.

"It's so good to see you again." She shook his hand firmly and offered a smile.

He ushered her into his office and closed the door. "I gotta tell ya, my wife loves the painting I brought home. She wants to come along next time. She wanted to know if you ever accept nude models."

Jade blinked, then recovered. "I don't know if I could get the venue to agree, but I would be happy to paint your wife outside of a classroom. The human form is a beautiful gift."

"Right you are. And my wife is the most beautiful of them all."

"I bet. Speaking of which—" She opened the Velcro on the pizza box. "I just finished up this series and I couldn't stop thinking about how gorgeous they would look on your walls. In the lounge, maybe?" She nodded her head in the direction of the cozy room with the crackling fireplace.

Vince reached out a hand, and she carefully handed over one of the canvases.

"Wow," he said. "This is great. This is the view from Rhodes?"

Jade nodded. "There are a couple other ones too." She pulled more canvases out. "The memorial chapel, downtown Hammondsport."

"They're beautiful." Vince handed the stack back to her. "I'm just not sure we're in the market for new décor right now."

Jade's heart plummeted. It had been a long shot anyway. She stood and filed the canvases back in the pizza box. No harm in trying urgency as a last-ditch effort.

"No problem," she said breezily. "I have an appointment with Avery at Glouchester Castle anyway. I guess they have a brand-new game room?"

Vince frowned.

"Anyway, she was looking for some art for it, but I thought I'd check with you first since we have a pre-existing relationship. I hope to see you—and your lovely wife—at the next paint and sip. Have a great rest of your morning."

She reached over and shook his hand again. He looked contemplative.

She turned around and put a hand on the door.

"Wait. Let me see the vineyard one again."

Jade smiled, then composed herself before turning back around.

"Sure."

When she emerged from the inn thirty minutes later, four of the six canvases were gone.

Rett looked like he was holding his breath. "How'd we do?"

"As long as Margie's not going to price gouge me, likely enough for first month, last month, and security deposit." She waved a check in front of his face.

He threw his arms around her and pulled her close. "I knew you could do it. See? You don't need the gallery."

"Well," she said, "if I ever manage to paint the way I used to, I might need the gallery. But for now, fuck 'em."

It felt amazing to take a step in the right direction. Her hope of an art career wasn't gone forever. And maybe she'd dabble in graphic design, at least enough to stay stable.

One trip to the Finger Lakes had completely upended her life. She had come here at rock bottom, weeks away from becoming homeless. She had folded herself into the fabric of this town stitch by stitch, and now it was home. A new future awaited her.

And if everything worked out, she just might help save the winery too. After she bribed him with a free portrait of his Chow Chow, Lindon had agreed to come to Rett's party. If it went well—and it would, thanks to Rett's unparalleled levels of control freaking—Antoine would write a glowing review, and New York's elite would visit the vineyard in droves.

The rest of the week passed in a blur.

Rett had visibly relaxed since Chris and Alexa had disappeared. While Jade's morning runs were less peaceful than they used to be thanks to Rett's swearing and sweating, they were falling into a rhythm. They showered together, made breakfast, and wrapped themselves in blankets to eat it on the dock. They stole heated moments together in the storeroom and his office between brainstorming and setup for the party.

It was the happiest she had ever been. Mornings were spent in the café, fiddling with the mural. She and Penny haunted the winery until closing time, experimenting with graphic design software and reading books in the gorgeous lighting of the tasting room and, on more than one occasion, sharing a glass and a story with Margie.

There was something intoxicating about seeing Rett in his natural element. He was so confident and charming. The way he schmoozed the customers, earnestly answering their questions and enthusiastically discussing his process. At some point during his shift, he would shrug his suit jacket off and sling it over the back of her chair, like he was claiming her in front of everyone. Together they mapped out the table arrangement for the party, planned the set list for the string quartet, and cleaned every crevice of the speakeasy.

Even her driving lessons were improving. Rett let her drive all the way to one of the decorating centers to procure some of the remaining décor. She hadn't even crashed into a single parked car.

At one o'clock on Friday, Jade put her brush down and stepped back. The wooden floorboards of the café creaked beneath her weight. Conversations buzzed around her and the seductive scent of the daily special beckoned, but she only had eyes for the mural.

It was done. Everything she loved about Hammondsport —every townsperson who had touched her heart, every friend she had made, every grain of sand that littered the beachfront splayed out in front of her. The illustrated story of her redemption. Of finding herself again. Learning that she could love again.

And here it would stay, a permanent part of the town that had come to mean so much to her in such a short period of time.

The door banged open, and footsteps thundered on the hardwood. She turned to find Cindy, Gemma, and Elena with scowls on their faces. They came up to her like they were about to challenge her to some kind of duel.

"Why did we have to find out from Tom that you're moving here?"

Jade's mouth froze in an O of surprise. With all the party planning, she had completely forgotten to pass the good news on.

"I'm so sorry. I finally talked to Rett and he said he didn't want me to leave. I was honestly convinced it was a fever dream and I forgot to tell you."

Cindy sidled up next to her. "So you're done doing the whole fake relationship now?"

"I think so? Technically we didn't put a label on it. But I'm moving into Margie's for good."

The girls surrounded her, jumping up and down and squealing. Finally, they stepped back to take in the mural.

"It's so beautiful," Gemma said, one hand outstretched to touch the unicorn leaving a trail in the cotton candy water. She snatched her fingers back. "Right. Shit. Wet paint."

"It's amazing," Elena said, coming around the front to administer one of her bone-crushing hugs.

Cindy grabbed her hand. "I can't believe you're really staying. Now you get to come to our legendary Halloween party. And if you think Hammondsport is adorable in the fall, just wait until you see Christmas. It's a whole-ass Hallmark movie."

"It's everything I ever wanted," Jade said.

The door opened behind them, and they all turned to greet the newcomer.

Jade's heart stuttered in her chest. There was Rett, a bundle of aster and goldenrod in his arms. Gemma, Elena, and Cindy offered hurried farewells on their way out the door, but he only had eyes for Jade. And the mural behind her.

"Hi," he said after the flurry of activity. He stooped down for a kiss, then took a step back to stare at the wall.

"It's finished," Jade said.

They stood together, staring at it for almost a full minute. He stepped forward, still holding the bouquet.

"Is that us?" He pointed to the couple on the dock, golden retriever between them.

"Yeah," she said. "I figured I'd give the book club something to gossip about."

"It's incredible." He reached out to touch it but stopped himself. "I knew you could do it."

She looped her arm around his. "Thank you. For everything. This place has truly changed my life. I have hope for the first time in a really long time. Did I tell you that Château on Seneca emailed me to ask if I could do a winter and spring series?"

"I'm so proud of you. Truly." He bent down for another kiss, and there was a flurry of activity at the book club table.

The sound of something ripping came from behind them. They both turned around, and Margie approached, tears in her eyes.

"I can't believe it. My own Jade Gardner mural. Your *first* mural. In my cafe," she whispered reverently. She reached over and touched the tiny David. "I don't know how you did it, but you can feel the town."

Thank god.

Jade, already overwhelmed with the emotions of the afternoon, threw her arms around Margie. She smelled like cinnamon. "Thank you so much. You believed in me even though you didn't know me."

"Heartache can take a lot of things from us. But it can't take who you are at your core." She drew back and held Jade at arm's length. A mother's pride beamed in her eyes. "Here, honey. You've earned it."

A check landed in Jade's hand. She blinked several times. Surely she wasn't reading the check correctly. "This is more than we discussed."

"It's a tip. I don't want to hear another word about it. I'll see you at the party tomorrow." And with that, she disappeared behind the counter.

The check in Jade's hand was basically a lifeline. She had done it—accomplished what she had stuck around to do, reclaimed her identity as an artist, and dug herself out of certain crushing debt brushstroke by brushstroke.

She took another look around, but everything was packed up. It really was finished. She clutched the bouquet and took an appreciative sniff. This moment would live in her brain forever—her redemption story spilled out on a wall in front of her, handsome, supportive man and teary-eyed mother figure behind her. New friends waiting in the wings. A fresh start.

"Here. Your favorite," Margie said, bustling over with a brown paper bag.

"I'm paying," Jade said firmly.

Margie shook her head. "Not today. You're still technically a contracted employee."

Jade threw her hands up. "Fine. Thank you." She leaned in for another hug, then allowed herself to be ushered out the door by Rett.

"Where's your truck?" she asked as he hefted her supplies over the threshold and out onto the sidewalk.

"Not here."

He fished around in his pocket and handed her a set of keys.

"What is this?"

There was a Mazda symbol on it. But Rett didn't drive a Mazda.

He walked over to a navy blue SUV that was parked along the village green and opened the hatch. He hefted the supplies inside and turned back to her.

"You bought a new car?" Something wasn't connecting here.

"No," he said carefully. "This was my spare."

Right. She had seen the Mazda lurking in the corner of the four-car garage.

"Don't get mad. It's for you." He cringed a little when he said it, like he was expecting an outburst.

"Excuse me?"

"It's yours," he said again. "You have a learner's permit now. You need a safe car to learn how to drive. And I don't particularly want my truck to crash through the wall of a Wegman's."

"Are you insane?"

A new laptop was one thing. But a gifted car was absurd.

"It's for purely selfish reasons. I worry about you on the bike," he said with a glance at the bike rack. "It gets really foggy, and people drive like assholes on the lake road. Plus it's going to be freezing here soon."

She opened her mouth to speak, but he shook his head.

"I don't want to hear another word about it. It cost me nothing, and your safety is priceless."

She reached over and shoved him. There was no use arguing with him.

"You're impossible, Everett Rhodes."

He shrugged. "You'll learn to ignore it."

CHAPTER FORTY-FOUR

RETT

IT WAS HERE. THE PARTY THAT COULD DECIDE THE WINERY'S
entire future. Rett surveyed the room. Invited guests milled
around glittering cocktail tables. Tiered trays of cupcakes he
had stress baked the night before waited on a banquet table.
He wasn't satisfied with his icing technique, but they had
been a welcome distraction. The sparkling wine was labeled
and chilling in ice buckets in the storeroom.

Thankfully, there had been no sign of Chris or Alexa.

The door opened, and Jade and Margie walked in. He
almost staggered. Jade was stunning in a glittering gold
gown with a sky-high slit up the leg. She smiled, and her
eyes lit up when she saw him. His heart lifted.

He opened his mouth, but nothing came out. A realization hit him like a meteor crashing through the roof. He was
in love with her. But that was insane. He couldn't be. They
had barely known each other for two weeks.

She came over and wrapped him in a hug. "Everything
looks amazing. How are you feeling?"

He shook his head, and slowly his ability to speak

returned. "Nervous. But there's nothing I can do about it now."

She pulled back and straightened his bowtie. "Your grandmother would be so proud. Seriously."

She leaned in to kiss him, and there was a gasp.

"I have to admit, Everett, I thought you were lying to us." Rett's dad, Gerald, adjusted his horn-rimmed glasses and smoothed his salt-and-pepper hair.

"Pleased to meet you, Jade." He reached out one hand. It jostled his tie, which had music notes on it. She shook his hand firmly.

"I regret to inform you I am very much real," she said with a smile.

"Jade, darling." Rett's mother, Teresa, glided over like she had snuck in wearing ice skates. She pulled Jade in for a hug, then drew back to look at her.

"It's so nice to meet you. Rett's told us so much about you," Teresa said.

"Has he?" Jade said with a teasing glance at Rett.

He swept his arm out, and she ducked underneath it. He tucked her into his side and she pressed a hand to his chest.

Teresa squeezed his arm. "I'm so happy for you both. Rett says you're an artist?"

"I am. Normally you could tell by my nail beds, but I made sure to scrub thoroughly for such an important event. Rett's worked so hard for this."

"Come have a chat with us, dear," Gerald said, offering his arm to Jade. "If you have the time."

"I have nothing but time." Jade accepted his arm and followed them to one of the glittering cocktail tables.

The calm that had washed over him at her appearance dissipated. Her absence was like a wound. He strode through the gift shop, straightening bottle labels and finding a small bit of order in this chaos.

The book club walked in and waved before beelining for the bar. Waiters milled around with hors d'oeuvres.

He snuck a glance at Jade and his parents. She laughed at something his dad had said, but he couldn't tell what it was from the distance. His hands shook, and he almost dropped a bottle. All of a sudden things felt very serious. He was in love with her, and she had met his parents. Their lives were intertwining. He wasn't in control anymore. Jade held his heart, and there was nothing he could do about it. And the last time someone had held his heart, they had put it through a wood chipper.

He shelved the problem to deal with later and greeted friends and neighbors as they filtered in. People exclaimed over the speakeasy, which he had opened for the first time. The winery was filled with laughter and warmth. A dedicated social butterfly, his grandmother would have loved it.

Half an hour had passed since his parents had taken Jade to the side. That was enough for one evening.

"All right," Rett announced. "You've grilled the poor girl enough. Come with me. We have guests to greet."

He kissed his mother on the cheek and swept Jade off.

"Sorry. I told you they can be a lot," he said quietly.

"They were nice," she said. "I think they were just happy that you found someone. Do you need help with anything?"

She had worked hard all morning, standing on ladders, draping bunting, and polishing glasses.

"Just moral support when I get up there."

"When will—"

Her question was interrupted by the opening of the front door. Chris and Alexa came inside, waving to Rett's parents. His chest tightened. He knew they were coming, but it didn't make their presence any less annoying.

"Want me to bounce those posers out of here?" Jade asked as she stared them down.

"No. I don't want to make a scene. I'm sure they'll leave after they've swindled my parents out of money." Rett took a sip of a grüner veltliner and turned his back to them. After tonight, he wouldn't have to see them again until Christmas.

"You've got this. Go wow everyone," she said firmly and kissed him on the cheek. She walked away and waved at a man he didn't recognize. How did she know someone that he didn't at his party?

There was no time to worry about that. It was time to stop teetering on the edge. The future awaited. Tom clapped a hand on his back as he passed, and Cindy offered a quick hug.

Rett made a pit stop at the drink table and reached beneath the tablecloth. He pulled out one of the bottles of sparkling wine and popped the cork before gingerly pouring it into a champagne flute. He carried both to the front of the room and set the bottle on a cocktail table.

With his glass raised, he struck it with a fork until the din quieted.

"Ladies and gentlemen, thank you so much for joining Rhodes Vineyard's golden anniversary celebration this evening. As most of you know, this winery was my grandmother Valentina's greatest passion and joy."

He turned the bottle so the label faced the crowd.

"She was an extraordinary woman. Completely unafraid of hard work, deeply involved in every step of the wine-making process. A devoted wife, mother, and grandmother. This business was built on her blood, sweat, and tears. Unfortunately, she passed before she was able to achieve her final piece of the puzzle." He raised his glass and looked at it, studying the bubbles. "Sparkling wine."

Waiters descended through the crowd, passing out glasses full to the brim with bubbles.

"This was her dream. The crown jewel of the legacy she spent her life building. There is an excellent chance that I've ruined it all."

A chuckle rippled through the onlookers.

"But I'll let you all be the judge of that. To Valentina," he said, raising his glass.

"To Valentina," everyone echoed.

His dad wiped a tear from under his eye.

Everyone raised their glasses and took a sip. Excited chatter broke out. Rett took a sip himself and closed his eyes for a second, half afraid that it had turned to vinegar overnight.

But it hadn't. It was crisp and refreshing and tasted like summer. Against all odds and in spite of a smashed case, he had done it. Applause broke out, and his dad rushed out of the crowd to hug him.

Their approval wasn't easy to come by. It kind of felt like winning the lottery.

"This is going to turn things around. I can tell," Gerald said. "She would have loved it."

"Thanks, Dad. I better go mingle."

A string quartet in the corner started playing. The crowd descended on him, but the only person he wanted to see was Jade. Her glass was empty, and she was still laughing with the stranger, who appeared to be squatting and miming something. He was incredibly muscular with a neck the width of a tree. Who the hell was he, and why was he talking to Jade?

Jade glanced at him and excitedly waved. "Rett, come here. I want you to meet someone."

He crossed to them cautiously and shook the stranger's hand a little more firmly than was necessary.

"Rett, this is Lindon. He's a CrossFit friend of mine from the city. And he's also a food and wine critic for the *New York Times.*"

Rett's head jerked back like he had whiplash. How had she pulled that off?

"Pleasure to meet you," Lindon said.

"I am so honored to have you here," Rett said. "Thanks for making the trip."

"Honestly? It was worth it. This is your first attempt at sparkling wine?"

"After a lot of painstaking research, yes."

"I would love to do a feature on the winery if you'd be open to it. And maybe take a half-case home if you have a spare."

Jade was grinning behind Lindon's back. She opened her eyes wide and stared at him. Right, he should respond.

"That would be amazing. Thank you."

Having a feature in the *Times* would be huge. Life-changing.

"Why don't I leave you guys to talk? I see a crab puff that is calling my—"

At that moment, Chris stepped to the front of the room and clinked his fork against his glass. The room fell silent.

Of course he couldn't let the evening pass without making it about him.

"Ladies and gentlemen," Chris said, "I just wanted to say I'm so happy to see you all here tonight. My brother has done such an incredible job carrying on the Rhodes family legacy. I would be remiss if I didn't do what I could to carry on the legacy in my own way."

He turned to Alexa, who was simpering nearby. With his eyes on her, he slowly came down to one knee.

A gasp raced through the crowd. Shock radiated straight to Rett's core. Heat flared in his face. Chris was going to propose to Alexa at his party? On the night of his triumph? Absolutely not.

Jade had gone rigid beside him, and her hands were curled into fists.

"Alexa Marie Dumont," Chris began. He fished a square box out of his pocket and clutched it in his hands.

Tears sprung in Alexa's eyes.

"I've been waiting to do this for two years. I've known from the moment we met that you were the girl I was going to marry someday."

Oh, the moment they met as in that time Rett had brought her home for Christmas? Fucking typical.

"Your laugh is contagious. Your heart is so beautiful, so pure. I love you endlessly. Would you do me the great honor of being my wife?" He cracked the box open, and Alexa gasped. It must have been a big one. Maybe that was the real source of this round of money troubles.

"Yes! Of course I'll marry you." She burst into tears, and he slid the ring onto her finger. It flashed under the overhead lights.

Applause broke out. Rett's parents converged on the couple, clapping Chris on the back.

The shock receded, and in its place rage boiled hot and overwhelming.

"Would you excuse me for a minute?" he said through gritted teeth. He dove out the front door and stood on the front porch, hands shaking.

The door popped open behind him, and Jade stepped out. Fear gripped his heart. He was looking at his future.

He had thought he was in love with Alexa, and her betrayal almost destroyed him. But what he felt for Jade was so much stronger. If she left and the future that he so desperately wanted disappeared, there would be nothing left of him.

"Are you okay? I can't believe he did that." She laid a gentle hand on his arm, and he shook it off.

She shrank back like he had screamed at her.

What was he thinking? They were too different. It would never work. She was a city girl who would grow tired of small-town life. Or she'd get sick of his work schedule or his need to control everything. She'd leave him just like Alexa had, and he would be left broken. It wasn't fair. None of this was fair.

Fear and anger poured out of him like a poison. "Are you kidding me? Of course I'm not okay. I have given everything I have to this place." He jutted a finger over his shoulder. "Spent years learning how to make wine, trying to make nice with my fucking cheating liar of a brother because it's what my family wanted. And on the night we were supposed to celebrate this final piece of the dream—her dream—my own brother proposes to my ex-girlfriend in front of me."

He paced, heels striking the pavement. "She's going to be in my life forever now. Every holiday, every family gathering. I'm tired of sweeping everything under the rug. I'm tired of trying so hard to take care of everyone else's dreams and feelings but my own."

"Does this mean you figured out what your dream is?" she asked gently.

Was she trying to redirect him like a fucking toddler?

"My dream is to be left the fuck alone," he shouted.

This time, she took a step back. "It's going to be okay. I'm right here. We can fix this," she said. Her tone was calm, but color had bloomed in her cheeks.

"Fix it?" He let out a bitter laugh. "How are you going to fix it when you can't even fix yourself, Jade? Are you going to run them over with your car? Oh, that's right. You don't have a driver's license. You don't have retirement savings. Not even a steady job. You have nothing."

Tears shimmered in her eyes. She squeezed them shut and turned away.

Shit. He had gone too far.

She shook her head. "I knew it. Deep down, I knew this is how you felt about me. You looked at me like I was a pet, a little project for your savior complex." She opened her eyes and turned to look at him. "I guess you're right. I have nothing." She turned on her heel and stormed off across the parking lot, nearly tripping on the hem of her dress.

Regret filled him immediately. Chris fucked with his head and now everything was ruined.

"Jade, wait—"

"Fuck you." Her car door slammed, and she fishtailed out of the parking lot.

CHAPTER FORTY-FIVE

JADE

TEARS STREAMED DOWN JADE'S CHEEKS AS SHE NAVIGATED THE country roads. Rett's words had lacerated her straight to the bone. She didn't even recognize that man on the porch.

She rolled to a stop at an intersection and let out a guttural scream. Back at square one. There wasn't a future for her here. Not with a man who could speak to her in that way.

There was no choice. She had to go back to New York. Her phone rang, and she whipped it out. Rett. She ignored the call and then blocked his number.

She had put herself and her heart on the line, and it had been returned to her mutilated and dragged through the metaphorical mud.

It wasn't fucking fair. She had lost her entire family, then Nate, then her basic ability to find any beauty or inspiration in the world around her. Her muse, her financial security, her future. And just when things were starting to look up, the universe pounded her back into the dirt.

As soon as she passed her driver's license exam on Monday, she was heading back to the city. It was time to build a new life. Without Rett. It had been insane to think that she could make a new beginning here. She didn't belong here. She didn't really belong anywhere. There were no roots, no family. Nothing to tie her to any one place.

Air whistled in and out of her nose as she took deep, steadying breaths. Penny still needed her. She couldn't break down completely. She wasn't entirely alone.

Even though everything had catastrophically fallen apart, things had been worse after Nate left. Something deep within her called out for release. She focused on the feeling as she drove back to Margie's, hands shaking with adrenaline.

The new canvases she had bought just in case—and also because they were significantly cheaper than the ones she had bought in New York—waited for her in shopping bags just inside the door of the cottage.

She dropped to her knees and took a moment to tearfully hug Penny. She let her outside, breathing in the crisp fall air like it would be the last time. And maybe it would. Maybe it would hurt too much to come back here. Every inch of this town was going to remind her of Rett.

Steven skittered past them, but Penny barely gave him a passing glance. Jade put his evening snack on the porch and closed the door behind her.

She unzipped her dress and let it slide down her shoulders, a mess of sequins on the floor. She grabbed a clean palette from the drying rack and angrily squirted colors onto it. Back to the deep reds, the blacks, the indigos. A canvas slammed onto the easel.

There was something primal and angry waiting to burst out of her. She took a moment to turn her focus inward, to embrace and accept without judgment the feelings that waited for her.

And then she painted.

———

THE NEXT MORNING, JADE WOKE WITH A START WHEN something rapped on her front door. She sat up like she had been struck by lightning. The colors of sunrise still bled into the sky.

Her heart raced. If that was Rett, she was going to answer the door with a can of Mace. But a quick inspection revealed only Cindy, who stood on the porch with a casserole dish covered in foil.

She whipped the door open, and Cindy's eyes bulged out.

The casserole dish hit the wooden floor with a clunk, and Cindy immediately started checking Jade's vitals.

"Hey—what are you doing?"

"What happened? Did you cut yourself in the kitchen? I have my kit in the car. We'll stop the bleeding, and then I'll take you into the office and—"

"What the hell are you talking about? I'm fine."

Jade looked down at herself and noticed for the first time that not only was she wearing only her beige strapless bra and panties, but she was also covered in splotches of red paint from her angry painting session the night before.

"It's paint," she said hurriedly. "Not blood."

Cindy deflated in relief. "Thank god. I'm a little hungover from last night, so I was not looking forward to suturing any surprise gaping wounds. What happened to you last night? I saw you go outside with Rett and then you disappeared. You didn't answer any of my texts."

The memories flooded back, and unwelcome tears formed in Jade's eyes for the millionth time in the past twenty-four hours. She had thought for sure she had cried them all out the night before.

Guttural screams and grunts had exploded from her for hours as she aggressively dragged the brush across canvas after canvas. Shreds of newspaper, splinters of a vinyl record, even pages torn from books joined the fray.

It was mixed media at its most unhinged. A return to her roots. It was probably all garbage, but at least it meant that she hadn't lost everything again.

Even if there wasn't hope for love, at least there was hope for her future.

Jade stepped back and let Cindy inside.

While Penny greeted Cindy, Jade slipped a sweatshirt over her paint-covered body.

Cindy set the casserole dish on the kitchen island and turned to look at Jade, arms crossed. "So?"

"He yelled at me and he asked me how I was going to 'fix this when I can't even fix myself.'"

Cindy's mouth dropped open. "No, he fucking didn't."

Jade smiled sadly. "It's better that I know. I always kind of figured he felt that way under the surface. How could he not? I am pretty pathetic."

"You shut that beautiful mouth. You are not pathetic. Do you see what you've overcome since you've come here? What you've created?" Cindy pointed at the stack of canvases drying in the kitchen. "You have such power, Jade. No one can take that from you. No one."

Jade sniffed and crossed her arms. She stared out at the silent gray form of the lake. More than half the leaves were missing now. It was time for her to go.

"I have to go back to the city. There's no future for me here."

Cindy shook her head and ripped the aluminum foil off

the dish. "I'm going to murder him. I meant what I said before. No matter what happens, you will always have us. Even if you purposely move five hours away. Now why don't you go take a shower? You look like a homicide victim. I'll brew some coffee and take Penny out."

"Thank you," Jade said. The kindness was almost enough to bring her to tears again. She needed to get it together. She wasn't going to be able to take her driver's test tomorrow if she stayed a weepy mess.

Twenty minutes later, she re-entered the living room with damp hair. Gemma and Elena now sat at the island, yawning into cups of coffee. They turned at her arrival and enveloped her in a group hug.

"You didn't have to come." Jade's voice was muffled in the hug.

"Yes, we did. Nobody disrespects our Jade." Gemma drew back to look at her. "I will happily troll Craigslist and find someone to put a curse on him if you want."

"I could go in and knock a bunch of bottles off the shelf," Elena offered.

Jade shook her head. "I don't think I need to bring any more bad karma to myself. But I appreciate you. All of you. When Nate left me, he took all our friends."

"Even though he cheated on you?" Gemma said in disbelief.

"Yep. I've been alone for a long time. I've forgotten what it's like to have close friends."

Cindy, Elena, and Gemma all looked at each other. Cindy's lip quivered.

"I can't believe that wine-slinging fuckface said that to you," Gemma said with a harrumph. She slid a plate in front of the empty seat at the island. "You need to eat," she said to Jade.

"I'm not really—"

"No buts," Elena said sternly. "Eat." She pointed at the plate.

Jade obeyed and sank into her seat. Even though her soul felt as battered as if she had just gone five rounds with a prizefighter, a sense of peace was creeping in. If it wasn't meant to be, it wasn't meant to be. She deserved someone who would choose her every single day. No matter what kind of emotional baggage they carried from their past, or whose brother was getting engaged.

Rett had gently reminded her that she deserved more than a string of one-night stands and emotional distance. She deserved a partner in life. Someone to share all the good and all the bad. Like her parents had. Like Margie had. And she would find them. Right after she fixed everything else that was wrong in her life.

Penny laid her snoot on Jade's leg, and she petted her. For right now, life with Penny and her new friends was enough.

Hours later, bellies full of coffee and the eggs Benedict casserole that Cindy had made, the girls had all piled into Jade's new car. The steering wheel was cool beneath her fingers. What the hell was she supposed to do about the car now that she and Rett had imploded? He said it was a gift, but the insurance and title were still in his name. And she would think about him every time she sat in it.

She shoved the thoughts to the back of her mind and drove to the local DMV branch.

Ten minutes later, Cindy pointed out the window. "Okay, this time, just watch the cones. I know you can do this."

It was Jade's fourth attempt at parallel parking, and none of them had been pretty.

"Pull up parallel to that car, slap it in reverse, then crank your wheel as hard as it'll go," Gemma instructed over the incessant clicking of the turn signal.

Elena slapped Gemma on the arm. "What if she cocks it too hard and she hits the other car?"

"She won't. I'm telling you, this is how my dad taught me."

"Okay," Jade said wearily. She cranked the wheel and started to reverse.

"When your back passenger door passes their bumper, turn your wheel straight."

Jade obliged and continued reversing.

"I think she's gonna do it," Cindy whispered.

Elena and Gemma shushed her.

"Now when your side mirror covers their taillight, turn the wheel the total opposite way."

"Oh my god. I'm doing it," Jade said.

The car slid smoothly backward and lined up with the curb.

"Boom. You can center it a little if you want to, but this is enough to pass."

Jade threw the car into park and clapped her hands excitedly. "I did it! An entire decade later than most people learn to parallel park, but I freakin' did it."

Cindy shook her. "I'm so proud of you. What time is your test tomorrow?"

"Nine."

"I'm taking you," she said.

"You don't have to do that. I'm sure you have patients. Margie already said—"

"No. I'm taking you. Margie will understand."

"Fine." Jade reached across the seat to hug her. "Thank you, guys. Seriously. Having a driver's license is going to change so much for me. I won't be stuck in the city if I don't want to be."

"Good. I still think you should consider moving here. I bet if we tried hard enough, we could drive Rett out of town," Gemma mused.

"He is terrified of heights," Cindy said thoughtfully.

"And cardio," Elena chimed in.

Jade laughed. "I'm not going to drive him from his home. But I won't let his presence here stop me from coming to visit. Maybe we could be friends someday. Lots of friends have intimate carnal knowledge of each other's bodies, right?"

"Sure they do," Elena said with a comforting squeeze on Jade's shoulder.

A few hours later, Jade was alone again. She spent some time doing laundry and packing everything up, then put it all in the car so she could make a quick getaway after the test. She would figure out what to do about the car later.

Wind whipped across the lake, loosing leaves from above. They drifted dreamily into the water. The damp smell of fall was all around.

The tingles were back. Surely she had earned a wine and paint break. If the canvases didn't dry by tomorrow, Margie would hold on to them until she came back.

When she planted herself in front of the canvas this time, she didn't feel the same anger and urgency. That would probably come back later. Anger and grief came in waves, stealing her breath when she least expected it. In the future, she'd probably be triggered by a picture, a song. But for now, she could take a moment to process.

When she prepared her palette, this time it came in bright hues. Yellow, pink, orange, royal blue, and lavenders. She took a breath and tapped into her deepest self. Her brush blotted and dipped over the canvas. A streak here, a line there.

Something was forming, but she wasn't entirely sure what it was. Her hand glided practically on its own until something formed. A naked woman, turned away from the onlooker, with butterflies and vines exploding from her voluminous hair. She was raw, natural, part of the earth.

When it was done, she took a step back and looked at it. *Rebirth*. That's what this trip felt like, and that was what this painting would be called.

Movement outside caught her eye. Margie was outside filling the bird feeders that lined her deck.

Jade plucked a painting from the pile and hustled out the door, Penny trailing behind her.

"Hi," she called to Margie.

"Jade, dear. I got your text. What am I going to do without you?"

"I'm sure you'll manage," Jade said with a smile. "You probably miss the silence."

"I did hear what sounded like some angry painting last night," Margie mused. "Is everything okay?"

"No. Things with Rett are over. He was hurting, but he was really cruel last night, and I'm not going to allow that in my life. Never again."

"Oh, sweetheart." Margie dropped the bag of birdseed on the table and came over to clutch her hand. "I'm so sorry to hear that."

"It's fine," Jade said hurriedly. "It was my sign to get back to the real world. But I wanted to thank you again for all your kindness. You honestly and truly changed my life. You gave me a place to stay and the second chance I so desperately needed."

"I don't know about all that," Margie said with a wave of

one hand. "I just selfishly wanted a Jade Gardner original. You should see the Instagram post I made with the mural. Over six thousand likes. I think the café will be pretty busy tomorrow."

"Really?" Jade asked.

"Oh, yes. The world's very excited to see you painting again."

"Wow." Maybe the gallery would work with her after all. The pieces she had produced last night were more like her old style. Maybe it would be enough.

"Well, thank you. For everything. Here." She held out the canvas.

Margie inhaled sharply. Her husband, David, was captured in brushstrokes sitting on a bench in front of the café. The sunflower hovered just over his head.

"This is too much," she said, turning to Jade with tears in her eyes.

"No. It's not nearly enough. I'm really going to miss you."

Margie threw her arms wide and pulled Jade into a tight hug. "You have to come for Christmas. I would love to have all my kids under one roof."

Damn it. The tears were back. Jade blinked them away and pulled back from the embrace.

"I will. There's nowhere else I'd rather be."

They looked at each other for a moment, smiling watery smiles.

"The invitation's always open, you know," Margie said. "As far as I'm concerned, the cottage is yours."

"Rett would say it's very fiscally irresponsible to not rent out a vacant property," Jade said.

"Well, he's also a bit of an idiot. So forgive me if I take any advice from him with a wheelbarrow full of salt."

————

THE CHILL FALL AIR TICKLED HER NOSE AS JADE STEPPED OUT of the DMV. A beam of sunshine blinded her as she looked at the plastic card in her hand.

"What's the verdict?" Cindy called across the parking lot. She had stepped out to do a teleconference with a patient. Penny's leash was wound around her wrist.

Jade triumphantly held her driver's license in the air.

Cindy's fist pumped the air. "You did it! Is it awful that I'm kind of sad you got it on the first try? Because it means you're leaving today, not because I don't want you to succeed."

Jade hustled across the sidewalk, enjoying the scent of decaying leaves in the air. Was that cinnamon? Did the air always smell like fall here, even outside a place as heinous as the DMV?

"I didn't expect to, honestly," she said. "But you guys helped so much, especially with the parallel parking. I can't thank you enough. This gives me...options."

"But you're still leaving?"

"I have to."

And she was taking Rett's car with her. It was the least he could do. Was she ready for a five-hour drive into a major metropolitan area with a freshly minted driver's license? Probably not. But she had been through worse.

Cindy stared off into the distance, in the direction of the mountains. "I still can't believe Rett did that to you. He's on my shit list now. My first stop after work is his rival winery."

"Don't punish him on my behalf. The next time I see him, I'll probably be six months pregnant and married to some smokin' hot basketball player or musician." It was a joke, but her tone sounded flat even to her.

"Not another artist?"

Jade shook her head. "Artists are too temperamental. We'd kill each other."

The truth was, she couldn't imagine moving on right now. As much as she was trying to be brave and confront her new reality, there was a gaping, Rett-shaped hole in her heart. He couldn't have been more opposite than her. While she flew by the seat of her pants, he lived his life by spreadsheets and plans. Everything was carefully regimented, every scenario prepared for. They would have made an amazing team.

He had given her so much—kindness, affirmation, support, encouragement. He had been nothing but a gentleman—well, outside the bedroom. Their future together had been as clear in her mind as if it were a memory. It would have been beautiful.

But he had royally fucked it all up. If that was how he acted when he was provoked, she would never see him again. Her new normal was going to be one of boundaries and self-care.

"I'm going to miss you so much," Cindy said tearfully.

"I'll be back at Margie's for Christmas. I promise," Jade said with a hug.

"Come on, Penny," she called. Penny hopped into the passenger seat.

Jade waved one final time and took a last look around. She drove over the carpet of red and gold leaves, waving at Cindy.

It was time to start over.

CHAPTER FORTY-SIX

RETT

"I'll be honest, it's hard to pick a favorite." Lindon sat on the velvet couch in the speakeasy, an array of glasses in front of him. "My husband will kill me if I don't bring a bottle of this back." He tapped a Blaufränkisch.

"That's high praise coming from you," Rett said.

Lindon lifted a glass to his nose and inhaled deeply. Ruby liquid swirled inside. "You really have something special here."

Had would be more appropriate. Sure, everything he could have hoped for had just come true—a feature in the *New York Times* would all but guarantee a boom in business. Everyone's jobs should theoretically be safe. He could dive in deeper on the sparkling wine and figure out what the future held for Rhodes Vineyard.

But all the success in the world meant nothing without Jade.

He had spent all of Sunday in bed, hoping that if he just slept enough, he would wake to find that everything had been a nightmare. He ignored calls from his parents, opting instead to hide in the dark, empty confines of his bedroom.

Jade had blocked his number after their fight, and he hadn't had the wherewithal to face the hurt written on her face on Sunday.

And now she was gone. After a lengthy interrogation, Cindy had revealed she had left town that morning.

He was such a fucking idiot. Something about seeing Chris propose to Alexa had broken his brain, and he had been unspeakably cruel to the person he cared about the most.

He felt her absence in every inch of the space around him. How could she trust him after that poison had poured from his mouth? He was an idiot, and he deserved to be alone.

When the tasting ended, Rett waved as Lindon's rented car disappeared down the driveway. He had promised the feature would be in the Sunday edition.

Rett flipped the lights off and locked the door. He had stayed open late to do a special tasting for Lindon. And now he was alone with nothing to distract him.

He tucked the day's deposit in the safe, and his fingers brushed against something small and hard. He withdrew a small box.

Fuck.

He flipped open the lid. A pear-shaped diamond glinted inside—the ring he had meant to give Alexa two years ago. At first, he had kept it around because he thought for sure she would come back to him. But the box sat there for weeks, then months. At some point, it became a reminder of the person he used to be. The Rett who had bought this ring was a different person entirely—fun, romantic, optimistic. He believed in love and the melding of two lives.

He squeezed it so hard the box creaked. He should throw it into the lake. Shove it up his brother's ass. Do something—anything—to take this pain away. He snapped it shut and slid it into his pocket. Fretting in the winery wasn't going to do him any good.

He locked up and returned home, greeted only by the emptiness echoing in the gargantuan house. The painting of Penny stared forlornly back at him. It didn't feel like home without Jade's frantic painting and Penny's army of tennis balls.

There wasn't even a way for him to apologize. What was he going to do, drive to New York and bang on her apartment door? She didn't want to speak to him. And he didn't blame her.

She deserved much better than him. But he couldn't let her go. He needed to apologize in a big way. But how?

On autopilot, he made a pan of brownies and slid them in the oven. Upstairs, he shed his work clothes and slipped into a pair of athletic shorts. He went to the gym and punished his body—bicep curls until his arms were screaming, weighted squats that nearly buckled his knees. But no amount of exertion was going to distract from his depressing reality.

Jade was gone, and Alexa was going to be in his life forever. Every holiday, every wedding, every funeral. He would be forced to stare into the eyes of the woman who slid into his brother's bed without a second thought.

He threw his dumbbell down with a roar and stomped back up the stairs. The ring box sat on the counter, mocking him with the lake in the background. He should just throw it in. Let it sink to the bottom and decay. He had one hand on the back door when there was a knock.

He stopped and checked the doorbell camera. Tom, still in his postal service uniform, stood on the front porch. At least someone was still speaking to him.

He tossed the box on the counter and opened the front door.

Tom rushed in for a hug, then drew back and slapped him lightly in the face.

"You fucked up, mate."

"I'm aware," Rett said, cheek stinging.

Tom handed him a foil-wrapped bundle and strolled inside. He took a seat at the island and helped himself to Rett's glass of wine.

Rett followed him and opened the bundle. A sandwich sat inside.

"Vegemite and cheese. My mum used to make them for me when I was sick," Tom said. "I know you're not sick, but being an idiot is kind of like being sick."

"Thanks."

The ring box seemed to have caught Tom's eye. He opened it and looked at Rett with his eyebrows raised.

"It was for Alexa," Rett explained. "I never used it, obviously."

Tom visibly relaxed. "Good. I was worried I was going to have to explain to you what a terrible idea an apology proposal would be."

Rett slumped at the counter. The ring had cost him almost $15,000. It would be insane not to sell it and be free of this burden. It could give him a jump start on the next batch of sparkling, or generous holiday bonuses for his employees.

Maybe he could use part of it to craft some kind of apology for Jade.

"So how are you going to apologize?" Tom asked as if he had read Rett's mind.

"I don't know. She blocked my number. She won't speak to me."

"You know where her apartment is, though?"

"For now. For all I know, she's signed a new lease." He buried his head in his hands.

Tom's hand landed on his shoulder. "I know what Chris did fucked you up, mate. But you can't keep using him—and your grandmother—as an excuse not to live your life. I can't keep watching you sabotage every chance of happiness you get. You need to make it up to her, and you need to sort out your priorities."

"I know. My hours at the winery aren't sustainable. They never have been. I was just so worried about driving it all into the ground. Which is exactly what I did. And the only reason there might be light on the other side is because of Jade. She brought that wine critic to the party. And I repaid her by yelling at her."

Tom took another sip of wine. "What would Jade tell you to do?"

Rett faltered.

Their agreement echoed in his mind—honesty always. But words weren't going to be enough. He needed to show her how much she meant to him. He hadn't even fulfilled her most basic request: identifying his dream. He didn't deserve to think about his dream. But no apology he made would feel complete if he didn't take it seriously.

What did he want? What was his dream? As if in response, the oven beeped behind him. He stared at the glossy, crackly top of the brownies. The warm scent of cocoa filled his kitchen. It was like therapy.

"I didn't know you baked," Tom said.

Rett slid them onto a cooling rack. He hesitated. Jade would tell him to be bold. It was stupid to be embarrassed about baking.

"I love to bake," he said quickly.

"Huh," Tom said. "What about an apology cake?"

Rett shook his head. "It's not enough. She deserves change. Action. Something that shows I listen to her."

He pulled out his laptop and sat at the island. In minutes, his browser was clogged with tabs of local community colleges.

Did any of them have pastry arts classes?

That had been his dream once, before his parents convinced him that business school was the more practical path. But now he had all the benefit of an education and first-hand experience of running his business.

The cursor hovered over enrollment information for a school forty-five minutes away. They had night classes, but it would definitely mean cutting back some at the winery. And it didn't guarantee that Jade would see he was taking her seriously. Was it insane?

Before he could second-guess himself, he signed up for a night class starting in January. Maybe it was time to follow that little voice.

Step one in his apology was complete. In the meantime, he needed to figure out how to make it up to Jade.

Tom cut into the brownies and took a bite.

"Holy shit, that's good. You've been holding out on us."

Rett straightened up. "Maybe I have. I need your help."

"Of course. With what?"

"Call everyone and tell them to come here."

"Everyone?"

"Everyone."

CHAPTER FORTY-SEVEN

JADE

TWO DAYS HAD PASSED SINCE HER FLIGHT FROM THE FINGER Lakes. After a somewhat harrowing five-hour drive during which she had nearly leapt out of her car and screamed at another driver for following her too closely, she had arrived home without further incident. Rett's car was in an over-priced garage in the Bronx, but at least she didn't have to see it every day.

It was strange to be back in the city, as if she had never left on that fateful trip to the doomed wedding. It felt like years had passed since the disastrous union of Ashley and Nate, even though it had been a matter of weeks.

Despite leaving the town that returned it to her, her muse tingle didn't disappear. Visions and images haunted all her waking and sleeping moments, begging to be transferred to canvas. A notebook next to her bed was littered with half-sketched ideas that would hopefully one day translate to canvas.

Some peculiar source of inspiration had washed over her. It was hard to describe in words, so she kept her titles short.

Rebirth. Karma. Feminist. Self-worth. They probably wouldn't be the permanent titles of these chaotic mixed media pieces, but they felt true.

Her experience in the Finger Lakes had pulled some kind of cosmic cork out of her. Everything she had bottled up since the day her world had shattered was pouring out.

Her parents, the crescent moon clinging to the cityscape outside her window, a tipped-over trashcan on the street outside. Everything was an inspiration. It couldn't have been more different from when she had left.

Was it the change of scenery? Something in the water or soil? Was it learning to open her heart again? Whatever it was, she'd be forever grateful that she had taken the risk.

Jade slid her headphones on and went for a run on her old route, Penny in tow. It was almost nice to be back on flat ground instead of fighting the never-ending hills and dips of Hammondsport.

But it wasn't the same without Rett's labored breathing beside her, panting and swearing. And then there was the scenery—as much as she loved the bodega down the block and the restaurants in her neighborhood, it just wasn't as beautiful as sunrise on the lake.

She sighed and quickened her pace, heading north to Central Park. There were a couple of lakes there. Maybe that would be enough to fill the holes in her heart.

Her feet pounded the pavement, canvasing the familiar park. She and Nate had picnicked on the grass by the carousel. Her mother had taken her on weekend walks here while her dad was at work.

This place, the city and the surrounding areas, had been the only home she'd ever known.

But it wasn't the same. She ached for the clean air and amber leaves. The empty roads, the small-town pace, and familiar faces. She had been in Hammondsport for less than a month and she had met half the town. But when she ended her run and clambered back up the steps to the fourteenth floor, she didn't recognize the woman locking the apartment next door.

Maybe a change of neighborhood would do her some good. After a shower and breakfast from her favorite café—yikes, she really needed to cut back on the spending—she took the train over to an apartment with an opening in January she had found the night before.

Throggs Neck. A hilarious name, to be sure. She didn't know much about the area, but Philip Avenue seemed, by all accounts, safe. She turned around on the front stoop and took in the street. She was a block back from the bay, which was a nice change of scenery. But the gray water didn't look anything like the lake she had come to love. And there was no grass, only a handful of trees next to the apartment building.

The door opened behind her, and she shrieked.

"Sorry." A middle-aged man chuckled behind the door. "You must be Jade?"

"Yes. Sorry for screaming in your face."

"Happens all the time. I'm Chuck. Care to come in?"

She took a moment to memorize him—deep laugh lines surrounding warm brown eyes, NYU sweatshirt, trusty pair of white New Balances. Just in case he ended up trying to imprison and murder her. Couldn't be too careful.

Chuck walked her through the apartment, explaining amenities and rent procedures.

"So you're an artist?" he asked. "I sure would love to brag about having an artist-in-residence."

"I am." For the first time in forever, the words were true. "The apartment's beautiful," she said.

It was almost twice the size of her current place. There was a decent amount of natural light, more than enough space for all of her current belongings plus room for her art supplies. Maybe it didn't have the shabby chic adorableness of her cottage by the lake, or all the amenities of her neighborhood in Midtown. But she had fared with far less.

"Thank you. We put a lot of work into these. It's someone's home, so it should feel like it. I did bring the lease along if you're interested in signing today. Either way, I'll need to know by Monday."

The "yes" was on the tip of Jade's tongue. It was, theoretically, perfect. A reasonable rate, no roommate, a short train ride to Manhattan and everything it had to offer. So what was holding her back?

In her heart, she knew it was because it wasn't Hammondsport. Against all odds, she had envisioned a whole life in that sleepy, quirky town. She could practically feel the thrum of an energized home team crowd at future homecoming games. It was easy to imagine her daughter or son's first art show at the local high school, attending festivals on Rett's arm. Maybe her own studio and gallery on the town square, a stone's throw from Margie's Café. Lazy afternoons spent on the lake, steamy evenings on the rooftop of the winery.

It was like a life she could look at behind glass. It was beautiful, but it wasn't real. Even so, she couldn't bring herself to throw it all away just yet.

Jade collected her thoughts and straightened her shoulders. "I have a great feeling about this place. I'll let you know by Monday," she said.

"Suit yourself," Chuck said. "If you need a great lunch spot, Wicked Wolf is about a mile that way." He gestured into the distance with a slightly crooked index finger.

"Good tip." She waved goodbye and stepped outside. Almost as if on cue, her stomach growled. Maybe a sampling of the local fare wouldn't hurt.

She pulled up the address for the restaurant on her phone and aimlessly followed the directions. Could this be her new neighborhood? It was quiet and unassuming, refreshingly middle-class based on the cars parked all around. The near-constant cacophony of sirens in the city was absent here. In the summer, it might even be charming. A decent place to raise a family, if it ever came to that.

An hour later, she washed her hands in the ladies' room in the pub. Chuck had been right. She could get used to having this warm, eclectic restaurant in her backyard. Her reflection caught her eye in the long, rectangular mirror over the sink. Physically she looked fine, but the bags under her eyes didn't lie. And something else drew her attention too—the stupid ice skate tattoo under her collarbone.

Images of Nate flashed through her mind. His fake remorse in the kitchen of what should have been their shared apartment. His condescending looks at his rehearsal dinner. Countless trips and adventures and galas.

He had taken so much from her. And lied the entire time. Had she even really taken the time to process that? The person she had thought she would spend the rest of her life with had been screwing around behind her back with her best friend. It should have been obvious from the start. But she was blinded by her love for him.

But no more.

She dried her hands and thrust the door open. It was time to remove this last tie to Nate and that dark time.

She looked up the nearest tattoo parlor that took walk-ins and strode off in that direction.

A few blocks away, she popped open the front door of a

parlor. A bell rang above her. She was immediately immersed in the dark, atmospheric space that kind of looked like it had been decorated by Spencer's. The Rob Zombie poster on the wall stared back at her. The smell of citrus was sharp in the air. A man looked up from behind the counter. He had a septum piercing, two sleeves full of what appeared to be gothic versions of Disney princesses, and, alarmingly, an orange covered in rose imagery.

"You here for a tat?" he asked.

She nodded.

"Take a seat. There's a special on lower back tattoos this month," he said.

"How about coverups?" She showed him the ice skates.

"Easy," he said nonchalantly.

She could only imagine what Rett would have to say about her latest impulse decision. He'd probably lecture her for forty minutes for not comparing costs between different parlors, let alone checking out reviews for someone who was about to permanently change her appearance. Pre-Rett, she wouldn't have given such an impulse a second thought. But maybe she should give this *some* thought.

"Do you have some examples of previous works?" she asked.

"Book's over there." He was a man of few words. He gestured at a black binder on the counter.

She picked it up and flicked through several pages. A sigh of relief slipped between her lips. What he lacked in conversation skills he clearly made up for in artistic ability. His work ranged from phrases written in departed family member's handwriting to floral works to watercolor, symbols, even cat tattoos. Satisfied, she closed the book.

He sat down and wheeled over to her. "Decided?"

She searched on her phone for a few minutes and

showed him a map of Keuka Lake. "What can you do with this? But maybe with a sunflower element at the bottom," she added. The café's front door and Rett's first bouquet burned in her mind.

"Consider it done."

He set to prepping his tools, and she walked out with stinging skin and a brand-new tattoo an hour later. It was everything she had needed in the moment. Even though her time away was now a bittersweet memory, it had given her so much life and purpose that the good eclipsed the bad. Gone were the ice skates and mistakes of her past.

Invigorated by this physical cleansing, she pulled out her phone and opened a folder with dating apps. If she wasn't careful, she would be tempted to backslide to her old ways. She couldn't even imagine climbing into bed with a stranger right now.

One by one, she deleted her accounts. It was time to put the one-night stands behind her. She wasn't going to find her future husband on Wink or Tinder. All she could do was trust that the universe would put him in her path when she was ready.

She took a deep breath and surveyed her surroundings. Maybe Throggs Neck wouldn't be so bad. A fresh start was exactly what she needed.

CHAPTER FORTY-EIGHT

JADE

When she returned home, Jade wrapped glassine paper over her last canvas and slid it into the pizza delivery box. Now that the explosion of inspiration had finally ebbed, her plan was to ambush the rep from her old gallery. Even if she had to press them against the windows until someone deigned to look at them, she would find a way to get their eyes on her newest work.

And if they didn't want it, she would figure out how to sell them online. Rett probably would have been helpful with such an endeavor, but she wasn't about to ask him for help. Her stomach clenched at the thought. But she was strong and capable. She didn't need anyone else but Penny.

She ducked out her front door, traipsing down the stairs to the familiar sidewalk. She hadn't yet made her decision on the apartment. There were still a few days to think about it.

She swung open the door of the gallery and stepped into the familiar space. A woman at the desk looked up. Her fingers flew to her parted lips.

"Jade! It's so good to see you. I'm sorry about the landscapes," the woman said. There was a hesitancy in her words like she was wondering what the hell Jade was doing there.

Lyric, her old broker, hadn't changed a bit since their last encounter. Cobalt blue bifocals perched on her nose. A loud statement necklace was draped over a simple black dress that was sure to be designer.

"I brought you something else. It's okay if you don't want them, but I had to try."

Jade put the pizza delivery box on the counter and slid it towards Lyric.

Eyes wide, Lyric pulled out the first canvas and carefully unwrapped it.

"So there's actually two series," Jade said. "I brought you three of each. The first is pretty dark, lonely, brooding. The second is my favorite. The theme is 'rebirth.'"

Lyric pulled out canvas after canvas, displaying them on the counter without comment. She pored over each of them, not speaking for several minutes.

Nerves twisted in Jade's stomach. Maybe they didn't have the promise she had thought. Maybe two years of no progress whatsoever showed more than anticipated.

Finally, Lyric whirled around. A pleased smile hovered on her lips. "You're back. I knew it."

Heat crept into Jade's cheeks. She could have collapsed with relief. "Well, it was a long time coming."

"These are incredible," Lyric said. She turned back to the canvases again, seemingly taking in each detail. "Incredible," she repeated. "We'll have to have a showing, of course. I'm picturing two rooms. The first collection—the dark one —in the front room. Then guests can transition through some greenery into the second room."

Lyric was an expert in creating atmosphere based on an

artist's theme, from coordinating scents to dramatic lighting and themed decor.

"I know you kind of hinted that you were low on cash," Lyric said carefully. "Maybe sooner would be better?"

"As soon as you can," Jade said. Even with the payment from the mural, an impending security deposit and first and last month's rent in the metro area would undoubtedly drain her reserves.

"Let's do it on Friday then."

"This Friday?" Jade's eyes widened. She had never had a showing on such short notice. "That's in two days."

"The artist we were supposed to have this weekend is sick." She gestured to a number of canvases on the wall, all which featured abstract shapes in varying colors.

"That's too bad," Jade said, but she felt lighter than she had since coming back to the city. Maybe this was the universe's way of making it up to her.

Her spine was tingling again. She needed to go home and paint.

"There will probably be more pieces coming. I'll try to get them dry as soon as I can," she said. "You'll hold on to these?"

"I will protect them with my life," Lyric whispered reverently. "We'll start the advertising push today. I'm so happy you're back, Jade."

"Yeah. Me too."

Jade left the gallery with a full heart and, for the first time in a long time, hope.

———

THE EVENING OF HER FIRST SHOWING IN TWO YEARS, JADE paced nervously in her apartment. True to her word, Lyric had put out a media push announcing Jade's return to the art world. She had put together a showing remarkably fast, and twenty pieces made up the roster. It was nothing like any of Jade's earlier shows—there wasn't as much social commentary, just raw emotion and imagery.

Lyric had hinted that the number of RSVPs was very encouraging, but Jade shied away from the specifics. Tonight would make or break her.

It was her triumph, her comeback story. And with any luck, after tonight she wouldn't have to worry about finances for a while.

She slid in a pair of dangling gemstone earrings. Her hair was swept back and bobby pinned in place, and a simple black dress adorned her figure. She paired it all with knee-high boots (mostly for warmth).

"Come on, Penny." She whistled to the dog, who was wearing a bowtie collar and black tutu.

Lyric gave her artists a number of allowances, including bringing their pets with them for support. Penny was sure to knock over a buffet table or snatch an hors d'oeuvre out of someone's hand, but at least Jade would have her furry companion there.

Maybe tonight would be an opportunity to make some new friends. Hell, maybe she'd even meet the future love of her life. Stranger things had happened.

Penny, at least, seemed to be happy to be back in the city. During their walk to the gallery, she ducked her head from side to side, dragging Jade all over the pavement.

Finally, after Jade had nearly face-planted thanks to Penny's desire to chase an errant squirrel, they arrived at the gallery. A crowd teemed inside, people filing around the space and staring at her paintings. The light had been lowered, with beams of red and deep purple mood uplighting spaced evenly in the front room. Golden light was just visible between the branches of some faux greenery at the back of the gallery.

There was no time to waste. People were more likely to buy if she schmoozed them first, and her future was riding on this showing.

With a deep breath, she flung the door open and stepped inside.

"Here she is!" Lyric's voice rang out loud and clear in the gallery. People turned towards the door. A hush fell over the crowd, and classical music tinkled softly in the background.

Clapping broke out until the entire crowd applauded. Heat rose from deep within Jade. Between the nausea and embarrassment, she probably looked like a half-ripe tomato.

Penny's nose was pressed to the floor. She tugged hard and disappeared into the crowd. Traitor.

Jade finally remembered to smile and waved sheepishly. Half a dozen people converged around her.

"Jade, tell us about your new collection." Oh, this one had a voice recorder. Must be from some sort of publication.

She chatted and made small talk with a number of critics, potential buyers, and previous customers.

It was an overwhelmingly positive flood. People gushed over the juxtaposition of the dark and the light. For the first time, she even felt comfortable answering some overly personal questions—the inspiration behind the darkness, why she had disappeared for a number of years.

Someone tapped her on the shoulder, and she turned around, already mentally steeling herself for more small talk.

"Kenya! What are you doing here?" She leaned forward and was wrapped in Kenya's sculpted arms.

"I was in town. Blake's here too," she said, pointing at the corner of the room. Blake appeared to be chatting up a Wall Street-looking thirty-something with carefully slicked-back brown hair. At least someone was meeting the love of their life tonight. "We saw the announcement and had to come. I'm so happy everything worked out for you."

"Well, almost everything. Rett dumped me. Long story," Jade said.

Kenya frowned. "You say the word and I will burn that winery to the ground."

Jade laughed. "As fun as it would be to see you do some kind of prison bootcamp workouts, maybe we should avoid arson. Thank you so much for coming."

"I'm buying one of the paintings in the back room. As a wedding present," she added, flashing an engagement ring the size of a Kinder Egg under the mood lighting.

Jade grabbed her hand. "Are you kidding me? Hakeem proposed?"

Kenya nodded. "I hope you'll come. We're thinking next September."

"Not in the Finger Lakes, right?" Jade teased.

Kenya laughed and shook her head. "Definitely not. Love it there, but it's forever tainted for me after that shitshow."

"I'm so happy for you," Jade said, administering another hug. "Have you talked to Ashley?"

"A little. Apparently the divorce isn't going well."

Jade shook her head. As much as Ashley deserved to have her marriage fall apart, it didn't bring Jade any pleasure.

"That's a pity. Well, thank you again for coming, and for buying. Which one's going home with you?"

"Karma," Kenya said. "It's perfect."

"That's one of my favorites," Jade said with another

smile. It made her heart glow to think of one of her creations nestled on Kenya's walls in Los Angeles.

"Go schmooze," Kenya ordered, pointing to the back room.

"Yes, Mom," Jade said. She should probably figure out where Penny had disappeared to anyway.

When she stepped into the back room she had a split second view of a floral arch.

"*Surprise*," someone shouted. Someone crashed into her, and something heavy sloshed between them. Was that a bag of wine?

She pulled back to find Tom, Cindy, Elena, Gemma, and Margie all crowded into the back room.

Her heart leapt into her throat. She hadn't even told them about the showing. "What are you guys doing here?"

"We came to celebrate you, dummy," Gemma said, throwing herself on Jade.

Jade laughed into her shock of red hair. She hadn't even consciously realized how important it was to have someone on her side during her first post-Nate showing. And now she had a small battalion of people just waiting to support and celebrate her. Even if Rett wasn't here. That fact bothered her more than she cared to admit.

"We've been waiting to talk to you for like an hour." Cindy elbowed Tom out of the way. "You're so popular."

"Everyone's just shocked to see I'm not dead," Jade said.

"Stop it," Elena said. "They're here for you. And to fight each other to the death in bidding wars, apparently. Did you see how many 'sold' tags you have?"

She glanced pointedly at the far wall, where there were indeed a lot of paintings with tags. She made a mental note to go to her bank on Monday. It was time to set up a retirement account and find a way to make sure that she was never again on the brink of homelessness.

"We are so proud of you, sweetheart," Margie said. "That one's coming home with me." She pointed to another one of the rebirth series.

"The rest of us would snatch them up, too, but we can't afford you. You weren't kidding," Tom said. His Australian accent seemed to have gotten thicker over the course of the bag of wine.

"What's this?" Elena leaned forward and frowned at Jade's collarbone. "You got the ice skates covered up!"

Jade's tattoo had healed enough to be unveiled to the world. A crooked lake with a sunflower at the bottom now covered the last remnant of Nate.

"Let me see," Cindy said. They all crowded around her.

"It's perfect," Gemma declared. "Now all we need for you is to—"

"Come home?" another voice interrupted.

Jade inhaled sharply.

Everyone turned around. Jade bristled. There, standing just around the corner from one of the pieces he helped to inspire, was Rett.

Come home? Come *home*? What the fuck was that supposed to mean?

He held a bouquet of sunflowers, and he was wearing one of his stupid three-piece suits. Penny sat on his foot, panting happily. Traitor.

"Did someone say hors d'oeuvres?" Gemma said loudly.

There was a murmur of agreement, and they all disappeared. Soon, it was just Jade and Rett standing in the room surrounded by her art.

Anger flared like a struck match. This was her night. A

lifetime had passed since their last conversation. "What the hell are you doing here?"

He reached for her, but she stepped back and briefly fantasized about delivering a roundhouse kick to his chest. But that might damage one of her paintings.

His face fell. "I needed to see you. I would have come sooner, but I was trying to figure out how to apologize. I tried to call, but—"

"I blocked you. For good reason. What makes you think I want to see you after everything you said to me? Do you know how hard it was for me to open myself up to someone again? Only to be told that I have 'nothing' by the person I decided to move five hours away for?"

Her angry air quotes almost knocked the flowers out of his hand.

"I'm so sorry, Jade. Of course you wouldn't want to see me. I made the biggest mistake. Something about seeing my brother propose to Alexa just broke me. You were trying to comfort me, and I lashed out. I just kept thinking about seeing her every Christmas on my brother's arm."

Her hostility dropped a millimeter. He *had* gone through something incredibly traumatic seconds before their conversation.

"Well," she said, "you clearly still have feelings for her if your reaction to her getting engaged was that strong."

He shook his head. "I promise you, I don't. I don't care what she does. I just didn't want her to be part of my family. I didn't want to see her ever again. Probably the same way that you never want to see me again," he muttered.

"But none of that is an excuse," he said. "What I said was cruel and untrue. There's nothing to fix, and you don't have nothing. You have everything. You *are* everything, exactly as you are . I'm the one who has nothing."

She raised an eyebrow. His winery and lakefront property would beg to differ.

"Nothing that truly matters," he clarified. "And the worst part is, I haven't been honest with you."

Oh, good.

"What do you mean?"

"I broke the rules of our agreement. I fell in love with you. And it scared me."

She inhaled sharply. The jagged edges of her anger softened.

"For the first time in a long time I could see everything—kids, a fall wedding, a little studio space for you in town. A painting shed in the backyard," he said with a sad smile. "And then I thought about what it would be like to have it ripped away—if you decided to go back to New York, or if things just didn't work out. I'm afraid of what you mean to me. Of what you make me feel. You have a hold on me. I've never let anyone in the way I let you in, Jade."

She looked away, preferring to study her own brushstrokes. "I don't know what to say."

He grabbed her hand, but this time she didn't pull away. "You don't have to say anything. I've thought a lot about what you said before—tomorrow is never guaranteed. I know it was stupid to come here on your big night and interrupt your triumph. But if I didn't tell you now, in person, I would have regretted it every day for the rest of my life."

There was a rustling in the corner, and Tom appeared, dragging the corner of something large and flat. Had the gallery forgotten one of the decorations?

Slowly, a miniature version of the mural she had painted for Margie crawled into the room. But it was different—abstract blobs in a multitude of colors spanned the surface.

Her brain was jumbled. Nothing was making sense. All she could see were the flashes of color around her. Rebirth.

"I haven't been at the winery all week," Rett said. "I was working on a project. The whole town helped me, actually. And I took your homework seriously. I enrolled in pastry arts classes. You inspired me. I don't know exactly what I'll do with it, but I know I want to learn. I clearly have a long way to go." He gestured at the miniature mural.

"You made this?" She took a step closer to the mural. Each spot of color was a tiny dessert. Orange macarons, tiny blueberry pies, dark chocolate brittle. Desserts of all colors and types spread over the scene. Some of them had uneven shapes and edges, but the resemblance was undeniable. It must have taken days. It was beautiful. Imperfect and beautiful. He had found his dream.

"You belong here." He gestured at the mural. "And I took that from you. I understand if you want me to go. I don't want to ruin your night. You've worked so hard for this, and I'm so proud of you. You clawed your way back from the brink with grit and determination. I had everything handed to me, and I still managed to fuck it up."

He buried a hand in his hair, and her hands clenched. She had almost reached for him.

"I just needed you to know how sorry I am," he said. "And I needed to tell you that I love you. You're it for me, Jade. If there's any way you can imagine finding your way back to me, I'll be there."

His face was ashen. He turned away and took a step toward the door.

Fuck. A big part of her was still afraid. Not that she would lose her ability to paint again—that power was entirely her own, and nothing and no one would ever take it from her again. She could see her future with Rett so clearly.

The idea of having it ripped away was torment. But her mom would have wanted her to be brave.

"Wait," she said.

No one was perfect. When Nate and Ashley had gotten engaged, she had almost thrown a dumbbell through the window at her CrossFit gym. It was a human reaction, but she had taken it as a sign from the universe to cut ties and run. And damn it if she didn't love that stuffy, suit-wearing workaholic too.

"You will never speak to me like that again," she said.

He shook his head. "Never. None of it was true."

"You need to work less," she added sternly. "Especially if you're also going back to school. Which I think is great, by the way."

"I already handed off weekends. It was time. I have new priorities."

"I'm living in Margie's cottage for at least a year," she said, arms crossed.

His expression shifted. Relief flooded those infuriating green eyes. "Does this mean you're coming home?"

She threw herself on him and kissed him. Electricity crackled between them like the first time in the rain outside the restaurant. Unspoken feelings rose and crashed like two seas meeting. Love, relief, lust, trust all swirled together in a maelstrom that would either bind them together for life or ruin everything. But she wasn't going to let the fear of the unknown hold her back. Not anymore.

She drew back and looked in his eyes. "I'm coming home."

BONUS SCENE
RETT

Three years later

"Why are we taking the food truck?" Jade asked.

Rett hoisted her into the vehicle. "It's good to start up the engine and put some miles on it every now and again."

It wasn't entirely the truth. A four-tier birthday cake and assortment of pastries were in the back awaiting transportation to Jade's surprise party. A night that would hopefully change everything.

He brushed a piece of dirt off the Rhodes Patisserie sign that Jade had painted and came around to the driver's side.

With any luck, the blustery winter weather was finally behind them. The pile of snow in the corner of the winery parking lot was now a puddle. Daffodils were popping up in the flower beds Jade mulched the week before. Or started to mulch. Her muse tingle had kicked in halfway through, and she had abandoned her post to paint wildflowers with leaves made of old wine bottle labels.

Rett reached for his keys, and his pinky brushed against

the small, square box in his pocket. His stomach twisted as they made their way down the gravel driveway and pulled onto the highway.

Could Jade tell? Something had been off about her all day. She hadn't wanted her usual post-run cheese plate that morning and she had disappeared for a couple hours in the middle of the day. Her phone was out, and she appeared to be frowning at something.

They had talked about marriage—more than once, in fact. While the proposal was a surprise, the intent behind the gesture was not. The proposal planner he worked with had made him answer an exhausting questionnaire before agreeing to work with him. He and Jade had talked about everything—finances, children, communication, and conflict styles. It wouldn't make sense for her to say no.

"Good birthday so far?" he asked.

Jade jumped like he had caught her doing something illicit. She put her phone away and turned her attention to him as they crawled down the hill into town.

"The best. Truly. Thank you so much. Don't tell Margie, but I think those were the best cinnamon rolls I've ever eaten."

"Good, because we're selling them on the truck for the next two days."

"I'm so proud of you." She scooted closer to him. His hand closed around hers.

Business at the winery was booming, rescued in part by the sparkling wine and feature in the *New York Times* but also by the rooftop wine bar Jade had insisted he open. The brand-new pastry and coffee truck had been a resounding success and was sold out by one o'clock every day. The potential for even more growth was there, but for once he was content with the way things were. All he needed was the final piece of the puzzle: Jade as his wife.

It had to be perfect.

They pulled to a stop outside Margie's. The streets were quiet this time of night.

Jade leaned forward and frowned. "Where are we going to dinner?"

"You'll see." He came around to her side and helped her down. He took her hand and led her over to a dark store-front. Was it his imagination, or was she paler than usual?

"Uh, Rett?"

"Yeah?" he asked as he fished around in his pockets.

"Why are we going to dinner at the thrift store?" She pointed at the faded sign over the door.

"We're not," he said. He slid a key into the lock. The door swung open into darkness.

She raised her eyebrows. "Why do you have keys to the thrift store?"

He pocketed the keys and took her hands in his. "Don't get mad. But there's one more gift."

"What is happening?" She squinted into the void.

He reached over and hit the lights.

"Surprise!" Thirty people shouted at once.

Jade's hands flew to her mouth, which cracked into a smile. She shoved him and ran into Cindy's outstretched arms.

The old thrift store had been spruced up considerably over the last four months. Everything had been cleared out and freshly painted. Shelves along one wall would soon feature local artists and jewelry makers. Track lighting showcased pieces of Jade's art on the wall. He had copied it from her vision board and brought her dream of her own gallery to fruition. But she didn't seem to notice as the town rushed in with birthday wishes.

A hand landed on his shoulder, and he jumped.

"All right, mate?" Tom asked.

Rett nodded. "Help me get the cake?"

They shuffled outside.

"She's gonna know something's up," Tom said as he opened the back doors of the pastry truck. "You're green."

"Maybe it was a mistake to do it in front of everyone." Rett grabbed one side of the massive cake, and Tom lifted the other.

The dessert was his magnum opus—he had poured every bit of expertise he had garnered from pastry classes into it. Ten different icing techniques and handmade chocolate truffles covered the surface of the genoise cake.

"Nah." Tom grunted under the weight of the dessert. "This town is her family. She would want everyone to be there."

"I hope you're right."

They hefted the desserts inside. Jade was still being accosted by half the town. A small pile of presents was forming around her—the latest Nora Roberts book that must have come from the book club, a set of brushes, a loose bag of wine that had Tom written all over it. Margie smiled as Jade pulled out a vase that looked handmade.

Rett slipped through a door into the back. Once a storage room, the cavernous space now teemed with paint supplies and canvases. A new picture window faced the lake. Would she feel inspired? Or would this all have been a colossal waste of time?

The ring box was burning a hole in his pocket. He wasn't going to be able to focus if he didn't do it. Immediately.

His heartbeat hammered in his ears as he dodged

between two waiters passing hors d'oeuvres. She smiled at his approach, and the stress subsided slightly.

She would say yes. He could feel it in his bones. So why was it so nerve-racking?

"Could I steal the birthday girl for a minute?"

"Of course." She smiled and took his arm. She was still holding Margie's vase. He led her around the desk in the center of the room and through a door into the studio space beyond.

"Rett, this is so amazing. You really didn't have to do—" She paused and swiveled to take in the space. "What did you do?"

"You know how we talked about your dream?" he asked. "A gallery-slash-studio space where you could feature your art plus other local artists? And have a dedicated studio space so you stop flinging paint on the gym ceiling?"

"Yes," she said slowly.

"This is that space. It's yours, if you want it."

Her mouth dropped open. "Are you fricken kidding me? This is mine?" She reached out to touch a canvas.

"Do you like it?" he asked.

She squealed and jumped into his arms.

They kissed, and he relished in her warmth.

"You're insane. I can't believe you did this for me. Thank you so much." She pulled back and put a finger in his face. "Hey. Wait. We set a hard limit on birthday gifts this year. You definitely violated it."

"This isn't a birthday gift."

She looked at him skeptically.

He drew a deep, shuddering breath. It was now or never.

"There's one other thing," he said.

"Wait." She unfurled her legs and dropped to the floor.

She was pale again. "I've been going crazy all day. I have to tell you something."

He froze with his hand halfway to his pocket. His heart jumped into his throat. What if the worst had happened and she had finally grown tired of him?

"Okay. What is it?" His voice shook a little bit.

She clutched her stomach, and the color drained from her face. In a second, she had bent over and retched into Margie's homemade vase.

Panic flared.

"Oh, no. Are you sick? What's wrong?" He gathered her into his arms, and they sunk to the floor. He couldn't propose to her while she had the stomach flu—or worse, food poisoning? What if something he made had caused this?

He drew back and stroked a finger over her cheek. "Let me get you some water."

She unwrapped a mint and tossed it in her mouth. "It's okay. I'm not sick. Well, I guess I am sick. But I'm also... pregnant."

Rett froze. Shockwaves were coursing up and down his body. Had he heard her correctly?

"You're pregnant?"

She opened something on her phone and turned it towards him. Lab results flashed onscreen. "I had Cindy do a blood test to be sure. I know we didn't plan this, but Cindy said it can happen even the first month after you remove your—oof."

Rett lifted her off the floor and gathered her in a bear hug. A tear leaked out. It was her birthday, yet she had given him a gift he had always painfully wanted.

A baby. *Their* baby. He was going to be a dad. Holy shit.

His brain immediately spiraled towards college savings

and nannies, but he fought back and re-centered himself in the moment.

"I told you your sperm have drill bits for heads." She was still pale, but smiling. "Are you happy?"

"I'm thrilled. Honestly. But are you happy?"

"I am, but there's so much uncertainty. So much can go wrong. Pregnancy is terrifying, and that's before we even consider the financial implications." She pulled out her phone and showed him the beginnings of a spreadsheet. "I want to be super present in this baby's life, but I don't want to give up my career, so that means at least part-time daycare or a nanny and we're really going to have to—"

His heart staggered, and he crashed his lips against hers. She had come so far from the directionless artist with no savings account who had arrived on his doorstep three years ago.

"You made a spreadsheet."

His hand pressed against her stomach. Somewhere in there was a brand-new life. The start of their family. Their lives were intertwining ever more deeply, roots spreading into the earth like so many vines.

She straightened up. "It seemed prudent." Her gaze swept the room, and her brows contracted. "Especially if we're going to also be paying rent on this place."

"More of a mortgage than a rent," he said.

Her eyebrows raised. "You bought it?"

"Real estate is a good investment. And I told you. It's a gift."

"But not a birthday gift," she clarified.

"No." It was time. The future awaited. He pulled back and lowered himself down to one knee.

Her sapphire eyes widened. Color bloomed back into her cheeks. "What are you doing?"

"Jade Alexandria Gardner," he began.

A tear slipped down her cheek.

He had rehearsed this speech a dozen times, but her announcement had derailed his concentration.

"There are a lot of reasons why this shouldn't work."

She frowned. "Okay, not where I thought this was going. Kind of misleading with the whole getting down on one knee thing."

"I'm not done," he said. "There are a lot of reasons this shouldn't work. We're fundamentally different. You're a dreamer, I'm a planner. I make wine, you make worlds. But when you walked into my life, those differences gave me something I didn't even know I needed."

He squeezed her hand, and she smiled.

"You taught me how to have fun again, how to take a step back and enjoy the moment. You've shown me the beauty in ordinary things. You reminded me how much richer life can be when you're not always fixated on work or the future. You fought for my dreams and taught me about boundaries. You gave back a piece of me that I thought was gone forever. You, Jade, are extraordinary."

He took a deep breath and pulled the velvet box from his pocket. "I know it hasn't always been a perfectly straight path, but you choose me every single day. And I choose you, Jade. Forever. Will you do me the honor of a lifetime and be my wife?"

The box creaked open, revealing an emerald set in a platinum band.

She sniffed. "Well, it will be easier to file our taxes if we're married filing—"

"I'm sorry, are you talking about taxes right now?" he sputtered.

"I'm just kidding, idiot. Of course I'll marry you."

She yanked him up to his feet and threw herself on him. Muffled cheering came from the door that separated them from the storefront. Half a dozen people were plastered against the small window, celebrating wildly.

They laughed and turned to each other. Their lips met again, and he held her. His fiancée. The mother of his future child. The legacy he had fought so hard and long for was only just beginning.

ACKNOWLEDGMENTS

TWSS for giving me gracious deadlines while I adjusted to having a newborn.

Editor Jess for expert guidance and empowering me to make big changes.

The following Finger Lakes wineries for inspiring this story: Dr. Konstantin Frank's, Heron Hill Winery, and Point of the Bluff Vineyards.

Lauren J for being my unpaid therapist.

Tim R for telling me what kind of objects he pulled out of people's rectums as a surgical resident.

Dr. Ciummei for nurturing my love of wine.

The hardworking teachers at my sons' daycare without whom these books would never be written.

Alexis for the life-giving contraband apple bladder.

My readers for making my dreams come true.

ALSO BY MADISON SCORE

Standalone:

Love Among Vines

Claire Hartley Accidental Mystery:

Book 1 - Bride or Die

Book 2 - Say Yes to the Death

Book 3 - Happily Never After